A DROWNING WAR

John Winton

A DROWNING WAR

Published by Sapere Books.

24 Trafalgar Road, Ilkley, LS29 8HH

saperebooks.com

Copyright © The Estate of John Winton, 1985

The Estate of John Winton has asserted his right to be identified as the author of this work.
All rights reserved.

No part of this publication may be reproduced, stored in any retrieval system, or transmitted, in any form, or by any means, electronic, mechanical, photocopying, recording, or otherwise, without the prior written permission of the publishers.
This book is a work of fiction. Names, characters, businesses, organisations, places and events, other than those clearly in the public domain, are either the product of the author's imagination, or are used fictitiously.
Any resemblances to actual persons, living or dead, events or locales are purely coincidental.

ISBN: 978-1-80055-895-3

CHAPTER ONE

It was like a small cloud, rising out of the sea, no bigger than a man's hand, just as the Bible said. Jay stood staring at it for a few moments. It was odd that nobody else seemed to have seen it, or was taking any notice of it.

The flight deck was deserted except for Jay and two sailors with brooms, sweeping up something beside the pompom gun mounting, showing its four barrels skywards just aft of the island. There were no aircraft on deck, and there had been no flying for hours. The RAF Hurricanes and Gladiators which had, with miraculous skill, been flown safely on in the early hours of the morning had all been struck down into the hangars below. The ship had a section of four of her own Sea Gladiators, and one Swordfish, at ten minutes' notice, but they too were still down in the hangar.

Jay dawdled, reluctant to reach the island and face whatever it was the Captain had to say to him. With this almost following wind it was quite warm on deck for the Arctic, although it never really got warm, not *bone*-warm, up here in these high latitudes, even in June. It was a very bright day, with the sea a milky blue colour, sparkling away to the south and west where the sun shone, the colour of one of those Southern Railway posters. COME TO SUNNY SOUTHSEA. *Come to Sunny Narvik for your holidays, the Holiday of a Lifetime. I don't think.*

The cloud was still there, almost in the north. Jay studied it more closely. It could not be just a cloud, on a day like this. Somebody ought to say something to the bridge about it. In wartime anything, anything at all, that looked suspicious had to be reported. At least they had all learned *that* off Norway. Now that it was over, or almost over, everybody could see what a right bloody shambles it had been. Now, they were taking the troops back to England — the Expeditionary Force, and all those bloody Frenchmen, and the Poles, and God knew who else, leaving the Germans in charge. *Good luck to them, I don't think. Norway was a beautiful country, but awful. Beautiful but bloody awful. Good riddance to it.*

The whole ship seemed fast asleep. Not surprising, after the last few days. Everybody had been up and about and on their feet for twenty-four hours a day for days, for as long as anybody could remember. They were all out on their feet long before the end. Jay was only up here himself because the Captain had sent for him. Otherwise, he would have had his head down like everybody else. Obviously the Captain was getting his ammunition together for the Big Row.

Jay had never understood what it was the Captain had against aircrew, and especially pilots. It was almost a kind of snobbishness. He was not so bad with the observers; he seemed to look upon them at least as naval officers and gentlemen. But pilots he could not abide, not at any price. He treated them as hardly officers, hardly human. Poor Wings, the senior Fleet Air Arm officer on board, was ashore in Scapa Flow, and the rumour was that he was going to be court-martialled as soon as the ship got back. The whole wardroom was seething with anger and resentment about it. The Commander, for the first time since he had been on board, was trying to keep the peace. What a way to go to war.

The cloud seemed to have shrunk. Maybe the bridge were right to ignore it, and Jay was wrong. Jay stood on the flight deck, looking up at the blank glass of the scuttles set in the island bulkhead. Part of the trouble was that the Captain had been a submariner, and a very successful one, in the previous war. There were strong rumours in the ship that the Captain had even been recommended for a Victoria Cross. Certainly he had a string of crosses and medals as long as your arm. The sailors liked to look at them. They liked a captain who had been decorated. It gave him, as they said, 'a certain mystique'. The Captain was as popular with the sailors as he was unpopular with the wardroom.

He might have been a brilliant submariner, but he clearly knew precious little about aircraft or what they could do. That was the root of the trouble with Wings. The Captain was always wanting the aircraft to go off on schemes which Wings, God bless him, thought were hare-brained, and said so. The Captain had said no submarine would ever be sunk by aircraft. Because he was the Captain, nobody contradicted him. In the meantime, the Captain behaved as though the ship were a battleship, not an aircraft carrier. Six months before, looking for the *Graf Spee* in the Indian Ocean, the Captain had breathed fire and brimstone, taking the ship swanning off on her own, and saying what he would do if he ever caught up with the enemy. The whole ship's company had kept their fingers crossed and prayed they would never meet anything. Nor had they.

That cloud was back again, bigger and higher now, and beginning to stretch further along the horizon. They ought to be flying off an aircraft to look at that. They ought, strictly speaking, to have an aircraft up already. That was one of the things aircraft were *for*. But maybe it was because the ship was dead on her feet. The ship was cluttered with RAF types, crashed out everywhere, all over the wardroom, in every sofa and armchair.

Jay had been thinking of getting up to have some tea when the Captain's summons came. It was almost certainly to do with the latest Big Row. The whole ship, and especially the squadrons, was still trembling over it. Poor old Wings had been the scapegoat. Back in Scapa, nobody knew what would happen to him. The Captain was going to have his blood for supper, that was for sure. That scene about the sparking plugs — Jay would never forget it, nor would anybody else who experienced it.

The sparking plugs in the Swordfish radial engines had given constant trouble in the cold weather. In wartime, off Norway, the ship got what stores she could, not what she should, and there were never enough spare sparking plugs. It seemed a trivial thing, but like the horseshoe nail it led to other things. Faulty plugs caused an engine to misfire, and a misfiring engine might cause an aircraft to ditch. So it was a question of taking the plugs out, over and over again, and cleaning them. But in the meantime, any pilot with a misfiring engine was going to return to the ship, not because he had cold feet, or wanted to go to the heads or left a lighted cigarette in the ready room, but because he didn't want to ditch and lose the aircraft.

Poor Wings had tried to explain this to the Captain, without success. One day, Jay himself had returned to the ship prematurely because of sputtering sparking plugs. When he went up to the bridge, he found Wings looking very white, and the Captain literally shaking from head to toe with rage. The Captain had sent for Jay's CO, and the Air Engineer Officer, and the Senior Observer, and the RAF Sergeant Engine Fitter, and in their presence gave Wings such a dressing-down that the Navigating Officer, who could not help overhearing, told Jay later he had never witnessed one officer of His Majesty's Navy address another in such language. Jay had read somewhere that you could scar a man's soul — or so the Greeks believed — if you spoke to him violently enough. Poor old Wings was certainly marked for life now.

Jay began to walk towards the island door again. He glanced over his shoulder as though somebody were following him. That cloud was a great deal bigger and blacker now. Everybody now looked back on those days, before this captain and this war, as golden days of golden Mediterranean sun. *Come to Sunny Malta* — now *there* was an idea! Hot sun, parties, Marsa Vin, hands to bathe, suntanned girls in their bathing suits, easy flying in lovely weather under blue skies. Now there was this bloody war, and days of fog and freezing cold. The wardroom was full of officers who knew not Joseph. Aircrew came back after a long sortie over enemy territory and found they had to wait to be served for meals behind some staff officer, or even some fat-bummed army liaison officer who most probably had had his head down all day, and had no intention of ever, but ever, putting his porky carcase into a situation of danger. And then to be given a bottle by the Captain when you got back, with the thinly veiled suggestion of cowardice! Pilots were treated like shit, after they had risked their lives. If *gunnery* officers were going over Norway, or even submariners, they would be dishing out gongs by the bushel by now.

Jay had reached the lee of the island, where there was very much less wind. That meant that it was blowing over the starboard quarter, just about on the bearing of that cloud. So, if they did want to fly off, they would have to turn through almost one hundred and eighty degrees and steer *towards* it.

The alarm rattlers had that terrible urgent sound, with a distinctive cracked note, which everybody had heard so often off Norway and knew so well. Then, as the sound stopped, there was that voice reeling off commands, all of them household words. 'Hands to action stations ... Main armament close up on the double ... Shut all X and Y openings ... Hands to action stations...'

Jay started towards the island door and then stopped. *Action stations. Hands to action stations.* He had no action station except his Swordfish, and that was down in the hangar. He ran to the after pompom mounting, and then stopped again, unable to decide whether to run aft, or forward, or go down the main island ladder to the decks below. The flight deck was deserted everywhere he looked. It was like standing on a wide field against a threatening sky, as though a storm were about to break at any moment.

There was a tearing, rending sound, like a thick cloth being ripped apart right overhead. Jay had never heard such a sound before and he watched, amazed, as a white tower of water rose silently on the port side of the ship and went on rising, silently and astonishingly, until it reared up its foaming crest many feet above the level of the flight deck. Still stationary, like a marvellous apparition, it slid aft, moving as the ship moved on. Beyond it, Jay could see their two escorting destroyers, changing course to steer out towards that cloud on the starboard side.

The four-barrelled pompom crew had arrived and manned their weapon. Jay could hear the mounting groaning as they trained it to starboard. Irrationally, he hoped they would soon be firing back.

Again, there was that terrible tearing sound, but this time Jay could see no white tower. Instead, he felt the impact of the explosion, somewhere up forward, through the soles of his feet. There was the piping of a bosun's call over the broadcast and a voice. 'Take cover. Take cover. Range one Swordfish...'

For one wild moment, Jay was sure they were addressing him, and he had time to ponder on the contradiction. How could he take cover *and* range one Swordfish? It was his Swordfish they wanted, and they wanted him to fly it. But his Swordfish was down in the upper hangar.

As Jay paused again, paralysed once more by the knowledge of what was happening and the need for him to make some decision, somebody came running past, arms and legs whirling and flailing, and then disappeared, just as though he had run straight aft and over the round-down and into the sea. The figure had shouted something, but Jay could not catch what it was.

The flight deck was throbbing underfoot as the ship increased speed, and Jay felt the deck tilting to starboard as the ship turned to port, to turn away from that cloud, to try and put the enemy stern on and make a more difficult target. Staring aft, Jay saw that the cloud had actually disappeared and had been replaced by something much more ominous: the hard dot of a ship, with a trace of light brown smoke. He saw the faintest blink, as of a carefully shaded light many miles away, winking from the base of the black dot. Jay had never seen such a sight in his life, but he knew at once what it was: the flash of big guns firing.

Jay turned and began to walk slowly aft, pleased by his own control over himself, restraining the urge to abandon all caution and run as fast as that figure before. Behind him, there was another impact, surprisingly, almost comically mild, like the sound of a brick dropping into a pat of mud. But when he turned his head, Jay saw a huge hole with jagged edges torn into the framework of the flight deck. He could actually see down it, girders and a frame like a fretwork, and part of an aircraft. That must have been a shell hit, maybe one which did not explode. That made at least two hits. At that range, and in that time ... how long was it? It could have been seconds, or minutes, or even half an hour.

There was somebody else on the flight deck with him. Jay could not remember ever seeing his face before, and could not at first recognise his light-blue uniform. Then he realised it must be one of those RAF types who had flown on board from Norway, risking a landing on a carrier rather than abandoning their fighters ashore.

'Better get below,' Jay said. 'I shouldn't hang around up here.'

'Who can that be out there?' The RAF type jerked his head, as though indicating the presence of a stranger just across a road. 'Out there. Not Salmon and Gluckstein, could it be?'

Jay recognised the reference: *Scharnhorst* and *Gneisenau,* the two big bad wolves who were such objects of fascination to the newspapers.

'Never,' he said, firmly. 'No, that's impossible. They're not at sea.' He felt obscurely pleased, oddly superior, with his naval knowledge, to this ignorant RAF type. There had, in fact, been rumours and even reports of German heavy ships at sea throughout the campaign. But not recently, and certainly not for the last two or three weeks. If there had been any chance of meeting them, they would have had at least one Swordfish airborne. Although, Jay reflected, with this captain nothing was certain. 'Anyway, I should get under cover if I were you. Next thing is, you'll get killed if you stay up here.'

'I must say...' The RAF type hesitated, and looked aft again, almost longingly, with his eyes shining. 'Is this a *naval* action?'

Jay did not reply to that, but climbed down into a small space just below the flight deck. It was not big enough to be a compartment, not long enough to be a walkway. Jay could see the top of a blue-green Carley lifesaving float projecting above the guard rail. Maybe this was where somebody released a Carley float, if it were ever needed. Although Jay had been on board over a year, and came on the flight deck almost every day, he could not recall ever noticing this space before.

The flight deck was now at eye level. Jay looked up in time to see a shell actually hitting the island. A wide portion of the after bulkhead melted physically away before his eyes, and the whole structure then vanished in smoke. Jay knew at once that that was the mortal blow. The ship would never recover. Her head had been snapped off.

Like a conjurer's device, the smoke seemed to thicken rather than clear and Jay had an eerie feeling that if it ever did clear, there would be nothing there. The Captain, the bridge, the whole of the ship's command structure had been obliterated, and that billowing smoke now hid an empty space.

There was another voice on the main broadcast. 'Belay the last pipe. Do not, repeat *not*, abandon ship…'

'How do we get out of here?' The RAF type had jumped down and joined him. Jay sensed the man's feelings of strangeness and insecurity. He obviously knew nothing at all about the ship or its layout, and wanted to stay with somebody who clearly did.

There was no ladder, or exit of any kind. 'We'll just have to climb over.' Jay looked over the side. Far below was the sea: the flight deck and its superstructure overhung at this point, so that Jay looked down directly at the water. But just below was another gangway, and Jay could hear voices. Possibly one could swing over and lower oneself down there.

The RAF type looked over the side. 'I can't do it,' he said. 'I hate heights.'

'Well, that's too bad.' Jay was surprised by his own briskness and ruthlessness. 'Either you go this way, or you stay up here. Up to you.'

Jay swung himself over, felt for a ledge with his right toe, found it, lowered himself hand over hand on some lucky rungs, and arched his back as he dropped. He found himself on familiar ground, actually on the main gangway along the battery deck. Men were hurrying aft past him, and he felt himself being jostled and bundled along with them. Everybody seemed to have a lifejacket on. Jay's was in his cabin, two decks down and on the other side of the ship.

Following the tide of men, Jay allowed himself to be pushed along, down a ladder, and out on to a broad space, forward of the quarterdeck on the starboard side. There was a gun sponson here, still painted a bright marine green on its inside; Jay remembered the gun's crew had painted it and filled it with goldfish for a children's party in Malta, long before the war. Here it was, still the same colour. The gun was manned. The crew stood, in their steel helmets, one of their number holding a projectile in his arms. They all stood immobile, as though charmed, waiting for the order to make a move.

They were much closer to the water here, and Jay was surprised to see how rough it was. Short steep waves were rising and falling with frightening speed. Something must have happened to whip up the sea like that. There was a grunting noise, and another tall spout of water shot up only half a cable away, followed by the crash and screams of another hit, down in the body of the ship. There was a man lying on the deck here, just groaning. The ship was being pounded to pieces and her men were being killed, as though one by one.

Somebody opened a door on the inboard side and somebody else shouted at him, but before either of them could do anything further, a shocking gust of flame and smoke hurtled across the quarterdeck with an almost solid draught of rushing air. The tip of flame actually cleared the ship's rail before coiling back. It swept around like a great eager arm, avid to embrace everybody standing there. Two men flung themselves upon the door and shut it, struggling to wind the wheel which secured the clips. Jay fancied he could hear something else: a sound from a nightmare, of somebody pounding and calling from inside.

Further aft, a sailor in a duffel coat was taking the lashings off one of the motor boats. A second man was tossing lifebelts up into it. 'Abandon ship, lads! This is it! Abandon ship! Fall in by divisions for abandoning ship...'

It seemed nobody knew what to do, or they could not believe what they were hearing. Nobody ever abandoned ship, not really. It was exercised, on a sunny afternoon. There was a proper drill laid down for it, so that everybody knew where to go and what to do. Both watches for exercise it would be piped: *Prepare to abandon ship. Boats' crews turn out and lower boats. Quartermasters provide boats' compasses. Marine band and stokers longest off watch provide timber from stowages. Officer of the Watch to inform engine room and main switchboard. Engine room provide hydraulic pressure for cranes and winches. Torpedo party man and work winches. Officers to see men go down ladders and ropes in an orderly manner.* It was all laid down in the Commander's Standing Orders. But nobody ever actually *did* it.

In any case, this was not like any of the exercises. Jay could see the Paymaster Commander, a pilot from his own squadron, the gunner, several petty officers and one of the shipwrights, and two or three Royal Marine wardroom flunkies. A mixed bag of ship's personalities. But none of them was moving.

'Abandon ship...'

At last, somebody obeyed. A stoker, wearing overalls and a singlet and oily heavy steaming boots, ran to the rail and, while another stoker called out a warning, put one hand on the top wire, which at once collapsed under him. A sailor had just loosened the bottle-screw slip, to let the guard rails down. The stoker fell sideways and then backwards, as though doing a trick dive in a swimming pool, with a smile on his face.

They could all see that the ship was still moving fast through the water. Anybody who jumped now would surely be left far astern and would never be picked up. That stoker's head and waving arms were already a long way off.

The deck was now noticeably heeling. The ship was listing to starboard, and the deck sloping so much that, in spite of himself, Jay had to take a step backwards to keep his balance. He had the weirdest sensation of mild outrage; he thought of being back at the seaside as a child, on a rubber raft which had too many bodies on it and would only right itself when enough children had slid or been pushed off.

The deck reverberated to another hammer blow, a long way away up forward. The angle of the deck steepened with a sudden lurch. The ship herself wanted them all to leave her. The blacksmith appeared, carrying the smithy black cat. Somebody had a handful of letters, scooped up from his locker as he left his mess deck. He was tearing them into fragments which he was scattering over the side, as though in a mad nautical paper chase. Another man, who looked like a stoker, actually had a mug of tea in his hand and was drinking from it. It was, after all, still tea-time.

Jay walked backwards uphill, until he felt the bulkhead behind him, to watch this grotesque parade of faces familiar and almost familiar, as though seen in a dream. Here came a man with no right leg, just the stump which was bleeding profusely all over the deck; if this were an exercise, Jay thought, somebody would already be shouting at him to move off because that patch of deck had just been scrubbed. As it was, the two mates helping him took him to the edge and there simply let him go. There was nothing more they could do for him.

A squad of Royal Marines had fallen in, just beyond the battery bulkhead door. They stood as though they were on parade. Somebody shouted, 'Royal Marines, turn forrard, *dis... miss...*' and they all turned forward, saluted, broke formation and went over the side. They were followed by a ship's cook, still wearing a white apron and a white cap. Another cook rushed to the edge, shaking his fist and shouting 'Come back, you silly bugger!'

'Would you like some barley sugar?'

Jay turned. The speaker was a paybob, a supply branch Sub-Lieutenant Jay had never taken any notice of before, except — if anything — vaguely to despise him.

'It stops you being sick.'

'Thank you very much.'

The paybob poked his fingers into a paper bag and pulled out several sweets.

'Do you think we could have one now?'

'Oh, no,' the paybob said. 'Not on the *upper deck*!'

'No, I suppose not.' Jay put the sweets in his pocket.

They both looked down at the sea, which was much closer now, rustling and rippling along the broad curves of the torpedo bulges in the ship's side. The ship still seemed to be speeding through the water and the sea looked just as rough.

'It doesn't look very inviting, does it? Do we really have to jump?'

'Either that or stay here,' said Jay. He remembered the RAF type, and wondered whether he had ever got down from that catwalk. 'You don't have to jump if you don't want to. Nobody's going to make you.'

The paybob's teeth were chattering. Jay could see that he was so frightened he could not move. Jay remembered the barley sugar. That was a really generous gesture.

'Come on. It won't be too bad.'

'No, I don't think I can ... Have some more barley sugar.'

'Thank you very much.'

Several large objects plunged into the sea, throwing up tremendous splashes. Somebody had jettisoned the Carley floats from above. They bobbed in the water, righted themselves, and began to float away astern, looking almost cosy and inviting.

'Shall we jump together?'

'No, no. I don't want to.'

The ship was heeling over, more and more. The sea almost lapped over the deck. In fact, they would not have to jump at all; all they need do was simply walk off. Jay had heard of the deadly suction of a sinking ship. It really was time to go. He *must* go.

'You coming?' Jay saw the pale face, the trembling wet lips, the bag of barley sugar crushed in one hand, and knew the other was never going to go of his own accord. 'So long, then.'

There was a row of people along the edge, looking over like children having their first lesson at a swimming pool. 'Don't blow up your lifejacket until you're in the water,' he heard somebody say. 'Don't want to break your silly necks, do you?' The ship seemed at last to have stopped, as though the force that had kept her going had finally bled out into the sea.

'Well lads, what about it? Do we go?'

Nobody moved. Jay still hesitated, along with the rest of them. This was the ship he knew. This deck was solid. This was his home, and still a refuge. There was nothing out there. Again he stepped out to the edge. He was not sure whether anybody jostled him or whether he went of his own accord, but he held his nose with the fingers of his right hand and went down into the sea.

Jay knew he must strike out and swim as he had never swum before, but nothing had prepared him for the cold of the water. It seized his whole body like a vice and drove all the breath from his lungs. He felt himself drowning already, although he was still going down. Swirling water immediately by the ship's side drove him further down. Shapes bumped and jarred him, knocking him sideways, and he thrashed and struggled, terrified that he was going to drown after all. He was under water a very long time, it seemed, and had acquiesced, and agreed that he was going to die and had let his head fall back, when he felt air on his lips. His face had broken the surface.

The ship was already some distance away. The water all around him was swarming with bodies, like the Mediterranean tunny fish in the killing season, all kicking and gasping and choking. An elbow or a fist struck Jay in the back, and he felt a hand close on the back of his neck. He fought back, and punched and kicked in fury, and thrashed his legs. He tried to strike out backwards in the backstroke he knew he could do well, but the lifejacket prevented him swinging his arms over. He thrashed even harder with his legs, with his hands folded across his chest. One finger felt something. It was a whistle. He blew it with all his might. The noise was shockingly loud. and now that he had blown his own he could hear other whistles all around, and voices calling out for God, and for their mothers, for life, for mercy.

Still thrashing vigorously with his feet, Jay saw that he was steadily moving away from the ship. He felt pressure on his head and turned. There was the painted rough surface of a Carley float.

There was even a rope to hang on to. He seized it with both hands, kicked the water, pulled himself out of the sea, and across the broad bulwark of the float and on to its slatted bottom, where he lay gasping like a stranded fish.

When he sat up at last, Jay saw that the ship was going, had indeed almost gone. There was smoke and the thudding of guns to the north. He fancied he saw the hull of a destroyer appear briefly out of the gloom, smoke and flames streaming from every part of her. The sea between his float and the ship was dotted with heads, dozens and dozens of them. It was just like 'hands to bathe', as they had done so many times in the Mediterranean. As he watched, the great stern of the ship lifted, the flight deck tipped until it was almost vertical, its colour changed from grey to black as it turned into shadow, and then it disappeared. There was a faint wisp of smoke hanging over a sea now coated with a thick scum of debris, and heads, and oil.

'Here, mate, give us a hand!'

Jay looked down and saw a bright red face, straining after its exertions, with a walrus moustache. Jay recognised him; it was one of the Royal Marine Band. He bent over to grasp him, but the face vanished. The man had used all his store of strength just to reach the float, and had nothing left to enable him to go on living. But other men were succeeding in getting in. Streaming shapes were rising out of the sea, each one gasping and shaking with the effort, as though each one knew he had just made the colossal expenditure of energy, like a birth, which made the difference between living and dying.

The wind was now taking Jay's float away from the ship, making it drift like some great water-lily pad, past the main mass of survivors. There seemed to be hundreds of them. There was an upturned boat, and the pinnace, used so often for libertymen, full of men, and more Carley floats, and the sailing whaler with only one man in it, and thick masses, like log-jams, of floating debris. Jay could hear a hoarse chorus of voices, calling and crying and swearing and coughing. Men were trying to swim out to his float but the wind was beating them. Two more did succeed, and painfully hauled themselves on board.

In the middle of the float, where a loose structure of ropes and slatted wood frames was free-flooding and open to the sea, two sailors had their knees drawn tight up under their chins, and their hands clasped over their faces. They sat, side by side, like children on a beach unable to bear the sight of a violent episode of Punch and Judy. One man, to Jay's right, was very badly wounded. There was a great gaping orifice in his chest. Jay could hear and see blood and air sucking and gurgling through it. There were scorch marks on his tattered overalls. It was a miracle he had achieved the upper deck, and an even greater miracle that he had survived this far. But even as Jay watched him, the dreadful sucking noise stopped. The man's mouth slackened, and some vital element of quickness left his body. Even the angle of his shoulders changed. Jay suddenly thought of all the trout he had ever caught. When you laid a fish on the bank you could see death spreading like a shadow over its shiny scales. So it was with that man. It was the first time Jay had ever seen a man die, had actually witnessed the moment of departure, the very instant when the spirit fled the body.

He began to count heads. It was difficult to be accurate, with all the movement of the float and his own low angle of sight, but he made it forty-one. No, forty-two, counting himself. He had forgotten to count himself. He counted again. Now it was forty, including himself. It was impossible to be sure. Say, forty. A round number. Not bad for a float which was only designed for … Jay did not know how many exactly, but it was certainly not as many as forty. It was extraordinary, but looking around him Jay could not see a single face he knew. There had been some twelve hundred men on board, so it was not really surprising. But a familiar face would have helped.

Then, two faces to his right, Jay saw Petty Officer Bracewell. He was Captain of the Fo'c'sle. Like many of the pilots, Jay had undertaken ship's duties. His was assistant or 'second dickie' to the First Lieutenant on the fo'c'sle, when entering or leaving harbour. Bracewell was a three-badge Petty Officer who had signed on for his pension and would in due course be a Chief Petty Officer. He had been a very present help in trouble, and an unobtrusive fount of good advice for Jay. If ever there was a man to share a life raft with, it was surely Paddy Bracewell.

Bracewell was leaning forward, to speak across their intervening neighbour. 'This man's a goner, sir. Can you help me put him over the side?'

'Surely not?' Jay was horrified by the suggestion.

'He's a goner, sir. Give us a hand, please.'

Jay was surprised by his own strength in such an undertaking. With Bracewell assisting from the other side, the corpse seemed as light as a feather.

'You're the only officer on board, sir.'

'Am I?' Jay did not know whether to be pleased or alarmed by the information.

'Yes, sir. I've had a good look. These are all marines and stokers. A couple of ODs. And you and me, sir.'

'What have we got? Have we got any water on board?'

They all looked and felt about them. 'No? What about food?'

They all shook their heads. No food.

'Have we got anything to bail with? Any masts, or sails?'

It transpired they had nothing at all: no water, no food, no masts, no sails, nothing to bail with, and no covering except their clothing. Just forty men, or forty-two, in an open float, open to the sky above, and open to the sea below. Already the wind was drying their clothing. Oddly, the sea water around their feet felt warmer than the air.

'Up the original shit creek without the primeval paddle, sir,' said Bracewell.

Jay grinned and at once winced, surprised to discover that his cheeks were already so cold and stiff the slightest movement of the flesh, even to smile, was painful. He looked up at the sky. It seemed to be getting dark, although it never got dark up here at this time of year. His watch was still going. It was a special type issued to aircrew. It said half past seven. They had been attacked at about tea-time.

The sea was much calmer, and the wind was actually dropping, but it was freezing cold. Jay's teeth were beginning to chatter. He wore flying overalls and a sweater underneath them, and his lifejacket. He had as good a chance as anybody. Better than some of the men he could see, sitting or lying on their sides. There seemed to be quite a lot of room in the float already. He noticed some men just watching him.

'Come on, we'll sing.' As he said the words, Jay himself found it hard to believe what he was saying. Singing in a life-raft. They had all seen it in films. The *Titanic* survivors had done it. But here they were, actually doing it themselves.

'*Roll out the barrel...*' There were quite a few singing — reluctantly, but they *were* singing. After 'Roll out the Barrel', there was one with a jaunty tune and ridiculous words: '*Run rabbit run rabbit, run run run ... He'll get by, without his rabbit pie...*' Then there was another one, very popular before the war. '*Any time down Lambeth way...*' It had been all the rage with Lupino Lane at the Victoria Palace, Christmas time two years before — it had swept the country. 'Anybody know the words? *Any evening, any day ... You'll find us all ... doing the Lambeth Walk, Oy!*'

The words and gestures seemed futile against that wide sky. The voice trailed away into that enormous distance. There was silence again, except for the sound of coughing.

A long way off to the south, Jay saw another float. He waved. A figure waved back. Jay waved again, but the other man's waving stopped. The sun had gone behind clouds, which made it feel colder, although it was probably just the same.

A man directly opposite Jay was coughing and retching, his whole frame heaving, as though he were trying to bring up the contents of the very bottom of his lungs, and indeed it seemed he was succeeding. A foul mixture of blood and oil and mucus was spewing between his lips and dripping on to his knees. Jay fancied he could even smell it from where he sat. The man went on coughing, on and on, regularly and deeply like a metronome, on and on and on, until somebody at last muttered 'For shit's sake,' but the coughing did not pause for a moment.

It was nine o'clock before Jay remembered the barley sugar. His fingers could only just hold the sweets. The tips were already numb, as though they did not belong to him. 'Have some barley sugar, Bracewell?'

'Ah, thank you, sir. That'd be nice.'

They both suddenly noticed the silence. The coughing had stopped.

'He's dead, sir.'

'Dead already? Good God!'

'He was in a bad way when he came on board, sir. The wonder is he lasted so long.'

The two on either side of the man were already lifting his legs. They tipped him backwards, over the side, and then moved closer together. It was as though that man had never been, had never existed. He was gone for ever, and there was no trace of him.

The barley sugar certainly did lubricate the throat. Jay thought of the paybob who had given it to him, and briefly wondered if he had ever left the ship. Jay decided that as the only officer on board he ought to organise games and exercises. He ought to exert himself to cheer the men up.

'Right,' he shouted. 'Pay attention. This way, everybody!'

Nobody moved, or even looked in his direction.

'Look here. You're going to do some exercises. If you don't, you'll all die.'

Even that word did not rouse them. It was an empty threat.

'First exercise. Hands on hips. Arms bending and stretching. First movement. Finger tips on shoulders. Extend the arms to their full extent, in front of you. Back to the shoulders. Arms upright in the air...'

Bracewell was following the movements, awkwardly but willingly. But he was alone. Nobody else was moving.

'Arms to the side...'

Several more men died that evening, or rather what would have been evening. In those high latitudes the sun did not actually set, but there was a discernible change in the intensity of the light, as though it were filtered through extra grey veils. Jay was shocked to see how little resistance some of the men appeared to have. One of those who died was a leading stoker who had played for the ship's football team; an enthusiastic gymnast in the dog-watches, that man had been one of the fittest in the ship, and certainly the fittest in that float. He was unwounded. Some of the badly wounded and burned obviously had less chance of survival, and almost all of them had died. This man was unmarked. He was perfectly well. But he died.

Jay decided that survival was largely in the mind of the survivor. After all, he thought, if forty men had been selected at random from the ship's company, told to jump overboard, swim to a Carley float some distance away, and stay on it for six, or twelve or even twenty-four hours, in sight of the ship, they would, at the very end, have been very cold, perhaps even frost-bitten, suffering from exposure, very hungry and thirsty. But they would not have *died*. It was that additional knowledge of being forsaken which did the harm. Jay remembered the story of a man lost in the Australian bush who died within a few hundred yards of rescue, not of sunstroke, or thirst, or a snake bite, or starvation, but from what could only have been sheer fright. Maybe it was a mental wound, just to be a survivor. It was the shock of their experience, and their fear of what might come, which was killing these men.

Trying to keep awake, Jake dropped off to sleep, lulled by the slight, gentle rocking of the Carley float. He woke suddenly, annoyed with himself and afraid for the rest of the survivors. Looking around, he knew at once that more of them had died. Only here and there now was the glint of a live eye. There was no darkness, just a shadow over the spirit which had carried them away. They had gone to sleep as though it were their proper bedtime and, unlike Jay, they had never woken up.

His watch had stopped at four o'clock. It was an effort just to turn over his wrist so that he could look at the dial. Salt brine and oil were hanging on his eyelids. He could feel the swollen length of his tongue, unaccustomedly pressing against the sides of his mouth. He had no feeling at all below his waist or elbows. All he had left was a warm core in the centre of his body. If that ever cooled, he would be — as Bracewell had said — a goner.

Bracewell was still awake and looking carefully into Jay's face. 'You all right, sir?'

'Oh, yes. Fine. How about you?'

'Fine, sir. Do you think we'll be picked up, sir?'

'Oh, yes.' Jay hoped he had said it with a confidence he certainly did not feel.

'Did they get a signal off, sir, do you know?'

'I don't know. I never went near the bridge the whole time. I didn't go there often anyway.' Jay suddenly had the thought that if he had been a little earlier on his way to the bridge he would have been there when that shell struck.

'You were one of those who kept out of the Captain's way, sir?' Jay hesitated. It seemed disloyal to the Captain to allow such a remark from a rating to pass.

'You needn't worry, sir. We all know what some officers are like. You know what they say: if he's an officer he must be a pig. In my time in the Andrew I've met some real officers. And I've met some pigs, too.'

Pigs. Jay knew the popular lower deck nickname for officers. It was justified, too, in a number of cases. Yet strangely he felt impelled to defend his fellow officers, from some curious loyalty to the Captain, and to the whole class of officers. He and Bracewell might both die, probably would, but they would still have this divide between them, even unto death.

'Oh, I don't think it's fair to say that. There are obviously differences between officers and sailors...'

'You mean, half the ship for the officers, half for the sailors — that's democracy, sir.'

Jay knew that old joke as well, but in any case it would have been too painful to smile.

'I've got a very funny feeling, sir, that we're in this float today — and there are a lot of men back there not even lucky enough to be in a float — all because some officer or some officers didn't do their jobs properly. Too bloody obstinate, that's what they were, or too bloody hidebound, to change with the times. The times *are* going to have to change, sir. That's one thing this war is going to do. You can see it already. When I think what happened back there, from what I know of it now, I'm so *bloody* angry...'

Jay nodded. Anger might keep Bracewell alive. It was too much effort to reply, and hurt too much. His lower lip was badly chapped and had a deep salt sore scored in it. Bracewell must feel deeply to discuss this at such a time. Jay had never suspected Bracewell of such revolutionary opinions — revolutionary for the Navy, anyway. Bracewell had always toed the line; never said a word out of place, or raised his eyes above a respectful level. It just showed how little one knew of a man, even though one served with him.

There were far fewer men left in the float now. But those who were still there would have to stay there, whatever happened. Those who were left would not have the strength to tip the dead over the side. They were all there now, for better or worse, the quick and the dead. Jay estimated their numbers at eight, although he was not sure of a stoker on the far side who was sitting with his head tipped back, staring at the sky in an attitude of utter and complete resignation, as though he had already decided to commit his body to its fate. But as Jay watched him, the man moved, for the first time in hours. So it was eight, after all.

On the second night the Northern Lights began to move mysteriously across the sky. They did not flicker — it was nothing so definite, but more of a continuous changing of shapes and faint colours — as with a random selection of slides, on a gigantic scale. In the morning, the horrors began. One man hoisted himself up into a sitting position, opened his fly, and urinated into his cupped hand. He dashed the urine against his lips. Jay was disgusted by the sight, although he conceded that it was probably harmless, apart from the repugnance it aroused. But even that could be fatal. It might be just enough weakness, the slightest amount of sapping of the will, to prevent a man from surviving. A violent recoil of disgust, a gagging of the throat at somebody's behaviour might make the difference between life and death. Another half-minute, a shade higher temperature, another lick of barley sugar, might decide between this world and the next. To be the slightest degree ashamed of oneself might be just enough to stop one living.

Jay's lasting emotion was, in the end, annoyance. The man's action had aroused his own thirst, which raged more fiercely, like a monster in his throat. He looked at the water swilling in the bottom of the float.

'It's tempting, sir.' Bracewell's voice seemed to come from a very long way away. 'But I don't think it would be wise.'

'What about that chap drinking his own…'

'I think when you get as far as he has, sir, it don't matter much what you do. It might even be a good thing, sir. He's a goner anyway.'

But now the man next to the urine-drinker was abusing him, shouting and swearing, and at last striking him in the mouth, accusing him of 'giving him lip'. While the mad shouts were still ringing in their ears, Jay and Bracewell and another man took garments off the dead and draped them around their own shoulders. They no longer had any feelings in their fingers or arms, and it took a long time. The urine-drinker watched their movements with a curious detachment, as though extra clothing was of no interest to him, after what he had done.

It became a day of visions, each more unlikely and disturbing than the last. One said he could see a dockyard wall, and palm trees waving in the wind. He said he could see an apple tree loaded with fruit, all ripe and juicy. Then he said he could see a canal with men and boys fishing. Another said he could see a Swordfish, and said he could see it going down into the sea. His account became excited when, to corroborate his story, he gave the aircraft's number. With a shiver of apprehension and recognition, Jay knew that the number was that, except for one digit, of his own Swordfish. The man was describing the scene he could see in some detail when he suddenly stopped, as though stunned into silence by what he had witnessed. They all looked at him. He was dead. He had died whilst describing his own terminal delirium.

Once again, Jay's sense of proportion, perhaps even his sanity, was preserved by Bracewell. 'Seems you and I are the only sane ones left now, sir.' Bracewell grinned. 'I'm not too sure of you, sir. Which only leaves *me*.'

At that, a man who had said nothing for two days got up and looked over the side. They were taken aback by his sudden strength. 'Just going to get my tot,' he said. 'Won't be a moment.' With that, he stood up, quite steadily, turned round and stepped over the side of the float into the sea. Jay did not even trouble to look and see whether or not his head reappeared above the surface.

During the third night, the man on Jay's other side died. Jay could not remember him ever saying anything since the time he'd climbed on board. Now, his weight slumped against Jay's shoulder. Jay pushed him away, but he fell back. Eventually Jay knew that he was only tiring himself out and resolved to bear the extra weight, until the man slid sideways across Jay's knees and he was at last able to joggle the corpse out into the centre of the float.

That third morning Jay and Bracewell devised a system of mutual help.

'Would you keep an eye out for me, sir?' Bracewell said. 'If you see me dropping off, give me a shake, a good hard shake. I'll do the same for you. We mustn't sleep from now on, either of us, sir. You rub my hands. I'll rub yours. Though I think we're much too late. Terrible sight, aren't they?'

They were indeed. Their fingers, hands and arms had blown up into obscenely white and puffy balloons of flesh. Skin did not react normally. Pressed, it stayed in the shape of the depression.

Jay felt somebody looking at him. There were two men still alive on the other side of the float. He nodded and forced himself to croak his advice to them. 'Should do this, too...' Jay held up one grotesquely swollen hand. 'Look after it...' Jay caught the eye of one of them, and nodded again.

It was as though Jay's voice was a trigger. Until then, that man had been staring at Jay with intense hostility. Now he began to fight the man next to him, struggling and pushing and punching with a clenched fist. Jay was astonished at the man's vigour. They both thrashed their legs frenziedly in the water, and their struggles jolted the float until it seemed they might overturn it. The assailant was holding the other's head below the water. They could all hear the fearful bubbling noise. It was murder. But neither Jay nor Bracewell could move a finger to prevent it. They were only a few feet away, but they might just as well have been a mile.

The winner of this appalling contest glared at them. It was clear that if he had been capable of it, he would have crossed the intervening space and attacked them.

'He's clean off his rocker, sir. Don't know what he's doing...'

'That may be.' Jay measured the distance between them. 'But if he went for us we'd be just as dead, wouldn't we?' The fear of attack gave fluency to Jay's chapped lips.

He did not know if it was then, or hours later, that he heard Bracewell say, 'He's a goner, sir. Do you know, sir, we're the only ones left. You told them, didn't you?'

Bracewell noted the puzzlement on Jay's face. 'You told 'em if they didn't do the exercises they'd die.'

Jay nodded. He tried to speak, but his mouth was too painful. He pointed at his lips and shook his head. His tongue had now swelled to fill the whole of his mouth. It was difficult to breathe, let alone speak.

'Shall we have another song, sir?'

Jay nodded again, knowing that he could not have sung a note to save his life. So he merely nodded, as best he could, in time, while Bracewell sang: *'Come cheer up my lads ... 'Tis to glory we steer ... To add something more ... To this wonderful year...'* Jay tried to nod sympathetically, to show support, but his nodding became slower and slower, and his head rocked as though it belonged to a clockwork toy that was winding down.

Jay knew that the end was now not far off. They were both still alive, and aware of each other, but unable to move. Only the knowledge of their mutual presence was keeping them alive. If one died, or if the other even suspected that he had died, then they would both die. They could no longer speak. Certainly there was no question of singing. They could only lie side by side.

It was thus that the small Norwegian tramp steamer found them, in the float, after some sixty-six hours. They were too weak to signal for help. The visibility was not very good and had the steamer steered a cable to either side it would have missed them, although it could not have missed the trail of Carley floats containing the dead and dying, which stretched for nearly two miles.

As it was, in the haze, the steamer nearly ran the float down. Jay had actually resigned himself, had prepared himself to die, when he saw a dark shape overhead. There was a bearded face which was not unfriendly, a wooden bulwark, and the sounds of voices, speaking something quite unintelligible.

It was Bracewell who was still capable of recognising the voices, and of himself uttering a further sequence of words.

'By God,' he said, 'they're *Jerries*!'

CHAPTER TWO

As always, it was Herr Kaleut himself who first saw the smoke on the far horizon. The captain always had the best eyes on the bridge.

'To starboard,' he said. He took a bearing on the compass ring. 'Due north.'

They stared out to the north, all three of them: Herr Kaleut, Hansi — the second watchkeeping officer — and the lookout. The other three lookouts kept on searching their own allotted sectors. That had been drilled into them: whatever happened elsewhere, whatever they heard or saw or felt, they were on no account to take their eyes away from their own sectors until the order was given to dive, or they had been properly relieved by another lookout.

'I'm sure I can hear gunfire, sir,' Hansi said.

'Well done, Hans-Dietrich Zschescher, I thought so too. For a torpedoman, you have very good ears. Stop engines.'

The noise of the diesels died away. The U-boat plunged on for some time, with way on, and they could hear the sound of the sea crashing over the U-boat's narrow bows and the long metal casing. When even those sounds had ceased, the U-boat swung and rolled, with a faint creaking of wire, in the heavy sea.

'Listen.' They all strained to hear. 'No, it's gone.' Herr Kaleut took his binoculars from his eyes, briefly cleaned the eyepieces, and put them back up again. 'I just thought ... I thought I could even see something. Looked like the tip of the mast of a big ship, a really big ship. But it's gone now. How long must we stay in this patrol area, Hansi, can you remember?'

'Till noon the day after tomorrow, sir.'

'Can't we go any further north now?' Herr Kaleut already knew the answer to that question.

'Not really, sir. We're at our limit now. From here northwards it will be *Kapitänleutnant* Siegfried Rollmann and his boat.'

Herr Kaleut laughed. 'That does it. We don't want to get in the way of that trigger-happy bandit, do we?' He bent down, to look at the chart, folded into a small square and pinned to a tiny stand beside the forward periscope standard. 'Here we are. Two hundred and ninety kilometres south and west of the Lofoten Islands.' He looked up sharply, his head on one side, listening. 'That was gunfire all right, then. No doubt. Heavy guns, too. Somebody's catching it. When can we go north? All right, I know, two days from now ... We'll get there as soon as we can.'

It was late afternoon when the U-boat, steering due north, closed the place where they had seen smoke and perhaps the tip of a mast, and had heard gunfire. Hansi was not on watch but standing in the control room below, and he heard Herr Kaleut's description down the voice-pipe.

'This is it, no doubt. Streaks of oil, lots of it. And *Überrest*, masses and masses. It was a big ship all right.'

Überrest. Literally, it meant the residue, the remains, the remnant. But it had a special meaning at sea. It meant the debris left on the surface, the survivors — if any — of a sunken ship.

'There are some floats, with bodies in them...'

Below, Hansi heard a shout, as though a lookout had reported something. Maybe they had sighted somebody still alive.

'Port wheel. Port twenty.'

There was another shout. '*Aircraft!* Dive, dive, dive, dive…'

As the bodies came tumbling down the ladder in the tower, Hansi reflected how, early in the war, nobody could believe that a captain, his officer of the watch and four lookouts could all get down a U-boat's conning tower in time to dive quickly. But it was amazing how actual war made everybody move faster.

Herr Kaleut was breathing hard, and Hansi saw that he was annoyed. Herr Kaleut always hated to be caught out. 'Up periscope.' Herr Kaleut was already sitting on the captain's periscope seat in the upper part of the tower. 'It was an English aircraft. I saw the roundels. It may see the *Überrest*. I hope so. They must have heard the news broadcast yesterday. Now they must know they have lost a ship. She was a big one. We shall stay down now until dark.'

When they surfaced, very cautiously — as always with Herr Kaleut — there was no aircraft, nothing to be heard or seen anywhere. When Hansi went up for his watch, he found Herr Kaleut, unusually, not looking out but leaning against the periscope standard, as though he were tired out. As Hansi took over the watch, getting the details of course and speed and future intensions from Klaus, the boat's *Eins WO* and First Lieutenant, he knew that Herr Kaleut was only waiting for a chance to speak after Klaus had gone down.

'All those dead men.' The captain's voice was so low Hansi could barely catch it over the wind. 'That was one of the most terrible sights I have ever seen.'

'Did we know what ship it was, Herr Kaleut?'

'We know she was a good ship, by her motto. It was on one of her lifesaving rings. I looked at the letters through my binoculars. *Explicit Nomen.*'

The words meant nothing at all to Hansi. He was not even sure what language they were.

'It's Latin, Hansi. And it's a very good motto. It means "Our name explains it all".'

This was not the first time Herr Kaleut had surprised Hansi with the range of his knowledge. For a *Kapitänleutnant* of the Kriegsmarine, known always to his crew by the traditional title of Herr Kaleut, he was surprisingly well read, a cultivated man. Hansi knew that he read, and admired, the Roman poet Horace. He had once said something that puzzled Hansi: 'One thing I really like about Horace — he really hated the sea!' He could also play the violin. Not well, but he could play and the sailors, the Lordly Ones, as they liked to term themselves up forward, loved to hear their captain play the flotilla song, '*So Klein ist das Boot, und so gross ist das Meer*'.

Herr Kaleut did not even look like an officer of the Kriegsmarine. With those thick, coarse lips, the tousled fair hair, the mottled red cheeks, the hair sprouting from the ears, that was more the face of a Pomeranian peasant than an officer of the Reich. Hansi knew that the captain's father had also been a naval officer, in the Kaiser's navy, just as his own father had been, though not an officer. Herr Kaleut had joined the navy as a cadet in the late 1920s, and had commanded a torpedo boat before the war and, after volunteering for the U-Waffe, at least one U-boat, a Type II, now used for training. This U-boat was a Type VII, the latest war canoe. Everybody said that the Sealion, the C-in-C, *Befehlshaber der Unterseeboote,* old BdU himself, had a soft spot for Herr Kaleut. He was the blue-eyed boy. Maybe that was just as well, because so far he had nothing to show for his war patrols. This Type VII was so far an operational virgin. They had laid some mines off the east coast of England which might possibly have sunk some poor unsuspecting ship. But they had sunk nothing at all with their torpedoes. Herr Kaleut always seemed to dive, 'like a married man' as the saying went, whenever he sighted anything. The Lordly Ones up forward were getting restive and on the defensive about their own boat's record. Hansi remembered seeing one or two black eyes the last time they all came back from shore in Wilhelmshaven.

Hansi heard the call up the voice-pipe, the phrase *'Offizierte Traffik!'* Certain signals were for officers' eyes only, some even for Herr Kaleut only. But whatever the classification, for security, the news always went round the boat at once, and was known to all.

'Shift patrol zone...'

Everybody waited while Herr Kaleut studied the secret chart with the squares marked on it. Dagomar, the Obersteursmann, the boat's chief quartermaster and also the catering and provisions officer, put the position of the new patrol area on the larger chart in the control room.

'New area just off the Faeroes Islands. Troop convoy expected. Faeroes,' said Dagomar. 'Never been there.'

'I have,' said Klaus, the First Lieutenant. 'The bleakest place in the world.' Oddly, Klaus had been a fisherman before the war, and his family came from Lübeck. 'If I were you, I would leave the Faeroes to the Faeroese.'

'Well, we're not going ashore there,' Herr Kaleut said, sharply. 'Maybe there will be a target. That's what we want.'

There was indeed a target. It appeared in the evening, when the sun had gone behind cloud, and sea and sky were a uniform cold steely grey. Far overhead, there were long streamers of mackerel-grey wind clouds, forming a huge vault of scales which shone in the light like the flanks of a tremendous fish. Again, it was Herr Kaleut who saw the smoke first, as the merest pencil shading on the hard horizon line to the east. But it grew quite rapidly bolder and blacker, until it became a sharply defined, confident little ship, with a single black funnel, trailing this long line of smoke. It was a tramp steamer, not much bigger than a trawler, possibly Norwegian, but she wore no flag.

A few months earlier, Herr Kaleut might have had to pause and consider whether this was friend or foe. But the operational orders were changing to keep pace with the mood of the war at sea. U-boats had begun the war bound by all manner of restrictions. They had quite literally filled a book with them. U-boats had to surface. They had to identify their targets and verify their nationalities. They had to obey Prize Rules. Then the rules were relaxed to include 'any enemy merchant ship', but not passenger ships. Then, French passenger ships were fair game, but not, not under any circumstances, Americans. The regulations were introduced and then cancelled, but their trend was clear and ominous. The gloves were coming off. The true nature of the U-boat war was emerging, like some monstrous shape which appalled everybody who saw it. But those who were part of it now recognised it, and realised they had known it all along. The U-boat was always the outsider, friend to none and enemy of all. The word soon would be *Sink them all, sink everything, do not hesitate, do not discriminate.* Nobody had actually said as much yet, but that was the way the war was going. BdU himself might publicly deny it, but his staff, whilst protesting that people were putting words in their mouths, were dropping hints and shrugging shoulders.

'Some troop convoy,' said Herr Kaleut, from the periscope. Hansi, at the torpedo firing calculator, looked round sharply. That was a rare mistake for the captain. He should exaggerate the importance of the target, not diminish it. After all, they had sunk nothing at all yet. They would welcome any scrap of success.

'That target, so-called, is tiny. Not much more than a thousand tons, maybe even five hundred. Heading for the Faeroes. Making about six or seven knots.' Herr Kaleut was muttering under his breath, so that Hansi had to strain to hear him. 'Could it possibly be a Q-ship?' he was saying. 'Surely the English would not be so stupid as to try that old trick again?'

The hydrophone operator, Franz Treumann, had been reporting bearings for some time. He classified the sounds as diesel engines, and gave his estimation of the engine revolutions.

'The target is a small merchant ship steering almost due west.' Herr Kaleut spoke loudly, for the benefit of everybody in the U-boat, not just for the attack team in the control room. 'Eight knots, maybe seven. Set speed seven. Making a lot of smoke for his size. His diesel injectors need cleaning. With any luck, he's going to need a lot more than clean diesel injectors in a very few minutes' time.'

The men in the control room exchanged glances. Some formed their lips into smiles without any appearance of humour. The attack team had fallen naturally into their various roles, which they had rehearsed and drilled so often. Theirs was ensemble playing, which Herr Kaleut had once compared to a team of actors from the old Italian *commedia dell'arte,* so used to each other they hardly needed cues. That was, to Hansi, yet another example of Herr Kaleut's unsuspected culture. For a U-boat captain, he was almost a poet.

'Up periscope.' None of them could see anything. All their eyes were fixed on the tiny spot of bright light reflected in Herr Kaleut's eyes. 'One torpedo will do. More than enough.'

Once again, Hansi's eyebrows lifted. One torpedo would certainly be enough, *if* it hit. But more, two or three at least, were needed to make a spread to allow for the inevitable errors in estimating the target's course and speed. It would need a sharpshooter to pick a ship off with a single fish. But, as Hansi realised, Herr Kaleut had a problem. He needed more than one torpedo, but the target was not worth more than one. Then why not surface and attack with the gun?

Herr Kaleut was training the periscope round to have a look around the whole horizon. Many a U-boat captain had become so absorbed in his immediate attacking problem he totally failed to notice an approaching destroyer attacking from another bearing.

'Target range ... is that. Bearing is ... *that*. Range three thousand metres. Target course, two-seven-eight. Open bow doors, number one torpedo tube, stand by...'

The team, crouched at their instruments, passed information from one to the other, as they had been taught and drilled to do so often: target speed, director angle, time to fire, torpedo depth setting, target course, target range, confirmed director angle, time left to firm ... Torpedoes could be fired from the bridge, or from forward, at the tubes, but normally by Hansi, with his hand on the firing levers in the control room. Herr Kaleut and his attack team, if all had done their work properly, had now constructed on their instruments a diagram of the target's position relative to the U-boat and had calculated the angle to which the torpedo must be aimed so as to converge exactly with the target: the director angle, known always as the DA.

'Stand by one tube...'

'Report from forward, one tube ready...'

'Up periscope.' There was time for a last look to check whether the target had been suddenly alarmed at the last moment and altered course or speed, or both. This was a familiar performance, every movement like a ritual, every word an incantation.

'*Rohr eins ... Achtung, Achtung...*' Herr Kaleut stood at the periscope, watching for the DA to come on. '*Lloooossss...*'

They all felt the jolt of the torpedo leaving and heard the muted hiss of air.

The Petty Officer Telegraphist*telegraphist* — the Funkenmeister, as the Lordly Ones called him — held the stop-watch, to count off the running time of two minutes, ten seconds.

'Torpedo running, Herr Kaleut.'

'Very good.'

At the precise running time, Franz Treumann held up his hand. 'A hit, a hit!'

There may have been a hit. But there was no explosion.

Herr Kaleut clenched his teeth, and drew in a long breath which everybody in the boat must have heard. They all knew that he had complained before about the performance of the torpedoes.

'Those infernal firing pistols.'

This, as everybody knew, was a running controversy. Nobody knew the rights or wrongs of it. The staff ashore responsible for maintaining torpedoes said that the pistols failed to detonate in the heads of the torpedoes because the U-boat captains could not aim straight. The U-boat captains retorted that it was the incompetence of the designers which had resulted in a torpedo that never exploded, even when they did hit, which they almost always did.

Hansi sensed at once the depression, which he knew would soon turn to scorn, now spreading through the boat. He had noticed before how extraordinarily easily depressed U-boat sailors were, just as they were so easily cheered up. It took almost nothing to make them gloomy, and little more to make them perk up miraculously. This captain was no good, they would be saying. A bad workman always blames his tools.

Hansi was the only one who met Herr Kaleut's eye, as he looked balefully around the control room. That was, perhaps, one of the bravest single acts of Hansi's life.

'What about it, Hansi? Is it the firing pistols?'

Hansi hardly knew how to reply. His loyalties were torn two ways. He was the boat's torpedo officer, responsible for their performance, and he knew how hard the men up forward worked, to withdraw the torpedoes from the tubes one by one, as they became due for overhaul, to carry out all the routines and tasks on them. They were complicated mechanisms, and could be temperamental. To look after them properly was a long, tiring and filthy, but extremely skilful job. On the other hand, it would be too easy a way out, just to blame the firing pistols. Those too were regularly tested and maintained by men dedicated to their work. But it did seem, on the evidence, that they were at fault. It seemed that Franz Treumann had heard the torpedo strike the target hull, but nothing had happened.

'It's those firing pistols,' Hansi said flatly, as though there could be no further argument, no dispute at all, about the matter.

At that, Herr Kaleut's shoulders slumped. His whole body seemed to go slack. He drew his lips into the form of a smile, but his eyes above it remained puzzled and furious. Then he nodded and turned away to give the orders for surfacing.

It was a gloomy return to Wilhelmshaven, itself the most gloomy and provincial of all gloomy provincial German cities. It was a sailors' town which appeared to dislike sailors. It accepted the business the Kriegsmarine brought it, while ignoring the men who brought the business. At least it was a harbour, and a change from the sea, but nobody on board looked forward to Wilhelmshaven. There were forty-five men in that U-boat and, curiously, not one of them came from Wilhelmshaven. *Just as well,* Hansi thought, with once again no success to report.

It really was the most melancholy of homecomings. In the Jade estuary the wind always seemed to blow straight off the North Pole into one's face. There were green shallows in the water beside the shoreline, and long desolate stretches of windblown reeds. Above them, there were flocks of seabirds, crying and wailing as they swirled to and fro. When the tide changed, there would be a roaring on the outer bar, like the ghosts of drowned sailors demanding God's mercy, or a drink anyway. There were fine churches with tall spires in Wilhelmshaven, but they always appeared reluctantly upon the horizon, as though they did not wish to give any help to returning mariners, not even so much as a leading mark for a bearing.

The U-boat was met by a small tender, flying the harbour commodore's pennant. The tiny wisp of red-and-black bunting at the mast was the only military-looking thing about the vessel. Otherwise, it must be about the same size and appearance of their late target.

But everybody noticed the new atmosphere ashore. For Wilhelmshaven, it was positively jolly. It was because Germany was clearly, unmistakeably, winning the war. There remained only a few loose ends to be tied up. The English army had been chased back across the Channel. General Guderian's Panzers were on the cliffs of France, looking across to England. Big guns were being brought up to bombard the English coastal convoys of small ships going through the narrow straits. The radio and the newspapers were full of German victories. Holland and Belgium had both been defeated. France had fallen prostrate and was begging for peace terms. Success in Norway, where the English had had to leave yet again with their tails down. Greater Germany now stretched from Poland to the Pyrenees. As somebody said in the U-boat bar, Germany goes from Brest to Brest-Litovsk.

Neither Herr Kaleut nor Hansi had much time to appreciate such puns. From the moment they set foot ashore, they were both engaged in a struggle with the Flotilla Commander's torpedo staff over the matter of firing pistols. The pistols had a magnetic device which detonated the warhead when it was activated by the magnetic field of the target's metal hull. Thus it was theoretically not even necessary to hit; a near miss would be enough.

Herr Kaleut continued to insist, and Hansi continued to support him loyally, that the attack had been good, the torpedo had hit, and the pistol firing device had failed. The shore bureaucrats continued to retort that the torpedo must have missed by a mile, and they were supported by staff officers who had arrived from the Marineleamt in Berlin, and by BdU's own Chief of Staff. It was recognised that a crisis was approaching. There had been too many misses to have a credible statistical basis. Too many U-boat captains had returned reporting failures. Even the shore staff conceded that they could not *all* be idiots.

Hansi began to sense that the shore bureaucrats were weakening, were arguing their case with less and less conviction. But that did not mean they would not stoop to use their dirty-tricks department. One evening, in the junior U-boat officers' bar, Hansi was approached by a man he had never met but knew all about. As an *Oberleutnant zur See*, the other was one rank senior to Hansi, but his actual rank meant little; he had the ear of much more senior officers. He was always to be seen hanging around in their company. He had the latest gossip, always knew who was now in favour, who was not. He was known as HK, because he was a *Hinterkriecher*, literally a backside creeper. HK knew of his nickname and, curiously, did not seem to mind, seemed even proud of it.

'Drink, Hansi?'

Hansi was annoyed by this use of his own nickname by a stranger. 'I have a drink, many thanks.'

'Oh, well, let me fill you up again next time. Did your boat get its mail OK?' HK continued in this vein, talking around several subjects in a casual manner, before he came to the point. 'These firing pistols, Hansi, what do you think? Is it true they're no good?'

Hansi looked around the bar. They were all making so much noise it was hard for Hansi to hear what HK was saying, let alone anybody else. Nevertheless, this was a very dangerous subject to talk about in a public place. After all, the performance, or the non-performance, of the U-Waffe's main weapon was a matter of the greatest importance to the enemy.

'Should we be talking about this here? Like this?'

'Purrh.' HK made an odd sound, like a startled cat, as he blew out his cheeks derisively. 'The war's nearly over. If there was anybody listening, it wouldn't do them any good *now*. What do you think, do you think your captain really hit the target?'

'Well, of course I do!' *Really,* Hansi thought indignantly — what did the man expect him to say? 'I was in the attack team. I saw everything that was going on...'

'Except through the periscope...'

Hansi shrugged. 'I don't know what you mean by that. The hydrophone operator said he could actually hear the torpedo hitting.'

'Ah yes. But it is not unknown for sailors to say what their officers want to hear, is it?'

Hansi looked at HK with contempt. 'I was *there*. I *know* it was a good attack. I *know* our hydrophone operator. We hit. It did not explode. That's an end of it.'

'Well, not quite. It is just that...'

'Just what?'

'There are such things as reputations. High reputations involved here. We would not like to spoil the good names of those set in authority over us.'

'I understand that,' Hansi said. 'But we are at war. Reputations may have to take second place to the war.'

'Psscht.' HK put his finger and thumb together in front of his mouth and blew them apart and away, like blowing thistle down. 'The *war.*'

Having, it seemed, said what he had come to say, or had been briefed to say, HK retreated smoothly out of Hansi's company, fading away to the other end of the bar as though he had never been. In a moment, Hansi saw him talking, like a conspirator, to someone else, and after a few moments they both looked in his direction. Clearly HK had just said something about him.

Hansi was glad to be left to his own thoughts. Aside from the firing pistols, there were aspects of that attack which needed some consideration. It had been a standard submerged attack with torpedoes, such as had been taught in the U-boat schools before and during the war. But it had seemed at the time, and the thought had occurred to Hansi many times since, a very elaborate way of attacking such a target, like laying a complicated ambush, using heavy howitzers, to catch a milkman and his pony. Why not stay on the surface?

It happened that Herr Kaleut invited Hansi to drink with him, a few evenings later, in the senior officers' mess. It was called the *Hoch Raum* — the High Room — and it was used by the flotilla captain, his staff, and senior officers, including the commanding officers of operational U-boats. Junior officers were not members, and were seldom invited, and Hansi was flattered — especially when he saw that Klaus, the First Lieutenant, was not included in the invitation.

The building itself dated from the nineteenth century, probably from Bismarck's day. The mess was a very long, high-ceilinged room, with portraits of uniformed men all around, but so dark it was almost impossible to distinguish their rank or features. There was a long bar of superbly polished wood, and stewards in white jackets with blue trousers and a red stripe down their sides.

Herr Kaleut came straight to the point. Hansi had already sensed he had something on his mind. Herr Kaleut was now seriously worried about the boat's lack of success. Apart from anything else, it greatly weakened his case against the firing pistols.

'You've been thinking about that attack, Hansi, I know. What *do* you think?'

Hansi told him of his misgivings, that he thought they had been using a very large and inefficient hammer to try and crush a very small nut. Although a U-boat was a submarine, any boat which dived at once lost a great part of its speed, awareness and manoeuvrability.

Herr Kaleut nodded quickly. 'That is *exactly* what I think, Hansi.' Herr Kaleut spoke rapidly and freely, so freely Hansi began to wonder how many of the schnapps they were drinking Herr Kaleut had enjoyed already. Hansi had never known Herr Kaleut unbend so much, or behave in such a relaxed manner.

At times Hansi had felt himself being nominated, by both sides, to act as the link between Herr Kaleut and the rest of the boat. When he had first joined, shortly before the outbreak of war, the captain had been as cold and aloof with him as with everybody. But slowly he had warmed to Hansi, as to a kindred soul. Hansi wished he would similarly unbend a little more to others. The Lordly Ones would like it, and do their duties better, if Herr Kaleut sometimes showed that he was human too. It seemed to Hansi that Herr Kaleut would like to be friendlier, but did not know how, as though he simply did not have the emotional equipment.

Herr Kaleut and Hansi sat together in front of the fire. Above the fireplace was a surprisingly modestly-sized portrait of Adolf Hitler. Its size suggested it was the smallest that could decently be hung in an officers' mess. Whenever Herr Kaleut nodded, a steward brought across to them glasses of schnapps and, later, brandy. Meanwhile the *Hoch Raum* emptied, until the two of them were left alone, sitting by the fire, which was itself dying, while the captain talked on and on, of U-boats and men he had known, of tactics and training, and firing pistols, and the sailing barque in which he had first gone to sea as a lad, and the torpedo boat he had commanded in the Baltic before the war, and of promotions and disappointments and scandals, some affecting U-Waffe men already lost at sea in the war.

Every time the steward brought a fresh drink, Herr Kaleut raised the glass to the portrait of the Führer, with a grimace of something close to contempt. Hansi listened, and nodded, and put in a word, acting his part as audience, sounding board, and junior confessor.

At last Herr Kaleut stopped and looked into the fire, which had long been dead embers. Hansi realised that his captain was drunk, so drunk he could not stand up. Hansi stood up himself, and at once Herr Kaleut looked round and up.

'*Treuherzig,* Hansi,' he said, and Hansi could see that he had the greatest difficulty in forming the words. 'I hope they don't spoil you. All this —' Herr Kaleut trained his gaze slowly around the *Hoch Raum,* to check if anybody else was there — 'is between ourselves alone.'

'Of course, sir.'

On the morning they left for their next patrol, there was the usual leave-taking. Herr Kaleut, Klaus and Hansi first went across to the flotilla offices — *pour prendre congé,* as the captain said to Hansi. They drank a glass of champagne with the flotilla captain. Hansi was given the cork, for luck. Then they all went down to the dockside berth, where there were some wives and girlfriends, with a scattering of officers from the staff and the U-boat base. There was also a party of schoolgirls, waving their white handkerchiefs. War pennants flew from the U-boat wireless aerials. '*Hals- und Beinbruch,*' everybody called out. 'Good hunting and a safe return.' The garrison brass band was playing, too, a fine oompah-oompah tune, which they were punching out against the steady wind from the north. '*Muss i denn, muss i denn, zum Stadtele hinaus...*' It was a splendid thumping tune, but the Lordly Ones always preferred something more modest and they used to sing '*So Klein ist das*

Boot, und so gross ist das Meer'. Best of all, they liked a plaintive little song on a gramophone record which the Funkenmeister had once brought on board. It was played by a solo violin, a gypsy-ish tune with some bounce to it. Herr Kaleut could play it, sometimes, when he chose. Some wag in the fore ends had put words to it, and the boat had made it their own song, because it seemed to sum up their feelings.

Behold, I heard a wise man say,
Come listen to my cheerful lay.
Don't take living with a frown,
Don't let the buggers grind you down,
Come on, cheer up, it could be worse!

That's good advice, I thought, though terse,
So I did cheer up, and I was so gay,
And it did get worse, the very next day!

They used to sing it whenever they went to sea, and standing on the bridge Hansi could hear the roaring chorus from below. *'So I did cheer up and I was so gay, And it did get worse, the very next day!'*

They had been a week at sea, and were in their patrol position off the Irish coast, two hundred and fifty kilometres from the Bloody Foreland, when the big ship came up over the horizon to the east. Hansi was on watch and saw the ship before the lookout for that sector. He took a bearing and called down for Herr Kaleut. He was studying the ship, still a very long way off, through his binoculars, when the captain joined him.

She was truly a monster. Already in the seconds since she had been first sighted as a minute grey speck on the horizon, her hull had swelled blacker and plainer. She must be travelling because, no sooner had Herr Kaleut put his binoculars up, than Hansi could make out two masts, two funnels and a superstructure which looked as broad and high as a mansion. Hansi even thought that he could distinguish her mauve-coloured hull as the evening sun caught it. As he watched, the great silhouette certainly lengthened, as though she had altered course. That was the second time she had done so.

'Zigzagging,' Herr Kaleut said. That showed she was aware of danger. Zigzagging might also indicate a guilty conscience. A neutral would surely steer a straight course, as though to proclaim by her actions her non-involvement in the war.

The range was closing very rapidly indeed. It was past high time to dive. The ship might see them at any moment. Already, Hansi could make out some detail on the bridge superstructure. On the nearest, port wing bridge, there was what could possibly be a gun…

'Dive … dive … *dive*…'

Below, the word had already gone through the whole boat that the target of a lifetime was approaching. Herr Kaleut's words, from the conning tower above, came down to the control room and the boat below, as Hansi thought, as though from Sinai.

'One, two, three and four tubes…'

There was the quickfire exchange of order and acknowledgement, everybody repeating the order and carrying it out, anxious to support Herr Kaleut in his attack. Hansi could feel the sensation of tremendous anticipation throughout the boat. A full salvo of four torpedoes — that was something like it! No pissing about in penny numbers, farting off single eels at tiny targets. This was a maximum salvo against something the size of the *Bremen*! At that thought, Hansi felt a tiny stab of unease; other nations, apart from the English, had giant liners.

'She's altered away again. Definitely zigzagging. My God, she's colossal! I can see the red and gold of the sun against her sides. She looks as big as a mountain!'

At each successive phrase, men in the control room hugged their sides. Everybody was beaming. Maybe this would break their long drought. The sounds of torpedoes exploding would be like the thunderclaps of a rainstorm deluging a parched countryside. It had been a long wait, a *very* long wait, but the biggest fish always came to the most patient fishermen.

As the range came down, the attack problem solved itself nicely. It was as though this giant sacrifice actually wanted to make things easier for her executioners. Hansi knew they were within some twenty-five seconds of a firing solution. Then he noticed a very slight but quite perceptible change in Herr Kaleut's manner, the lightest but clearest hint of doubt in his voice. The seconds passed, until the firing moment, and nothing happened. Herr Kaleut said no more. Everybody was now keyed up to fire. If the captain said anything, even so much as a whisper under his breath, those torpedoes would go. All their training had led up to this very moment. The next order, the next sound of any kind, must be *Fire!* If Herr Kaleut only cleared his throat those eels would be on their way.

The firing solution came, and went. Herr Kaleut stood motionless. He continued to stare through the periscope. Below, they knew now something must have gone amiss. Finally, and very slowly, Herr Kaleut withdrew his eye from the attack periscope.

'Down periscope. Keep twenty metres.' He called down the ladder from the conning tower. 'It was an American. I saw the stars and stripes on her side as she turned the last time...'

An *American* ... a great groan of disappointment and anguish passed through the boat. Would their bubble of bad luck *never* burst? An American ... of all the things to happen. But Herr Kaleut was quite right. Nobody, least of all U-Waffe crews, wanted the Yanks in the war. It might come to that, but happily not yet. Everybody knew about the *Lusitania* in the last war. That had been an expensive success, in blood and treasure, for Germany in the end.

It was Hansi, with his acute sympathy for Herr Kaleut's feelings, who realised most clearly what the decision not to fire had cost him. It had been much braver to refrain. It was moral courage which was so often harder to show than physical.

The Lords up forward might understand the need not to annoy the Americans, but that did not mean they were pleased by events. When Hansi next went up there to the fore ends, there was an atmosphere of open criticism, close even to insubordination. Hansi himself was amazed, not for the first time, that any men could live in such conditions for weeks at a time. The cramped space was restricted even more by the reload torpedoes, which of course had not been fired, lying in their racks. Then there was the smell, the dirty clothing lying everywhere, the stores and food packed and hanging in every crevice, the ugly metal surfaces, the faces and bodies pressing into view, always, and from every side. Nobody had any privacy, physical or mental. The Lords did not even have a bunk of their own to which they could retreat into their own thoughts. Every man 'hot-bunked' with his opposite number, climbing into the bunk vacated at the end of the watch. The wonder was not that the Lordly Ones were sometimes cheeky and restive, but that it did not happen much more often.

Their complaints were laced with a characteristically bitter wit.

'This torpedo, do they want it for a museum?'

'Will they take away our pay if we go on like this?'

Even the torpedo petty officer, Charley the *Aalmeister*, was unusually sarcastic. 'We could never fire *this*,' he said, gingerly patting the shining greased surface of the nearest reload. 'We've looked after it so long it would be like losing a *brother*!'

'Don't you worry,' Hansi said, 'there's plenty of time. This war is going to go on a long time.'

To Hansi's own surprise, that remark quelled everybody. It was not actually what he himself believed. Surely, by all reports, there could not now be long to go before it was all over. But the mere mention that the war might be long-lasting was more than enough to quench the spirits even of the Lordly Ones. Hansi was sorry he had said it, when he saw their expressions change, the witticisms wither on their lips. He had forgotten how mercurial U-boat crews were. It took nothing at all to depress them.

Happily, they all had good news almost at once. 'Lorient,' said Herr Kaleut, looking at the signal book. 'Lorient after this trip is over.'

Lorient. The news went through the boat like a draught of some miraculous tonic. Wine, warmer weather, *women*: legendary, fabulous Frenchwomen. Hansi was not surprised to discover that Herr Kaleut was a Francophile, who had travelled extensively in France before the war and could even speak passable French. 'After all,' he told Hansi, 'we both speak a form of bad Latin. It is a pity we are at war with the French. Our real enemy is not in the west. Have you been to France, Hansi?'

'Never.'

'You'll like it.'

Certainly, Hansi liked what he could see from the bridge as they closed the coastline of France. He was struck first of all by the deep, intense, almost voluptuous green of the countryside. Germany was green in the summertime, but not like this. This was an altogether more sumptuous colour, a healing green, like a balm to a seafarer's eyes. It was a dramatic coast, with its cliffs, and the rock of St Michel on the approach, and hillsides, and more green fields. Hansi could see a small beach, of white shingle set in a green cleft; what a heavenly place to take a girl, with a basket of food and some wine, for a fine afternoon in the sun. Beyond, there was the spire of a church, and some red-roofed houses. This was not a countryside at war, this was rich and lush, and ripe for plundering.

There was not a sign of war — not a scar, not a mark — in Lorient itself. There were large trees growing even alongside the jetties, and a road as broad as a boulevard leading from the town. Ahead of the U-boat's bows, as they steered in, was the old fortified city of Port Louis. With its crowding houses coming down to the water's edge, the busy traffic on the streets, and above, a clear blue summer sky, it all looked like an eighteenth-century painting.

Men were ready on the quayside to take the U-boat's lines. Their faces were not at all hostile, but seemed almost welcoming.

'*They* look healthy enough,' Herr Kaleut said. Hansi took his point at once. There was an ironic contrast between the grey, beard-fringed faces and the filthy, oily-grey leathers of the U-boat men, the victors, and the healthy colour, the tanned skins and rosy cheeks, of the defeated.

Some French sailors stood in the crowd in their smart blue uniforms with those ridiculous pompoms on their caps. Should they, Hansi wondered, should they still be allowed to wear that uniform? Surely they were a vanquished navy?

'Probably Bretons,' Herr Kaleut said. 'Half the French navy comes from these parts. Great seamen.'

Hansi was about to comment, but Klaus took the words out of his mouth. 'They haven't done very well so far,' he said.

'Ha, don't you worry,' the captain said sharply, as though he had almost been waiting to reprove Klaus. 'The war's not over yet, not by a long way indeed. Don't believe everything you read in the *Völkischer Beobachter*!'

They could hear the sound of a band now, and following the band a procession of women dressed in black costumes with white lace caps on their heads. The men, gathered like pall-bearers, carried a shrine, roofed and curtained like a howdah. The curtains were drawn back to show the blue-painted, brightly gilded effigy of a saint. Other men were striking large metal triangles, and blowing long horns. It was an unexpected, almost a pagan sight in a foreign port in the midst of a war. For one moment, Hansi wondered whether this was some hostile demonstration by the French against their conquerors.

'Saint Anne of the sea,' said Herr Kaleut. 'She's the patron saint around here. St Anne's festival, this must be. The Bretons have a prayer. It's famous. Do either of you know it?'

Klaus and Hansi both shook their heads.

'O God be good to me, thy sea is so wide and my ship is so small…'

'But that's the same as our song!' said Hansi. *'So Klein ist das Boot und so gross ist das Meer!'*

'It's not surprising. We're all sailors together. We happen to be at each other's throats just now. Although that is hard to imagine, looking at this place.'

It was indeed hard to imagine. After the bare, bleak coastline of northern Germany, and the regimentation and regulations of its daily life, Lorient was like some summertime paradise. There were no sentries, and hardly any uniforms, except those of the U-boat sailors themselves, who could stroll into town, wander under the trees, and have a drink in the nearest bar. The food, wine and coffee were superb. There were lobsters cooked in cream and wine; crabs, delicately simmered until their flesh melted, in cream and wine and herbs; prawns, and langouste, and chickens, and fish soup, piping hot, served with cream and the most delicious bread crumbs. Really, the only signs of the Occupation — as the French were already calling it, but offhandedly, as though they were merely referring to some unfortunate but unavoidable disease of some remote relative — were the signposts. The French street and route signs, with their neat and old-fashioned blue-and-white enamel plates, were already overhung and obscured by fresh-painted signs in German: *SOLDATENHEIM* and *STANDORT KOMMANDANTUR*, instead of *LA PLAGE* and *ST NAZAIRE*.

The more they looked, the more they found, and the more amazed the U-boat crews and the technical staffs were by the wealth, the sheer prodigality of the place. Across the harbour there was a small dock and repair yard, sited on a narrow peninsula where two rivers joined and flowed together towards the sea. When Hugo, Herr Kaleut's Engineer Officer, went across there he found German staff and French employees, foremen and machinery, all ready to carry out major repairs to hulls and engines. The flotilla had asked for offices, storerooms, accommodation, dumps for ammunition, and suitable work spaces for maintaining torpedoes, and periscopes, and heavy electrical machinery. Everything was provided. The flotilla asked for fuel tankage, and lubricating oil drum storage, and fresh water distilling machinery, and an electrical generating plant, and metal-working shops, coppersmithing, iron foundry, brazing and welding and casting and pattern-making. It was all provided.

Finally, BdU himself was expected to move his headquarters to Lorient, and proper buildings were needed. A château was commandeered, only a little one, but a château — a *Schlösschen,* in fact — two or three kilometres away, looking from above the old town, down the estuary and out to sea. It had belonged pre-war to a sardine-canning magnate, everybody said. So they called it the little sardine castle: *Sardinenschlösschen.*

The only activity which was at all regulated at Lorient, as Herr Kaleut said, was drinking. All drank according to rank and status — the senior officers in the Hotel Beau Séjour, the junior officers in a bar always known simply as The Café' the petty officers in the Napoleon Bar, and the Lordly Ones in Le Pigeon Blanc. But on the Saturday night, their first Saturday in harbour, most of the officers in the flotilla were driven in several large cars out into the country to a great house, much bigger than the sardine castle. Hansi had no idea where he was, or why he had come, or who had told him, but when he climbed out of the car he thought it was like something out of the *Arabian Nights.*

The sun was almost setting behind trees at the end of the drive. Lines of coloured lights ran from tree to tree in front of the house. The visitors were, apparently, expected. There was a joint of meat roasting over an open fire, tables crammed with bottles of wine, chairs, and carpets, and a gramophone playing, and there were girls. How many, Hansi could not see, but there were enough to go round; indeed, there was enough, and more than enough, of everything.

They all drank wine carefully, eyeing the girls. It seemed the girls were all French and none of them had a word of German.

That was a disadvantage, at this stage. It would not matter later on.

The wine was delicious. Hansi allowed himself to get pleasantly drunk. Normally, he hated the feeling that he was not entirely in control of himself. But surely he was entitled to some dispensation now, if only for tonight. Herr Kaleut, he could see, was much more drunk, in fact fast approaching that state he had been in that night at the *Hoch Raum*. He had a bottle with an expensive-looking label. Trust Herr Kaleut to choose the best of everything.

Herr Kaleut sat down beside Hansi, who was not at all sure he welcomed the captain's company that night. 'Tell me one thing, Hansi, before you get too big for your boots...'

'I beg pardon?'

'Hah! *Hansi!* You don't know your own talents. The U-Waffe is going to need men like you. It's young men like you who are going to *fight*...' Herr Kaleut said the word with an explosive hiss, using *raufen,* the word for schoolboy brawling. But the way he said it lent it a deeper and wider meaning: the real fight, he meant, that was going on outside, out there, beyond the Rock of St Michel.

'Tell me, Hansi, what are they saying about Herr Kaleut up forward there, with the Lordly Ones? Are they furious with me?'

Hansi had defended the captain to the sailors, and now, curiously, he felt bound to take the sailors' part with the captain. 'They are very disappointed, of course. Some of them say things they should not.'

'What sort of things do they say that they should not, Hansi?'

'Things that should not be repeated to Herr Kaleut.'

'Loyal Hansi. That's right. That's quite right. You're going to be one of the good ones, Hansi. I can tell it. They'll follow you to the ends of the earth, and the sea. I prophesy it. They'll have to, too, before we're finished. And I hope to God I'm still there to see it.'

'I didn't mean to say that they are seriously concerned, Herr Kaleut. If anything's worrying them, it is that the war will be over before they have done anything much. Of course, they don't want any trouble. Maybe they don't want the war to go on, really, they want a quiet life. But still…'

Herr Kaleut was laughing, spluttering, choking even, so that for a terrible moment Hansi thought he was going to vomit.

'Is *that* what they think? I don't believe you! They'll get all the *war* they want. The little innocent ones! The *lambs*! Have you ever met an Englishman, Hansi? Ever *seen* one, even?'

Hansi shook his head.

'Well, I have. I have been to London. Twice. I can even speak some English. Nothing like as good as my French, but I can get by. I'll tell you something about the English, Hansi. They are not beaten easily, because they never believe they will lose. No matter what happens. No matter how many ships they lose, when ships are sunk, no matter how many men are drowned, deep down they still believe they are unbeatable. As for us, now, you know us, Hansi. No matter how big and powerful our ships are, no matter how successful we are, still deep down we have this anxiety, this little voice that says *This can't be, this can't last*. It's what it means to be a German, Hansi, to have this little skeleton voice on your shoulder. All the time.'

Hansi knew exactly what he was saying. It was something he had seen in the sailors' faces. It was a perspicacious, and still a dangerous, comment for Herr Kaleut to make. Nobody, not these days, cast any doubts upon Germany's fighting men.

Herr Kaleut called across to one of the girls. She clearly had no German, but he spoke to her in rapid and obviously idiomatic French. Hansi studied her face in the firelight as she replied. She might have been talking to a neighbour over her fence. The French themselves were, of course, quite the biggest amazement of all. Their manner towards the Germans was not in any way apologetic, certainly not in any way defeated. They seemed instead to be making tacit appeals for understanding, for lenience, even, during a period of temporary, but only temporary, embarrassment. They were not abashed by their new situation, not at all. Indeed, Hansi and many of the younger officers had already begun to think that the French did not take their present predicament nearly seriously enough. They had an irresponsibly frivolous attitude towards the war and towards those who were winning it. The French — and especially their girls — should be paying them, especially the younger Germans, a great deal more deference, and even respect.

'Shall I introduce you, Hansi? I think she likes you.'

The girl said something in French.

'She does, she does, she likes you! She says you look like a sausage, with your clean round face, all pink and shining. She says she could stick a fork into you. She says she could *eat* you, Hansi!'

Hansi grunted, at a loss to know what to say. 'What's her name?'

'Yvette. They're all called Yvette.' Herr Kaleut exchanged another rapid tirade with the girl. 'I told her you were a fighting man, Hansi. It was the war that brought you here. And do you know what she says? She says, "Booofff!"' Hansi had seen the gesture, and Herr Kaleut imitated Yvette's expression and tone of voice perfectly. 'The war, the *war,* she says, who cares about the war? Good advice, Hansi. I should follow it if I were you…'

'I will.' Hansi got up, surprised, after so much wine, that he could stand so easily.

'Well done, Hansi.' Herr Kaleut had his violin and he now took it up, put it to his chin, and drew from it a long, tuning chord.

Hansi had nothing he was able, or wanted, to say to the woman. There was only one thing to be done. They walked away, hand in hand, in a manner which might in other circumstances have been called companionable. From behind him, Hansi heard Herr Kaleut playing 'Behold, I heard a wise man say', in the rhythm of a *gigue,* the traditional wedding dance.

Further into the trees, where the lights stopped, the wood was full of the whispers of other couples; but no giggles, as there would have been in the park at home in Leipzig. This was a serious matter.

There were murmurings from every tree, it seemed. They had to walk further and further. Looking back, Hansi could see the glow from the fire and in it, the movement of Herr Kaleut's bow arm. He almost stepped on a body in front of him. The girl beside him, and the couple below, all laughed.

Somebody, somewhere, Hansi thought, knew what U-boat crews needed. Here there was no waiting, no wooing, no *war,* merely acquiescence and complete submission. Her body was very pale, with very dark hair by contrast. She kept slapping herself, lightly, on the side, as though trying to kill midges. Looking down at her face, he could see no expression whatever. As for himself, after that first blessed physical relief, he felt no emotion at all.

CHAPTER THREE

In peacetime it had been a well-known five-star hotel, where the rich came to eat large Scottish meals and go for motor drives in the hills and glens of Perthshire. Even now, there was still an air of peacetime about it, with food borne on silently rolling trolleys, and arrays of clean linen, and glass and cutlery. There were even whiffs of cigars and perfume which were only occasionally overcome by the cruder, more animal smells from the wards. There were even some guests, still staying there, still paying their bills weekly or monthly, as though they had been caught by surprise by the events of 1939 and had not yet decided what to do next. Sometimes, the guests even saw some of the patients, by staring at them through open ward doors, or encountering them walking or being wheeled through the grounds. They seemed to regard the patients with a curious mixture of emotional detachment and pity. It was, as Hamish the young Scots Guards subaltern in the bed next to Jay said, just as though this were a dispensary for sick animals. 'And we're the puppies, with injured paws.'

There was even, so Jay had heard, a psychiatric ward — a 'funny farm' — somewhere in the grounds, but most of the wards had been converted from the larger bedrooms and the pre-war ballroom, and the patients were, like Hamish, casualties from Dunkirk, with one or two from a destroyer which had been badly shot up, and her captain killed, in the Firth of Forth in the very early days. There were also a handful of survivors from Narvik and some aircrew, including one burned fighter pilot who died shortly after Jay arrived, and several cheerful bomber pilots and navigators.

There were no other officers from his ship, so far as Jay knew, and no sailors in that hospital. In fact, Jay had seen none of his fellow survivors since they were all brought ashore in Rosyth. He had heard that Bracewell and the other sailors had been taken to a hospital in Aberdeen. He had heard that Bracewell had lost some toes and one finger from frostbite. But he could get no confirmation, no hard information at all from anybody. Nobody would admit to knowing anything. Jay fancied he had seen some newsreel cameramen filming when he had first been carried ashore on a stretcher. But he had heard nothing since, and nobody else mentioned that they had ever seen that newsreel.

Sometimes Jay felt that at least part of his nightmares was coming true, that he really was quite alone, and that everything had happened only to him. He lay awake every night, in pain, sweating and crying, feeling that he was back in that float, convinced he was all alone, enduring that action, the sinking, the ordeal, by himself. Maybe he really did belong in the funny farm, alongside that man he had heard about who was sure he was Adolf Hitler's uncle.

But there was nothing imaginary or fanciful about the pain in his hands and feet as his circulation patiently, remorselessly, restored his sensations of feeling. Jay would not have believed he could ever have sustained such pain for so long. It was there constantly, for days on end, always waiting for him. His sleep was brief and broken because of his pain. His meals had to be fed to him. Everything had to be done for him because he could do nothing himself. Always the terrible, grinding pain was there, like a burden which was crushing his body deeper and deeper into his bed. Yet he knew he was better now, and he was lucky. All his fingers and toes had survived with him, he had been told, although the sensation had not returned to his fingertips. He could not have tied a shoelace or picked up a pin from the deck, but at least those grotesque and obscenely white swellings had gone down, and his members were back almost to their normal size. On good days he could even swing himself upright and sit on the side of his bed while he put slippers on, very gingerly. But the slippers, he noted, were at least two sizes larger than before.

Possibly worse than the pain, or anyway just as bad, were the interrogations. They said that very few officers had survived, and none of them were in any condition to answer questions yet. 'You're by far the liveliest,' they told Jay. So they asked him again, and again, and again. More and more officers, ever more senior, attended his bedside. Jay discovered, from the shape of the questioning, that it had literally been days before anybody had realised that his ship had been sunk, and then all had been struck aghast, stunned into immobility by the scale of the catastrophe. So now they all centred their enquiries upon Jay. They seemed to home in on him as their only possible source of information, every scrap of which they snatched eagerly from his lips, delighted when it seemed to confirm their preconceptions, frowning when it did not.

Jay told his story again and again until he began to cringe whenever he saw anybody new in the ward or heard footsteps approaching his bed. It was like being suspected of some serious crime and kept in custody, being questioned repeatedly in case one changed one's story in some vital aspect. But his ordeal remained essentially the same: the shock of the action, abandoning the ship, the floats, the cold, the Norwegians who had sounded like Germans, the fear of open daylight, with everybody wanting to be down below. The Norwegian skipper had said something about a torpedo attack; he said he believed that a U-boat had fired at them on the way back to the Faeroes but missed. Jay did not care either way. He knew that he could not have been a survivor a second time. Another visit to those cold waters would have killed him.

While Jay was concerned to tell the story of his ordeal, his inquisitors were much more interested in the action. Had he personally seen any German ships? What size were they? Cruisers? Bigger than cruisers? Smaller? What calibre shell had hit the ship? Eleven-inch? Larger? Smaller? How many hits? *Where* were the hits? Impossible to be sure. Jay could only lie in bed and think again of that terrible thunder, rolling up the ship's side, like a pillar of fire advancing along the deck, devouring all who stood in its path, and covering their last moments in a pall of dense smoke. But was it true the order to abandon ship had been first given, and then belayed, then given again? Whose voice gave the orders? Was it a different voice the second time? Jay tried his utmost, but he simply could not remember.

Above all, the questioners pressed Jay on the matter of the disagreement between the Captain and Wings, and any possible bearing it might have, or he thought it might have, on the loss of the ship. Jay wondered why they did not ask Wings himself. Ironically, the Captain had saved Wings' life by putting him ashore. Wings must still be up there in Scapa Flow, and he probably would be most glad to tell them everything they wanted to know. Maybe they would go up there and ask Wings, but in the meantime they asked Jay. What was the row about, basically? What had the Captain actually said? Did he say anything to Jay himself?

Again, Jay did his best. But as he said, over and over again, he was only a junior aircrew member of a squadron. He was not in the Captain's confidence. He retailed the great sparking plug affair again. But apart from that, he doubted if he and the Captain had ever exchanged more than half a dozen words since he joined the ship.

Jay did his very best to help Wings. As very probably the only surviving aircrew officer, it was his duty to defend him as best he could. He told his story, under intense pressure, to show Wings in the most favourable light, even to the point where, he suspected, he was almost being disloyal to his dead captain.

Jay was surprised to find that his visitors did not agree with him. They were surprised by his surprise. 'This is a big war,' they all said. 'One man isn't important. It's the big picture that counts.' Even the nurses seemed to disapprove. 'Your job is to get well again,' they said. 'You should leave your friend to look after himself.'

Even Hamish, in the next bed, sounded a warning note. 'I don't know anything much about the Navy,' he said, 'but I sense something going on here. I smell faggots being piled under somebody and the fire being lit. This chap you're all talking about, he's much older and senior to you. He ought to be able to look after himself.'

Privately, Jay doubted that. Wings seemed so very isolated and vulnerable. Even the stars in their courses seemed against him. All his accusers were dead now, but that seemed to make no difference. They were all acting as though the accusations could still be supported by evidence. Nobody made allowances for the fact that all Wings' defenders were dead, too, except Jay.

One day, when Jay had been allowed up and had managed to walk four and a half lengths of the ward unaided, his father arrived to visit him. Jay had the greatest respect and love for his father, who had set out on his own naval career before the First World War with the highest hopes and expectations. But his father had had to leave the Navy because of the Geddes Axe in the 1920s. His experience had not made him bitter. Rather, his view of life and his opinions had set solid, just as they were when he was serving.

In many ways, his father was a fossilised specimen of the naval officer of the First World War. Jay knew his father's qualities: his loyalty, his bravery, his sense of humour, his ability to lead men. But Jay sometimes wondered whether the officers of his father's generation had quite the subtlety of mind, the flexibility, to combat the present enemy. Maybe what was needed was an officer who was less of a gentleman and more of a low, cunning cad. Yet his father and his contemporaries were supremely jealous of the Navy's reputation, and were quick to avenge what they saw to be a slight upon it. They had a way of dealing with those who transgressed, or even threatened to transgress, their code; they compromised them, by involving them. *If you can't beat them, make them join you,* was their motto; and a very good one, too. Jay's late captain and his father were very like each other. After all, they were almost exact contemporaries. His father had been a couple of terms senior to the captain at Osborne and Dartmouth. But, while his father had been beached, the captain had carried on and had been promoted.

Jay had not expected his father to sympathise with his desire to defend Wings. His father was horrified, by the prospect and by his presumption.

'Jonathan, that is not up to you. That is for Their Lordships to deal with. With the officer concerned.'

'But, Father, I'm one of the very few aircrew — I think almost the only one — to survive. If I don't speak up for the truth, it will never come out. Never be known. There could be lessons to be learned from this, important lessons, Father, which everybody ought to know about. Don't you see? I don't *want* to cause trouble.'

'There are times when it is better for the Service that the truth, as you call it, does not come out. Because it is *not* the truth.'

'But, Father, I must...'

But Jay could see from the flush, the tightening of lips, that his father had made up his mind and there was nothing to be gained by discussing the point further. It was always thus with his father. His mind seemed to snap shut on a particular point of view, or rather, his mind had never really been open to argument. His father had decided views, the views of his generation, on everything, and nothing would alter them.

'Let's not talk any more about that. How are you, anyway?'

'Very well, considering. I'm lucky I haven't lost anything. My feet still feel peculiar. Partly numb, partly red hot, I never quite know which. But I'm still all there. I hear some of those who survived have lost toes and even fingers. So I'm lucky.'

'So you are indeed,' his father said decidedly. 'You'll soon be up and about and ready to go to sea again. Wish to God *I* could. Did I tell you about my new job?'

'No, you didn't.' Jay could see that his father was pleased and yet somewhat abashed by his new employment.

'In the Admiralty. In charge of collecting and categorising postcards and holiday snaps.' His father saw Jay's look of blank incomprehension. 'Not as stupid as it seems at first sight, let me tell you. Didn't you see our special appeal in *The Times*?'

Jay shook his head. He had not, in fact, read *The Times* or any newspaper for weeks. He would have had difficulty holding the pages and, anyway, nothing in them seemed to relate to him. It seemed that his mental calendar had stopped, on some bulkhead somewhere, when the ship went down.

'We've appealed for people to send in their holiday snapshots and postcards of beaches and holiday resorts all over Europe...' His father had seen Jay's amazement. 'Just a minute, I'll explain. You can get a quite astonishing amount of information from a picture postcard or a snapshot. Behind Mum, on the beach there, there's a pier, just waiting. It looks big enough to land troops on, big enough to take a destroyer, perhaps alongside. Where that girl is lying in her bathing suit, you can see the gradient of the beach exactly, and you can see that it's a good firm shingle surface; you could drive vehicles up that. And so on.'

Jay stared at his father. 'But surely...' *Surely we won't need anything like that for* ages, *Father,* he nearly said, but refrained just in time. 'Surely it's the *Germans* who should be studying postcards of *us*?'

His father seemed piqued by Jay's expression of astonishment. 'Of course we'll need information on the beaches, and sooner than anybody thinks.'

His father seemed impervious to the edgy mood in the country which even Jay, in the fastness of his hospital ward, could sense. The nurses were ever more punctilious about the blackout curtains. Jay had heard stories that there were roadblocks on all the main roads in the Home Counties, and East Anglia, and obstacles like old cars and mangles and waggons placed in all fields likely to be used as landing strips, and the Local Defence Volunteers were drilling all over the place. There was even a code word, Jay had heard, which meant that the Germans had invaded — *Cromwell* — and then all the church bells were going to ring out an alarm.

Nor was his father much dismayed by the fall of France, or the prospect of waging the war without French help. 'Good riddance,' he said. 'Bloody Frogs. I've never had any time for them. Always look after Number One, the French do. The most selfish, self-centred people in the world. No, it's a good thing they've packed up. No more nonsense from them. No allies. Nobody to let us down. We shall just have to get on with it and finish it ourselves. We'll win, you'll see.'

His father's sublime confidence was impressive, and in the end convincing. Maybe he was right. Jay recalled a story Hamish had told him of how he finally got away from Dunkirk in a ferry which normally ran between Liverpool and the Isle of Man. Hamish had found, quite unexpectedly, a bar deep down in the bowels of the vessel, where a steward was selling cups of tea. There were dive bombers overhead, the occasional crash of bombs, and exhausted soldiers and their gear lying all over the place, but the steward was still charging twopence a cup for his tea, although as a concession he was accepting foreign coinage. 'As I was drinking my tea,' Hamish said, 'I had a sudden thought, and I asked this steward if he had any whisky? He gave me a very old-fashioned look and said yes, he did; but, he said, the bar was always closed in harbour. In *harbour*! There were swarms of bloody Stukas all over the place, every now and again the whole ship shook with near misses, and every moment might be our last; and no, he said, no the bar was never opened in harbour! I must say, all of a sudden, I had the funny feeling that we were going to win this war after all. With blokes like that, keeping the bar shut in harbour, how can we lose?'

Jay found that his father was riding an old hobbyhorse. 'Maybe this time, with the French out of the way, we'll get the fleet action we've always longed for. Finish that bit of unfinished business at Jutland.'

'I think it'll be the U-boats this time, Father. That is certainly what we in the air branch are preparing for.'

His father looked at Jay as though he had suddenly found him speaking an alien and incomprehensible language. 'No, I don't believe that. They're no problem. Although the figures are going up. They don't put those in the papers. Especially now they've shifted their bases to France. *That's* a bit of a blow, I must admit. While they still had to make the passage around the British Isles we had a chance of hammering them on their way. Now, they can slip out and in a few hours they're in the Atlantic.'

When his father had gone, to have lunch with the Surgeon Captain whom he had known in the Grand Fleet and then on to catch his train, Jay thought over the implications of their conversation. Wings' reputation had been damaged. His honour had been brought into question. It behoved anybody who knew the truth to speak up, whatever the consequences. One should be loyal to one's ship, one's Service, one's country. But surely that grander loyalty began more humbly, with loyalty to the man sitting across the wardroom table, the man on the other side of the bridge, the man sitting behind you in the observer's seat. That was where true loyalty began. After all, it was Bracewell's loyalty which had kept Jay himself alive.

The physical test, which Jay had to pass before he could be discharged, was to walk ten lengths of the ward, which was some thirty feet long, unaided. Jay passed the test much more easily than he had expected, indeed he felt slightly guilty at not having attempted it earlier. But the doctor and the two ward nurses seemed pleased. 'That's very good,' they said, 'after only eight weeks.' Before he had properly realised what was happening to him, Jay found himself sitting in the train going south on leave. It was the first time he had been left to his own devices and resources, the first time he had been called upon to organise his own life, for what seemed months. Jay had looked forward passionately to the day of release. Now that it had come, he wondered whether he was as capable of meeting the outside world again as he had thought.

His father met him at King's Cross and bought him a ticket and guided him through a maze of underground trains. They sat together in the darkness for some time in their final railway carriage of the Metropolitan Line, which was to take them out to Harrow on the Hill, where Jay's father had rented a semi-detached house. Jay assumed there was an air raid on. The train did not move, and Jay sat for over half an hour waiting for something to happen. The carriage windows had been pasted over with some webbing material to avoid splinters after a blast; small diamonds of space had been left clear for passengers to look out. Jay looked out. All he could see was a brick wall of Baker Street station with a pattern of pipes or cables running along it.

The house was half a mile from the station in a quiet residential avenue. It was past midnight when they arrived, and there was no chance of a taxi. With astounding forethought, his father had left a bicycle ('Next door's,' he explained) at the station. By night, with searchlights above, his father wheeled Jay's suitcase on the bicycle home to their house in the avenue.

His mother was welcoming, but, as usual, abstracted in manner and preoccupied with problems. The problem here was that there seemed very little food in the shops, especially in the butcher's. His mother, being new to the district, had had no chance to lay down those ties of long custom and loyalty to any particular tradesmen. Thus she was a stranger, served last and least.

Jay found himself left on his own for much of the time. His father went up to the Admiralty every day on the Metropolitan Railway and stayed most evenings until late. His mother shopped every morning, and went to whist drives or to the local WVS every afternoon and some evenings. Jay listened to the wireless for hours on end, to somebody playing the theatre organ seemingly interminably, and to programmes for schools every morning and afternoon, which were more informative, on a huge range of subjects, than any other source Jay had ever encountered. As the days went by, Jay heard over and over again a particular song which seemed as appropriate as it was popular. 'I don't want to set the world on fire,' it went, 'I just want to start … a flame in your heart…'

From the sanctuary of the small living room of that semi-detached house, it seemed to Jay that the whole country was numb, and only came back to some semblance of life for an evening ritual: an ARP warden riding down the avenue on his bicycle, the putting-up of the blackout shades and curtains, and the reading of the nine o'clock news.

As the days went by, Jay marvelled that nobody bothered about him. There was no mail, no messages, no word from the Navy. The weather eventually turned wet and cold. It had been the most marvellous summer and early autumn, Jay was told constantly. He had hardly seen any of it. For him, it was like going from one winter straight into the next. Every night, he lay in his bed, looking up through the window. The window faced the avenue and beyond it, two or three rows of houses away, the railway. Every night, he watched the flashes from the conducting pads of the trains grinding against the rails. They lit up the sky with their tremendous splashes of light. So much for the blackout. But they did stop the trains running when there was an air raid.

Outside, the raids had started in earnest. As somebody said on the wireless, as the nights draw in, the bombs come down. The sirens sounded every night almost. A huge round metal tank, labelled EWS, appeared at the corner of their avenue. For some time Jay thought the letters stood for East, West, South, and wondered why, until he discovered they meant Emergency Water Supply.

One early morning, there was a very loud explosion close to their house. Later in the forenoon, Jay walked round to the next avenue. There was a large hole in the road, with boards and railings, and red warning lamps, like roadworks. There was still a curious smell, like rotten apples mixed with steam and marsh gas, which for some reason made Jay think of the ship. Jay saw that all the trees nearby had had their leaves blown off. That was instant winter.

It was an avenue just like theirs. It could have been theirs. There was a small Austin Seven Ruby, a dear little car of the kind Jay himself had coveted, which had been blown over on to its side. All its windows had been broken. An LDV man in a khaki uniform with an armband was looking inside it. A policeman was watching him.

'Any casualties?' Jay asked the policeman.

'Who are you?'

'I'm a lieutenant, in the navy. On survivor's leave. I got frostbite.' The policeman showed no signs of being impressed, or even noticing what he had said. 'Quite badly, actually.'

'Oh.' The policeman still showed no interest or sign of recognition. 'Bit off your beat, then, aren't you?' He jerked his head towards the hole. 'Landmine.'

'Anybody...' Jay searched for the proper euphemism. 'Anybody *bought* it?'

'Milkman. On his rounds.'

'You mean the ginger-haired one?' Jay knew him. He was their milkman.

The policeman nodded. 'Him, and his horse, and his float, all gone. Vapourised, I expect. All they found so far is the horse's head.'

'Oh, my God.' Involuntarily, Jay put his hand to his mouth, in mourning for this milkman he had never even spoken to. If he had been sick that day, or late for work, he would still be alive. His punctuality had killed him.

'Yes,' the policeman was continuing, conversationally. 'All the lot landed in front of that pub up there. That's a good three hundred yards from here. That's a good distance.'

'Yes.' Jay shook his head. He knew the pub, although he had never been in it and did not even know its name. He felt he ought to say something more. 'What's it called, do you know?'

'*Nag's Head.*'

Jay studied the policeman's face. There was not the slightest vestige of amusement upon it. He had not been cracking a joke, he was not even conscious of any other connotations in what he had just said.

A young man wearing white running shorts and a red singlet ran towards them and stopped, level with the hole. He continued to 'run on the spot', as the Navy's PTIs always called it, raising his knees to an exaggerated height and panting as he spoke.

'Good ... old ... Gallipoli...' the youth gasped, and put his head down, and ran on.

Jay went back to the empty house. On the wireless there was a schools programme about a boy who had been crippled, but who became one of the world's finest middle-distance runners. Soon it was time for the daily theatre organ again: excerpts from *Chu Chin Chow*, played with thunderous *rubato*. This morning, there was also a woman singer. 'I don't want to set the world on fire...' she sang. She pronounced the word 'fire' in a curious way, as though it had two syllables. 'I don't want to set the world on *fi-yah*...'

I don't want to set the world on fire either, Jay thought, *but there is something I must do.* He sat down at the desk in the front sitting room, took out some sheets of writing paper with their address embossed on them — obviously the property of the house's real owners — and there, looking out on the tiny garden, with its paved path, sodden hydrangeas and low brick wall, he began to write a letter to the Admiralty.

Jay had kept a rough diary on board, in direct contravention of King's Regulations and Admiralty Instructions, and although it had gone down in the ship he could still remember many of the original words and phrases he had used. Now, as he called upon his memory, he could describe in detail what had happened in the ship in those two tremendous last months. His pen flew across the page, the words poured out, the events came flooding back: the arguments, the clashes between personalities, the almost unbearable strain of long hours operating off a hostile coastline, the anger, the unforgivable language.

It was, as Jay himself realised, the most valuable therapy, and he was still writing when his father came back that evening. His mother was out, helping to make the preliminary arrangements for the organisation of their neighbourhood's Poppy Day which, in that area and in that year, was clearly close to a major religious festival.

Lately, his father had been growing more and more concerned and worried about events at sea. He had stopped claiming that the U-boats were under control. Even the postcard-collecting and the holiday snapshots had lost their urgency.

'What are you writing? I saw you at the window as I walked up the avenue.'

'What happened in my last ship, Father.'

Jay saw his father stiffen, his body posture expressing his alarm.

'I'm going to send it up to Their Lordships. They've always been asking me what happened. They never gave me a moment's peace when I was in hospital. So now they'll know.'

'Do you mind if I read it?'

Jay watched his father's face, twisting and grimacing as he read the 'report', as Jay had already begun to think of it.

'You can't send this to the Admiralty. I forbid it.'

'I must, Father. I *must*!'

'No son of mine is going to send a letter like this.'

'Father, so far as I know, I'm the only one left now who can really say what really happened. That puts me in a very important position.'

'Don't flatter yourself! Jonathan, let me explain some things to you. Maybe I should have done this before.' His father's voice held a note of real desperation which, in a peculiar way, almost amused Jay. 'I don't like to see anybody, and certainly not any son of mine, rush on this from ignorance. Do you know how this letter of yours will be received? I'll tell you. It will be seen as insubordination. As disloyalty. It is quite out of order and out of place, it is *unseemly* for a junior officer such as you to write of his seniors as you have done here. Especially when those senior officers are dead, and had such distinguished records. You won't do any good with this. You will only do yourself harm. You won't do the officer you hope to help any good either. If there is any truth in what you allege happened, then it is up to that officer himself to clear his own good name. Not you.'

'But he might not be able to do that without my help, Father.'

'I forbid you to.'

'I'm sorry, Father. I *must*.'

There was a long silence. His father put the sheets of the letter back on the desk top. The longer the silence lasted, Jay knew, the more certain he was of winning. Finally, his father said, 'What do you want to do when you go back to sea, have you thought about that?'

'I want to fly again, of course.'

This was another, very old, bone of contention in the family. Jay knew that his father did not look upon aircrew as officers and gentlemen. He could hardly bring himself to regard them as fellow human beings. In that, his father had much in common with his late captain. The earliest naval pilots and observers had mostly been Dartmouth officers who had chosen flying as their specialisation. But lately, as Jay knew his father had heard through his contemporaries' own grapevine, a shortage of aircrew had brought in officers on all sorts of entry schemes and from all sorts of backgrounds. Now, in the eyes of older officers such as his father, aircrew was not much better than having a job in the motor trade. Worse still, aircrew tended to be a navy within a navy, and a navy which by all accounts could do with some old-fashioned discipline. Worst of all, aircrew represented a threat, as yet improperly defined and whose full effects had yet to be realised, to the old and proper way of things. Jay knew very well that his father would much prefer him to do as his older brother was doing, serving in a Home Fleet destroyer at Scapa Flow, waiting for *Der Tag* to come round again. Jay had often seen his father's eyes moisten, and his wistful expression, at the mere mention of Scapa Flow. That was more like it, more like the last war — *his* war — or as his father himself always called it, 'the last spot of unpleasantness with the Central Powers'.

But the very next day, his father came back looking relaxed and pleased. 'Well,' he said, 'I've done what I could for you. Done my best. Hope you'll be pleased. Pulled a few strings. Your appointer is an old term mate of mine. I hope I've got you a destroyer in a Med flotilla. The very best job of all for a young officer.'

'But I did say I wanted to fly again, Father.' Once again, Jay saw his father bristle. He bitterly regretted, but could not see how he could avoid, offending and hurting the old man.

'They've got more than enough pilots. *More* than enough. We won't need pilots this war. It's destroyer flotillas we need.'

Jay hung his head and bit his lip. He knew his father in this mood. There was no talking to him when he was like this. All the same, it was *his* life they were talking about.

'Can't I go myself and see about another job?'

'I've fixed it, I tell you!' His father was shouting now. 'But first you'll have to go and do your medical.'

Jay went up to some building off the Horseferry Road, near the Thames. He went by train and then by bus. There had been a raid overnight and the journey took several hours. At one point the bus stopped opposite where a house had been. There were men in helmets climbing over the rubble and hoses littering the road. There was a striking example of the strangely selective effect of bomb blast. Facing Jay was the wall of the house, stripped of floors and roof as though by a giant knife.

There was a fireplace in the lower room, which had been a sitting room, and another in the room above, plainly a bedroom. But there were still ornaments on each mantelpiece, and a calendar and two pictures still hanging on the walls.

The Surgeon Commander who examined Jay just grunted when he apologised for being late for his appointment. He looked closely at Jay's hands and feet. He tested his blood pressure, his eyesight, and his hearing. He tapped his knee with a little hammer, and made Jay touch his toes, studying him carefully the while, but not saying a word, either of approval or dismay. At last, he said, 'Do you want to fly again?'

'Yes, please, sir.'

The Surgeon Commander pursed his lips and drew in a long audible breath. 'Well, you're just about fit enough. Just about. I'm not enthusiastic, mind you.' He did not look to Jay to be the sort of man to be enthusiastic about anything. 'But I do happen to know how short they are of aircrew now, especially experienced aircrew.' The Surgeon Commander put the horns of his stethoscope back round his neck and sat down again at his desk. 'Nobody but the medical branch of the Navy seems to have hoisted in one bloody obvious thing about the Norwegian campaign.' He looked up at Jay and went on without waiting for a reply. 'It wiped out a goodly part of the Fleet Air Arm. You were there?'

'Yes, sir.'

'And you want to go back?'

'Not to Norway, no, sir.'

'Back to flying. Well, I'll say that, then. You've got a good chance, I suppose.'

Jay's new appointment arrived ten days later in a brown envelope — which, in those days, so often portended bad or at least uncomfortable news. So indeed it was with Jay's appointment, which surprised everybody. Jay's father was not so much surprised as horrified.

'*Whitby!* Good God!'

'What is she?'

'Sloop. Sort of corvette. Built long before the war. Convoy sloop.' His father made the two words sound like some fatal disease or a long prison sentence. His father got out his copy of *Jane's* and turned the pages with practised hand and eye. There she was: 990 tons. Complement 100. Built 1934. Two 4.7-inch guns. Sixteen-and-a-half knots. *Good God.*

Jay acknowledged his appointment, writing in his own handwriting to the Commanding Officer, c/o GPO, London, as they had all been taught to do at Dartmouth. A railway travel warrant arrived in answer, with joining instructions. The ship was at Rosyth dockyard and Jay was to join forthwith.

His father was on duty at the Admiralty and his mother had something on with the WVS, so Jay went alone to King's Cross, going by taxi to Harrow, the Metropolitan to Baker Street and then by Inner Circle. His fingers could not bear his two suitcases' weight for long. He had again and again to stop and put the cases down after a few steps. Sometimes, a passer-by, loaded himself, would stop, look into Jay's face, pick up one or both of his suitcases, and walk on for a little. Jay was grateful, though he wondered what these benefactors could see in his face.

The platform for the night train to Scotland was dark and full of soldiers running up and down and shouting at each other. A small party of sailors walked by, almost surreptitiously, humping their kit bags and hammocks, and went into a carriage at the front of the train. Jay's seat was in a first-class compartment which was so dark he could not see who else was sitting in it. He guessed, from their boots and conversation, they were all army officers. When they moved off at last, after a wait of over ninety minutes, Jay could see searchlights over northern London. One of them looked as though it might be over Harrow on the Hill.

They spent the night sitting up in their compartments and at dawn the train was stopped — somewhere near Grantham, Jay heard someone say — for another air raid, or a locomotive failure, or to await some connection that never came. Nobody knew. At York there was a trolley selling tea and sandwiches on the platform, but there was only tea left by the time it reached Jay's window. By the afternoon, the train was gliding through the green fields of the Border counties. At one station, where all the name-boards had been removed, Jay looked out and saw a company — perhaps even a regiment, there were so many — of Sikh soldiers, wearing turbans, fallen in all along the platform.

They reached Edinburgh under a cold, clear autumn evening sky. There was actually a car to take Jay, and a Lieutenant Commander who had been sitting in the next compartment, to the ferry. Beyond the Forth Bridge, a cruiser was lying out in the stream. The Lieutenant Commander, who was supposed to join her, began to fret in case she sailed without him.

At the gate of Rosyth dockyard, a sentry made the most cursory examination of Jay's identity card, and as they drove through he became aware of an extraordinary air of lassitude, with nobody about, and nothing visibly being done. On the newsreels, shipyards and dockyards were always hives of frantic activity, with showers of welding sparks and a deafening soundtrack of hammering and riveting. Here, it seemed it was perpetually Sunday afternoon.

Whitby was alongside a wall at the north end. She looked, as Jay knew his father would have said if he could have seen her, like a 'glorified trawler'. She even had a crow's nest on her foremast, like a small barrel, with room only for a very small lookout. She had a gun forward, and another aft, and an upper-deck gallery running from amidships aft to the quarterdeck, which suggested she had been designed for the tropics. Now that Jay looked more closely he could see another gun, a 3-inch anti-aircraft gun, above the forward 4.7-inch, and immediately in front of a small, stumpy superstructure. She had battered-looking depth charge rails aft, and a motor cutter and a whaler, but her ship's sides were rusty, and she had a general air of dilapidation. Her deck, from where Jay was standing, looked a jumbled mass of cables, and boxes, and crates, and wires, and sacks of vegetables, and pipes, and drums of oil, and pieces of metal which Jay could not identify, but which clearly belonged to some vital aspect of the ship. Yet, for all her grime and dishevelment, the ship still had a workmanlike, serviceable look about her.

The Quartermaster was standing at the salute as Jay crossed the gangway. Jay was just asking him if someone could get his gear on board when he heard a great bellowing voice from forward and above. There was a large red face looking at him from around a door, high in the bridge superstructure.

'That our new First Lieutenant?'

'Yes, sir.' Jay saluted. 'Just come aboard to join, sir.'

'Come on up here.'

Jay's new captain was a man approaching forty, with the medal ribbons of the last war on his reefer jacket. He was broad-shouldered, almost stout in build, with the beginnings of a pot belly. His large, red face had purplish veins in the side of the nose and along the cheekbones, his thick black hair had noticeable lines of grey in it, and bushy 'bugger's grips' grew down his cheeks, close to his jaw line.

'Everybody knows me as Gussie,' he said, shaking hands. 'Sit down, sit down. Like a drink?'

Jay knew that on his almost empty stomach alcohol would have a rapid and dramatic effect, but he nodded.

'*Townsend!*' Gussie roared. A sailor's face appeared at a small hatch in the bulkhead. It clearly belonged to the Captain's steward. 'Horse's Neck for the new Jimmy!'

Jay watched as Townsend brought in a tray and mixed him a brandy and ginger ale. For Gussie, Townsend sprinkled red cayenne pepper in a large glass, and swamped it with neat gin to a depth of some two inches.

Gussie took up his glass. 'Cheers. You Trapper's son?'

'Yes, sir.' Jay knew of the old nickname his father had had in the Navy, but he could not recall anybody actually using it before.

'Thought I recognised the name. I used to know your father quite well at one time. Well, fancy that. Trapper's son coming here. You've got an older brother, haven't you? Well then, what have you done wrong?'

'Nothing, sir, that I know of.'

'Come on, you must have done something,' Gussie said. 'Nobody gets sent to this Fred Karno's navy who's kept his nose clean. What you see here are all the deadbeats. The castoffs from Scapa Flow. Escorting convoys is such a low-grade exercise they only send the third division to do it. The *bright* boys escort the Home Fleet around the ocean.'

Jay felt the tingling of the ginger ale in his nostrils, and the first insidious fumes of alcohol reaching his brain. He was thankful that so many of Gussie's questions were so obviously rhetorical.

'So. Here we have a straight RN two-striper, as they say nowadays. New. Just out of the egg. But still a straight ring

RN. A fully qualified pilot, I see. A Brylcreem wallah. And a survivor, I'm told. Just off survivor's leave. Have you done an anti-submarine course, at *Vernon,* or anywhere? No? You must have done *something,* in more ways than one. Do you know why you're here? No? You're a replacement. Our last First Lieutenant very carelessly fell overboard, and as it was blowing force eleven, gusting to twelve, at the time, we couldn't turn round and pick him up. And the same wave that carried him off also damaged our depth charge rails. It should take forty-eight hours at most to straighten them out. We've been here four days. Long enough to whistle up a new First Lieutenant. It was *twelve* hours before anybody even came and asked us what the devil we were here for. Anyway, we're sailing tonight.'

Jay had been wondering, if what Gussie said was true, then what had he, Gussie, done wrong?

'You're wondering why *I'm* here, aren't you? What did *I* do wrong? I'll tell you. I was a submariner before the war, on the China Station. I think that was the finest submarine flotilla God ever gave any navy out there. Most of them gone now, poor buggers. But one Christmas we were having a lunchtime session down in my boat, and suddenly we got a signal to sail. That evening. On Christmas *Day,* I'm telling you. Well, I went inboard to try and talk them out of it. Half of them were tight as owls. This was peacetime, remember. Well, I succeeded, but somebody must have stayed sober. I got our sailing signal cancelled, but at what a cost for me. That was the end.

'I went to a battleship next, instead of a submarine staff job, as a common-or-garden watchkeeping two-and-a-half, along with about two dozen other poor sods in the same predicament, all hoping to be noticed somehow. Then I was passed over. Got a job ashore. Next, another job, in the barracks at Chatham. The usual pattern. You wouldn't know.

There's a long, long trail a-winding, laddie, on to the gash heap. And then the war, and then lo, behold, the half was not told you ... They suddenly decided they needed blokes like us, after all. They need deadbeats like me to go out in crap barges like this and try and sink submarines, though what *with*, the Lord and Their Lordships only know.'

Actually, Jay did know something of the bitterness of Gussie's experience. His own father had endured something very like it. But, while his father would never have breathed a single word of it, not even to his sons, Gussie was prepared to tell an officer who had not been on board his ship fifteen minutes.

There was a knock at the cabin door. It was a Petty Officer, a Yeoman of Signals, with a signal pad. 'Sailing signal, sir.'

Gussie read the top signal and briefly scanned the ones below it. 'Meet a WN convoy,' he said to Jay. 'Take it round the north coast of Scotland. Escort of two corvettes, three armed trawlers, and us. More than usual. Should make Jerry shake in his shoes.' Gussie looked at the clock on the bulkhead. 'Two hours. Just time for you to sling your hammock.' He got up and shook hands. 'I'm very glad you've come.'

The wardroom was one deck below the Captain's cabin and aft of it. It was a small musty-smelling compartment, with one scuttle opening to the outside air, and one punkah louvre fan slowly rotating in the centre of the deckhead. There were the two obligatory royal portraits, two leather armchairs, a sofa, a table running the length of one side of the compartment, a bar cupboard in one corner, a fireplace with an electric fire, and a magazine and letter rack on the bulkhead beside the door. It was in its way a miniature of every wardroom Jay had ever seen, but he found its atmosphere quite different to any other.

Those others had been mostly big-ship wardrooms with easily recognisable personalities, in the Commander, the Paymaster, the Major of Marines, and the Padre and Guns and Torps and the Schoolie and the India-Rubber Man, all, even just before the war, exactly as described by Bartimaeus thirty years earlier. But this wardroom consisted of an RNR Lieutenant called Blackstock, who seemed to know what he was about, a thin-striped, thick-lipped Warrant Engineer — Mr Beamish, a man of few words — and two RNVR Sub-Lieutenants. One of them, a young man called Drury, was quite the youngest-looking officer Jay had ever seen. Jay had often met aircrew officers who looked as if they had just left school, but Drury looked as though he were just going to school.

It was an awkward meeting; Jay knew that his predecessor was still in their minds. He could see they were all very conscious of two stripes and pilot's wings. He conceded he must appear a somewhat exotic sight for a convoy sloop's wardroom at Rosyth, on a raw cold October evening.

There was not time for much more than an exchange of names, but Drury did contribute a piece of ship's history. He was responsible for handling the ship's correspondence. 'We keep getting *Whitley*'s mail, sir. They keep getting our names wrong. They were sunk, bombed off Dunkirk. But they should have been *Whitby*. There was a typist's error, from somebody's handwriting, when they were launched. And we still get their mail. Gruesome, ain't it?'

Jay was able to see his suitcases into his cabin before the pipe for 'Special Sea Dutymen'. There was a pair of boots and some oilskins behind the cabin door. They fitted, so at least he had something left from his predecessor.

But on deck, taking charge of leaving harbour, Jay felt himself floundering in his ignorance. He had no idea where anything was, and in the blackness, no means of finding out; he knew nobody's name and, for the same reason, could not even see their faces. When the Coxswain told him that all hands were on board, and he went up to the bridge to report it, Jay sincerely hoped he was telling the truth.

'Ready for another tussle with our gallant merchant marine, Number One?' said Gussie, and went on, as usual, without pausing for an answer. 'Brave merchant seamen we read about in the papers. They're the thickest, stupidest, most bone-headed collection of ... words fail me. They won't stay in convoy, even for their own safety. They prefer to straggle behind, or romp on ahead, just to show their independence. They make clouds of smoke for hours on end. They ditch gash at all hours for miles on end. They can't keep in station for toffee. They're a menace to themselves and to everybody else. What we need is a depth charge or two to sharpen them up. Or a survivor. *That* concentrates the mind wonderfully. Ever seen a survivor, Number One? I'm sorry ... I was forgetting. But don't expect any sympathy from me.'

'No sir. Not at all. I was just listening to what you were saying.'

'I'm still getting used to the fact that I now have a pukka RN First Lieutenant, with angel's wings and a heavenly smile. Straight stripes and straight morals, we trust.'

Once again, Jay realised that Gussie often did not need an answer.

They sailed in almost complete blackness. There was one lighted buoy winking out in the fairway. Gussie aimed for it. As the ship was turning to head downstream, a searchlight woke up on the southern Queensferry side and made one horizontal sweep which momentarily lit up their bridge. Possibly it was somebody taking over the watch and testing his equipment.

But it was a foolish thing to do. Maybe they were a little too nervous of air raids here.

They met their convoy far out beyond May Island. To Jay, in his inexperience, it was all strange and new, and he had great difficulty in following what was happening. But he could see a dimly shaded blue light, with the shapes of some ships, and there was a voice on a loud-hailer. Soon, it was clear that the rendezvous had been made safely, and they were all on a course heading up the east coast of Scotland.

Jay's predecessor, as the most experienced watchkeeping officer, had always kept the middle watch, and Jay was bound to follow suit. He guessed that Gussie seldom left the bridge at sea, but he was flattered when Gussie said he was going below for an hour. It was a nice compliment. Gussie had not even asked him if he had a watchkeeping ticket. It was tacitly assumed that he had.

Jay did indeed have a watchkeeping ticket, but he had hardly any experience. He had been preoccupied with his flying duties in his last ship, and had not kept a watch of any kind on the bridge for over a year. He had only kept the bare minimum to qualify before that; in fact, he had seldom kept a watch on his own at sea. In pitch darkness, with darkened ships, in wartime, in the outskirts of a convoy, close to land on the port side, were not the best circumstances in which to start again.

Just after two o'clock, the lookout on the starboard side called out something. Jay crossed the bridge. He could see the shape of a ship, already so close he did not need binoculars, and knew that she was steering directly towards them. There had been no convoy alteration and there was no reason for that ship to be steering in their direction. But there she was, closing on a steady bearing.

Jay stood paralysed, his body incapable of any movement and his mind able to encompass only one thought: the terrible realisation that if there were a collision and he should go into the water, he would not survive. As in that time in the trawler, a second immersion would kill him.

But Jay could not have given an order, could not have made a sound, even to save his own life. He stood frozen into immobility, knowing that he *must* make some sound.

A blue light shone, and began to blink as though somebody were signalling. Jay could even see the sharp angle of her funnel against the lighter sky, and he could smell tea brewing, and frying, and a whiff of funnel smoke, and he heard the rustling of the water being pushed away from her bows and towards himself. At last he managed to make a word audible, the one word: 'Captain...'

'*Well*.' Gussie was already standing beside him, leaning over to peer aft at the rapidly receding ship. He turned back to look directly at Jay. '*Well* ... that took some nerve, I must say! I don't think *I* would have been quite so confident he'd draw clear. Next time, I really would appreciate a call a lot earlier than that, if you wouldn't mind. All right?'

Still, Jay could not bring himself to utter another sound.

'OK? You OK, Jay? All right?'

Jay knew that if he did not say something he would give himself away. He swallowed very deeply. 'Sir ... that's right, sir ... thank you.'

'Poooh, don't thank *me*. Just keep an eye on that bugger. I don't share your confidence in his ship-handling. This isn't the Med Fleet, you know. These are merchant skippers you're dealing with here. Liable to do anything at any time.'

'Yes sir.' Jay had now almost wholly recovered himself. 'I'll certainly keep a sharp eye open for him, sir.'

Before dawn, they went to action stations. As the pale light strengthened, Jay watched the various shapes of the ships emerging from the darkness. Looking around, he knew that he had never been in company with so many ships before, not even in the Mediterranean Fleet during an exercise. Nor had he ever seen so many small ships together. They were all *tiny,* jutting along with their blunt little bows, and their funnels raked back, and their wakes streaming astern in faint lines. It was a very grey day, with cloud extending right to the horizon in every direction. It was, as Jay had already learned, good protection.

But not quite good enough. Just after action stations had been stood down, a Heinkel bomber flew in from the east very low over the convoy. Jay heard the alarm in his cabin, where he was just finishing shaving. By the time he reached the upper deck, the 3-inch forward was thumping away and, as he stood for a moment in the daylight, the aircraft actually passed low over his head, throwing a great black shadow over the ship. One of the armed trawlers astern had also opened fire. But nobody else had. The rest of the convoy seemed totally taken aback.

There was a column of mottled grey water, well over on the port side, close to the Scottish coast. Jay saw it rising, and it seemed minutes before the sound of the explosion carried across on the wind.

'Anybody hit?' Gussie was sweeping the lines of the convoy with his binoculars.

'Don't know yet, sir,' said Tottenham, the other RNVR Sub-Lieutenant, who was keeping the forenoon watch with the Captain very much standing at his shoulder.

'Bloody hell, nobody ever knows anything.'

The furthest trawler, now a very long way astern, was signalling by light.

'*Signalman*! Get that! Chop chop chop.' The lamp the trawler was using was small and faint but, for a trawler, the flashing was fast and furious. 'Must have been in the Sea Scouts before the war,' Gussie said.

'From *Aston Villa*, sir...' Leading Signalman Hutchings was standing on the step of the bridge, reading the message. '*Cameron Lady* near miss. Reduced speed. Am standing by. End, sir.'

'She looks all right to me,' Gussie said, rubbing his stubbly chin. 'But we don't want her straggling. *Cameron Lady* nearly a miss. That's very witty, Hutchings. Now make to *Aston Villa*: "Rejoin me. *Cameron Lady* divert to Aberdeen. At best speed."' Gussie looked at Jay. 'I don't want to reduce the escort just to escort one ship. We've got the whole convoy to think about. Although, sometimes I think we'd do better just to let the buggers get on with it themselves.'

It seemed to Jay, looking around the ships, that the convoy was like a flock of hens, smoothing ruffled feathers into place. There was something actually affronted in the lines of the masts and the funnels. There had been a loss of dignity rather than of life. The attack had been not so much dangerous as impertinent, not so much risky as cheeky. But then Jay recalled a sailor who had dashed past him as that aircraft went overhead, its wings shutting out the light. Jay had not been on board long enough even to know the man's name, but he knew the expression in his eyes, that look of naked, quite unconcealable fear.

They arrived in the Clyde without any further incident and their ships dispersed in a sharp squall of rain mixed with sleet. Jay's fingers ached forebodingly in the cold. Gussie's temper matched the weather. He bellowed in a most uncivil manner at the oiler when they went alongside to refuel at the Tail o' the Bank, and he chivvied the Stoker PO and his two stokers who were hauling their hose across and getting ready to connect it. But it seemed the Stoker PO was as impervious to Gussie's language as he was to the weather. He and his stokers just grinned and carried on bawling at their opposite numbers in the oiler. Jay watched them working on that oily deck, with oily hoses, in the driving rain. It was not a job he coveted.

The Senior Naval Officer had sent a harbour launch to take Gussie and other captains to the convoy conference ashore in Greenock. Jay was left by himself to try to come to some kind of grips with his new status. He quickly found out that his predecessor had been as careless in his duties as he was in his manner of death. Stores and spare gear of all kinds had not been ordered or properly mustered. Valuable items such as binoculars and sextants were not accounted for, consumable items such as electric light bulbs had not been reordered, and were now scarce on board. There was a shortage of bedding for the sailors, and galley utensils, and signal bunting, and flour for making bread. There was not enough reserve food for emergencies. Ratings were overdue for courses, or for advancement, or for the award of good conduct badges, because nobody had reminded them to put in their requests. These were all bread-and-butter issues which were the normal province of a First Lieutenant but which, as aircrew, Jay had never had to deal with before. The correct procedures to carry out, the right forms to sign, the right quantities to order, were all matters he had learned on his courses as a Sub-Lieutenant. He had been taught the theory. He had never dealt with the practice.

Jay found his first hectic day oddly exhilarating. As a squadron officer in an aircraft carrier he had become detached from the everyday hurly-burly of ship life. Now he had jumped into it up to his neck. This was the *real* Navy, which was, after all, only asking him now to do what he was supposed to have been trained to do. In a way this was like getting one's hands healthily dirty after a long period of being unnaturally uninvolved.

They sailed to join another convoy as soon as Gussie came back on board. Again, there were some thirty or forty ships, but though they were much bigger they proved to be no faster. The escort was stronger — three corvettes, and *Whitby*, and two fleet destroyers who would join them after refuelling at Londonderry.

The barometer dropped steadily as the convoy cleared the North Channel and steamed westwards into a rising gale. By dawn on the second day it was blowing a full westerly gale and the sea had risen to match it. Ships plunged down into the side of a wave and disappeared into sheets of spray, thrown astern over their whole lengths, before reappearing, as though hauling themselves laboriously up a steep slope. Sometimes the escorts rose so high in the air they showed their smooth forefoot and keel as far back as the forward edge of the upper-deck superstructure. A freighter just ahead presented a curiously foreshortened view: as her round bows rose, her whole upper deck became visible as though in plan view, and then her stern took its place before the ship vanished again in spray. Considering the weather, the convoy's station-keeping was excellent. A purist from the Med Fleet might have criticised the exact distance between ships and the precise distance apart of the lines, but every morning at dawn, the ships were still in sight, still in company, still in convoy.

At longitude 19 degrees west, the destroyers left to refuel at Reykjavik in Iceland. The convoy steamed onwards, while the corvettes and *Whitby* waited for a rendezvous with another incoming convoy eastbound. They arrived that afternoon, in a miraculous feat of navigation in that weather and that ocean, every ship laden down to its marks, wallowing much more heavily and deliberately than those in ballast in the first convoy. Gussie exchanged identities with the Convoy Commodore in the leading ship of one column, and then they were on their way again.

It seemed that the U-boats also had a rendezvous, and had waited to meet the incoming convoy along with the escort. It seemed, too, that the U-boats knew enough to strike when it suited them best — as the sun was going down, flooding the whole western sky with a deep red background, against which every ship stood out in silhouette.

The first torpedo hit was so surprisingly mild, so unobtrusive, that Jay, who was on watch, noticed nothing. It was Gussie, who was just taking a bearing on the leading ship of the nearest column, who suddenly looked up, as though sniffing the air, aware of the very scent of danger.

There were rockets, tracing vivid lines against the deepening gloom, far down at the rear of the convoy. There was a ship, already hull down, sagging away badly, dropping out of the convoy formation with terrible finality. Now that he knew what to watch and listen for, Jay saw in the gathering darkness another subdued flash and a second ship heeling away out of her proper place. He could even hear the siren bleating desperately.

As Jay looked out on the bearing of the stricken ship, he fancied he saw another ship intervene, crossing his line of sight. Perhaps it was a larger wave, because there was no ship in the convoy there. It was less substantial than a ship, no more than a shadow, the merest suspicion, some wraith, some sea spirit passing momentarily across his field of vision. Jay took his binoculars from his eyes and stared.

'Sir.' Jay pointed in the direction. 'Is that a ship, or ... it just looks like a ripple of something...'

Gussie was already searching the bearing. 'That's something, all right ... That's not a ... *Hard-a-starboard!* Full ahead together! Pass the word to the quarterdeck: Stand by depth charges, 'A' gun load with starshell. That's a U-boat! Well done, Jay, well done *indeed*!'

CHAPTER FOUR

Hansi felt Herr Kaleut's hand pressing on the back of his neck, forcing his head down. The captain did not want even the paleness of their faces against the blackness of the night to give them away. At that moment, a large ship over on their port side blew up. Crouching, bent down, but looking back and over his shoulder, Hansi saw the sky above glow brightly for some time, and then slowly fade.

When Hansi straightened up, Herr Kaleut was already leaning against the side of the bridge, concentrating on the sea out to starboard. 'Is it coming towards us? That destroyer there?'

They had already sunk two ships, briskly, one after the other. Hansi had been quite astonished by the lack of fuss those ships had made about dying. Those fat morsels had just vanished away, quietly, as though melting down into butter. But this third ship, evidently sunk by another U-boat, had been a tanker, and her passing had lit up the whole scene in a bright glare, which picked out every wave, every detail of their U-boat's bridge.

'Is he turning? Has he seen us?' Hansi could only just hear what Herr Kaleut was muttering, above the pounding of their diesels and the rush of the wind of their passage. They were heading at full speed directly into the heart of the convoy. 'It's only a small one. Tiny, really.'

Hansi could hear Herr Kaleut murmuring over and over again, 'Mustn't dive, mustn't dive, mustn't dive,' when a flare or a starshell burst almost above their heads, drenching them in a baleful light which made them all duck in spite of themselves. This was far, far brighter than that burning tanker. That had been a pale moon. This was like the noonday sun.

'Dive dive dive dive...'

They fell rather than climbed down the ladder, in a frenzy of arms and legs and boots and binoculars and curses, drowned in the roar of air escaping from the ballast tanks and the last thuds of the diesels as their pistons came to a sudden stop.

'My God, the Tommies could hear all that back in England...'

In the control room, Hansi landed next to Hugo, their imperturbable engineer. He was squinting at his gauges, calculating weights and adjustments to their trim. As Hansi struggled to get his breath back, he saw Hugo, absolutely calm and impassive, as though this were just one more practice dive back in the friendly Baltic.

'Fifty metres ... Quiet as the grave, everybody. Quiet, quiet...'

Hansi clutched at a valve handwheel, to steady himself as the deck angle steepened. He saw Herr Kaleut looking upwards at the lower hatch. He too, Hansi knew, was calculating odds, for and against an attack. It was possible that destroyer had not seen them. On the other hand, the weather had improved a great deal in the last six hours, making an attack quite feasible. Yesterday, no destroyer's crew in the world could even have kept their feet on deck, let alone made an attack.

Neumann, the hydrophone operator, was already reporting propellor noises on a threatening bearing, in that stage whisper which made everything sound so dramatic, and which annoyed Herr Kaleut so much. But, as they all waited in silence, they heard the tiniest *tick, tick, ticking* noise, lighter than the merest flick of a whip, against the hull. There was no longer any doubt that the destroyer, or trawler, or whatever it was, was in contact — and attacking.

The deck angle eased as the boat gained depth, with the slightest shudder of the hull under the thrusting of the propellors. There was still some time left to prepare for the ordeal ahead. They shut off pipes to gauges, shut bulkhead doors, isolated all systems except the hydraulics, converting the boat into an assembly of separate cells, each sealed off from its neighbour, each ready to take its chance on its own. Most men lay down on their bunks, but those who had to stay where they were sat on the deck, loosened their shirt collars, and took off their shoes. Most were still optimistic about what was to come. They had all heard that small practice charge, dropped by a *Sperrbrecher* off Kiel, quite close, 'to give U-boat crews some idea of depth-charging'. It had been very alarming, and quite frightening, but bearable.

The truth, when it came, was worse than anything anybody could ever have imagined in their most shocking and violent nightmares.

That practice charge was a pinprick, a scratch of a nail against a pane of glass, compared with the colossal sledgehammer blow of the reality. The concussion was so loud they seemed not even to hear it but to allow it to take over and possess their bodies. Their mouths swam with saliva, and their lungs seemed to fill with some choking fluid. Their arms and legs felt infinitely heavy, weighed down by some unnatural gravity. Small bits of metal and shards of paint and debris spun in the air, and crackled and hissed like a fierce hailstorm as they swept the deck plates. The very air itself in the boat seemed to thicken and darken as though it were being forcibly compressed, until they could actually taste its texture and foulness on their tongues.

They had not recovered from the first, when there was a second impact. They could not have imagined anything louder than the first, but the second was so much worse that they wished for the first again. They all gave a great gasp of agony. Hansi felt as if his lungs had been paralysed, so that he could not take a proper breath. Large fragments broke off the bulkheads, and one just missed his head. He had had his hands out, palms down, on the deck to support himself. His hands were both numb, as though smashed by a hammer.

Herr Kaleut was sitting on the deck, his back against the helmsman's chair. He had his arms folded across his lap, and his cap was tipped down over his eyes, so that nobody could see his face. Just beside him, Hugo had a pad of paper and a pencil. Hansi saw that he was making a tick, or some mark, for every detonation.

The U-boat's hull was still shaking, like the flank of some terrified horse, when the third charge detonated immediately above. It pressed the boat bodily downwards, so that they could all feel the sensation of it in their stomachs. The noise rumbled on and on, and was followed by a gurgling and rushing of waters, as though a space had been blown in the sea, which was now crowding in to fill this hated vacuum. It was a chilling and triumphant sound, of the sea itself searching for them, confident that it would eventually repossess the space they now occupied.

Somebody a little way aft was actually beginning to sing. *'And it did get worse, the very next —'*

'Be *quiet!*' Herr Kaleut silenced the singer, but his admonishing finger made it plain he did not resent the song. Any sound at all might betray them.

The propellers, and the tick-tick-tocking, were coming back. Once again the charges descended and filled their ears and mouths and their bones and their very bloodstream with thunder. Hansi climbed into his bunk and pressed his hands against his ears. But he found that he had to listen in case he missed something. Terrible though the explosions were, it would be even worse to be caught unaware. In his mind's eye, he could see the charges coming down, turning end over end as they dropped silently through the water. He fancied he could even hear one bouncing against the hull. He started up from his bunk in a movement of sheer animal terror. But there was only silence, in which he could hear the air rasping in and out of his throat.

The explosions seemed to have come to a pause, although there was still that very gentle ticking. They had all become hypersensitive to it. The lightest whisper, the least suggestion of it, made the hairs prickle on the backs of their necks.

Listening to the sound of it on the hull, which was only a few inches from his head, Hansi suddenly became aware of a change in the note. The impulses seemed to be striking the hull at a different angle, with a less confident, more questioning sound. Hansi got up and looked around the partition into the control room. Herr Kaleut had tipped back his cap. He had already noticed the change. Their attacker had actually lost contact. Temporarily, their pursuer was at a loss. There was still that threatening tick-tick, and still those tremendous explosions, followed an infinitesimal fraction of time later by the waters rushing together. But the sounds no longer had that imminent menace. One explosion was noticeably more distant, the next even further away. There was then an interval of time, nearly a minute, before the next salvo. An even longer gap followed, of over three minutes, followed by one last detonation, a comparatively long way off. But it seemed to Hansi that that final explosion was like a signature. *Don't go away,* it seemed to say. *We won't forget you. We'll remember you next time. You will know us. If you're still there.*

Neumann said he could still hear convoy noises, but that the steady whirring of a destroyer's propellers passing to and fro overhead had stopped. Neumann picked up another propellor noise, moving astern of the convoy.

'He might have gone to pick up survivors,' Herr Kaleut said. 'Very understandable, but very foolish of him. We may give him some more survivors to pick up before the night's over.'

Herr Kaleut might have intended that remark to be encouraging but, looking round the control room, Hansi saw that it had been a mistake. It did not suit the present mood in the boat. Their ears were still ringing with the sounds of explosions. They were not yet ready to attack again.

'Stand by to surface!'

Hansi saw the faces around him wincing at the order, as though they had all been rapped smartly upon an old bruise. They certainly wanted to surface and breathe some fresh air again, to prove that they had survived. But Hansi knew they did not want to attack again. None of them ever wanted to see that convoy again. It was quite possible, Hansi thought, that this crew might never be the same again. He had heard that severe depth-charging could change men. Until now, they had all had the keenness and freshness of ignorance. But no longer. Now, they knew. Now they knew what their enemy could do to them. A boxer, hit too hard, knew what could happen to him again. A spring, compressed too much and for too long, might never regain its former resilience.

Neumann had listened carefully all round and reported no propellor noises or Asdic anywhere. But when they surfaced, they were horrified to find they had emerged very close to a merchant ship. But it was apparently derelict, motionless —

which was why Neumann had heard nothing — and had been abandoned by its crew. There was no sign or sound of life. But it was still a target. They fired one torpedo and, as the sound of the explosion was dying away and before the column of water had fallen, Herr Kaleut had ordered the helm put over and the boat shaped course to the east, where the convoy had gone.

When Hansi came up later to take over the watch, there was still a pale afterglow, which could be flares on the water, far down on the western horizon. Possibly that was where they were still trying to pick up survivors. Meanwhile, the wind had lost most of its violence, and the sea had also moderated. Towards midnight they dived for a time, to get a hydrophone bearing of the convoy, and to give a steady platform for the fore-ends men to finish reloading the torpedo tubes.

Herr Kaleut looked over the *Obersteuermann*'s shoulder as he plotted the likely course and speed of the convoy on the chart. 'It's a good trace,' he said. 'Twenty ships, I would say. Perhaps five destroyers, who knows. Plot a mean speed of six knots. Allow for zigzagging.'

'*Will* they be zigzagging, Herr Kaleut?'

'Almost certainly, yes. If they weren't doing it before, they'll be doing it now that we've attacked. And they're getting nearer England all the time. Nearer and nearer within range of *us*.'

Watching Herr Kaleut standing in the middle of the control room, at the very centre of affairs, with his men and his instruments all around him, unselfconsciously thinking out loud, Hansi could not help noticing how the captain had gained greatly in stature from his battle success. Before, he had commanded the U-boat because he had been appointed to do so. Now, he seemed to wear it all, the men and the equipment and the weapons, like a familiar garment which fitted him well. There was a new confidence, even in the line of his arm and hand as he thoughtfully scratched his chin, pondering out loud what to do next.

'What would I do, if I were him? He's probably told one of his destroyers, perhaps even two, to drop back and pick up survivors. I wouldn't do that. But he probably has. They ought to have a ship specially fitted to do that, to pick up survivors. They'll need them. I would put one destroyer on the windward bow of the convoy. That's the port bow. They must have noticed by now how often we like to come in to the attack down wind. Although we shan't be doing that tonight. Another destroyer immediately ahead of the convoy. For myself, I would put myself in the rear, just slip in behind the convoy, just astern of the rear ship. I'd wait for any U-boat which had finished its attack to come out just there, like a rabbit bolting out of its hole. Also, any U-boat just catching up. If they had any sense they would always have somebody bringing up the rear. Like the last pallbearer. *So* —' Herr Kaleut looked round the control room, as though to gather in all their attentions and to sum up — 'we shall steer east on surfacing, and then northeast. And we should find the convoy again, very fine on our port bow and crossing us from port to starboard, after about three hours. We will have time for just one more attack before dawn. But when the sun comes up, we shall be gone. Like the vampire. That's a thought. We should paint a vampire on the side of our tower!'

Herr Kaleut grinned at the looks of disapproval all around. The Lordly Ones were horrified by the very suggestion. That, in their opinion, would be taking quite unnecessary risks. It was true their U-boat had as yet no insignia, no unofficial badge, as many boats already had. But a badge was best left to luck, to suggest itself. One boat in the flotilla, they all knew, had two red devils painted on its sides. Not a sailor in the whole U-Waffe, and certainly not those in that U-boat, approved of that, although as it happened, that particular boat had been very successful, so far.

Hansi could see the captain's own returning confidence was affecting the whole crew. Assurance was flowing back into them all, as though the battery of their morale had been recharged. Already, they seemed to have forgotten the recent terrors of that depth-charging.

It all came about just as Herr Kaleut had forecast. They surfaced and steered east, and then north-east. After about three hours, there indeed were the ships, at first no more than a single indeterminate shape, then three, then a line of ships. It was the convoy, which had closed up its ranks again, and was steaming onwards, seemingly invulnerable. The wind had gone down to a light breeze, and there was no moon. Dawn would help the U-boats, making the sky pale first behind their targets. But that would not be for another two hours at the very earliest.

Herr Kaleut had four lookouts up, and Hansi as officer of the watch. 'No,' he said, when he saw Hansi's questioning look, 'we shall *not* be diving this time. That was the mistake we made last time. I want every possible pair of eyes up here. We shall fire from the bridge. *You* will fire, Hansi. We're going to make one run through the convoy, like the last time, and then out to the north on the other side.'

The wind seemed to spring up and bear them down upon their targets, as if the boat itself were part of a storm cloud. The ships leaped into sharp focus so quickly that, almost before Hansi was ready, Herr Kaleut had taken and passed him the firing bearing, and ordered him to fire. There was the expected pale gush of water, like a cliff rising suddenly out of the sea, but again curiously little sound. Not pausing even to look at their victim, they went on, and took a second bearing, and fired again. A second time there was a muffled detonation, and a more dramatic column of water. This was the most polite and discreet killing, like hitting a man with cotton-wool gloves.

This time, as they passed the spot where the ship had already gone down, Hansi saw something in the water, like a boat or a raft, with a few pinpricks of light in and around it. He saw what he thought was a man's face, just coming into sight on the flank of a wave, being lifted up, and then vanishing. Then there were more rafts and lights, and Hansi was sure he could hear men calling out, voices pleading or even cursing, and there was the suspicion of a fist raised, maybe the whisper of an oath, or perhaps a prayer for forgiveness. Somebody, Hansi was sure, was damning them all to hell. A shiver passed down him. Those men would surely die if they were not picked up very soon. Their faces should be hidden. Sailors always covered the face of a corpse, lest its eyes draw them down with it into hell.

Now, there was a third firing bearing, and a third ship sinking. This was becoming mechanical. Beyond their target, Hansi fancied he could see another U-boat, just like themselves. It was like looking across and seeing Herr Kaleut and himself. The other boat was outlined in fire, lighting up the faces of the men on her bridge.

There was still no sign of any of the convoy escorts. Possibly the destroyer had dropped astern to pick up survivors, and they had approached through the gap it had left. They were now cutting through the convoy on a diagonal, at right angles to the wind, as though sailing on a broad reach, the 'soldiers' wind' as the sailors called it. Their last target was the leading ship of the extreme port-hand column of the convoy. She was much, much bigger than the others. Her great sides seemed to tower over their heads as they approached her. She looked like a passenger liner, perhaps a troopship. But still one torpedo was enough to dispatch her. This time Hansi actually saw the dark space, the vacuum made in her side by the explosion as though all the metal there had been torn bodily apart. The great soaring masts and superstructure began to lean and then heel over. After they had passed her, Hansi heard the after starboard side lookout murmur something. He looked back, in time to see the two enormous funnels looking directly at him, and still glowing like the huge red eyes of that dog which guarded the entrance to hell. The funnels dipped underwater and were extinguished. Hansi heard steam escaping, shrieking like a man under torture. It did seem these ships had lives of their own.

They were free now, out on the port side of the convoy, and nobody had laid a finger on them. There was no destroyer on that side, either. They had sunk four ships with four torpedoes. Other U-boats had been present and must have sunk other ships, perhaps nine or ten ships in all. This had been a major naval defeat for the British.

They dived before the sun rose. Hugo caught his trim at once, as though as usual, he had spent the time on the surface doing sums in his head. The boat was immediately stable at periscope depth. It was dead quiet below, with no sound of propellors or Asdic, no sound from the sea itself.

Herr Kaleut was sitting in the periscope chair, gasping for breath, as though he had run many miles at top speed. He asked for a drink. Hansi saw his eyes filling with tears. The strain of the last thirty minutes must have been immense. Hansi himself felt drained of energy. For Herr Kaleut, who bore the full responsibility, it must have been much worse. But just as the captain was sipping the coffee and obviously beginning to relax, he suddenly stiffened and sat bolt upright.

'Have we still got a torpedo in the after tube?'

'Yes, Herr Kaleut.'

The men in the control room had been relaxing along with Herr Kaleut, responsive as always to his changes of mood. Now they saw he was genuinely annoyed. He had thought he had fired all his torpedoes. There went a fifth ship, escaping, which should have been sunk.

'Maybe we shall get another target, Herr Kaleut?' As usual, it was Hansi who volunteered to speak first and take the captain's wrath.

'Maybe. But next time, *you* remind me. That is your *job*!'

But the recall signal came that evening, to break off patrol and return to Lorient. They surfaced and steered south and east, the Lordly Ones up forward singing, 'And it *did* get worse' at the tops of their voices.

As they left their patrol area, there was on board the most extraordinary lull; the whole boat seemed to drop its guard. On watch, Hansi found the lookouts disposed to chatting one to another, instead of concentrating upon their sectors. With the singing and the smiles up in the fore ends, there was an atmosphere of holiday, like children escaping from school. Even Herr Kaleut himself left the bridge for hours on end to stretch himself out on his bunk and sleep deeply. He had not done that since they left Lorient. It was as though everybody on board now believed they were immortal, and nobody could harm them, or even see them.

So it seemed, even when there was an aircraft alarm on their second evening. Hansi was on watch and, like a true U-boat captain himself, saw it first, before the lookout. The boat was dived and safe long before the aircraft could arrive overhead, if indeed it had ever seen them. Once more they all waited for bombs which this time never came, and surfaced to an empty sea and sky. This was now, as they all recognised, the regular pattern of their lives: diving and surfacing, waiting and hoping, attacking and evading, striking and hiding.

The ignorant were often rude about U-boats and their crews. English propaganda was fond of calling them sea-wolves, or pirates, or outcasts. In a sense, that was right; they *were* outcasts. They were outside the main war, on land, which everybody knew about. Theirs was a war known only to those who were in it. They were predators known only to their prey. Even the enemy still did not know what was involved in this Atlantic war. He was still feeling his way, although, as Hansi reflected, he was learning fast. That last destroyer had certainly known his business. Those charges had been dispatched with a knowing and a hostile hand.

Even the weather seemed to be relaxing its attack. For late November it was positively benevolent. The wind blowing steadily from astern wafted the boat on its way, while the mighty Atlantic swell gathered and pushed the boat to the south-east, onwards to harbour and safety. Waves surged up from astern, gurgled and washed through the casing, and subsided, leaving the boat wallowing in foam and broken water.

Dawn on their last day at sea was a broad band of saffron yellow, deep and clear to the east; and below the sky, unmistakeably, the hard, black line of the French coast. Hansi still wondered at the lack of tension, the absence of precautions, on board. Their U-boat was hastening down upon one of the most treacherous and dangerous landfalls in Europe, perhaps in the world, after several days without a proper navigational fix, and without any lights to guide it.

Navigation was not Hansi's responsibility, and it was not his place to criticise Herr Kaleut or the *Obersteuermann*. But if he were ever captain, Hansi decided, he would exercise much more seaman's ordinary prudence. More ships were going to be lost to the shore than to the enemy, on both sides.

Winter was only a few weeks off, but the French coastline was as green as in high summer. This time the boat had victory pennants to fly, hoisted on the radio aerial. Hansi watched them tugging at the wire, and felt so proud of their crew and of the whole U-Waffe that he could not prevent the tears in his eyes. In the end, those little bits of colours, literally scraps in the wind, made it all worthwhile.

Herr Kaleut seemed to have timed their arrival, or perhaps it was a fortunate tide, so that the boat came alongside in the basin just about eleven o'clock in the forenoon, that time when every admiral in the world, and all their staff officers, were sure to be up and awake and appreciative. As the first lines went ashore, a bitter, unwelcoming wind sprang up from the hills behind the town and came sweeping down the narrow funnel of the harbour, but it made their victory pennants flutter all the more bravely. There were more flags ashore than usual, and there was a band thumping away, and a crowd of U-boat officers and sailors and hangers-on. Some of the trees on the quayside still had their last leaves, and they looked surprisingly fresh in the sunshine.

There was one slight mishap. The order to put the electric motors astern was not obeyed quite as quickly as Herr Kaleut anticipated, and the boat's bow nudged one of the jetty support pillars. It was hardly noticeable to those ashore, but Hansi could feel the boat shivering. It was a prolonged shudder, as though the whole boat now remembered that depth-charging. Looking down at the casing plates, Hansi could scarcely believe that this metal had withstood such pressures. Those plates had been deep down in the sea and subjected to enormous forces. Now, they looked damp and rusty but otherwise unharmed. In fact, it was remarkable how little damage the depth-charging had actually done to the boat and its fittings. The only casualty was very probably Klaus, the first officer. He had been very quiet on the voyage homeward, and Herr Kaleut seemed to have stopped consulting his opinion or even talking to him. It was likely, Hansi thought, that Klaus would not be going to sea with Herr Kaleut again.

BdU himself was waiting on the jetty, and soon he came on board to meet and shake hands with everybody. Everybody always said BdU looked more like a Lutheran pastor, in the days when there were still Lutheran pastors in Germany, than an admiral. He was a very short man, surprisingly short considering his reputation, a slight figure wrapped up in his greatcoat. His eyes and face were shadowed under the great beaked peak of his Admiral's cap. He seemed almost a caricature of the BdU of legend, a caricature drawn by an unsympathetic artist. But there was nothing comical about the look he gave each man, and the way he shook each hand.

Herr Kaleut was introducing his crew, knowing that they were all self-conscious about their stinking seagoing leathers, their beards, their pale faces. BdU had a firm handshake for Hansi.

'I hear you fired your eels to good effect?' The slang word, used by all U-boat men for torpedoes, came quite naturally to BdU's lips.

'Yes sir, I hope so, sir.' Hansi was aware of the keen expression, the eyes summing him up, estimating his temper and his morale.

'Well done. Keep it up!'

'I thank you, Herr Admiral.' Hansi had heard that a visit, even a social visit, up to the little sardine castle to see BdU was no picnic, even for the most aggressive and successful U-boat captains. But everybody knew the other side of it: BdU fought like a tiger for his U-Waffe, especially against those Luftwaffe idiots.

Some pompous security officer had tried to rename the Hotel Beau Séjour the Hotel Göring, but everybody still called it the Beau Séjour, and the senior U-boat officers still used it. The junior officers still drank in the little bar down the street called The Café. It was a dirty little room, which stank of stale spirits, kept by a woman and a girl whom everybody assumed was her daughter. They both wore check-patterned dresses with a vaguely Tyrolean look about them. Sometimes, when Hansi was on the way to getting drunk, he half expected them both to break into song. Something from the White Horse Inn, perhaps. There was a glass-beaded curtain guarding the door, and rows of dusty bottles behind the counter, and a picture of some local dignitary — the mayor, perhaps — and several cuttings, browning with age and exposure, from local newspapers. The cuttings were all news stories about cycling. The owner of the bar — perhaps the husband of the woman and the father of the girl — was a man nobody had ever seen, but he was supposed to have been a cyclist of some repute before the war. Hansi sometimes wondered what sort of Frenchman had used the bar in those pre-war days. Maybe other cyclists, enjoying a break in their training. No Frenchman ever came into the bar now. He would not have been welcome. Also, it was possible that the bar was actually out of bounds for Frenchmen.

Hansi's first glass of wine was delicious. It was red, exactly at room temperature, with a velvety, yet piquant taste. Here they served it over the bar, like beer. It was a claret which, at home in Leipzig, they would have drunk only on special days, if they had been able to buy it at all. Or maybe, Hansi conceded, it tasted like this because it was his first glass of wine for weeks.

There were some additional decorations to one side wall of the bar. There were three rows of portraits, all photographs, of faces of naval officers in their caps. All were grinning, and all had a black band pasted across the lower left-hand corner of the frame. Hansi knew who they were. He could even remember some of their faces, as men he had known. There was no need to ask why they were there. They were all dead. Smiling, but dead.

'Cheers, Hansi,' somebody said. 'Rogues' gallery.'

There were several U-boat officers in the bar, sitting on stools or at tables down in the main part of the room. Hansi did not know any of them, but they seemed to know him.

'There seem to be many more of them?' Hansi said. 'I can only remember half a row, at the most. There's six or seven of them, new faces. Does that mean two or three boats lost? It does, doesn't it?'

'Bound to be losses, Hansi. What's two or three? *C'est la vie.*'

'*C'est la mort,* you mean,' somebody else said.

Hansi could not hide his dismay. 'But we've hardly started here yet, as a flotilla.'

'We'll get better.'

So will the enemy, Hansi thought, but he did not say that aloud. 'What happened to their boats?'

'Nobody knows, for sure. Didn't signal. Never heard from them again. Just guesses now, about what happened to them.'

Once again, Hansi could not repress that shivering sense of foreboding, which made all his back hairs prickle. The U-Waffe was successful, beyond anybody's dreams before the war. The war was being won, there was no doubt about that. This was their *glückliche Zeit,* their happy time, of successes and explosions and exultations. For every sunk ship there was a flag, and for every homecoming, garlands and girls and music. It was preposterous to be gloomy at such a time. Maybe, Hansi thought, he was being too introspective.

All the same, there had been a dreadful purposefulness, a shocking readiness to learn, about that destroyer's depth-charge attack. Somewhere out there the enemy was still waiting, like a wrestler who was always thrown and who always got up again, stronger than before, like a punchbag that got bigger and harder the more it was punched, like some elemental force which was always killed off and always sprang to life again, growing new and more menacing heads, like that monster from the mythology Herr Kaleut liked to read and quote. It had already begun, that slow, patient chip-chip-chipping away of the U-Waffe's strength and confidence. Hansi suddenly had the ominous, chilling feeling that no matter how many U-boats they built, no matter how many ships they sank, the enemy would still be waiting, with inexhaustible patience, to begin all over again. When the waters had subsided, when the noise had died down and all was quiet again, there would start that chip-chip-chipping away, like the ticking of the Asdic in a silent sea.

Hansi and his contemporaries were always being told that they were very junior officers, to be seen and seldom heard. Nevertheless, they did have something to contribute. For example, Hansi confidently expected the flotilla staff and BdU's staff to interrogate him closely about the events of that attack, which had apparently been the most violent any U-boat had yet experienced and survived. They should want to know *everything,* every single last detail: times, courses, speeds, depths, the rates and bearings of the escorts' approaches, intervals between depth charge salvoes, the number of the charges, and estimate of their distance from the U-boat on detonation. They should want to know, or at least to try and recreate on a plotting table, precisely what the enemy did to attack and what their boat did to evade. The enemy had left, to their great relief. But *why?* Had he run out of charges? Was there a change of sea water density, a temperature layer perhaps, which deflected his Asdic beam; or was it now enemy policy to keep the U-boat down only long enough to allow the convoy to draw ahead?

There were, in Hansi's opinion, all manner of lessons to be learned, by anyone who bothered to look. For instance, Neumann had actually heard the depth charge splashes as they hit the surface of the sea. Measuring the time, from that moment until the detonation, would give a good estimate of the rate of sinking of the charges, and from that could be calculated how long a U-boat had to evade a particular salvo. There was bound to be a critical interval when the attacking destroyer was 'blind', when the target U-boat had left the Asdic beam ahead of the destroyer, but the destroyer still had to run over its target and the depth charges still had to sink through the water. How long *was* that interval? Hansi suspected that it was a great deal longer than anybody in the U-Waffe had yet realised, and a U-boat had a much greater chance of evasion than anybody knew.

Hansi did not like to be disloyal, or even the least critical of Herr Kaleut, but in Hansi's opinion Herr Kaleut had been too passive during that attack. There had been a chance to get away. Hansi could recall a distinct period, of some three or four minutes, when some further avoiding action could have been taken. There was a lull, their attacker had seemed temporarily nonplussed, and a quick sidestep or dart to one side, or even a drastic change of depth, might have thrown him off. But it seemed that Herr Kaleut, like everybody else, had been stunned by the sheer venomous weight of those hateful detonations. But surely, Hansi thought, it was the *business* of the captain to keep one move ahead even when the charges were raining down? Simply to loosen one's collar, take off one's shoes, and hunch one's shoulders and wait for the enemy to give up and go away, surely that was to present him with the initiative?

But Hansi could find nobody, least of all on the staff, who seemed concerned with the operational lessons to be learned. When he transgressed perilously close to a breach of security and ventured near the subject in The Café, he was almost shouted down. 'Don't be morbid, Hansi,' they called out. 'Just be thankful you survived. Be grateful.'

It was as though they all believed that it would bring bad luck to hold post mortems, that these things were like acts of God, and to enquire too closely would be like prodding the dreaded *ankou,* whom the Bretons believed was the very personification of death, and inviting it into one's life. Such was the force of local beliefs that many U-boat sailors believed that the *ankou* appeared — as a skeleton, or as a white-haired old man wearing a wide-brimmed hat which hid his face — whenever somebody was about to die. Sometimes the *ankou* was alone, sometimes he appeared with two companions, to knock on the doors of those who were to die before the year was out. There were men in the town who said they had heard the sound of the *Crierien,* the rattling of bones of sailors who had died at sea and were asking to be buried. Everybody knew of local cemeteries where there were empty graves — real graves, not just headstones — for those lost at sea. With the strength of such local superstition, it was no wonder the U-boat sailors were sensitive on such subjects as boats' badges and insignia, and sailing dates, and whistling on board. Perhaps, Hansi thought, they ought to do as Herr Kaleut said the ancients did, and pay due attention to the flights of birds, and omens in the sky.

The next morning, when Hansi went down to the boat to clear out his locker and take the last of his personal belongings away before going on leave to the U-boat rest centre, he saw an unaccustomed crowd on the casing.

'Here you are,' he heard somebody say. 'Here's just the man. Look at that blond hair and blue eyes. They'll *love* him.'

The sailors on the casing had gathered round two strangers, both wearing grey overcoats and grey felt hats. One of them had a cinema camera, the other a small apparatus like a suitcase. Hansi knew they were from the *Propagandakompanie*. They were always hanging around the U-boats and the U-boat berths, looking for patriotic stories to send back to Germany.

The man with the camera still looked a little doubtful. Clearly he had come to interview Herr Kaleut. But the other man held out what Hansi could now see was a microphone. 'Your name, sir, please?'

'Hans-Dietrich Zschescher. Everybody calls me Hansi.'

'And your rank is? *Oberleutnant zur See*? How long have you been in the Navy, Hansi?'

'I joined at the end of nineteen thirty-eight. I have been in U-boats nearly one year.'

'And where is your home?'

'Leipzig.'

'Ah, Leipzig,' said the man. 'City of books and battles and Johann Sebastian Bach! And what does your father do in Leipzig?'

'He is a printer.'

'Is he a member of the Party?'

'Oh, yes. He is the *Blockführer* for … for…' Hansi hesitated. He really did not know why he could not complete his sentence.

'For your street … where you live?'

'That's right. He was in the navy, too. The Kaiser's navy, that was.' Hansi saw the expression on the cameraman's face alter slightly, as though tensing. 'My father is still a big gun man at heart. He thinks U-boats are not fair!' Hansi began to laugh, but saw the other was not laughing.

'Not *fair*?' The man with the microphone was wetting his lips. Hansi realised he might be speaking a little indiscreetly, but there was a seductive pleasure in talking to these two men, with all their camera and recording equipment, all so *interested* in what he, Hansi, had to say. It tempted one to be indiscreet.

'How do you think the U-boat war is going, Hansi? Lots of victories?'

'Of course. Lots of victories. But there could be more. And we could avoid some defeats.'

'Oh?' The microphone man was all attention, while the cameraman was looking intently at Hansi, almost as though he were wondering whether he should go on filming this. 'What do you mean, *avoid* defeats?'

'We should look more closely at why we lose boats. Why torpedoes sometimes miss, for no reason we can see.'

'*Do* they miss?' Both men looked incredulous.

'Oh, yes. Often.'

'And you think we should look more closely at this, and also why we lose U-boats?'

'Yes. I do.'

'Thank you very much, Hansi.'

The first sign that something might be amiss was the sight of Herr Kaleut coming down to the boat later that forenoon. This was an unusually early appearance for a submarine captain in harbour, and Herr Kaleut himself was looking uncharacteristically concerned.

'We have both to go up to the sardine castle, Hansi. To see the Sea Lion.'

The juxtaposition of the words 'sardine' and 'sea lion' made Hansi laugh out loud.

'It's no laughing matter, Hansi. What have you been saying to the propaganda sharks?'

'Nothing of much interest, Herr Kaleut.'

'It's enough to interest BdU himself.'

BdU's office was a very large room, possibly the former dining room, on the ground floor of the château, with tall windows looking on to a terrace, a low wall, and beyond that a view down the harbour to the sea. On one wall was a portrait of the Führer, and on the other a painting of a girl carrying a basket of flowers, posing against a country landscape. Very possibly it was the property of the former owner.

BdU sat at his desk, which was an expanse of polished wood, quite clear except for a blotter, a penholder, an inkwell and a silver-framed photograph of a young man in naval uniform. BdU's sons, Hansi had heard, were also in the navy. Behind BdU stood the *Kapitän zur See* who was his operations officer, and two other officers from the staff. For whatever reason, this was to be a full audience.

BdU came straight to the point. 'What have you been saying to the *Propagandakompanie*?'

'Herr Admiral, that I joined the navy in...'

'No, no. You know what I mean. That we should learn why we lose boats.'

'Yes, Herr Admiral. I meant just that.'

'Were you aware that we do check every boat's patrol record very carefully? That my staff go through everything that happens, to try and learn from it?'

'No, Herr Admiral, I was not aware of that. We in the boats do not see this going on, nor do we ever hear the result of the — the — the —' Hansi could not think of the proper word — 'checks.'

Hansi saw one of the staff officers standing behind the BdU stiffen, and guessed that he was the officer he had just indirectly criticised.

'Well, then, you tell me what we should be doing. You say we are not examining things closely enough. *You* tell me what we should do.'

'Herr Admiral...' Slowly, but with increasing confidence, Hansi related to the Admiral his thoughts from the last patrol, the lessons he thought they should learn, the tricks of the trade the enemy was using, the deadly necessity of lifting out every shred of evidence which could help their side. Hansi could sense the alarm of Herr Kaleut, standing at attention beside him, that one of his officers should be talking to the Admiral like this, but Hansi plunged on. It was now or never. 'There is lots of time for thought in a U-boat at sea. Lying there, just waiting for things to happen, waiting to surface, or to go on watch. Just waiting, thinking about the enemy...'

'What about the enemy?'

'Herr Admiral, when you are fencing...'

'You are a fencer?'

'Yes, Herr Admiral, I was in the sabre team for the college at Flensburg. It is a fact that when you first cross weapons with an opponent, you know at once, the very first touch of the blades, how good he is. We have had a first touch with the

Tommy ships, and I think they are much, much better than we give them credit for. We should try to analyse what they are doing.'

BdU was nodding, as though agreeing. 'And you think you are the man to do that?'

'Oh, not at all, Herr Admiral. I can only see what happens in one boat, my own. It needs somebody to look over every boat, in every base, every flotilla, to see the whole pattern, to see if there is anything that happens to everybody. Compare all the reports, so that every time, for instance, a torpedo fails to explode…'

Hansi saw the other staff officer behind BdU glare at him and purse his lips and recalled, too late, that this was the flotilla staff torpedo officer. That man would now work as hard as he could to discredit everything Hansi was saying. That was too bad. It was too late for regrets now.

'You will not find torpedoes failing to explode. We have enquired into it. There were faults on both sides, ashore and at sea.' But BdU was now smiling. He was standing up, to shake hands. 'Very good, you may go now. And good luck.'

Hansi saluted. 'Heil Hitler.' He turned on his heel, while BdU crooked a finger at Herr Kaleut, to detain him.

Hansi never discovered what BdU said to Herr Kaleut, because the captain did not volunteer any further comment, and Hansi dared not ask him. But at lunchtime, Herr Kaleut seemed pleased by the forenoon's outcome. 'I learned a lot this morning, Hansi. But I wonder how many others will learn?'

Somehow, the date of the start of another patrol always became known. Somewhere, a staff officer looked at a signal and then at a calendar and within a very short time, only minutes, it seemed, that date was known throughout the flotilla and all over town.

Their date was to be Saturday 21 December, the shortest day of the year, the day of the winter solstice. For over a week beforehand, the activity of storing the U-boat mounted to a steady crescendo. Lorries and horse-drawn carts crowded the jetty. There were torpedoes to be loaded, and tins of preserves, and hams and sausages, and bread, and coffee, and spare parts for the diesels, and ammunition, and fuel to be embarked, and a last charge and topping-up of the main batteries. All day long a line of sailors formed human chains across the gangways, handling endless boxes and packages and bundles of clothing from one man to the next. At times it seemed quite impossible that such a mountain of objects could ever be packed down into such a small U-boat hull.

On the Friday before sailing, they had a deserter, a fore-ends man, one of the Lordlings, who was absent over his leave and, so the rumour was, had said he was not coming back. Hansi found that his name was Ernst — Ernst Webo, a leading torpedoman — and it was believed he had a liaison with one of the local French girls, one of the myriad Yvettes, Janettes, Babettes ('Why is it that they all have names like hand towels?' said Hugo the engineer) in the town. The girl's mother was half German, it was said, and did not object to a U-boat fore-endsman for a son-in-law.

The flotilla had contingency plans for deserters, and provided a replacement from spare crew. The police would look for Ernst, and might recover him before the boat sailed. If they sailed without him, he was officially a deserter, and could at the worst be executed by shooting.

For Hansi, any event on board was of interest and he made enquiries. It seemed Ernst had not liked the depth-charging. A particular friend of his in the same watch, who slept next door to him, said Ernest had lately been crying in his sleep, and calling out loud, and complained of suffering from bad dreams. He was moody and sulky and silent, where before he had been a notably cheerful, talkative youth. One day he would work hard, the next he would loaf and skulk off by himself.

Hansi suspected that the other Lordly Ones knew more of Ernst's whereabouts than they would admit. He wondered at their silence, at their readiness to conceal him. There was such a thing as loyalty, but surely they must also know that any desertion, any weakening of the fibre of the boat, of its temper and fitness for war, any failure, indeed any change at all, was bound to affect them personally? Evidently their mistaken loyalty to their shipmate was stronger than their instinct for survival — at least, it was for the moment.

On the Saturday morning, the day they were to sail, the whole crew went up to the *Sardinenschlösschen* for an address by BdU. They stood, formed up in four lines, in a small courtyard. When BdU arrived with his staff, once again Hansi found it hard to associate this little man in a big coat — with the dried-up-looking countenance and the high piping voice — with the strident messages, echoing blood and thunder, which he sent to his U-boats. On the very first day of the war, back in September 1939, he had begun with his Secret Standing Order No. 154: 'We must be harsh in this war! The enemy began it, to destroy us. So nothing else matters.' That had been his motto ever since.

BdU walked along their lines, followed by his staff. Herr Kaleut went with him, to tell him a man's name if he should ask. BdU said nothing to Hansi, or made any sign of having met him before. Hansi was aware only of the grey eyes, that pale, tired-looking skin, and the folds on the neck.

BdU made a speech. The message was still the same. That piercing voice rose and fell, rebounding thinly off the courtyard walls. It had a hypnotic cadence, rising and falling in a steady rhythm which plucked at his listener's deepest feelings. The speech was full of emotive words that chimed with their own emotions. *'Ran an den Feind!'* was his theme, repeated again and again. 'Go after the enemy! *Versenken!* Sink him!'

The boat was to sail at midnight, on the tide, a time which might have been specially chosen so as most to embarrass Herr Kaleut and the other officers. Saturday night was always the worst night for drunkenness and leave-breaking, even without the prospect of sailing at once on a war patrol.

So it was no surprise that when Hansi went up to the bridge to join Herr Kaleut for leaving harbour, he had to report several men still missing. Hansi was now *Eins WO*. As he had forecast, Klaus had left the boat, nobody knew where. They had a new *Zweiter*, a very young man straight out of U-boat school. His name was Siegfried, and he seemed keen enough, but as he had straight fair hair, brushed back, pale grey eyes which were rather protruberant, and two very prominent front teeth, the Lordly Ones were already calling him *Kleines Kaninchen* — 'Little Rabbit'.

There were still some shaded lights burning on the jetty, but they went out as Hansi looked at them; probably an air raid precaution. It was now very cold, with a north wind gusting over the roofs of the town. It was sheltered where the boat was lying, but Hansi could hear the wind blustering over his head. He could guess what it would be like when they reached the open sea.

A lorry came grinding towards the boat. Somebody let down the tailboard, and it fell with a crash. Hansi recognised six or seven of their sailors climbing out of the back. One of them had to be supported, he was so far gone. Hansi watched, disgusted, as they giggled and quarrelled as to who should go across the gangway first. The most drunken one slipped and almost fell. Hansi thought he could smell the booze and the vomit on them from where he was.

Hansi was surprised to see Herr Kaleut grinning. 'This is St Lucy's Day, Hansi. The shortest of the year. And we're sailing at midnight. It is the year's midnight and the day's. It couldn't be a bigger omen, could it? Must get better. *Bruma recurrit iners.* "Lifeless winter rolls round again." There are two references to the winter solstice in those three words, Hansi. But you don't read Horace, do you?'

'No, Herr Kaleut.' Hansi was impatient with this kind of talk. He had just noticed that the most drunken of the men was the *Obersteuermann*; as quartermaster, a warrant officer, and a man with a most responsible duty on board, he should have known better. But here he was, reeling and staggering on board like a junior sailor on his first run ashore in a foreign port. All these drunks would have to be put in bunks. Somebody else would have to do their work until they sobered, at a time when the U-boat would be in great danger; it would be like starting on a patrol having already granted the first few tricks to the enemy. They ought to make an order that *all* U-boat personnel should report back on board at least twenty-four hours before sailing, to leave them time to dry out if they had to. It was preposterous to expect men to come straight out of a bar and go straight to war. In fact, they ought to go to sea for a couple of days, for a shake-down cruise, just to let everybody, from Herr Kaleut downwards, get his eye in again. But obviously they would not want to go through that whole business of getting a U-boat out to sea, the escorts, the minesweepers, the opening of the boom at the entrance, the air raid precautions, the signal traffic — naturally the people ashore would want to do all that only once for each U-boat. But still, it seemed to

Hansi, that *not* to do all that was improperly cutting corners, was gambling with the crew's lives. It was *unkriegerisch* — unwarlike. There was another, better word for it: *unberufsmäßig*. Unprofessional. The enemy would never be *unberufsmäßig*.

Their own song was now coming up from the control room below. 'And we *did* cheer up ... And it *did* get worse ... The *very* next day!' Herr Kaleut made a wide gesture with his hand, as though sweeping imaginary bouquets of flowers off the bridge rail.

'*Halb fahrt zurück.* Half speed astern. *Leinen Los!*'

The last line dropped away and was hauled inboard. They took no wires with them. A U-boat had none of her own. She would never need them, and they took up space and added extra weight; also, they might come adrift in depth-charging and foul the propellers. There were three cheers, *hurrah, hurrah, hurrah,* coming on the wind from shore. As the boat backed away, far enough, a fierce gust of wind hit it and made those on the bridge actually step back a pace with its force. There was now one light on the jetty. Hansi watched it get smaller and then go out.

The patrol vessel that was supposed to lead them down harbour seemed to be showing no lights at all, as though scared of attracting aircraft. It was an anxious passage down to the sea. The patrol vessel did give them the faintest of blinks at the harbour bar: *Fare thee well, my friend.* Then they set out into the Atlantic.

From the first they all knew that this was the worst weather they had ever experienced. Day after day the boat wallowed and plunged and rose again, and sickeningly dropped into a trough. The watch and the lookouts came down from the bridge soaked and exhausted. Water poured never-endingly down the tower, and the pump was at work on the control room bilge constantly.

On Christmas evening, when the weather seemed even worse than it had been, a handful of men off watch gathered in the control room, hanging on to valve and handwheels as the boat bucked and plunged, and sang some Christmas carols. *'Stille Nacht, heilige nacht...'* In the circumstances, Hansi thought, they sang very well.

'Alles schläft, einsam wacht
Nur das traute hochheilige Paar
Holder Knabe im lockigen Haar
Schlaf in himmlischer Ruh ... schlaf in himmlischer Ruh!'

Then they sang *'O Tannenbaum, o Tannenbaum, wie treu sind deine Blätter?'* They ended up, of course, with their own 'And it did get worse...'

During that night they received the signal. In a moment the news was around the boat. Another large convoy. They were in the best position to intercept. Once again, Hansi could not help noticing the great surge of high spirits, the lighter steps, the smiles. Truly the men of the U-Waffe were the most temperamental warriors of all time.

CHAPTER FIVE

'Well, well, well,' said Gussie. 'What have we here?' He was looking through his glasses at a strange destroyer approaching from ahead. She looked unusually long, but had a low freeboard, and four very thin and very tall funnels. The water of Liverpool Bay was as smooth as a steel mirror and upon it the destroyer, with the curl of her bow wave and the whiffs of smoke from her funnels, had an oddly antique appearance, as though she had steamed straight out of a late-nineteenth-century engraving. As Gussie said, 'Like something off one of those old cigarette cards.'

'It's one of the Lend Lease destroyers, sir,' said Drury. '*Yank* destroyers, sir. They gave them to us in exchange for bases, or something, sir.'

'Well.' Gussie was still studying the new apparition. 'I suppose we knew what we were doing. We need every ship, God knows. But there are limits, surely.'

'They've got a turning circle larger than Hood's, sir. Did you know that, sir?'

'No, I didn't know that, as a matter of fact. Thank you for the information, Sub.'

The first portion of their convoy had spent most of the forenoon forming up in Liverpool Bay. Astern, on the starboard quarter, were the flat sandy wastes of Southport. Ahead, just visible on the port bow, were Llandudno and the Great Orme. It was a day of exceptional winter visibility, with one of those clear skies through which one felt one could see the North Pole if one looked hard enough. It was certainly too chilly for Jay's hands, which were still very sensitive to cold indeed, so that he now had to wear some kind of gloves almost all the time he was in the open air. He had also found that he could not stay on his feet for too long without weariness and actual pain. Jay knew that Gussie was already looking questioningly at him, considering how long he could last as a small ship's bridge watchkeeper in winter time. Gussie would always be slow to axe another officer, bearing in mind his own past experience. But, as Jay had come to know, in matters of his ship's operational efficiency, Gussie was quite ruthless.

Jay himself knew that, if it came to that, he would be very sorry to leave. Of course, he would have liked to return to flying, but he had already grown very fond of this little ship, with Gussie and her wardroom and her ship's company, with all their small-ship idiosyncrasies. Jay had never had so much personal responsibility before, and he found himself enjoying the ordering of a ship and her ways. It was pleasantly fulfilling to see one's own organisation and arrangements actually working.

The Lend Lease destroyer passed quite close down their starboard side to take up her position astern. As she passed, an officer on her bridge took off his cap and waved it to Gussie, who took off his own and did the same.

'Clive Broadrigg,' Gussie said. 'I knew him in China. Ambitious sod. Someone must be remembering the affair he had with someone else's wife in Hong Kong. He always wanted a destroyer. Now look what he's got.' Gussie turned his gaze on the convoy. 'Come on, come on, come *on*. We'll never get to New York at this rate.'

This convoy was as slow and awkward in forming up as they all were. There was always something maddeningly deliberate about merchantmen. Their blood actually seemed to flow at a slower rate. Even the quickest of them seemed to move at snail's pace. The sun always cheered them up. Their blood, like that of great saurians, quickened in its heat. But cold always deadened and slowed them even more. They spent hours steering in various directions, occasionally sheering off hurriedly to avoid collisions. They never signalled to ask anything, least of all for advice about where they should go and what they should be doing. Instead, they continued to plunge and thrash about, like desperate men fighting to find a way out of a locked clothes cupboard.

The Escort Commander, in a V and W-class destroyer dating from the previous war, was pounding up the other side of the convoy, his signal lamp flashing and his halliards streaming with flags.

'*He sings each song twice over,*' said Gussie, '*lest you should think he never could recapture* ... How does it go on, Sub?'

'I'm afraid I don't know that, sir.'

'Hah! *Lest you should think he never could recapture, the first fine careless rapture.* Not much point in signalling to *them.*'

Gussie had learned, as all escort captains had to learn sooner or later, that it was indeed fruitless to signal to merchantmen. The Convoy Commodore's ship had a naval signal staff, but the signalling of every other ship in the convoy would depend upon the importance accorded to it pre-war by her owners, or on the presence in her crew of an enthusiast. Very occasionally, they would encounter one of the 'ex-Sea Scouts', in Gussie's phrase, who responded with a torrent of fast and accurate flashing. But far more generally, answering a signal meant somebody had to be rousted out of his bunk, and most ships preferred not to bother.

'That's Coolie Colclough,' Gussie said, nodding at the Escort Commander's ship, now taking station ahead of the convoy.

'Coolie was Chief CC at Dartmouth, you know. The high point of his life. I don't think he's ever really got over the glory of it all.'

It was one of the chief delights of Gussie's conversation, Jay had found, that he knew everybody — everybody, that is, in the regular Navy. Gussie was a walking Navy List, but his Navy List had a strong flavour of *Tatler* and *The Bystander* about it. He seemed to be aware of everybody's foibles. He seemed to know the inside story of every mishap and every success in everybody's career. Gussie mentally saluted, and gave every credit, to those of his own generation who had risen in the Service. But he also had a wry, consoling concern for those, like himself, who had rather fallen by the wayside.

'The trouble with Coolie,' Gussie was saying, 'is that his father was an Admiral, and Coolie himself has always wanted to command the Grand Fleet, or something like it. So he treats every convoy as though it were the Grand Fleet. Isn't that *Padstow* calling us up by light?' Gussie had eyes in the back of his head. Even when he was gossiping and not apparently paying attention, he still sighted ships, signals, anything untoward, before anybody else.

Padstow was their chummy ship. The sailors of the two ships had always got on well together. *Padstow*'s Captain was also a passed-over Lieutenant Commander of about Gussie's own vintage. Occasionally, when the two ships secured alongside each other, Gussie and Tich — so called since his Dartmouth days because he was six foot six inches tall — would go ashore together on drinking bouts described in tones of awe in the escort groups of Liverpool and Londonderry.

'From *Padstow*, sir: "Let's all hope for a quiet trip, sir."'
'Make to *Padstow*: "Hear hear."'

The late-afternoon sun came out for a few moments and briefly lit up the hulls of all the ships around. Momentarily, their convoy made a cheerful, composite scene, with the long grey hull of a tanker, and the short black hulls of the tramp steamers, the tall thin funnels and the squat tubby ones. For a little while, there was an atmosphere of confidence and comradeship, a belief that if they kept together in convoy they would be safe.

They lost the first ship just as the sun was setting, before they were even clear of the North Channel. A German bomber dropped out of the sky, like a pigeon on to a field of greens, and hit the leading ship in the third column with one bomb, and near-missed her with a second. None of them on *Whitby*'s bridge heard the sound of the explosion, but they all saw the tower of water and the smoke, quickly blown away on the hard, steel-coloured sky. The ship sank very quickly, going down by the bows. They could see one boat only, moving out and away from the tipped-up hull.

Some of the merchant ships were armed, and they opened fire unavailingly at the aircraft as it crossed the convoy. The aircraft streaked through a trail of smoke and banked, so that they could see the light flashing on its cockpit canopy, before climbing easily out of sight.

'They keep on doing that,' said Gussie, as he bent to take a bearing of the ship's lifeboat. 'Steer zero nine seven. We never get any of them. It would be a miracle if we even hit one. We're much more likely to hit each other, the way they spray ammunition around. Any pre-war Gunnery Safety Officer would have a fit if he saw what goes on around here. But it's no use. What we really need, I suppose, is our own air cover, right with us. Take it along with us. Like Mary's little lamb.'

'There aren't enough aircraft carriers to do that, sir,' said Jay. 'Not to go with convoys.'

'Got more important things to do, I suppose you mean. I know we haven't got enough carriers. But we don't need a big fleet carrier, one of *your* lot, Jay. That sort of thing is for the Med Fleet in peacetime, and Royal Reviews at Coronations…' Jay knew that Gussie loved to poke fun at the Fleet Air Arm whenever he could. 'No, what we need is a *little* carrier. Something cheap and cheerful.'

'We haven't got any of those either, sir.'

'Why not put some sort of a flat deck on top of an ordinary merchant ship?' said Drury. 'If the ship was long enough they could probably take just a few aircraft. That would be cheap and cheerful, sir, wouldn't it?'

'What a *brilliant* idea, Sub!' said Gussie. He was pretending to be awe-struck, but his voice and manner showed that he really was impressed. They were all suddenly impressed by the possibilities of the notion. 'That's the germ of a *bloody* good idea! But I don't suppose it'll ever come about.' Gussie turned his attention back to affairs of the moment. 'Here you go, Jay, stand by to pick up survivors, if there are any.'

But far away, up ahead of the convoy, Coolie Colclough was flashing. "From the Escort Commander, sir, *Padstow* take survivors. *Whitby* rejoin."

'Short and sweet, I must say,' said Gussie.

That, it struck Jay, was an abrupt and callous way to put it. But he had already noticed the hard, ruthless streak in Gussie's temperament. Whatever his shortcomings pre-war, Gussie was coming into his own now. Everybody in *Whitby*'s attack team had noticed how thoroughly Gussie had enjoyed their last attack on that U-boat, when they had thought at one time that they had sunk it, although Gussie refrained from making any claims. Jay recalled the rapt concentration upon Gussie's face as he took his ship in and over the target in a series of attack patterns, the crouched stance, like a wrestler searching for a weak point in his opponent, as he stood at the voice-pipe, and the gleeful eyes watching the sea astern boil and split and erupt from the exploding depth charges. Gussie had led his team onwards by example, shepherding them, reassuring them, impressing them all with his own conviction that they would surely find and nail down their target. None of them would ever forget Gussie's rage and self-disgust when he realised that he had inadvertently turned the wrong way, distancing the ship unnecessarily from the target. The added range was not much, two or three hundred yards at the most. But it had been just enough to make them lose their firm Asdic contact.

Their first task when they had rejoined was to nudge the two rear ships of the port column back into their proper station. Gussie and the other escort captains had long since realised that this convoy was unusually undisciplined. Station-keeping in every convoy tended to be empirical, but no matter how much ships 'ebbed and flowed', they generally managed to keep together. But this convoy's station-keeping was appalling. Every morning, the escorts had to range around its edges, like sheepdogs around their flock, nipping at the heels of stragglers and wanderers. Every convoy had 'Smoky Joes' who stained the sky with their funnel smoke and, not infrequently, lied about the speed they could maintain. This convoy consisted of Smoky Joes. Every convoy ditched gash. This one left a trail, like a broad highway of wooden boxes, potato peelings, paper bags and cardboard cartons, stretching for miles astern and proclaiming to every U-boat, in Gussie's phrase, 'Come see, come buy.'

The Convoy Commodore, a retired Vice Admiral who had volunteered to go to sea again when hostilities began, evidently knew Coolie, or of him, and clearly did not like what he knew. 'Probably served with his father,' said Gussie. There was almost constant agitated flashing between Coolie and the Commodore. Much of the signalling complained of unnecessary signalling, and the rest were recriminations and accusations — of bad station-keeping, smoke-making, gash-ditching, and straggling. But, although the Convoy Commodore was a Flag Officer who had been Commander-in-Chief of a foreign station, and Coolie was a Commander, many ranks junior and many years younger, Coolie was the Escort Commander, and had charge of everything concerned with the conduct and defence of the convoy and its escort.

Nevertheless, it seemed to be a lucky convoy, untouched after that first early loss. By their last night in company, when they were due to detach in the morning and join an incoming convoy, *Whitby* and the other escorts had grown fond of their wayward charges. It seemed that a special providence, like that which takes care of drunks, had watched over this convoy. When Jay came up on the bridge at five to midnight to take over the middle watch, he was just about to remark that he hoped their luck would last, when a brilliant flash lit up the sky well astern, where a straggler had begun to drop back unnoticed.

Whitby was the stern escort of the convoy's port flank and, as the ship's company went to action stations and Gussie took over again from Jay, the ship steered for the stern of the convoy. They had hardly steadied on their new course when there was a second and even bigger flash on the far side of the convoy, and it was followed at once, and slightly to the right, by a third. The watchers on *Whitby*'s bridge had not had time even to consider what this meant when a ship quite close to them, in the extreme port hand column, blew up with a detonation so loud it had an actual physical impact upon their eardrums. The U-boats had clearly caught the convoy up and, whether by luck or judgment, had begun two perfectly synchronised attacks, from its port and starboard flanks.

For a space, it seemed that the whole convoy and its escort were utterly taken aback by the suddenness of the onslaught. Jay could think of nothing to do except take a bearing of the nearest stricken ship. Gussie said nothing, gave no orders, no course to steer, had quite apparently not yet recovered from his shock. Then, over the loudspeaker from the Asdic office, they all heard the solid, metallic, unmistakeable echo of a firm sonar contact.

The sound seemed to snap Gussie out of his shocked trance. 'Blood for supper!' he shouted. 'Bearing, bearing, what's the *bearing?*' Gussie's shouting drowned the Asdic operator's voice, already trying to tell him what he wanted to know.

'Zero eight nine ... Bearing zero eight seven. Range two thousand five hundred. Bearing zero eight *three* ... bearing moving rapidly *left,* sir...'

'Port thirty. Steer zero seven eight.' It was important, as they all knew, to steer to head off their target and not simply run directly at it like a greyhound at its hare.

'We have not exactly *shone* tonight,' Gussie said to Jay. 'We're going to make up for that now.'

With thirty of port wheel on, *Whitby* continued to swing in towards the convoy, but the target bearing was still running left, until *Whitby* was astern of it and actually chasing it into the heart of the convoy. In daylight, Gussie might have held on. In the dark, and with the convoy in such a state of nervous confusion after the attacks, he dared not follow. Once again,

Jay sensed his captain's uncertainty. It was not at all like Gussie to be so hesitant, but events seemed to be conspiring against him this night.

Gussie happened to break off the chase to starboard and there, immediately ahead, and only some two miles away, were the tiny lights of the survivors of the ship sunk nearest them a few minutes earlier. Some at least of her people must have got away. Here was something definite for Gussie and his ship to do.

'Stand by to pick up survivors, starboard side.'

Jay went down to the upper deck and walked aft to take charge. They had exercised this many times, laying out their lifelines and lifejackets, and breaking out the scrambling net, and taking down the guard rails. But this was the first time in practice.

It was pitch dark on deck, and there was no sign of the convoy or of any other ship. At this much lower level, Jay could see that there was a tremendous sea running. The waves were brushing the deck edge and hissing along it as they passed astern. Larger waves came over and flooded the deck up to where Jay was standing. Now and again, there was a crash of broken water and spray flew overhead, drenching everybody as though in a heavy rain storm. Jay could see that they had never exercised in anything like this sort of weather.

Leading Seaman Blakey, who was in charge of the quarterdeck and the depth-charge party, had already taken down the guard rails. Two of his sailors, both wearing lifelines, carried a scrambling net to the ship's side and let it go. A wave gathered under it and lifted it until Jay could actually see it floating on the surface of the sea, like the tendrils of some grotesque water weed. Jay felt the ship slowing down and turning to port. Looking out on the starboard, leeward side, he could see the lights, much brighter now than they had been, but still terrifyingly small, and dim. Each light was a man. Jay fancied he could see white faces looking at him. For a moment he felt a frightening sense of unreality: was he really here, were those out there really flesh and blood, or just phantoms? Jay thought he could even hear shouts now, and long wailing cries, somebody pleading for God's charity.

There was a sudden rush of water and a wave swelling up the ship's side and, to Jay's amazement, a large Carley float appeared right alongside them. It rose and then disappeared again. That was brilliant ship-handling by Gussie, in this sea. Now, to Jay's utter astonishment, Blakey actually had hold of a man, who was shouting at the top of his voice, and was dragging him on board. The rescue technique was actually working. Men were being saved. Now there was another, lying still, who had to be lugged and dragged forward like a sack of wet coal. Jay took hold of a third man's hand as he stepped calmly on board, as though arriving for visitors' day. He stood for a second or two on their upper deck, clasping both hands on the light on his lifejacket, as though that represented life itself; as long as the light burned, he would live. Jay brusquely motioned him to go forward. There was a long cry, so loud it made Blakey and the others wince, as a fourth man was dragged across; it took less than a second to cross that abyss, from the float to the ship, from death into life.

A much larger wave lifted the float so that it rose almost to Jay's eye level and he could see its round painted canvas side. The water poured inboard and they all stopped what they were doing to clasp stanchions, a deck ventilation outlet, anything to prevent them being carried away. Jay felt the sea tugging at his own calves, with a shockingly strong pull, as though it really did mean him to follow the water over the side. At this rate, they would be all night recovering the men in the float.

The head and shoulders of yet another man had appeared above the deck at gunwale level. His feet were entangled in the net and he could go no further. Jay saw the man's face gleaming brighter and brighter as though painted with luminous paint. Before anybody could move, another sea crashed over his head and swamped him, but when it ebbed, he was still there, still looking up at Jay. The ship heeled violently to port as Jay and Blakey seized him, and the motion helped them to lift him upwards and in.

The deck was throbbing underfoot. The float had vanished. The deck was now heeling further over to port as the ship turned to starboard. They were going ahead. They must be abandoning the rescue. Jay could see the Carley float some way astern.

'What's happening now?'

Leading Seaman Blakey shrugged. 'We're going ahead, sir,' he shouted against the wind. 'Looks like the finish of that.'

When Jay reached the bridge, he could hear that same sound over the Asdic office broadcast — the hard, solid, indisputable sound of a contact.

Gussie was staring out ahead. 'Not sure if it's the same bugger, but he's trying the same tactic. My God, these bastards are going in for the convoy as though they were diving for prizes. Bearing, what's the *bearing*, goddammit?'

'Zero six four, sir ... Bearing moving very rapidly left...'

It was the longest night of the war, the longest night of Jay's whole life. Series of events, the same events, seemed to follow each other in sequence. They attacked, and had to break off, and set about picking up survivors, and had to stop, and got another contact, and attacked, and had to break off. At dawn, they closed yet another boat load of survivors. It was a very large boat, packed with people. It had a cabin superstructure, and what looked like a green-painted funnel. 'Looks as if it's come from the Thames,' as Blakey said. 'All out on a spree.'

But there was nothing amusing about the contents of the boat. With the coming of daylight, and the sea calming and the sky clearing, they were able to bring the boat actually alongside and secure it. When Jay first went down into the boat with Blakey, he thought they had rescued a crew of Hottentots or pygmies. Most of the survivors were tiny. But then, Jay realised they were children, all completely covered in oil, which made them look like old men. Most of them were naked or almost naked: they had had to abandon ship in their pyjamas. The rest looked like Lascars, and there was one officer still wearing his reefer jacket with gold lace on its sleeves, sitting at the tiller. He had a great raw wound, clearly visible in one thigh. The other leg was broken and the powerful leg muscles had tucked the limb up underneath him, as though he were performing some grotesque circus trick of acrobatics.

As they began to pass the survivors up to the waiting hands on the upper deck, Jay realised that most of them were already dead. There were some sixty people in the boat, and only six or seven were still alive. The children had died of shock and cold and exposure, the sailors of massive burns which covered much of their bodies. Those still living screamed and cried in agony whenever they were touched.

They approached the officer sitting in the stern sheets last. He had made no move to save himself or anybody else. Jay saw his lips moving but could hear nothing. Only his eyes seemed really alive, and Jay saw that the man was crying. His fingers gripped the tiller still, so tightly Jay had to prise them apart. They lifted him, his body still dreadfully contorted, up to the gunwale. It was not possible to be gentle with him, and Jay dared not think of the added pain they were causing him. They laid him on his back on the upper deck while somebody went to fetch a stretcher.

The children were taken to the Captain's cabin, in Townsend's care. The officer from the stern sheets was carried to the wardroom. The three surviving sailors, who did not look as if they would last the day out, were carried to the forward mess deck and laid out on the cushions. There were three bunks in the small sick bay, but they were already occupied by survivors picked up earlier in the night. None of them were half so badly injured as the sailors, but Jay did not feel he could move them. The bodies of the others were laid out on the upper deck aft. They made a shockingly long line. Blakey and passing sailors looked askance at them, and Jay knew they must hold a burial service as soon as possible. Corpses like that were bad joss.

On his way forward, Jay paused at the wardroom door. The officer from the lifeboat, by some unimaginable physical effort and mental victory over pain, had apparently moved himself off the stretcher already and was sitting, with his legs tucked up underneath him in a Buddha-like posture, on the wardroom sofa. His eyes were open and he seemed to be looking directly at Jay.

'He fought me off, sir. I couldn't do anything.' The face of Prescott, the wardroom steward, was grey and shocked. 'I think he's gone, sir. He's gone, I'm sure.'

The eyes did not follow Jay or look up as he came towards the sofa. Jay picked up one loose, floppy wrist. He could feel no pulse. Jay put his hand inside the man's vest. The flesh of his chest was as smooth and cold as marble, with globules of water standing out on it, with the horrifying likeness of sweat exuded from living skin.

'Get somebody to help you take him down aft with the others.' Jay felt inside the jacket. There was a Merchant Navy Officer's identity card, but the ink was illegible. A stamp showed that it had been issued in Liverpool. It reminded Jay that they ought to note the particulars of all the bodies before they disposed of them. There was a lot still to be done.

On his way towards the ladder to the forward mess deck, Jay heard voices raised in the main passageway. One of the survivors they had picked up first had his arms clasped around a stanchion, near the watertight door leading out to the upper deck. Hutchings, the Leading Signalman, was trying to persuade the man to unclasp his hands.

'Come on, mate. We've got a nice cup of tea down the mess. Come *on*.' Hutchings seized the survivor's shoulder with both hands and tried to pull him. 'Come on. *Tea*. You won't get nothing up here.' Hutchings looked at Jay. 'He's been here like this for hours, sir. Come *on,* mate.'

But the man shook his head emphatically. His whole body posture made it clear he meant to stay where he was, literally within stepping distance of the open air. When Hutchings' urgings made him at last look down the passageway, he stared at it like a rabbit looking into the neck of a poacher's sack. Nothing on earth would persuade him to go down there. Luck had brought him out of the ship and into a float. Luck had plucked him out of the float and brought him here. Luck might just run out if he went any further.

'Leave him be,' Jay said.

Standing at the foot of the ladder leading down into the forward mess deck, Jay was surprised to find the place so full of men. He had not realised they had picked up so many.

There were some twenty to thirty survivors, sitting at the tables or lying on the mess stools. The mess-deck deadlights were screwed shut and there were only a couple of lights burning, so it was very dark, but Jay noticed that survivors from the first ship were already sitting together, as though they had formed their own individual mess. It seemed that, left to themselves, sailors' first acts were to mark out a space of their own, to establish their own identity. There was a smell of oil and sea water and iodine, but the men were making no sound. The only voice was the Coxswain's, asking one man to lift an arm so that he could get a bandage under it.

Blackstock appeared from the other end of the mess deck. He had a list in his hand. 'I make it thirty-five. From three different ships.'

'Yes,' Jay said. 'We've done very well. Can't we brighten this place up? Put some lights on?'

'No, they don't want it. They want to stay in the dark.'

'They're very quiet.'

'That's happened in the last, well, just now. They were coughing and sobbing and generally kicking up a bit of a row. But now they seem to be a bit numbed by it all. Don't blame them.'

'What about those last three?' Jay asked the Coxswain. The three sailors were lying on adjacent seats. Their brown faces looked a curious purple colour in that light.

'Fifty-fifty, sir, I'd say. Motton's looking after them, sir.'

Motton was the ship's Leading Sick Berth Attendant. They had been promised a qualified Surgeon Lieutenant, but he had not yet joined. Meanwhile, Motton was the only man on board with any proper medical training other than a basic first aid course.

'How's it going, Motton?'

'I wouldn't say fifty-fifty sir. I've never seen *anything* like those burns. It's not a case of a patient with burns, sir. They're just one big burn. Must have been a boiler flashback or something, sir. How they ever got down into the boat in the state they are beats me. They can't speak any English, sir, it seems, and I can't speak their lingo. So we don't even know their names.'

Jay looked down at the sailors' faces. They were going to die, and nobody would even know who they were. He remembered that he had not yet reported to the Captain.

Gussie was having his breakfast, brought up to him by Townsend. 'Strange about those children,' he said. 'I thought they'd stopped that scheme, after the *City of Benares* disaster. How are they now? How is everybody?'

'As well as anybody could expect anybody to be, sir,' Jay said.

'We have thirty-five in all, from three different ships, sir. And, sir?'

'Yes?' Gussie looked round warily, as though he knew the request was bound to be unpleasant.

'There are quite a lot of ... bodies, sir. Down aft. Would you read the service, sir? We really ought to do it quite soon.'

Gussie glanced up at the sky. 'It's blowing up again, thank God. Let's say we'll have the service at noon. That'll give the buffer time to finish all his sewing. We must do this as properly as we can.'

'Aye aye, sir.'

It was a sign of the distorted, upside-down world they now lived in, where even nature and all its expectations were reversed, that Gussie should ever have thanked God at the prospect of bad weather, in winter, in the north Atlantic. But bad weather was good. It had been discovered that heavy seas and high winds hampered the U-boat attacks more than the convoy's station-keeping.

Jay was so tired he could hardly stand up, but he was ashamed to find that he was afraid to go below. He now had a fellow feeling with that terrified wretch, clinging to his stanchion in the passageway below. The act of leaving the upper deck might be his last. Jay could not disguise his fear from himself. He was sure of it. He had no appetite for breakfast and he went to his cabin reluctantly, as though the decision might be irrevocable. It might mean him ending up like those men on the mess deck, in somebody else's ship; that is, if he was lucky. Jay was thankful he had not thought of this when he was on the mess deck. Those survivors would have known that he was afraid.

Jay stretched himself fully clothed on his bunk. Normally he looked forward to that delicious headlong plunge into oblivion. This forenoon, he let sleep come to him reluctantly, ready to start up at the slightest untoward sound or movement.

At noon, Gussie waited, hoping for a sight of the sun. But the clouds stretched down to the horizon, with every sign of growing thicker as the day went on. Gussie put away his sextant and took up his prayer book instead. It was the first time Jay had ever known him leave the bridge, or his sea-cabin, once they had left harbour.

Gussie was away some time, and came back irritable and out of sorts. 'God, how I *loathed* that. Do you know it's the first time I've ever had to do it, in all my years at sea. Was Coolie flashing us just now as I came up, or was he giving the Commodore another piece of his mind?'

Jay grinned. Gussie never, ever missed any trick. Dawkins, the signalman on watch, was just finishing writing the message down.

'Let's have a look.' Gussie glared at Jay. 'You didn't tell me there were so many back there. Now what have we here?'

'"Aircraft reports damaged U-boat. Suspect unable to dive. Go and finish it off."'

The position given was over forty miles away, back along the convoy's track and some distance to port of it. The direction was south-east, which would be down wind and sea, but in this weather it would still mean nearly three hours' steaming, even at full speed.

Jay's first reaction was to expect the order for the new course to steer. Surely there could be no doubt about that. But he was surprised to see Gussie looked puzzled and indecisive.

'I'm not sure about this one,' Gussie was saying. 'If it were me…'

Jay waited, impatient for the new course to steer. It seemed to him there could be no possible reason for hesitation. After such a night, and when their own ship had a mess deck full of the shocked and injured results of that night, the situation cried out for vengeance. When Jay remembered those survivors' faces, with their lopsided smiles — whether of gratitude or hatred it was impossible to interpret — he knew the whole ship longed for revenge. Here was one of the perpetrators of that night, apparently helpless, and on the surface. Yet still Gussie hesitated.

'I know it's tempting, but it's a long, long way from the convoy. I've just got a funny feeling in my water this one is going to be bad joss…'

However, it was the Escort Commander's order. Still shaking his head, Gussie gave the new course to steer.

Any doubts about the propriety of their action were, in Jay's opinion, laid to rest almost at once. For a little while they were doubling back on the convoy's track and soon they passed the scene of a sinking. No ship disappeared without a trace. Here, there were shattered lengths of timber, clothing, scraps of debris, and patches of oil. Worst of all, there was a small white dog, a Highland terrier, standing upon a floating box lid. Jay could hear it barking at them, like a thousand small dogs asking to be taken for a walk. Again, Jay saw Gussie shaking his head and pursing his lips. They could not stop to pick the dog up.

'Dog on the port beam, sir,' said Dawkins, the young signalman.

'I know, I know, I *know*,' said Gussie fiercely. 'Helmsman,' he said down the voice-pipe, 'watch your *course*!'

Jay watched the little dog, which was still barking, slide aft. As he followed it, he caught sight of the three children on the lower wing of the bridge where Townsend had taken them. Three pairs of round, wondering eyes looked up at him. Jay was very glad when the dog was finally out of sight.

The ship had settled for the run down wind and sea. It was a pleasant easy motion after days of driving into the weather. This would certainly be a long chase. The U-boat would be heading south, trying to open the range, slipping down the west coast of Ireland towards its base in France.

'This is where we could use bases in Ireland, sir,' Jay said.

'Indeed, indeed.' Gussie was quite clearly grateful for a change of subject and a chance to think about something else. 'But that's one battle we've already lost. The Irish won't have it. There's no blackout in Eire, I'm told, and there's a Nazi flag flying over their embassy in Dublin. Makes you think.' Gussie looked round the horizon, at the sea and cloud. 'It's looking quite fair at the moment. Send everybody to clean and get some hot food inside them. This is a good chance. And make sure those children stay below. What are their names, incidentally?'

'John and Eric, sir, and Sophie.'

'They related to each other?'

'No, sir. They've all lost brothers and sisters.'

'It's just one *bloody* awful thing after another, isn't it?'

Changing one's clothing before battle, Jay thought, was like it was in the days of sail. It was a very sensible idea: dirty clothing might infect a wound, a very serious matter in a world without disinfectant or proper anaesthetics. Jay's cabin was a shambles, as it almost always was at sea in rough weather, but he picked out clean underclothing and put it on. By the evening, Jay was satisfied that everybody had hot food inside him and was as ready for the enemy as Jay could make him.

But, as evening came on, they saw that their first enemy was the fading light. The sun was setting and the light ebbing out of the sky when they were still some miles short of the datum position. Gussie urged the engine room on, faster and faster. The diesels pounded as they had never done since the ship's acceptance trials. As darkness approached, the wind strengthened and the sea got up. Great waves gathered behind the ship's stern as though willing to waft her onwards towards her target. As the ship plunged down into a wave hollow and swooped upwards again, the watchers on her bridge scanned the dark horizon ahead for the first break in it, the slightest unevenness in that faint line where the sea met the sky.

They were still a full three miles from the datum when the light finally faded. Looking forward from the bridge, Jay could just see the gun's crew mustered around the 4.7-inch, discernible by the pale shapes of their anti-flash hoods under their steel helmets. A larger wave crashed against the side of the fo'c'sle, and its spray drifted aft over the gun mounting and the bridge above it. It was only just safe enough for the guns' crew to stand there in this weather, but they could not afford to give up the chance of that first, and very possibly the only, shot at their target. Meanwhile, the wind had increased so much it was becoming difficult to hear anything else on the bridge.

When they reached the datum, it was quite dark. The fierce wind had blown away the clouds and the sky was full of stars. Gussie slowed the ship down and set her swinging in a wide turn, whilst he, and everybody on the bridge, stood with their binoculars set, hoping, expecting, to see the glimmer of a wave breaking against a hull as the ship swung round. Once somebody grunted and gave a half-strangled murmur, and they all tensed as though waiting for game to spring. But the moments passed, and there was nothing more. Now that they had slowed down, the Asdic was working, but its sound fled away into the depths with no returning echo. The U-boat, if it was still there, was still on the surface.

The ship had turned through nearly 180 degrees, and was heading back into the wind. The setting sun had left a lighter patch on the horizon, on the starboard bow. Gussie concentrated his search to port, to the darker side. The least movement out there would be enough. A glint in an eye would do. Maybe after such a day and such an ordeal, one of that U-boat's watchkeeping officers would be lunatic enough to light a cigarette, which would be visible for miles around.

'He's there,' Gussie said. 'I bloody *know* he's there. I can smell him. He's down there. Port twenty. Steer south. Let's get down there, into that blackness. Stop engines. Let's listen.' As the ship swung, ever more slowly, to the south, they heard the sound of the sea slapping against the ship's side, and the engine-room fans aft, and the thrashing of the halliards in the wind. The ship heeled over violently. Clearly, they would not be able to stay stopped, without any control over the ship, for very long.

Nothing in sight. Nothing on Asdics. *If only he would dive,* Jay thought, *if only he would.*

'"A" gun load with starshell. Target bearing red four five. Fire when ready!'

The gun barked, with a suddenness that made Jay jump. When it exploded, the starshell was disappointingly faint, giving what seemed an ineffectual light. But it was enough.

'By God there he is! I *knew* it! Full ahead together! Port thirty! Alarm U-boat, port side, engage, engage ... engage...'

In his excitement, Jay could hardly focus his binoculars. But Gussie was right, there was no doubt about it, the enemy was there. It was not so certain, so definite as a shape, it was more of a presence. But he was there, and furthermore was already drawing very quickly right across their bows. There was now the noticeable white line of a wake, lengthening all the time to starboard.

The gun fired again and the flash blinded everybody on the bridge for several seconds. The port-side Oerlikon below was also firing now, and its streaming tracer flowed out towards the target and seemed to bounce off the surface of the sea.

'Midships! *Starboard* thirty! Ye Gods, the bugger's slipping us!'

Again the gun fired and, though Jay did not hear the sound, he was dazed by the intensity of the flash. It was impossible to concentrate upon anything, let alone actually pick up the target again, for some time afterwards. The U-boat could not have been more than three hundred yards away when it was first sighted, which was almost point-blank range. But so far their firing had been counterproductive.

'Check check *check*...' Gussie was bellowing. 'Check firing. We can't see a damned thing!'

'There's a hit!' But it was wishful thinking. Jay had picked up the wake again, and he could see that it was still drawing even further and more rapidly right, and the range was steadily opening. As he watched, the wake seemed to thicken and the bearing steadied. The target was now heading directly into wind and sea.

Another starshell exploded above, and this time Jay had a clear sight of the U-boat. It was very much smaller than he had ever expected, and its appearance was somehow distorted and out of shape, as though mangled in some way. Jay was reminded of a squashed opera hat, made of chocolate which had half melted. It looked nothing like anything Jay had ever seen in any of the official publications.

When the next starshell ignited, the conning tower had disappeared. Jay could see nothing at all.

'It can't be more than a thousand yards away. He's bloody well getting away from us!'

It seemed that the U-boat, whether it was able to dive or not, was some two or three knots faster when steering into wind and sea. Whatever else was wrong, there was nothing the matter with its main engines, and it was driving up into the weather much better than *Whitby,* with her high freeboard and greater bulk.

'If only he'd gone downwind,' Gussie said. 'But he obviously knows that. Whoever that is on that conning tower, he's certainly got his wits about him.'

The same thought had occurred to Jay. Hanging on to the bridge rail with one hand, his fingers already ominously numb, Jay could not help thinking of their opponent. That U-boat was being admirably handled, damn him. That captain had not dived, when every submariner's instinct must have been screaming at him to get down to safety. Damaged his boat might have been, but he had worked out the best course to shake off his pursuer. And now, it seemed, he was getting clear away. Another starshell showed nothing. The gun was silent. So too was everybody on the bridge. The sounds of wind and sea came back, to drown everything else.

'We've lost him,' Gussie said. 'We've lost him. The bugger's gone. We *almost* had him. Right *here.*' Gussie clenched one hand, and the intensity of his voice conjured up for them all a vision of his crooked fingers, and the sheer desire, the *longing* to get at their enemy. 'I could smell him, and his pork sausages, and his *eau de cologne.* Crafty Kraut. You could almost admire them if they weren't such *scum*!'

'I'm very sorry, sir,' Jay said.

'Oh, it doesn't matter. It was fated from the very beginning. Let's work out a course to steer to rejoin the convoy. And we can slow down a bit. No need to keep plugging on like this. We'll never catch him now. I wonder how badly damaged he really was?'

It took them most of the night to catch up the convoy. Gussie leaned against the forward bridge rail muttering, 'Come on, come *on* ... I've got a horrible feeling we ought to be back there.'

Jay's middle watch was almost over, and he was about to be relieved when they first sighted the convoy. They headed towards their proper station in the screen. Drury, who had just come on watch, said brightly, 'At least we didn't lose anything by our little jaunt!'

Jay had opened his mouth to tell Drury never to say such things, when there was a huge detonation on the other side of the convoy and a flash which lit up the sky for several seconds.

'*That* looked like an ammunition ship,' said Drury.

'Do shut up, Sub,' said Gussie, harshly. 'There are no ammunition ships in this convoy.'

Jay knew that the truth must have flashed in on him at the same moment as it did on Gussie. If there were no ammunition ships, then a conflagration like that meant the victim was an escort. Further, Jay reasoned, the U-boat must have entered the convoy through the gap left by *Whitby* herself when she went to pick up survivors, and had made one of those diagonal traverses through the ranks of ships which the U-boats had been doing so often and so successfully of late.

It was too dark for flashing, and Gussie hesitated to break radio silence. They had to wait until dawn, when they saw the masts and funnels of Coolie's destroyer coming up from astern. Coolie had taken further risks by going back himself to look for survivors. The message did not take long to pass.

'*Padstow*. No survivors. Sorry.'

Padstow must have encountered the very worst set of circumstances for a small escort vessel. She must have been hit in her forward magazine and blown up while travelling at speed, and the shattered remains of her hull had simply gone on and down, taking all her people with her.

But this was *Padstow*, their chummy ship. This was Tich and his merry men. This was their own *chummy* ship. They knew every man on board her. They had secured alongside each other more times than anybody cared to remember. They had gone on runs ashore together. They played football against them, and darts, and punched their heads when they got above themselves.

Gussie was standing at the front of the bridge, his arms apart and braced against the rail. His head was down, and Jay had never seen him looking so defeated.

'There was a chance that we would get that U-boat, sir.'

'*Never.*' Gussie's voice was dogmatic, almost contemptuous. 'Not a chance. It wasn't our night. I knew it was bad joss from the off.'

Jay had served long enough with Gussie to trust his instincts. In some ways, Gussie was almost supernaturally perceptive.

'And you could even say that Coolie was taking unnecessary chances by going back to look. Although, dear God, I bless him for doing that. Signalman, make to the Escort Commander, "Thank you so much."'

The ship's company took *Padstow*'s loss much more lightly, on the surface, than Gussie did. Jay was surprised by the sailors' stoicism, amounting to indifference. But Gussie was very subdued, and even a signal received late that afternoon failed to cheer him: there was no incoming convoy to meet, and *Whitby,* instead of going on to Reykjavik, was to refuel at Londonderry.

Londonderry was one of *Whitby*'s favourite runs ashore, as indeed it had been *Padstow*'s. It seemed that, by some mysterious Irish bush telegraph, Londonderry was ready for *Whitby.* As the ship entered the Foyle estuary, she was met by a man wearing what looked like a tartan blanket around his shoulders, steering a tiny cockle-shell of a motorboat. The ship stopped and a heaving line was lowered, to which the man in the boat attached a crate of eggs. The line was hauled up and again lowered. When six crates of eggs had thus been brought on board, the Coxswain took out his wallet and, holding them so that the man below could see them, counted out bank notes. The Coxswain held up the bank notes, the man held up his thumb, the notes were lowered, and the ship proceeded whilst the man waved farewell.

Jay had never been to Londonderry before, and he enjoyed the pilotage trip up the Foyle, with its bends, and its little bankside houses, and its soft, green scenery. It was odd to reflect that those green fields and low hills on the starboard side were in Eire and not at war. There were rumours of U-boats coming in to spend the night at Moville, just on the other side of those hills. Maybe that little Irishman, or perhaps his cousin, sold them crates of eggs.

They secured alongside an oiler at Lisahally, on the way up river. The mail came on board, as did a questioning staff officer, whom Gussie took away into his cabin. The visitor had known Tich well and his call was not just professional. He had a personal interest in the story of how his friend and his ship's company had died.

Drury, as the ship's correspondence officer, was logging in the official mail. He held up a small, thin book with a blue cover.

'Monthly Intelligence Report,' he said. 'It's got some dope about our attack in it. Lessons learned. They've analysed our attack charts and plot.'

Jay frowned. 'Let's have it here,' he said. He had noticed that Drury treated him with only just about enough respect. Drury deferred to his straight stripes and seniority, but only just. Drury needed taking down a peg, or several.

There was indeed a very full report and analysis of their attack. The conclusions were hardly original: deeper depth charges were needed, longer attacks, more than one escort taking part, coordinated attacks — there was nothing much new there. But further on, there was a list of names. 'Look at all these, all the U-boat captains who have won the Knight's Cross. Goodness, you can have it with Oak Leaves, Swords and Oak Leaves, Swords and Oak Leaves and Diamonds, if you're a very good little U-boat captain. How come we know so much about these people?'

'We know much more than that about them, much more than just their names,' said Drury.

'How do you know?'

'My elder brother is in army intelligence. He's a German speaker. He listens all the time to their equivalent of the BBC Home Service. They're on it almost every day, telling the German public what good blokes they are, and what they've done and how many ships they've sunk, and what they're going to do to us and how they're winning the war. My bro' listens to them all the time. Gets all their names. Very Teutonic names, he says. He says there's almost a Class of Thirty-Nine. Endrass, Schuhart, Heinrich Liebe, and Fritz Julius Lemp. And that chap who got into Scapa Flow. By the way, there's a very official-looking *billet doux* for you, Number One.'

'Well, I must say, you might have given it to me before!' But Jay's heart began to thump when he saw the buff envelope, and the franking from the Second Sea Lord's Office, and the OHMS slogan. This normally meant more uncomfortable news.

'To *Daedalus*, for *Phalarope*, as Commanding Officer Anti-Submarine Air Warfare Course. New appointment.'

'What's a Phalarope?' Drury asked. 'It sounds vaguely indelicate.'

'*That,*' said Gussie, with emphasis, 'is a first-class job. You deserve it, Jay.'

'It's very kind of you, sir...'

'Oh, don't thank *me*. Nothing to do with me. *I* didn't organise it.' Gussie had a mischievous look on his face. 'Although I'm not above a spot of arranging, where I think it merited. But not this time. No, you got this on merit.'

They were in Joe Cassidy's bar, at Gussie's invitation. It was where Gussie and Tich normally went, and Jay realised that to some extent he was substituting, in dead men's shoes. Jay could see already that it was the start of a big evening. Gussie had his fingers wrapped around his fifth pint of Guinness of the evening. 'It's good to be saving shoe leather in here again,' he was saying. 'There are times, at sea, when I think I'm never going to see this bar or any other bar ever again. Do you know that feeling, Jay?'

'I do, sir. I do indeed.'

'By the way, what about those children? I'm afraid I barely had time to speak to them. They must have thought me *very* remote, like some wicked old uncle…'

'Oh, not at all, sir. Townsend looked after them very well, and so did all the sailors. We made it up to them as best we could, for what happened to them. A large matron from some hospital ashore came and collected them.'

'I wonder if they'll ever recover? And that bloody *dog*. That was almost as bad. It still haunts me. That bloody *bloody* day, every single thing went wrong. I shall be very sorry to lose you, Jay.'

'Thank you, sir.'

'No, I'm serious, I think you've got the makings. If you behave yourself and don't go writing any more indiscreet letters to the powers that be.' Gussie caught Jay's look. 'Oh, yes, I heard about it. I salute you for your loyalty. But I still think you were ill-advised. You certainly wouldn't have been able to send a letter like that from my ship, I can tell you. But I don't think there's any harm done, in the end. Maybe even some good. How long you been on board now?'

'Just over six months, sir.' It was long enough at least for Jay to grow used to people staring at his pilot's wings when they came into the wardroom.

'That's quite long enough. Anybody can be Jimmy of one of these crap-barges. We're just convoy-fodder. But flying, we need some specialists for that. You'll be much better employed back doing that.'

Jay did not agree with those sentiments at all; in fact, quite the contrary. Anybody of the dimmest intelligence, with good physical coordination, could be taught to fly. But *Whitby* and her sisters were fighting a skilful, vital war, which demanded the greatest ability, stamina and expertise from its participants. It was Gussie's officers, not aircrew, who needed the best, the most special training in the world.

'The Navy's always been a bit hidebound about aircraft,' Gussie was saying. 'A little bit silly and reactionary about them. We've never really taken to them wholeheartedly, not as a service. Always had reservations. Always been suspicious of them. Not quite the *thing,* if you understand me. Most of the officers of my generation tend to think of aircraft in terms of something that would be nice to have for gunnery spotting. But where we need them is out *there...*' Gussie jerked his head towards the north. 'It's getting clearer and clearer to me that there's nothing like them for making the U-boats keep their heads down. And, after all, if you can keep them down while you get your convoy past, you've won, haven't you?'

Gussie glanced around at the other drinkers at the bar. Jay knew what he was thinking. That was as far as he could go, in public. This was Ireland, after all. The Irish were good eavesdroppers, and there was no border between north and south. Jay recalled, all of a sudden, somebody in that train coming up to Edinburgh from London talking loudly about a torpedo that hit his ship and did not explode. Nobody asked him to keep quiet. That was precisely the sort of information the enemy wanted most badly to know.

Jay acknowledged freely that he owed Gussie a great personal debt. He had arrived in *Whitby* badly needing reassurance and guidance. Looking back, he could see that he had passed through a crisis. Certain of his basic assumptions, his basic tenets of faith — in his senior officers, in loyalty, in the Navy itself — had been seriously undermined. He had very nearly suffered what in religious terms would have been called a loss of vocation. But Gussie had restored him, seemingly effortlessly, with his own brand of good humour, his urbanity, his calm in a crisis, his sheer professional competence. Jay knew that his bridge watchkeeping ticket was now a genuine one. He really was capable of taking over a watch at sea in any conditions. He had learned a great deal, about himself and about the Service, just from watching Gussie.

'This is really a wake, you know,' Gussie was saying. 'I think this is the little city we both liked best. It's a beautiful place, you know, Londonderry. It's got an eighteenth-century air about it, that little city, the walls, the bridge. Sometimes when the sun is going down you can stand on that bridge and it's all like something out of an old watercolour. He was in my term, you know. We were both Exmouths. Started out together. But we both fell by the wayside a bit. Here's to *Padstow*. I've never even been there. Now I'm getting maudlin. I shall be weeping into my Guinness soon. Won't I?' Gussie had not turned his face, but Jay could see that the tears were indeed coursing fast down his cheeks. 'Won't I?'

'No, sir.'

'You're a loyal little bugger, Jay. You'll go a long way, do you know that?'

CHAPTER SIX

The aircraft must have come suddenly out of the clouds without being sighted by anybody on the bridge. Certainly there was no alarm given below. Hansi was off watch, lying asleep in his bunk, and he woke to the loudest bang of the war, seemingly directly over his head, much louder and more immediate and threatening than any depth-charging. For a stunned moment, Hansi thought it was the end and they were all dead men. He could hear cries from the control room, and water flooding down the tower. Somebody shut the lower hatch and the main diesels stopped. Hansi leaped from his bunk and in the short silence, as he landed on the deck and tried to hold his balance, the U-boat itself seemed to lose all its momentum and sag away down, downwind, as though sick of the war and the weather.

When Hansi reached the control room the helmsman was calling up the voice-pipe to the bridge and, evidently not being able to hear the response, was leaning his head to get his ear closer to the rim. As Hansi watched him, the man recoiled in a gesture of disgusted revulsion. A great slow teardrop of blood and gristle had formed on the rim, and dropped from the metal tube on to the deck. It was followed for a very short while by a steady trickle of thick liquid.

Hugo the engineer had appeared from aft, and was examining the rows of gauges above the helmsman's head. He looked at Hansi, without any expression. Hansi wondered if he would ever see Hugo frightened or concerned.

'A bomb,' Hugo said. 'There'll be nothing left up there. You going up?'

'Of *course*,' Hansi said. The boots he was putting on were still cold and soaking wet inside. Somebody gave him a leather watch jacket. He put it on and an oilskin on top of it, with an oilskin hood. He nodded upwards at the hatch. 'Open up!'

But the main engines had drawn a considerable vacuum in the boat after the hatch had been shut, and two men wrestled for some time with the hatch before they could get it open. Then Hansi, swollen with his bulky clothing, could hardly force himself up through the narrow opening.

The upper hatch was only partly open, although water was splashing over its rim. Hansi had to use all his strength to open it further, and even then he had to wriggle and struggle to get his body through. As he felt his way through a strange tangle of twisted metal and wires, he heard the sound of another wave gathering below. The water rose and swilled around him, buffeting him and drenching him to the skin.

There was nobody left. Herr Kaleut, Siegfried the Little Rabbit — who had been on watch — and all four lookouts, had all gone, blown away into eternity. The forward gun had disappeared. It had taken the first impact, and it was lucky for all those who still survived that the bomb had detonated on the gun barrel and not on the boat's hull. The bridge and tower were barely recognisable. The whole front had been pushed bodily down and back, as though some giant hand had capriciously palmed it backwards until it was tired or satisfied with what it had done. The periscope standards were bent like celery stalks. The voice-pipe was broken off at deck level. Every fitting and piece of equipment on the bridge had been blasted away or distorted beyond repair.

Holding on to some unfamiliar projection of metal, Hansi stood up, lost his balance and had to kneel. There was nothing in front of him, no protection at all from the sea. He was looking out over the whole length of the forward casing and, as he watched, a great wave smashed along it and swamped it. The remains of the gun mounting could still be seen, like the gap in a gum after a tooth has been wrenched away. The wave swirled around it, rose, and hit Hansi solidly, forcing his head down. As Hansi crouched even lower, he could hear the water falling down the hatch behind him, with a roaring sound that went on for some time after the wave had passed.

Hansi realised that the U-boat was now propelling on main electric motors, and at full speed. They would need their battery capacity before they were safely home. He shuffled aft until he was kneeling beside the upper hatch. He could feel something slippery underneath his knees. The waves were washing it away, but it was still squashy, like dung in a farmyard heap. Hansi refused to look at it as he called down the tower. Hugo's head appeared below.

'There's nobody left up here!'

Hugo nodded, as though that were no more than he had expected. 'Do you want me to send up lookouts?'

Trust Hugo to make a practical suggestion. 'Not yet. I'll let you know. Can we get back on main engines?'

'Of course, Herr Kaleut.'

Hansi was taken aback by the title. But then he realised, as Hugo had already done, that he was in fact — and now in name — the captain.

'Start main engines, then.'

'Course to steer?' Again, Hugo with a practical point.

'South. And let me know as soon as you can what the position is down below.'

Hugo was back long before Hansi expected him. It seemed that things could have been much worse. Everything had survived below. They had no torpedoes left, and nobody knew what state the tubes were in, but that was the least of the problems. The main engines were intact, although some fuel tanks might have been ruptured and contaminated with sea water. Time would tell. There were a few leaks, but only one serious: the starboard shaft stern gland. They had to keep one pump running continuously to hold the water level in the motor room down.

'And what about lookouts, Herr Kaleut?'

Hansi was gratified by the title — although, strictly speaking, it was really only deserved by U-boat captains who had the actual rank of *Kapitänleutnant*. But maybe Hugo was trying to boost his morale as well.

'No. There's hardly space for them, and they might get tangled up if we had to dive quickly. Pass me up a lifeline. I'll secure myself.'

It seemed a sensible decision but, when the sun went down, it was shown that Hansi did not have Herr Kaleut's famous awareness, and one pair of eyes were not as good as four. Cold and tired as he was, Hansi allowed the destroyer to get quite close before he saw it. It had been approaching from astern, the most awkward direction, but nevertheless Hansi was furious with his own failure, which might still jeopardise them all.

His first impulse was to dive, but he controlled it. If they dived, the destroyer would certainly find them. If they stayed on the surface he might run past.

'Stop engines.' Hansi had heard that destroyers now had a device which could smell diesel exhaust fumes. The U-boat plunged on, making what seemed to Hansi a lot of noise for a long time. He prayed it would soon lose way and stop crashing through the waves, with that booming, betraying sound. He dared not even order the propellors to go astern, and lose way more quickly, lest the water turbulence give them away.

Looking back, Hansi could plainly see the white bone in the destroyer's teeth. It was overhauling them very rapidly, and its course would take it quite close up the U-boat's starboard side. Hansi had already decided to do nothing. His own carelessness had allowed their enemy to come so close that almost anything he did now would give them away. He would lie low, stay stopped, and hope for a miracle.

The destroyer came thrashing past, across their stern and up the starboard side heading south-east. Its course seemed to be converging on theirs. As it passed, Hansi could pick out its dark mass against the lighter sky to the west. He could hear its bows driving into the sea and the waves throwing spray across its upper deck. He fancied that if he listened just a little harder he could hear voices on her bridge. It certainly did not look a very big destroyer. It was much like the one that had attacked them before. Maybe, as Herr Kaleut once said, the Tommies could only afford one kind of destroyer.

'Starboard twenty,' Hansi called, quietly, down the tower. There was just enough way on to turn the bows. With luck, Hansi would start the main engines and make a dash for it, across their opponent's stern. In that wind and sea, they stood a good chance of making better headway into the weather than that destroyer. They might just, *just,* have the legs of it.

The destroyer had now turned to port and was steering a collision course, only some four hundred metres away. In spitting distance, as Herr Kaleut would have said. Before Hansi could make up his mind, a starshell exploded behind him. He knew he would now be presenting a broad target, in perfect silhouette.

'Full ahead together! And for God's sake give it everything!' They would have to cross their enemy's bows instead of his stern, but that could not be helped.

There was a cough, and then silence, and Hansi for a moment thought the diesels were not going to start. That would definitely be the end of them. But then there was a series of belches, like a giant burping, and a steady drumming. Spurts of water and exhaust smoke flew out in two long plumes, one on each side. Hansi found himself grinning. The sound those donkey engines made, and the chance of escaping after all, were actually very funny.

It seemed some seconds before they were seen. It was long enough, in fact, for Hansi just to have the hope that they might get clear away. But then there was flash from the destroyer. Hansi had no idea where the shot went, but it meant the chase was on. They must have heard it below, because the U-boat seemed to gather more speed, and then more speed again. There was nothing like a good explosion for encouraging the black gang to do their utmost.

There was another flash. This time, Hansi saw the shell burst, rising well forward of them, and a good distance to port. He altered course to port, as a larger wave swept over the tower and cascaded down into the boat for several seconds. It was too bad. Hansi could do nothing about that now. The next shot was astern. He could see it clearly. But he could do nothing about that, either. For those gunners, the bearing must be swinging very quickly right, and the range opening. It was a question now of how quickly they reacted. Hansi knew that the chances of a direct hit, and nothing else would suffice, were remote, but he still ducked involuntarily when another starshell burst very close to his port side.

The boat was responding very well. The range was clearly opening. That last flash was noticeably further away. Hansi hoped Hugo was pumping water out of every tank he could. That might make it difficult when they next dived, but he had no intention of diving now. That would be fatal. That would be giving themselves up into the hands of their enemy. It was surface now, neck or nothing.

Hansi noticed tracer now, from some smaller-calibre gun. This seemed much more likely to hit them. It swung over Hansi's head and he watched it pass, noticing that strange optical illusion he had often been told about: how tracer always seemed to be travelling slowly until the last moment, when it suddenly accelerated. Another monstrous wave swamped the bridge, rose to Hansi's waist, and poured in a torrent down the tower. They would just have to keep on pumping and pumping. The boat was punching up into the head sea, every wave jarring the boat, trying to make it turn back.

The next starshell burst right overhead, so close Hansi could almost smell it. It was now or never. If they were ever going to get a hit, they must get it now. They would never present a better target. But the column of water was so far away Hansi almost missed it. It was five, six, seven hundred metres off. Hansi shouted for joy. A miracle was coming to pass. They were going to escape. They were going to live, and go on living, after all. 'And it *did* get worse, the *very* next day...' Hansi shouted the words into the wind. There was nothing more he personally could do. He had told them the course. The engines were running. Now it was up to the gods.

The next wave was so big it lifted Hansi clear off his feet. Without his lifeline he would have been over the side. As it was, the force of the water picked him up and dashed his face against some wreckage. His nose was numb and he felt the salty taste of blood on his tongue. He looked down and saw the water actually draining away into the tower, like bath water out of a bath. They would be pleased about *that* down in the control room. Hansi laughed out loud. There was no doubt, this all had its funny side. *Again* a flash, and *again*, but both very much further off, and no sign of the fall of shot. They were weakening! They were giving up!

At that, a shell pitched right alongside, deluging the bridge and Hansi in a torrent of evil-smelling water. It was like being ducked in bilgewater. Hansi coughed and blew furiously. For one terrible moment he thought the engines had stopped. The entire stern of the U-boat was underwater, and the waves had flooded back up to after base of the shattered tower, as though they still believed they could hold the boat up. But, in a second, those two blessed plumes of water and exhaust reappeared, pouring their reassuring clouds out to port and starboard. That marvellous steady drumming of the engine beat had never paused for an instant. The whole boat was shuddering and straining, like a horse that knew it must go on to win.

This time the wave was larger and more powerful than ever. Hansi gripped the nearest metal fitting with both hands, but he could feel the force of the wave working at him, loosening his grip and finally dislodging it so that he relied entirely upon his lifeline. The wave was trying to suck him over the side. Well, even if it did, the boat would still go onwards.

There had been no flash for some time. Hansi guessed it was over a minute since the last. He put up his binoculars and stared astern. But the glasses were muzzy and blurred. German glasses were the best, and U-boat glasses were the best of German, but even these had been waterlogged.

The time since the last flash lengthened. Hansi knew that their enemy would not fire again. He had really given up. It was now time to think of the future. Every moment on this north-westerly course was taking them further and further from France. It was, in fact, double fuel consumption. There was no knowing yet how much usable fuel they had left, but however much it was they would have to husband it. Now, if that Tommy destroyer had paused to *think,* he would have reasoned that north-west was no direction for a damaged U-boat. The boat would surely, sooner or later — and sooner rather than later — have to turn back south. If he had simply *thought,* he could have plotted the U-boat's probable course, and cut across the corner to intercept. No U-boat would ever continue to steer out into the Atlantic. Surely that would be obvious.

But maybe he did not know the U-boat was so badly damaged. And, after all, his first care must be for his convoy. He was probably now steering to rejoin. But, Hansi reasoned, his course to rejoin would be north-west, or very nearly. That meant he must now be coming up in their wake. If only they had some torpedoes left...

After some ten minutes, Hansi turned the boat to port through ninety degrees, to steer across wind and sea, and reduced speed. In the beam sea, the U-boat rolled prodigiously, throwing Hansi violently from side to side, to the full extent of his lifeline. It was very uncomfortable, but soon Hansi had the satisfaction of seeing the shadow of their pursuer pass, without stopping, across their stern, from port to starboard. Hansi cupped his hands to shout after it, but changed his mind. It would not do to tempt the gods.

Hansi heard somebody call from the tower. It was a sailor with some soup and a portion of sausage. Hansi drank the soup. His brain told him it was very hot, but his lips could feel nothing, and he was not conscious of the heat until he felt the soup going down his throat. He finished the sausage in three huge bites. His stomach felt as though the bottom had dropped out of it.

Next in the tower was Hugo. As he had said before, it could have been worse. The main engines were working, and the electric motors were available if they had to dive. The steering was also working properly, but the leak from the stern gland had increased and was still increasing. They had no periscope, no guns, no torpedoes. They could dive, but only in emergency. They would then be blind, and surfacing again would be very dangerous.

The sky cleared during the night and the dawn was fine. Hansi hoped they would be able to stay on the surface, but just after the sun came up the expected aircraft appeared, low on the horizon to the east. It was flying out of the sun so that it was quite close before Hansi sighted it, clearly heading towards the boat.

'Dive! Dive! Dive!'

Hansi turned to make the familiar movements, and for a fleeting moment he was baffled by the tangle of wreckage on the bridge. He had to struggle down through the hatch again, and as he shut the lower hatch he could actually hear the thump of water striking the top of the tower, and the pouring tearing sound as it began to fill the space above him.

Hugo was crouched in front of his gauges. This would probably be the trickiest dive of his career as a trimming officer. The boat might be too light, or tons heavy, there was no way of knowing.

Hugo had pumped out tanks to give the boat more speed. Now he was flooding as hard as he could to get the boat down. It became clear that he had misjudged it. The boat was already too heavy. The depth gauges unreeled as though spring-loaded. The boat gained depth rapidly and continued on downwards. There must be hundreds of litres of extra water in the flooded tower above, and the leak aft must have added much more than Hugo had calculated.

At last, Hugo caught his trim, precariously, by puffing high pressure air into the midships ballast tanks. This was an unstable method, not to be recommended. The tanks were normally open to the sea and either completely flooded when the boat was submerged, or completely empty when the boat was on the surface. Pockets of air in them at depth would expand should the boat happen to rise and the sea pressure lessen; this would make the boat effectively lighter, and it would continue to rise, even faster. Conversely, should the boat go deeper, increased sea pressure would cause the air to be compressed, and occupy less space, allowing more water into the tanks; this would make the boat effectively heavier, and cause it to go deeper, even faster. But, under Hugo's expert touch, the boat seemed to remain stable, at depth, and going slow ahead to the south.

Looking at the faces around him, Hansi realised that he had not told the Lordly Ones anything. They had heard the bomb explosion. They had seen him go up top. They had heard the helm orders and the distant sounds of the destroyer's shell fire. But he had told them nothing. That was neglect on his part. Nothing was worse for any U-boat crew than to be kept in ignorant suspense.

It gave Hansi a curious and quite unexpected sense of achievement to know that they were all now looking at him, as to the captain. He had assumed Herr Kaleut's mantle. He was now the captain, and they were looking to him to get them home.

Hansi raised his voice, so that it carried along the passageways, forward and aft.

'Pay attention! We were hit by a bomb on the forward gun. Herr Kaleut is dead. So too are the Second Officer and the four lookouts, whom you knew. The bridge and the tower are badly damaged, but not impossibly so. We have a very good chance of getting back safely. We are now dived for an aircraft approaching.' Talking of that aircraft, it could not have seen them after all. There had been no bombs, no sounds of attack. 'We shall stay dived until dark. Steer south.' Hansi nodded at Hugo. 'All right? Can I leave it with you?'

'Of *course*, Herr Kaleut.'

Hansi drew across Herr Kaleut's curtain, and stretched himself upon the captain's bunk. This was the first time he had ever known privacy in a U-boat. It was a great privilege, worth more than anything else, and conferring upon the man who enjoyed it an absolute confirmation of his command and authority on board. This, Hansi decided, was what he wanted to do most. He lay for a time, listening to the creaks of the boat as it rolled slightly, to the sounds of low voices, and footsteps outside, and liquids rushing and thumping through pipes. Then he fell into one of the deepest and most peaceful sleeps he could ever remember. It was as though the brief experience of command had calmed and reassured him. This was something he could do best. Other men might shrink from responsibility and its weight. Hansi welcomed it. This was the life for him. It would be unbearably flat to go back now to the position of being first officer. Command was infinitely better, on another plane of existence.

That evening, after dark, Hansi faced the problem of surfacing. Neumann listened very carefully, all round, and reported that there was nothing, no propellor noise, no possible sound of a ship. It seemed to take hours to drain down the flooded tower, all the while the boat rolled blindly on the surface. Anything might be up there. They might even have surfaced next door to a destroyer which, unable to believe its luck, was even now waiting and laughing at them.

But when Hansi was at last able to climb up through the dripping tower and out through the upper hatch, he found an empty sea and a night brilliant with stars. They had come some way south and the weather already seemed warmer. There above was Orion and his belt, there were Altares and the Pole Star. Even an idiot could steer his way by them. But there would be navigational problems. They could not surface until well after sunset and would have to dive well before dawn. There would thus be no chance of sun or star sights. They would rely upon dead reckoning, the sailor's oldest friend and helpmate. But even there they had problems. They could work out the tides on the surface from the tables. But nobody knew what, if anything, the tides were at depth. But Hansi felt confident enough even to surprise himself. It would for sure be an interesting exercise in navigation. But he and Herr Obersteursmann were up to it.

That night, Herr Funkenmeister rigged an emergency wireless aerial from the remains of the periscope standard, and signalled Lorient. Shortly after midnight, they had an acknowledgement, asking them to report their fuel state, number of torpedoes remaining, even the weather in their vicinity. It was the usual state report required of U-boats. Hansi ignored the request. Lorient now knew they were still alive, and that was enough for the time being. Hansi always felt uneasy about signalling. He had no evidence of it, but he suspected that in some way signalling betrayed a boat's presence.

Later that night, just as Hansi was considering the question of diving, Hugo appeared in the tower with bad news. The stern gland leak had got much worse during the dive and was making water in the bilges faster than they could pump it out, even on the surface. If they dived it might get out of control. That would mean they might never surface again. Hugo did not say so, in so many words, but the clear conclusion lay between them, unspoken. But it might still be the lesser fate to dive and risk it, than to stay surfaced and be certain of destruction. Meanwhile, they must obviously stay on the surface for as long as possible.

Hansi's resolution was tested at dawn, when the boat was steering south-east, on the last leg for France. There were only some hundred kilometres to Lorient. A twin-engined aircraft appeared over the port quarter, from the north, and headed directly for them, as though it knew they were there. Hansi ordered main engines stopped while he and the lookouts hid in the tower. Possibly the absence of a wake might save them. The aircrew might see the streaming white wake, while missing the small dark shape of the tower.

The aircraft flew directly over the boat, so far as Hansi could judge, at a good height. It did not change course or react in any way, but flew on towards the French coastline, and altered course to the east to close the land. Clearly, it had been looking for U-boats, possibly even for one U-boat in particular, and unknowingly had passed right over one.

Their landfall was good. Herr Obersteursmann had done an excellent job. Their errors, as Herr Kaleut would undoubtedly have remarked, had cancelled themselves out. Thinking of

Herr Kaleut reminded Hansi that he had a bottle of schnapps in his cabin, somewhere in one of the drawers below the tiny folding desk. He passed the message down for it and soon heard a tapping behind him. The bottle was being waved at the top of the tower.

Hansi uncorked the bottle and took a deep gulp. It scorched down his throat, making him cough and his eyes water. He took another great gulp, and then another. He would have liked more, but he had to keep his wits about him for the passage up harbour.

Hansi handed the bottle back. 'Finish it below,' he said. He could hear sounds, but he was so tired he did not know whether they were cheers from below, or crying seagulls, or some twisted portion of the bridge protesting again as the sea washed through it. It was not until he saw the minesweeper waiting for them at the entrance that Hansi realised how tired he was. Except for his sleep on the middle day, he had been standing on the wrecked bridge, soaking wet, in the open air, in the Atlantic, in winter time for three days. He had not gone below for any reason. He had waited until his bladder was almost bursting before relieving himself inside his clothing.

There was also a small tug waiting to assist them, but Hansi was determined to finish the patrol unaided. He felt he owed that much to Herr Kaleut. He ordered full ahead and to his delight the boat surged up the estuary, so that its heightened wake buffeted that silly little tug, and the minesweeper had to flash urgently and fussily for them to slow down.

The band was there on the jetty, but it was not playing. There was something about the look of the U-boat's misshapen bridge that stilled all joy. The bandmaster had his baton raised, but he was looking at Hansi's face, not at his players. There were girls, but they were not smiling and waving. There were many officers and men from the flotilla, many more than usual, but their faces were solemn. Hansi saw somebody point and, for the first time, he looked over the side. There was a human foot protruding from the base of the bridge structure. Its boot and sock had long since been washed away. It was a dead, bone-white colour, as though all blood and feeling in it had long since been leached away by the sea. Hansi had not seen it before and had no idea who it might belong to, or whether there was any more of the man hidden underneath. It might even be the last human remains of Herr Kaleut.

The lines were passed from the jetty, and a gangway. The fore torpedo-loading hatch opened and out stepped Hugo and Herr Obersteursmann, and the rest of the Lordly Ones. Hansi saw them staring and exclaiming. Of course, this was the first time they had seen the wreckage in which Hansi had been keeping watch for the last three days. Hansi climbed down unsteadily and rested against the remnant of the gun mounting. He found himself wanting, needing, to cry, but no tears came. He was too tired to be embarrassed as Hugo stepped forward, saluted and shook him by the hand. Hugo put one of Hansi's arms round his shoulder, Herr Obersteursmann took the other, and together they carried him over the gangway and ashore.

Hansi wanted most of all to be left alone, to sleep, but he found himself caught up in a whirl of activity — a bath, a shave, new dry clothes, hot food and coffee. He was being prepared, as a calf for the sacrifice, he thought, for an interview with BdU. At least, he had to concede, they were showing some sense of urgency this time.

Hansi only had one brief chance to pause, to look at himself when he was shaving. He hardly recognised himself. He had a growth of greyish stubble on his chin, and his eyelids were red-rimmed, as though touched by some lurid ointment. There were red traces of strain in his eyeballs, and the corners of his mouth were pulled down. His face should have been raw and ruddy with wind and weather. But it was dead white, the colour of that protruding foot, and when he rubbed his cheek, he could feel the vibration but had no sensation of touch, either in his fingers or on his cheek. It was as though that grotesque, ghastly face in the mirror belonged to somebody else, somebody very much more tired and frightened, somebody, oddly, very much younger.

There was a car to take Hansi the short way to the château. They drove through the courtyard, where Hansi could see sentries and men marching, and there was a great gate leading into an inner yard. BdU was in the same room, with the same staff officers ranged behind him, but he was sitting in an armchair, warming his hands in front of the fire. The room smelled very faintly of decay and lack of cleaning, but Hansi dismissed the thought as being very unlikely. To Hansi's surprise, somebody gave him a glass of brandy. He sipped it, and supposed it was the very best from that part of France, but he could not appreciate it. In fact, he seemed barely able even to taste it. His hands could only just hold the glass. He could feel his fingertips tingling, and beginning to be painful, as the sensation returned to them.

Prompted by BdU himself, Hansi began hesitantly, and almost apologetically. He saw it as his first duty to justify Herr Kaleut. the captain's famous, almost psychic sensitivity had let him down for the first and last time. But the aircraft had come suddenly out of heavy cloud. Nobody had seen it, but in some mysterious way it seemed that the aircraft had been able to see them. As he grappled with this professional conundrum, Hansi began to warm to his story. BdU himself nodded, to encourage him, when he paused for a moment.

Hansi tried to explain how and why he had done what he had done; the course he had chosen to steer to escape from the destroyer, his decision to stay on the surface, the moment he chose to steer south; his vindication when he saw the destroyer pass their stern and go on onwards, towards the convoy; his decision to risk diving for the first aircraft, but to remain on the surface for the second; the navigation by dead reckoning; the leaks; the damage to the bridge. As he went on, Hansi felt as though it had all happened to somebody else, somebody not all that competent. He became ashamed of his story; no efficient U-boat commander or officer would allow his boat to get into such a state.

Towards the end, BdU began to interrupt, to ask questions, to ask for parts of the story to be told again: how did the attack on the convoy go; how long did it last; how many bombs did the aircraft drop; what calibre gunfire did the destroyer use; how many rounds; at what range did it stop firing; how bright was the starshell; what speed did the boat make up into wind and weather; what height was the aircraft which failed to see the boat.

At the end of the inquisition, BdU sat for a long time looking into the fire. Hansi became aware of the ticking of a large ornate clock on the chimney piece. It had a peculiar resonance, uncomfortably like the sound of an Asdic beam.

At last, BdU swung round and looked up at Hansi. 'You did well,' he said. 'You did *very well indeed*. There are men alive today who would have been dead but for you. We have a boat, thanks to you, which would have been lost. We have some knowledge of the enemy and his ways, through you. I shall see to it that you are properly rewarded. You will write all this down in your report. But I wanted to hear it all from your own lips, while it was still fresh in your mind. Now you will want to get back to your boat and your crew…'

But, as it happened, Hansi never saw that boat again, nor any of its crew. He never knew whose body it was that lay under that crushed metal. If it was Herr Kaleut, as he suspected, he was not able to go to his funeral and pay his last respects. As he came out into the château courtyard after his interview with BdU, he felt the reaction of the strain and danger of their patrol. He was dizzy, and stumbled, and fell to his knees. When somebody helped him to his feet, he stumbled again, and began to shiver so violently his teeth rattled in his mouth. He was half-helped, half-carried into the motor car, half-carried again up some steps, undressed and laid in a bed.

Hansi lay for some days in bed, while his body and mind sloughed off the after-effects of his ordeal. There were days of furious bodily sweating, and dreams so vivid and terrible he had, as a matter of sheer self-preservation, to make himself wake up from them, which he did, again and again, his body drenched in sweat and a foul, rank taste in his mouth. It was like a fever, but a fever of body and mind, in which both fought to rid themselves of an infection.

One morning, when Hansi woke, clear-headed and determined to get up, a Korvettenkapitän, a senior officer from BdU's staff, appeared at his beside.

'Good morning, *Herr Held*,' he said.

Hansi frowned, wondering whether his ears were playing him tricks, or whether the staff officer was really serious. He had never thought of himself as a hero. That patrol had been a disaster. Herr Kaleut was dead, and so was the Little Rabbit, and all the lookouts: men he had known. The owner of that foot must have been buried by now. Hansi had not been able to go to his funeral. He did not even know who it was.

'You have been promoted to *Kapitänleutnant* immediately, and you have been awarded the Knight's Cross. That is a great honour, as I am sure you will know. The Knight's Cross is almost unique for an officer of your rank. What is more, the Führer himself wishes to present your Cross to you personally. Arrangements have been made for you to go to Berlin at once.'

Once more, Hansi felt himself caught up in a whirl of organised movement. There was a car to Merignac airfield, and a plane to Paris, and then another on to Berlin. Hansi had time to reflect that he wished they had used as much effort and efficiency in bringing up spares for the U-boat as they had in transporting him across Europe. As the Lordly Ones always said, and believed, 'They can do it if they want to.'

Tempelhof from the air looked enormous, with a row of planes, all silvery-grey and important-looking, in front of the main building. There was another, even bigger and blacker, motor car to take Hansi to the Kaiserhof Hotel which, like the car, was clearly for the use of very important people only. There were giant columns in the hotel foyer, and huge gleaming crystal chandeliers, and all around the very smell of richness and opulence. There was no war here. All this was a very long way indeed from the smell of oil, and the sight of blood, and the heart-jolting explosions of depth charges.

Hansi's room was enormous, too, with a vast bed, gold sheets, and a gold curtain around it. There was a colossal bathroom next door, marble and gilt, with a marbled bath as big as a swimming pool, and great gleaming gold taps. When Hansi turned one tap, hot water came coughing and spurting, and then streaming out of it. Hansi could not help being reminded of the first coughs and spurts, and then the steady drumming of diesel engines starting on the surface. In spite of his rich and ornate surroundings, Hansi could not rid his mind of such parallels. Watching the bath water draining out, he suddenly had a stomach-turning memory of the sea swilling down the upper hatch from the wrecked bridge.

It was only another very short drive to the Reich Chancellery. Again, there were huge stone pillars, ten times larger than ordinary life-size, with a mighty German eagle soaring and towering above, and a flight of steps, which made every visitor feel only two feet high, leading up and up towards a row of red-and-black banners, the emblems of National Socialism.

The whole building, inside and out, was made on a titanic scale, designed to make ordinary human beings feel dwarfed and insignificant. Even the Führer's own naval *aide de camp*, who darted out to intercept and greet Hansi, was like some brilliant insect which had been hiding behind great, dark plant stems. He was a man of about Hansi's own age, wearing a beautiful naval uniform with some medal ribbons Hansi did not recognise.

Hansi was led towards a short queue of officers, mostly from the Luftwaffe, some of them very senior and already much decorated. But there were two other U-boat officers, both Korvettenkapitäns, who were getting Oak Leaves to their Knight's Crosses. They looked curiously at Hansi, but made no attempt otherwise to acknowledge his presence.

The Führer himself was a very much shorter, slighter man than Hansi had ever expected. He was below Hansi's own height, and he had puffy cheeks, and a face which Hansi found difficult later to visualise and describe. But Hansi did remark the surprisingly bright, pink, moist lips, which pouted like a child. The Führer had very dark hair, slicked down, and that direct, almost hostile stare, as in all his photographs. He was wearing a light-grey uniform with a tunic and horn buttons, and a swastika armband. His pale face, his clothing, was an ensemble of grey.

The Führer did not actually say anything to Hansi, but nodded and handed him a long box with a swastika embossed on its lid, and shook hands. Hansi noticed that the handshake had a limp, wet feel, but before he knew it, somebody had him by the elbow and was steering him away and across and into another room, where the *Propagandakompanie* men were waiting.

Hansi opened his box and looked at the Knight's Cross, with its handsome red-and-black ribbon. 'Put it on, put it on,' somebody said. Hansi ducked his head and arranged the ribbon around his neck. 'How does it feel?'

'Oh, very good, very good indeed. It is a great honour.' Yet somehow it all seemed rather flat and disappointing, after such preliminaries and the nervous waiting to meet the Führer. Hansi's passing-out parade at the cadet school had been a great deal more exciting.

Nobody had been allowed to smoke in the Führer's presence. The *aide de camp* offered Hansi a cigarette from a silver case, and took one himself. 'Would you mind talking to the radio men for a little while?'

'What shall I say?' Memories of his previous awkward experience crowded Hansi's mind.

'Say? Why, just tell them what happened. You've already been very much in the news. We shall have a look at it afterwards, in case you say anything…' The *aide de camp* paused, as though deciding to go no further. Hansi wondered if the man had heard his previous broadcast.

'What was it like?' The *Propagandakompanie* had gathered round.

What *was* it like? Hansi tried to marshal his thoughts again.

'It was terrible,' he said at last. He knew now the utter futility, the hopelessness of trying to describe what happened to somebody who was not there, who knew nothing of U-boats. 'It was really frightening, the most frightening moment of my life. When I got up there and saw the state everything was in, and there was nobody left up there ...' Hansi could see, by their faces, this was not what they wanted to hear. 'I never thought we would ever come out of it alive.' That was not at all what Hansi had felt at the time, but the words just escaped from him.

'But you did.'

'Yes. By the grace of God.'

'And the Führer,' the man said, sharply.

Hansi said nothing.

'And the *Führer.*'

'Of course. The Führer is always with us.'

Hansi was well aware he was being a disappointment. But how could he explain, for all those people out there, how it had *really* been: the death of Herr Kaleut, who had been his friend, the sound of his voice, the cold, the smell of the sea? The sea did always have an evil smell about it, sharp and unmistakeable and menacing. The sea was like some permanent implacable enemy, who would never forgive, never overlook a weakness. The sea beat everybody down, in the end. No matter what you did, how hard and how well you tried, you could never beat the sea. It would just wait and wait and wait: a moment's carelessness, some gear not properly stowed, a man not paying attention, some work neglected or skimped, and the sea would enter and win at once, just as if nothing had gone on before.

'Now you are going on leave?'

'Yes, I am going home to Leipzig.'

'I'm sure there will be a welcoming party there for you.'

It seemed a long time since Hansi had been on the Leipzig train. It was slower and dirtier and smellier, much more crowded and with many more uniforms. Hansi wore his Knight's Cross at first, but it attracted so much attention, with people walking up the platform and staring in through his carriage window, and an officer of the Landwehr actually pushing open the compartment door and coming in to shake his hand, that Hansi eventually took it off and folded it and its ribbon inside the handsome case.

But Hansi cheered up, as always, at the thought of going home to Leipzig. City of books, and battles, and Bach, as that radio man had said. Also, the city of Luther, and lotteries, and Leibniz. Goethe had called it *klein Paris*. It was a cosmopolitan city; Hansi's father loved to quote that old saying that Leipzig was the only city that represented Germany, where every German could forget that he was a Hessian, a Bavarian, a Swabian, a Prussian, or a Saxon, or even a Berliner.

Hansi knew, from long experience, just when to stand up and look away to the south to catch sight of the great dome of the *Völkerschlachtdenkmal*, the monument to the Battle of the Nations when Napoleon himself was defeated. Hansi had an uncle who had a farm by the river Partha. He could see it from the train. But there were six Panzers drawn up in the lane, obviously on exercise, beside the farmhouse. That, Hansi thought, was bringing the war a little too close to home.

But there was very little other sign of the war. Leipzig had not yet had an air raid, and the station still wore a peacetime air. Leipzig, of course, had the biggest station in Germany, bigger than Berlin, the biggest in Europe, in the world, in the U*niverse*, as they used to crow when they were schoolboys.

Hansi thought at first there was nobody there to meet him. But that would be typical Leipzig. Leipzigers were famous for their self-control, for never showing any emotion. Leipzigers even had a special meaning for the word *Absonderung*: detachment, aloofness, somewhere between separation and indifference.

Then Hansi heard the band. It seemed they were playing some war marching song, maybe some Wagner. But then he recognised it as *their* song: 'And it *did* get worse, the *very* next day…'

Hansi had to blink the tears from his eyes as he climbed down from the train. All those men, all that pain and fear and courage, it all stabbed like a spear-thrust in the side. Was he going to be the only survivor in the end? Was it going to go on and on and on until everybody in the whole world was dead?

'Hansi, *Hansi* … Hans-Dietrich, my little kitty cat!' His mother was there, in her best pink and perfume and her Sunday hat. 'But you're not wearing your medal! Put it on, put it on!'

Hansi took the thing out of its box and slipped the ribbon over his head again. At once, as though that was all they had been waiting for, the station platform sprang into hectic life. His mother kissed him. There was a flash of a camera bulb. His father wrung his hand. There was an audible cheer from several bystanders. '*Prima!*' they called, '*Prima!*' with a most un-Leipzig-like display of enthusiasm.

Even the taxi cab they had waiting had a Navy ensign draped and tied over its bonnet. His father must have arranged that. As they drove along, his mother fingered his Knight's Cross and said, over and over again, 'So you saw the Führer. You actually spoke to the Führer. He shook your hand, the Führer! You spoke to the Führer!'

Hansi looked out of the taxi window. Nothing much seemed to have changed in his old home town. Perhaps there were a few more boarded-up windows, and certainly a lot more posters. The whole city seemed to be plastered with black and red official lettering. They had always lived in the Altstadt, in one of the narrow streets behind the citadel, the *Pleissenburg*, where there had always been a regiment stationed — to keep the Leipzigers in order, they always said. They lived above the printing works; Hansi's father had been manager before the war. Now he appeared to own the works.

Solomon, the old Jew, the owner, had left the city before the war. Gone to America, Hansi had heard, and was probably never coming back. Meanwhile, Hansi's father ran the business: probably he printed most of those posters in the streets. Meanwhile, neither Hansi nor anybody else asked after old Solomon.

'Were there other U-boat men there with you?' his father asked, prodding the taxi driver in the back, to make him pay more attention to his driving and less to Hansi's Knight's Cross.

'Oh, yes. Two very famous captains.'

'Ah. That's good.' But Hansi saw the uncertainty pass like a shadow across his father's face. He so clearly wanted to say something complimentary, but he remained a man of the Kaiser's Navy, who thought the whole U-Waffe an unfit weapon for a *proper* sailor — underhand, below the belt, *unter der Gürtel*.

'So you saw the Führer himself, and you *spoke* to him!' said his mother, for the twentieth time. 'The family will be so delighted, and *honoured*!'

All the family and all their friends gathered at their house in the next few days, to admire the Knight's Cross, to congratulate Hansi, and themselves. Hansi was the first hero in the family since Uncle Leopold, who had served in East Africa — and he was not really a hero because he had never come back. They all patted Hansi as though he were a mascot. They talked endlessly amongst, and about, themselves. To please his mother, Hansi wore his cross every day, but said less and less about it as the days went by. Nobody wanted to talk, not *really* talk, about the things he wanted to talk about. Whenever he mentioned the U-Waffe, which was now his real life, they all seemed mentally to shy away from him, whilst composing a careful, solicitous smile on their faces, as though he were somebody who had a painful and embarrassing disease and kept on wishing to discuss his unfortunate affliction.

It was still bitterly cold for the time of year. It had been warmer, they told Hansi, but that was just *falsche Frühling* — the false spring.

One night it snowed, and in the morning Hansi went out and stood in the street. The stillness of the air, the smoke rising straight up from the chimneys, the bread cart with its horse snuffling in the cold, the women with their brooms sweeping the snow from their steps, all made a scene of such familiar peacefulness it made Hansi's heart ache. Even the air smelled quite different here, hundreds of miles from any ocean. But there was a deficiency here of some vital vitamin for living. The peacefulness was very close to stagnation. There was a lack of stimulus, of exciting movement, of unpredictability.

The truth was — and soon Hansi had to admit it to himself, if not to anybody else — that his leave was boring. He had always loved coming back home, but now it was an anti-climax. It was dull. His true life was no longer here. He listened to his father dictating, as though to a secretary, statistics from the *Völkischer Beobachter* of the number of ships sunk by the U-boats. It amused Hansi to watch his father's obviously mixed feelings that such an illegitimate weapon should have such success. But he would much rather his father continued to read out figures than talk about 'that day off the Skagerrak in 1916', when, according to his father, 'we had the chance to see the Tommies off, to get rid of Trafalgar for ever. But we let them off.' Hansi knew better, as did his mother and all the family, than to argue, for that would 'set him off on his favourite hobbyhorse.

But otherwise, the beer seemed flat and the girls ugly and dull, even Hedwig, who was not his girlfriend, although she was certainly the girl next door. Hansi had no girlfriend. He had left Leipzig a boy and had come back a man, with no intervening period of maturity. Hedwig had put on weight and become even more bossy, and now had a disturbing physical resemblance to her mother. As for the rest, they were not like the French girls, and they were all safely locked up at night. Leipzig girls were noted for their off-handedness. Wartime did not seem to have changed them. A Knight's Cross was supposed to act like a charm, a door-opener — a leg-spreader, as the Lordly Ones would say. But not in Leipzig. Hansi remembered Hugo the engineer telling him of a holiday he had spent in the Austrian Tyrol, shortly after the Anschluss. He had discovered a quaint local custom, Hugo said, where every Austrian girl over the age of eighteen was granted what they called *die Freiheit aus die Leiter*, literally, 'the freedom of the ladder'. It meant she could put a ladder up to her bedroom window and climb down it, or permit a young man to climb up it, just as she pleased. What Leipzig girls needed, Hansi thought, was a few more ladders.

Hansi's father had his optimism about the progress of the war, not just from the newspapers, but from the men he drank beer with every night. They came up to his table, all of them, and shook his hand and said, 'All over this year.' Hansi inwardly doubted it. This was the second spring of the war. Where the end of the war was concerned, it was another false spring.

One evening, as Hansi was sitting with his father, there was a commotion outside. He heard motor car engines, and running footsteps, and the word *'Razzia! Razzia!'* A police round-up. The very word itself had an urgency about it, with its flat, harsh sound, ending in a menacing hiss. Hansi did not ask who was being rounded up, and his father said nothing. He was *Blockführer*. His son held the Knight's Cross for gallantry against the Führer's enemies. Nothing more need be said, or explained.

But one night his father did surprise Hansi. He was growing close to being drunk; maybe that accounted for it. 'I'll be honest with you, Hansi,' he said. 'I never knew you had it in you. I never would believe you had *die Hoden*.' His father used the plain, coarse word for 'balls'. Hansi had never heard his father use such a word before. It was as though he were now talking, not as father to son, but as sailor to sailor. Hansi thought he could even detect the merest inflexion of his father's voice, of having slipped into the characteristic Hamburg accent, somewhere between a drawl and a whine, of the typical sailor, and especially the U-boat Lordly Ones. Hansi himself could even put the accent on if he wanted to.

'I only think it a great pity you have to do it in those things.' His father laid a forefinger along the side of his nose. 'But we have a ship getting ready. A *proper* ship. In the *Baltic*. That's where *you* ought to be!'

Hansi had heard rumours of the new battleship *Bismarck,* on her trials. From all accounts she certainly was a proper ship.

But his father should not be talking like this, even in the heart of Germany, even in his own home town, in his own street, as *Blockführer*, even to his son. Nobody knew these days who was listening.

'Well, maybe one day I'll be lucky, Father,' Hansi said, placatingly. 'I wouldn't mind serving in her. But her officers are all specially selected. Maybe I've been in the U-Waffe for too long.'

Ironically, Hansi's next appointment was indeed to the Baltic. His father looked expectantly at the brown envelope, with the large swastika and the *Marineamt* official stamp.

'The *Baltic*!' Hansi saw his father's eyes light up.

'It's the U-boat commanding officers' course.'

'*Pah!*' His father blew out his breath in one great gust of disappointment.

'It is a great honour, Father. I am a very junior officer to take such a course.'

'Rubbish! You should be in the Baltic with the rest of the *proper* Navy.'

Hansi made up his mind: he must try at least once more to make his father see reason. 'Father, I owe this to all the men I served with in that U-boat. I *owe* it —' Hansi waved the piece of official paper — 'I owe *this*. I learned things in that boat, Father. I learned things from them. Now I owe it to them. I am *good* at it, Father. I don't want to boast, but I am a good U-boat officer and...'

'Hansi, you're not a proper sailor. You're a prig.' But his father used a much coarser, sailor's word.

CHAPTER SEVEN

'It's very good of you to come all that way to meet me, I must say.'

'You've said that several times now. It's all part of the Phalarope service.'

'By the way, nobody seems to know, what *is* a phalarope?'

'A small wading bird, of the family *Phalaropodiae*,' she answered easily, as though she had been expecting the familiar question. 'Related to the snipe. And HMS *Phalarope* is the newly established anti-submarine air warfare school.'

'Dear me, at least I knew that.'

It was a long drive from Glasgow. They had started early that morning, and were now, nearing midday, only halfway up Rest And Be Thankful. In places the roads seemed to be reverting to grass. Scottish road metal was not well looked after in wartime. Jay admired and envied the confident way she eased the big Humber staff car around the bends.

'I'm afraid I can't drive a car myself.' That seemed a very lame admission to have to make to a Third Officer WRNS. 'Not even a motor bike.'

'But you can fly an aircraft. We've been expecting you for some time.'

That remark seemed to need some supplementary reply. 'Well, first I went on leave. Then I did a flying instructor's course at Lee, and a weapon training course, and a course on RDF. Then I had briefings in the Admiralty on the current state of the art. I seem to have been briefed by absolutely everybody on absolutely everything. Then a consolidation course on Swordfish, as if I needed it. A course on explosives, and a course on flight-deck medicine. It seemed as if somebody actually wanted to delay me for as long as possible. Then I was going to fly up here, but the cab went US at the last moment.'

'Of course. You're here now, anyway. Who organised your briefings for you in the Admiralty?'

'A red-headed Third Officer Wrens, who…'

'Sarah One.'

'Who?'

'There were three Sarahs in our batch when we all joined the Wrens. For some reason we were all called Sarah One, Two and Three. I know Sarah One got a job in that section.'

'Which are you?'

'Sarah Three.'

'Is that in order of seniority, or … I was going to say, good looks, or … I shouldn't have put it like that…'

'Alphabetical order.'

Jay remarked privately on the fact that these two girls knew each other, kept in touch, knew where the other was serving. Obviously, the Wrens had their own system of jungle drums, their own service grapevine. The Fleet Air Arm itself was like a great worldwide whispering gallery, and the Wrens in it had just added another tier. It was amazing how quickly some Wrens had been assimilated into the naval world. They had taken to it at once, as though their family background and upbringing — their education, their outlook on life, had all fitted them for it, to the manner born.

They were driving past a structure on the right-hand side of the road. It was not a building, not even a hut but a kind of rough shelter, made of bracken and a strip of corrugated iron and various odds and ends.

'The hermit,' Sarah said. 'Lives there all the year round.'

'He must be *mad*. The winters up here must be terrible.'

'Not all that bad, actually. But the hermit thinks *we're* all mad, to have a war.'

'Well.' Jay laughed. 'He could have a point there.'

The big car surged over the shoulder of the pass and began to descend the slope on the other side. As they went down, the great humps and shapes of the hills around changed their silhouettes, like scenery moving. Jay had had to clear his ears on the way up. Now he felt himself descending, just like losing height in an aircraft.

Their road went round the top of Loch Fyne, and at a particular point, which Sarah obviously knew of in advance, she slowed the car and then drove over and on to a gravel reach, leading down the water's edge, and stopped.

'Lunch,' she said. 'I got some sandwiches and some soup from a friend at Abbotsinch.'

'Was that Sarah Four?'

'No, it was Pauline, about a Hundred and Sixteen, I should think.'

From where they sat in the car's front seats, they could look right down the loch. It was a day of silver splendour, with the water stretching away in a great shimmering path down to the south. The sun, shining through thin cloud, seemed directly overhead, and by an accident of atmospheric conditions its rays were concentrated in radiant columns of light which seemed to stalk across the water surface in succession. On either side were green landscapes, and beyond, the misty grey of the open sea. Far down, at the limit of visibility, Jay saw a dot on the water.

'What's that? Looks like a launch.'

'My golly, you must have good eyesight!'

'Necessary for survival.'

'I can barely see it. I wouldn't, if you hadn't mentioned it. If it's a launch, it's one of our HDMLs.'

Jay noticed how familiarly she used the initials. Harbour Defence Motor Launch.

'We use them to tow targets and things. They also do a spot of quiet lobster fishing on the side. It is a bit far up the loch here. We've got miles to go yet.'

As they crossed the bridge just before Inveraray, Jay saw the castle for the first time. It was even more fantastic than its postcards; with its turrets and pinnacles and battlements, it looked like Walt Disney's vision of a Highland laird's fastness, with additional advice from mad King Ludwig of Bavaria.

As Sarah drove out on the other side of the fishing village of Tarbert, she jerked a thumb towards the hillside on her left. 'There's one of our ranges over there.' Jay had no idea whether she meant right beside the road, or miles away over the hills. 'It's an even worse road than this. La Belle Dame Sans Whisky runs it.'

'La Belle Dame ... who on earth is that?'

'Third Officer Farquharson-Farquharson. She comes from these parts. She's tall and pale and teetotal. Hence the name.'

Their road had now crossed the Kintyre peninsula and was running on the western side, next to the Atlantic. There were islands out to the west, no more than dim blue shapes in the glittering sea. The road was getting worse, with more and sharper bends, but Sarah was still taking the corners smoothly, passing the huge knobbed steering wheel expertly through her hands.

'Another range, over there,' she said. 'The live range, where we actually drop live depth charges. Where the *boys* actually drop depth charges, I should say.'

He noticed the correction, and the word 'boys'. It was not familiar, nor slang, but natural usage, obviously second nature to her.

'What is your function, exactly?' Jay asked.

'Function, exactly?'

'I'm sorry ... What do you do on the station?'

'I'm the senior Wren officer at the moment, believe it or not. The place is still very new, and it is growing all the time. I look after the Wrens, their routine, their welfare, see they're all in the right place at the right time, see they go on leave, get their advancement, and all that. Standard divisional officer's course stuff. I'm also the staff operations officer.'

'Crikey, sounds as if you run the place. I must say I'm very flattered to have the queen bee herself come and meet me.'

'That's a funny way of putting it. *Queen bee.* I was due to go down to Greenock anyway and see some people.'

So that was it, Jay thought. *So you needn't flatter yourself.*

'In fact I don't run the place. We've got a captain, a four-ring captain. I gather you know him?'

'We served together. We're now just about the only survivors.'

'You were in one of the life-rafts. I heard about it. Are you all right now? Your hands and feet and all that?'

'"And all that?" Yes — well, more or less. I still get painful twinges when the weather gets cold. Rather like those old boys whose corns give them gippo when it's going to rain. But now the summer's here I should be OK for a bit.'

'It must have been bad. On those rafts.'

'It was. But it's over now.'

They were passing a small church, with a tiny graveyard. 'Your predecessor's buried there.'

The matter-of-fact way she said it made him laugh out loud, despite himself. He stopped, embarrassed by his own lack of self-control. 'What happened? I'm sorry I laughed.'

'He just went on, and in, and out. We've got another range here. There's the hull of a U-boat, full size, painted on the ground. You can't actually see it from here, on the road, you can only see it from the air. He was giving a demonstration. The first real run over that range. We hardly had a chance to see what went wrong. Perhaps you'll find out. He just turned inland — I can see him now — and seemed to fly low into a hillside. Just like that. Nearly there now.'

There were some rows of huts near the airfield runway, and some more substantial brick buildings further away. It all looked much bigger than Jay had expected, like a small town, which had grown up, like a colliery village, for a special purpose and to serve a special sort of villager. There was a golf course, a relic of peacetime, and it was odd to see a flag flying from a hole, so close to the White Ensign flying in front of the buildings. There was a large Victorian-looking hotel, another relic of more than one peacetime, almost at the end of the runway. It looked as though it had been built by the architect of Inveraray in even more gloomy mood; compared with this hotel, the castle was almost frivolous.

'The Wrens live there,' said Sarah. 'I'll take you to see the Captain.'

Wings was standing, waiting for Jay, in the sunlight outside his office, which was a little brick building close to the flagstaff. He was wearing the four gold rings of a captain, and Jay was pleased to see those. But Wings himself looked much older, and thinner, and much more bent in his stance. He really had aged a great deal in a year. But the sight of that familiar face brought all the memories back, of their time off Norway, all those friends gone for ever. Jay felt a spasm of grief, so pure and intense, it was more painful and vivid than anything that had happened since the sinking. He was very nearly in tears as he shook Wings' hand. Wings had always been such a confident, reassuring personality. He was so slow to anger, it must have taken something like an earthquake to shake him. But it had happened, and now he looked so much more frail and vulnerable. Layers of his personality — those defences which every man put up to guard himself from his fellows — had been ripped away, and Wings had not yet succeeded in re-erecting them. Jay realised that Wings had not recovered, and never would recover, from his experience. He himself might, in time, recover his full fitness in every way. But Wings never would.

'Good to see you, Jay. I heard you'd been getting on well. Did I write to you in hospital? I meant to...'

'You did, sir. Thank you. I couldn't reply then. I couldn't hold anything in my fingers, and I didn't like to ask anybody else to do it for me.'

'I can guess.' Jay saw by Wings' face that he did understand precisely what Jay meant.

'What I meant to say, sir, was that I eventually did write it all down. When I got better.'

'I heard. You shouldn't have done it. Although I am very grateful to you.'

'I would have given evidence on your behalf, if it had ever come to that.'

'I know you would. But there won't be a court martial now. I asked for one ... but what's the point? Everybody who knew us has gone. I got this the other day.'

Wings had plainly brought the letter with him to greet Jay with, to show to him specially as soon as he arrived. It was an extraordinary gesture, as though Wings wished to make his point at their very first meeting.

It was from the Secretary of the Admiralty, and it was brief.

Their Lordships have had under review the circumstances which led to your leaving your ship in May 1940, and I am to inform you that in the official view of the Admiralty no charges involving your honour or professional reputation stand against you. The notation of the reason for your removal from the ship has been erased from your record.

'What were the charges, sir, did you ever know?'

'Not specifically, no. They never told me. It would have been something like cowardice in the face of the enemy.'

Every word still hurt like the lash of a whip. Jay could sense Wings still wincing inside. The psychological hurt was still there. 'The *bastards*.'

'Well, that is all over now. Have a day or so to sling your hammock. The next course arrives on Thursday. I'll take you up for a bit of a flip tomorrow and show you round the parish. Sarah will show you your cabin and all, won't you, Sarah?'

Jay had quite forgotten that Sarah was there, and must have overheard their conversation. As they walked away, back to the car, to get Jay's gear out of the boot, she said, 'That was a most interesting conversation.'

Jay said nothing.

'I think I learned a lot about you both in that.'

Again Jay said nothing at all, but humped his bags out of the boot and followed Sarah to his cabin.

'There is a wardroom, two huts along, just to eat in. The bar is in the hotel,' she said.

'I'll see you in there later.'

'Maybe.'

The bar ceiling was at least twenty feet high, and there was actually an organ in the hotel hallway leading to it, with its dull metallic tubes in rows, the holes in them all grimacing like gargoyles forced to smile against their will. The room was full of antlers, and pictures of stags and girls mending fishing nets, and cases of stuffed fish, and a very large stuffed ptarmigan with a moth-eaten breast on a stand immediately by the door. The decor was dark mahogany and brown paint, with shiny tiles showing grapes, and vine leaves, and cornucopias spouting streams of fruit and vegetables of unknown species. The bar itself was a huge slab of very dark mahogany, its leading edge carved to resemble a long row of bulbous, anthracite-coloured beads.

Waiting there to greet Jay was Bonzo, his chief assistant and senior pilot. Bonzo had been on board off Norway. He and his squadron had been fortunate enough to fly ashore just before the ship left for her last sortie to the north. Jay knew him well, and there was no need for curiosity.

'Welcome, oh depth charge king,' said Bonzo. 'Good to see you looking so fit. What'll you have?'

'Oh. Glass of beer would be fine.'

The bar was staffed by two Wren stewards. Jay was conscious that he was being summed up for future reference.

'Cheers,' said Jay. 'Good to be back. Now, let's have the lowdown, Bonzo.'

'Well, you're the chief anti-submarine wallah. I deal with the rest — because this is also a holding air station for front-line squadrons when they're disembarked, and waiting to go on board their carriers. We're the last gasp before they go to sea. Trouble is, they don't go to sea, because we haven't got any carriers, not for the sort of job we want. So half the Fleet Air Arm is busy still training to torpedo the German High Seas

Fleet. Evidently nobody has told anybody yet that the High Seas Fleet scuttled itself more than twenty years ago. Another problem is that the squadrons that come here should know what they're doing. Trouble is, they don't. And accidents can and do happen.'

'Such as?'

'Last month. The usual balls-up. We're still new here, you must understand.'

'Yes, but what happened?'

'Momentary aberration of the brain, I suppose. He and his flight were doing an exercise with the army. Coldstream Guards and the Royal Fusiliers. All very *Tatler and Bystander*. Down in Kirkcudbrightshire somewhere. Dive-bombing the army positions and didn't pull out. Nearly took the colonel's tin hat off into the bargain, I heard. One of our most experienced pilots, too. Cast a great gloom over the place.'

'I can imagine.'

'No, it was more than that. He was keen on young Sarah. And I think she was *very* keen on him, too.'

'You mean…'

'*Our* Sarah, yes.'

'Good God, I would never have guessed…'

'I know she's no oil painting, but still…'

'No, no, I didn't mean anything like that. I meant, from her manner.' Jay remembered his own laughter as they passed that graveyard, and cringed inwardly.

'No, you wouldn't, not from Sarah. She'd make sure of *that*. Never mind … the first turn of the screw mends all broken hearts. Here it's the first turn of the prop. There are millions of Wrens here, and more arriving every week.'

On his first flight over the 'parish', as the Captain had called it, Jay was able to solve the problem of the accident at the painted U-boat range. It was simply an optical illusion. There was a low, bracken-covered hill immediately inland. But in front of it, and slightly lower, was another ridge, also bracken-covered and merging perfectly into the hill behind it. In flying to clear the hill, the Swordfish had clipped the ridge in front with its undercarriage. The mark of the accident now lay like a warning beacon, as a dark scar, the shape of a bat's wing, on the ridge-top.

The first squadron arrived for their three-week course. There was a full programme of depth-charge attacks on a dummy U-boat hull, towed by the HDMLs; radar tracking exercises, using the ASV sets newly fitted in Swordfish; torpedo attacks on target vessels in the Clyde; army co-operation exercises in Ayrshire; navigation exercises, flying across to the Irish coast and back again; homing exercises on Ailsa Craig; and practice deck landings on an old carrier which came up for a week and steamed sedately up and down off Arran whilst the Swordfish landed and flew off, and landed again and flew off again, like bees around a pool of water.

The whole programme was organised with unobtrusive skill by Sarah and her assistant, a large, buxom Leading Wren, with horn-rimmed spectacles, from Yorkshire, who was known for some reason as Biggles. Every day, Sarah and Biggles shuffled timings, rearranged rendezvous, laid out exercise serials, brought availability state boards up to date, and even, as Bonzo said, brewed a very good cup of tea.

There was only one flaw, which was beyond Sarah and Biggles to remedy, and that was a lack of information from sea. Nobody knew, for instance, whether the dummy hull towed by the HDMLs actually looked like a U-boat's hull, because nobody had actually seen a U-boat's hull from the air.

'The trouble is,' Jay told Bonzo, 'we don't really know what we're doing.'

'Situation normal.'

'It's not funny. We get no word back from sea. No feedback. Do you realise, the Fleet Air Arm hasn't sunk a single U-boat yet for certain. Not for certain. We think we might have done. Nothing confirmed. There was that Swordfish which sank one up in the fjords while we were there. But I'm talking about in the open sea, in the Atlantic, in defence of a convoy, or a fleet.'

'Well,' said Bonzo, 'the reason we hardly get anything back from sea is that we've hardly got anybody *at* sea.'

'True.' Jay looked round the bar, which was filling up. 'What are we celebrating tonight?'

Every night, or almost every night, there was a party — for somebody arriving, or somebody leaving, for somebody getting a good score on the range, for somebody who had missed everything. There were celebrations to 'wet' one stripe, to 'wet' two stripes, to 'wet' a baby's head, to 'wet' an engagement ring. The pre-war aircrew, as Jay very well knew, were far from teetotal. But the drinking here had an added energy literally a *Drink before we die* attitude to it.

There was even a party one night to celebrate a failure to complete the course, a failure indeed so complete that the celebrated one was being removed from flying and returned to general service. Jay and the Captain had to watch such cases carefully. If it ever became known, or even suspected, that *Phalarope*'s course was a soft touch, a likely route out of flying, more than one might try to swing his ticket. They were all volunteers. They had already survived basic and operational training, and it would be unusual for anyone to back out. But it would not be unthinkable.

The squadrons had the services of an ancient submarine, an 'O' Class dating from the 1920s which had spent years on the China Station; maybe it was one of the boats Gussie had served in. She was known as HMS *'Orrible* and she was based at Campbeltown, on the other side of the Kintyre. Jay, still preoccupied by the problem of identifying submarines from the air, invited himself over to see her, although he knew that she was so obsolete as to be the only survivor of her class: all the others had been readily sunk by the enemy.

The submariners lived in a gloomy hotel facing the sea front. There was whisky there only three times in a normal week; they drank it all on the day it arrived and spent the other days seemingly pacing up and down the town. Campbeltown was a town of many church spires and dozens of shuttered windows belonging to the twenty or so, it was said, old distilleries which had closed down. It was an oddly isolated place, in mind as well as in space. It was many miles from anywhere by land. Steamers did come in from Glasgow, especially in summertime, so life flowed in and out of the town mainly by water and not by land. The ragged children on the streets spoke a largely incomprehensible dialect. But the war and the Services had brought a kind of prosperity and, though the townsfolk would have perished in eternal hellfire rather than admit it, servicemen and women were welcome, if not for themselves then at least for the money they brought in.

The submariners clearly took life a great deal more seriously than the aviators. Jay found them solemn men of solemn mien, even when there was whisky.

'This is really quite lively, for Campbeltoon,' *'Orrible*'s Captain told Jay, 'when you compare it with pre-war. There was tremendous unemployment then, I'm told, nothing but a few fishing vessels. There used to be gangs of rowdies roaming the streets in the evenings. I understand it was quite an ordeal for holidaymakers to go out at all after dark. Trouble is, it's still very isolated. There used to be a narrow-gauge railway here. I'm told you can still see the station, and bits of the line here and there. Closed sometime in the thirties, I believe. We've got palm trees here, did you know? The Gulf Stream, of course. You say you want to come out with us? Sure you know what you're doing?'

'No I don't know what I'm doing. That's why I want to come out with you one day.'

It was some years since Jay had been in a submarine, and he found it still another world of strange commands of unfamiliar but powerful smells, cramped space, and an easy familiarity between officers and men.

Jay had arranged for an aircraft from *Phalarope* to come out and do a dummy attack whilst he was on board. Although he was expecting the aircraft, and although the Swordfish was a particularly slow marque, Jay was astonished by the speed at which it approached them, and by the difficulty of spotting it. Surely, with those advantages, the aircraft was the ideal anti-submarine weapon?

'How many do you normally have up here?'

'This is a training boat, but I always have the full number, as though we were on a war patrol. That's me; the Officer of the Watch; four lookouts. Six in all. The lookouts each have their own sectors. The Officer of the Watch pays particular attention to special factors, like the direction of the sun at dawn, and at sunset — in fact, the sun at *all* times — the weather side if it's rough, the windward side at night…'

'And can all six of you get down in time when you dive?'

'*Easy*. It takes us about sixty-five seconds, going flat out. That's a hell of a long time, in submarine terms.'

'What does a Type Seven C U-boat do, then?'

'Oh, thirty seconds, I would say. Thirty-five at the outside, but quite possibly less than thirty seconds, if they're properly worked up and have their wits about them.'

Thirty seconds. Fully loaded with depth charges, a Swordfish would just about top ninety knots, and that was downhill with a following wind. That was a mile in forty-five seconds. Say a first sighting of the U-boat at five miles. It would still have a long, long three minutes and forty-five seconds to get down.

'What would you say we had to do to sink a U-boat? What would be your advice?'

'First, try and get overhead before he dives, or if you can't do that, as soon as you can afterwards, while he's still going down. Because once he gets down to about sixty feet or so, better still to a hundred as far as he is concerned, you've not got much chance of hitting with a charge. And U-boat hulls are very robust. You've got to get your charge literally within a few feet to breach the hull.'

'And even when the U-boat has gone, disappeared, would it still be worthwhile going on with the attack, would you say?'

'Goodness me, yes! If you've got a good datum, you want to *plaster* it! Nobody likes being depth-charged. Even if you don't sink him, a near miss would shake him up very badly indeed. You'd certainly spoil his day, and you might even damage something so that the boat couldn't go on with its patrol. You could even shake the Captain's nerve a bit. Might *just* make him think discretion was the better part of valour and not press on quite so hard.'

'Would you do that? Is that how you would react?'

'I've never been depth-charged. It may make some more cautious, others more bloody-minded and even more anxious to get their own back. I like to think that with me it would be the latter. I would guess that most U-boat captains would react the same way.'

'I expect you're right.' Jay watched the Swordfish droning off back to the field. It was Bonzo, delighted he had caught his boss napping. *'Orrible* was only halfway down when Bonzo was overhead. 'I wish we knew a little bit more about them. I'd love to *talk* to a U-boat captain. Even just to have a look at him would be worthwhile. Just to get an idea of what sort of bloke he is, what makes him tick.'

'Why don't you go down to one of these interrogation centres, where they ask captured U-boat crews questions?'

'*Have* we captured any of them?'

'Lord, yes! Dozens, I'm told, and they ask them questions about life in U-boats, life in Germany now. Just generally shoot the breeze with them, obviously hoping they'll say something indiscreet.'

'Can you do that? Can you go and see them being interrogated?'

'Well, you can only ask, can't you? I think all aircrew, all escort captains for that matter, ought to be able to have a good hard look at their enemy.'

'That,' said Jay, 'is a simply *brilliant* idea!'

It was Sarah who arranged it, through one of her Wren contacts.

'Was that Sarah Two you got on to?' Jay asked.

'Veronica Six,' Sarah grinned, 'if you really must know. There might have been a bit of a problem about intelligence clearance for you, but I've managed to fix it. Fly to Abbotsinch on Tuesday. On to Hendon. Train to London. Stay the night. Another train out to Aylesbury in the morning. Somebody will meet you.'

It all went as Sarah said. Jay was met by a plump Lieutenant RNVR, who wore large spectacles and an air of pleasant, though somewhat remote, benevolence. He resembled a very amiable hospital almoner, who always thought the best of his fellow men, and indeed as their car drove through the main gate Jay noticed above it the legend MIDLAND COUNTIES HOSPITAL.

'Needless to say, this is *not* a hospital,' said Jay's host, who asked to be called Colin, 'and please try not to remember anything of what you see here. We've got a subject for you. A very young *Oberleutnant zur See*. Hans Gerfried Bruetzer is his name. He's just come in. We like our meat fresh. We hate anybody else to question them. Spoils it if they do. Contaminates them. This chap thinks he's the only survivor of his U-boat.'

'Isn't he?'

'No.'

'Won't you tell him?'

'Oooh, *no*. Not till we've finished with him. A man'll always tell you much more if he thinks he's alone. Nobody left to betray. Nobody left to check up on him. And nobody left to give him any moral support, and warn him what he should or shouldn't say. He's a stranger in a strange land, with nobody to stick up for him, or point the way, or say you shouldn't do this or that. In any case, it seems none of these characters have ever been warned about what might happen if they were ever captured. The thought never seems to have entered their heads.'

'Nor should it,' said Jay, with some heat. 'What sort of an attitude would that be, if you went into it *expecting* to be captured?'

'That's it.' Colin grinned, with the utmost amiability. 'That's it. That's the right attitude. *That's* the attitude we like!'

Colin led the way down a long corridor and into his own very small office. 'Let's have a cup of coffee, and I'll brief you. Now, please, when you get in there, I want you to be as anonymous as you possibly can be. I don't want him to look at you too much, or even notice you. I don't want any distractions. It may all seem rather casual to you, and inconsequential, but I don't want you even to catch his eye if you can help it.' Colin looked at his watch. 'Nearly ready. He's just had a meal. Long enough to think about it all and wonder what's going to happen. In any case, I doubt if this little troglodyte will tell us much. *We* know more about the U-Waffe as a whole now than any of them do. I could tell *them* things.'

'Do you just rely on questions?'

'Yes. More or less. Sometimes we put a microphone in their rooms, up in the electric light fitting, but that all seems terribly dramatic. Sometimes we use a two-way mirror.'

'Don't they find that?'

'The microphone? Not yet. One or two of them have looked for it. Sometimes we use a stool pigeon — one of us dressed up, perhaps with his leg in plaster or something, pretending to be a U-boat survivor kept back for extra questioning or until his leg gets better, or something. But as I say, that is all very dramatic sort of stuff. Normally it's much lower-key than that.'

'How long do you keep them here?'

'Not long. Few days. A week. Depends on how much they tell us. But as I say, most of them don't know as much as we know. We listen for specific words sometimes, for instance if we get the message to look out for particular code words or names of new weapons or new techniques. We sometimes drop a few hints ourselves. We know that one or two have codes, to write home with, just as we have. You would know all about that, being aircrew. So we sometimes give them some material. At the moment I'm plugging the notion that we've got some way of sniffing out diesel fumes from a U-boat on the surface.'

'Have we?'

'Not that I know of. But it's not impossible. Perfectly feasible technically, I should imagine. Who knows, it might make U-boat captains just that bit more cautious. Make them think the whole world's against them and they can't even start up their diesels now without giving themselves away. But largely, we let *them* ramble on, for as long as they like. It's all done by kindness, you see. This is a joint Services interrogation centre. Some of the army bods are much rougher — sentries with fixed bayonets, and a lot of shouting. We find that sort of thing counterproductive. All done by kindness. *Much* better.'

Jay felt a peculiar chill at Colin's affability. There was something infinitely cold and calculating, something much more menacing than threats, about this well-mannered approach.

'This shouldn't take very long.'

Nor did it. The interrogation took place in a small room furnished with a table and chairs and nothing else. There were no pictures on the walls, no window, nothing to take the prisoner of war's attention away from Colin. Jay sat behind Colin, studiously avoiding the prisoner's eye.

The *Oberleutnant* was a very young man with long fair hair. His fingers were heavily nicotine-stained and his gaze travelled constantly from Colin, to Jay, to the soldier standing as sentry on the door, and back again. But in general he seemed at his ease, and if anything anxious to please. Colin spoke to him in rapid and obviously idiomatic German. The *Oberleutnant* responded readily, almost eagerly, as though trying to prove his own worth and importance as a capture. Jay noticed that Colin spoke less and less. The *Oberleutnant* took over the dialogue, while Colin looked thoughtful, and impressed, and at last very struck by something the *Oberleutnant* had said. Colin gave him coffee, which the man clearly enjoyed, and plied him with cigarettes, which made him first cough, and then laugh out loud.

At last they shook hands, and two more soldiers came in, each with a rifle slung over his shoulder. The U-boat man stepped in between them, then turned back, and hesitated, and held out his hand, tentatively, as though afraid of a rebuff. But Colin took the proffered hand and shook it warmly. He said something which made the prisoner grin as he went out. It had, as Jay now realised, been a brilliant demonstration.

'What was that you said?' Jay asked.

'Nothing much. Just a private joke. We know all the U-boat jargon, all their slang. We can even imitate that particular slow drawl they've got. They like to speak a special way — it's like a club, like a sort of occupational dialect. I could go on board a U-boat tomorrow and pretend to be one of the ship's company. I bet I could pass it off — until we were depth-charged. From what these men tell me, I don't think I'd enjoy that. It's the one thing they're sensitive about. *Not* one of the world's most enjoyable experiences.'

'Did you get much from that chap?'

'Not a great deal. About what I expected. You'll never believe it, he said he'd heard about a device that could detect submarine diesel exhaust gases! He had one or two suggestions about increases in torpedo speed and range, and a hint they're producing a new sort of U-boat. A *wonder weapon* which will win the war. But then, they all say that, all the time. You can read *that* in the German newspapers every week.'

'You read the German papers?'

'Goodness me, yes. Keeps me up to date on the questions I can ask. We even sent a letter to one once. To the agony column. I said I was ambitious for my husband who was a member of the Party and I wanted him to get on. Should I submit to the blandishments of my *Blockführer*, I wanted to know? Signed myself Hilde of Hamburg.'

'You're joking.'

'Not at all. I even sent a picture of myself. I was a blonde. Rather blowsy, but there's no accounting for taste. The original was given me by a U-boat man.'

'Did they print it?'

'No, not yet, so far as I know.'

'But was that wise, to send the photograph? There might be some way that could be traced? You might even give away the secret of this place in that way.'

For the first time since Jay had met Colin, his face looked less amiable and more concerned. 'I've said too much already. There was a reason. Let's leave it at that.' Colin looked at his watch. 'I'm sorry we didn't have an English speaker for you today. Some of them do speak English. They're very proud of it. I once took one of them out to dinner with me; and I took him mushrooming in the fields at the back of this place!'

'Now you *are* joking.'

'No. He was much better at mushrooming than I was. Obviously had lots of practice in the Black Forest, or wherever it was he came from.' Colin was searching in his desk drawers, clearly looking for some document to show Jay. 'If there's one thing I hope we can get across to you blokes, it is that you've got some real opponents in these U-boats. Don't be misled by all my jokes about them. We're getting a different sort of captain now. They did have some good ones, the aces, as they liked to call themselves, although they weren't *quite* as good as they thought they were. Against independently routed ships, or against weakly escorted convoys, or inexperienced escorts, they were good kids. But now that *we're* getting better, they're finding themselves on harder times. I can tell by what they say under interrogation. Where the hell is it? But most of the early prima-donna types are gone. Sunk or captured. Now we're starting to get a new type. The children of the war, you might call them. They've been brought up in it, graduated in the war. No flies on them. Much more cautious. The percentage players. Much more dangerous. But they're the sort that will beat us if anybody can. Now, where the hell did I put it?'

'You don't seriously think we're going to lose?' said Jay.

'Let's just say we've got to come to terms with these men we get passing through here. Ah, here we are. My rogues' gallery. Look at this.' Colin lifted a large book, as big as two or three telephone directories, full of photographs and newspaper cuttings, and put it on his desk. 'Cast an eye on your enemy. Youngest officer ever to win the Knight's Cross. Went up to Berlin to receive it from the Führer's own fair hand.'

Colin thumbed through the pages. 'Here we are. Hans-Dietrich Zschescher.'

Jay looked at the thin lips, the high cheekbones, the fair straight hair. It was the face of a capable, confident young man. In other circumstances, this could have been the face of a chief cadet captain at Dartmouth.

'Right little stormtrooper, isn't he?'

'How did you get all this gen on him?'

'Pictures, cuttings from the papers. We keep tabs on them all. It helps if we know something. Gives us a lead in when we're interrogating someone. We first heard of this chap through interrogation. Somebody who knew him, served in the same flotilla in Lorient. Rather jealous of him and his success, we thought. Well...' Colin looked at his watch again, for the third or fourth time.

'You want to get back to your torture chamber,' Jay said. 'Thank you so much for your hospitality.'

'My dear chap ... *delighted*. If you ever want to do a spot of ... *mushrooming,* you'll know where to come, won't you?'

Colin was still grinning widely, like a hospital almoner after an unexpectedly successful case, as Jay's car drove out through the gate.

Jay had only been away a very short time, but when he returned the season seemed to have taken a great step onwards. Full summer had arrived and, as sometimes happened in the far west of Scotland, July was a magical month. The sun shone down every day with such force it flattened the surface of the loch into a smooth plain, the colour of bottle-green glass. A sea-bird alighting, or a sea-trout splashing, sent out surface ripples which spread seemingly for ever. A launch going up the loch trailed a sharp ripple of wake which could be heard later actually breaking on the pebbles ashore, long after the launch itself had vanished into the heat haze. In such conditions, the Swordfish pilots complained of difficulty in judging their height above the water accurately. Several times Jay saw planes' wings dipping close, until the propellor churned up whirls and water turbulence on the surface.

Jay now had what Sarah called his new toy: a short-range radio set, which he put in the big staff Humber, driven off its battery. With a Wren driver, he set out most mornings along the eastern coast road which wound up and down like a switchback and was so narrow it was little more than a track, with the occasional passing place. But in all the days he went there, Jay could not remember ever meeting another vehicle.

From a favourite position sitting up on the hillside opposite the depth-charge range, Jay would watch and comment upon the bombing runs. Waiting for the Swordfish to arrive was like a peacetime picnic, with the heat coming off the tussocks of grass, the noise of insects, the smell of gorse and heather, and far below, the sight of the silvery shining loch. On days when they were using live charges it seemed a sacrilege to disturb the loch with those spouting, leaping columns of water, which subsided into broad dishes of creamy froth. It seemed to Jay from his vantage point on the hill that the ripples from depth charges did not last as long as those from fish, as though the loch itself resented these violent unnatural disturbances and erased their traces sooner than usual. As the waters cleared, Jay would tell the pilot over the radio whether he had hit, or missed, and by how much.

Some pilots missed more often than others. The worst was a young man called Jessop who, in Jay's opinion, was not safe, to himself or to others. It mystified Jay that Jessop had passed first his basic and then his operational training without being 'scrubbed' from the course. There were always borderline cases, and Jessop must have been given the benefit of a very large doubt. Many squadrons had a weaker member, just as litters had their runts, and Jessop was certainly the runt. It was not that he was unwilling or resentful. On the contrary, he was embarrassingly keen, and that made him an even bigger menace to himself and others.

'The trouble is,' he told Sarah, 'that it *is* wartime, and what would not do in peacetime will do now. What are those birds?'

'Oystercatchers, maybe. Sandpipers or something.'

'You're a great birdwatcher.'

It was Sunday afternoon, and they were walking along the beach north of the airfield. The sands really were wide and golden and empty, just like the railway posters promised. There were no holidaymakers, nobody swimming in the sea — neither were there any mine sentries or barbed wire barriers, as there were on the south coast of England. The Germans could land here at any time. But, as the sailors said, what would they do when they got here? There were no buses or trains, and if they came on a weekend they would have to wait until Monday morning.

It was Sarah's suggestion that they walk along the beach. 'Get you out of yourself,' she said. 'You've got your head stuck too far down in the bucket. You've got to let up sometime.'

Jay picked up a large pebble and threw it. It hardly reached the water. 'I'm too weak even to chuck a bloody stone.'

'You're very thoughtful.'

'Well, it's this Jessop business. Do we chop him or not? He's useless. He's worse than useless, he's keen. Keen and useless is a very dangerous combination, worse than being stupid and industrious. And he's affecting other people. The last thing we want is people working their tickets. But if he goes on I think he's going to kill somebody. Probably himself, and maybe, others too.'

'You take a very hard view.'

'Good God, you've *got* to. This isn't some sort of game, you know, where we've all got to be good chaps, and never do anything that isn't cricket. I've *been* a survivor, I *know*. It's a hard war. That sounds melodramatic, but it's true. A few hours in a dinghy, a few days on a Carley float — believe me, it concentrates the mind wonderfully. Anyway, the final decision is not up to me. It's up to the Captain, and his CO, to sort out eventually.'

'Yes, but what *you* say is bound to have a good deal of influence.'

They had reached a point where the beach narrowed to go round a small spit of land. There was a path leading up and across the minute headland. They walked up and found some stones and a clear grassy space amongst the gorse. From where they sat they could see the coastline for miles to the north and south.

'You've been here before?' Jay asked.

'Yes, I used to come here with Joe. Sometimes you can sit here and watch when the sun is going down, it looks as if the whole surface of the sea, the whole lot, is on the move, streaming away down south, in a great, great wide river, which looks as if it's made of solid silver. It's the most beautiful sight, even though you know it's an optical illusion.'

'What's that island up there?'

'Gigha.'

'And we in dreams behold the Hebrides...'

'Funny you should say that. I was just thinking the same.'

Jay stood up to declaim: *'From the lone shieling of the misty island ... Mountains divide us, and the waste of seas ... Yet still the blood is strong, the heart is Highland. And we in dreams behold the Hebrides.'*

'It sends a sort of shiver up your spine.'

'That's what it's supposed to do. I don't even know who wrote that. I must ask the Schoolie, our pet weatherman. He's RNVR, he's probably got a degree and knows about these things. Not like us boorish, uncouth, uneducated NOs...'

'Boo-hoo. You don't have to be so prickly and defensive.'

'All as thick as deckhead planks. Lot of boneheads who pound the gravel at Whaley.'

'Oh, come off it. You know you don't really think like that. Quite the opposite, in fact. Everybody I've ever met in the RN has this disgusting sense of personal superiority over the rest of creation. Although I must say, you do seem to give a lot more thought to things than most of them.'

Jay sat down again, with his back to a large stone. Sarah sat beside him, in a curiously comforting, companionable way.

'It's my job, isn't it,' he said, 'to think about things? It was my job before the war. That's why I joined. Not like all these RNVR types. They were doing all sorts of things before the war. It was *us* who were supposed to be thinking how things should be done in wartime, how it would go, what we should do, what weapons we'd need, how we should use them, and so on. But we don't seem to have done it very well. Not as far as the air side is concerned. Do you know, my first captain when war broke out got us all together and told us, quite seriously, that in his view no submarine would ever be sunk from the air! He meant it. Every senior officer always seems to be permanently amazed when anything happens in the air. We took a hell of a licking in Norway, you know. Everybody knows it wasn't exactly a success, but it was a bloody disaster in almost every way.' Jay saw Sarah staring intently at him. 'What are you looking at?'

'I was just seeing how intense and serious you are. I think if I was in those U-boats I'd be beginning to get a bit scared. Because you're not like the pre-war naval officers at all, even I can see that. Not you younger ones. You've sort of *graduated* in the war, in some odd sort of way. I would say that made you that much more dangerous.'

'Hope so. I don't *feel* dangerous.'

Sarah had drawn her knees up under her chin and was looking out to sea. 'It was never like this when Joe and I came up here. It was absolutely foul all the time. The weather, I mean. We had to wear coats and hats all the time. Still, it was fun.'

'Watch out. Mustn't get sentimental, whatever you do.'

'I've learned that. Like more than one girl around these parts. Whatever you do, don't get too keen on aircrew. You'll break your heart every time they take off and go out there. And if they're delayed for any reason, you die all over again.'

'Well then, live a little.' Jay put his arm round her and kissed her.

'I am not, repeat *not,* going to get involved.'

'Of course not. Just give me … several kisses.'

He was surprised, and stimulated, by her lack of resistance.

'Take your jacket off and put it underneath me. It's all prickly here on my bottom.'

'I was very…' Jay searched for some word that was not too banal. 'I was very attracted to you that first day, when I first met you on that trip up from Glasgow. I didn't realise it at the time.' Now that he had said it, it seemed the most natural and self-evident truth in the world.

'That's the last time I give somebody a lift up from Glasgow.'

'It was very enjoyable. So is this.'

'You're just lonely, that's all. And you've got a lot on your mind, a lot of responsibility.' But her body contradicted her words.

'No it's much more than that.'

'Well, you've never given me any inkling at all. Suddenly you just pounce on me like this. I'm not a U-boat, you know.'

'Not all *that* suddenly.'

'No. Not really. I suppose I liked our trip up from Glasgow, too. And I didn't realise it properly till afterwards either.'

That, Jay thought, with all its implications, was probably the most thrilling and delightful remark anyone had ever made to him.

'Don't wrestle with it. Let me do it.'

'I'm not wrestling with it.'

'Maybe. But I don't want to have to sew any buttons on again. You know, I feel as if I've just found somebody.'

'So do I. I know just what you mean. And I feel I've got to hurry, too, in some way — we haven't got much time.' It was extraordinary, Jay thought, that even a minute earlier, before he had had this conversation with her, already seemed ages ago.

A flock of seabirds fled screaming overhead, so close and so low that Jay, preoccupied as he was, could not help hearing them and ducking his head. As the birds' wailing died away, he heard another sound, like somebody calling. He sat up. A Wren was cycling along the coast road towards them.

'It's Biggles. Gosh, she can pedal, can't she?'

Sarah buttoned up her blouse before sitting up. 'Do you think she's looking for us?'

'It looks ominously like it.'

Biggles had climbed off her bicycle and was waving. They both stood. Biggles looked from one to the other. They knew what she was thinking. She knew they knew. But, strangely, neither of them resented Biggles' knowledge. Sarah carefully picked a scrap of heather from the collar of her blouse.

'The Captain would like to see you both, sir. It's a *flap!*'

They found the Captain in Sarah's ops room, with several other officers, including Andy, the CO of the Swordfish squadron on course, and the CO of *'Orrible*, who had come over from Campbeltown ostensibly to discuss the next week's programme, but actually — as everybody knew or suspected

— to see a newly joined Third Officer WRNS.

'It's a Polish merchantman, or rather it *was*.' The Captain straightened up from the chart. 'Probably going to join a convoy. Possibly a straggler. Sunk in the North Channel.' He looked at Jay and Sarah. 'If you'd gone down to Southend you could probably have seen it.'

'That's right on our doorstep,' Jay said. 'He torpedoes a ship on the front doorstep of the anti-submarine air warfare school. At a weekend, too. That's what I call cheeky. That's very, very cheeky.'

'Well,' said the Captain, 'what do you think we should do?'

'It's the obvious place, sir. If I were a U-boat captain that's where I'd be. The North Channel is only about ten miles across, between the tip of the Mull and the Irish coast, where the convoys go in and out. The time to catch a convoy is early, just as they're forming up, before the escorts have had a chance to get to know each other's form...'

'All right. But, to answer my question ... *'Orrible*, what would you do now if it were you? Setting a thief to catch a thief, so to speak.'

'Thank you very much, sir. Well, first, what's the tide doing?'

'It's setting southerly,' said Biggles, who had already taken out the tide tables, to everybody's surprise. 'Quite strongly, too. Two or three knots down through the North Channel.'

'Well then ... I'd stay down, if it were me, just stemming the tide, or trying to make some headway to the north if I could, until the tide changed; and then I'd stay with it, letting it take me back up again through the Channel, until dusk or thereabouts. All depends on the vis. As soon as it got dark, or if the vis got very bad, which is unlikely, I'd surface and get the hell out of it as fast as I could, around Rathlin Island and away like a dose of salts.'

'Do you know,' Jay said, 'I never *thought* of the tide like that.'

'Well, you wouldn't, would you — you wretched flyboy with your head and your thoughts in the clouds all the time!'

'So,' said the Captain, 'we keep one aircraft overhead in the Channel, to make sure he keeps his head down. Then, we have an armed strike ready, with depth charges, ready to get him as soon as he surfaces and starts for home, thinking he's well away. Who's going to go?'

They all looked round and they all became aware, together, of Jessop's beaming face, standing behind his squadron CO. *All bright-eyed and bushy-tailed,* Jay thought. Just like a spaniel, knowing there was a day's shooting coming up. If he had a tail he'd wag it. But the man wasn't safe. Jay had said so, and believed so. He was still officially on the course and a member of his squadron. The wheels had not yet begun to turn which would dispatch him back to general service. But he should not be allowed on a night sortie like this.

Jay saw that they were all looking at him. It was time to speak, if he were ever going to say anything. *Therefore if any man can show any just cause ... let him now speak, or else hereafter for ever hold his peace.* He saw Jessop's face and the expression on it. He allowed the silence to lengthen, knowing that his silence would certainly be taken to mean approval.

'Right,' said the Captain. 'We'll do a search now, just in case he is an amateur and comes up too early. Then we'll all go away, just to encourage him. He'll have to wait a very long time for it to get dark up here at this time of year, so he'll be good and ready for the sun to go down. He may even warm the bell a bit. Then we'll nail him!'

As they broke up, Jay caught Sarah's eye. Although there was no accusation in her look, Jay felt a sense of shame. He had betrayed his own profession by being disloyal to his own standards. He really ought to have said something about Jessop. But it was too late now. It was curious how quickly his elation of that afternoon had been dissipated.

It was, as somebody said, the First Eleven: Jay himself, and Bonzo, Andy and his senior pilot, and seven others, including Jessop. All aircraft had ASV radar, newly-fitted in Swordfish, and were armed with three depth charges.

'This bugger's going to get well plastered,' Bonzo said. 'I hope we're not going to get in each other's way.'

The afternoon patrol sighted a boatload of survivors, and a destroyer came out from Londonderry to pick them up. By dusk, the Channel was empty again. Cloud spread from the east as the sun went down. The western light glowed on the surface for a time, and then withdrew rapidly, as though it could not bear to stay and witness the execution. As Jay led the three flights around the tip of the Mull to start the first radar search, he felt events beginning to unreel like the perfect textbook demonstration of anti-submarine warfare. His observer soon reported the blip on the radar tube. The other Swordfish, flying in close formation, waggled their wings one by one as they picked up the target.

There was nothing to be seen of the target when it was first detected, at just under five miles' range. Jay felt himself flying up a long black channel, with nothing to distract him to either right or left. At three miles, his observer had established a plot of the target. It was steering north-west, and doing, he said through the communication tube, more than seventeen knots. It was just as *'Orrible* had predicted. Their man was no beginner. He was now on the surface, and going at full chat for home.

At two miles, Jay could see him, a black blotch on the sea, trailing a swirling pale wake of foam. This was clearly going to be one for the scrapbook. Jay had pushed forward his joystick and begun his shallow attacking dive when there was a colossal explosion behind him and to starboard, and a sheet of flame so bright it blinded everybody.

'Fucking *Malony*!' shouted the observer. 'That was a collision! Target's gone, Boss!'

Jay grimly flew down his attacking glide-path but, as he expected, there was nothing there. The sleepiest lookout in the world could not have missed that explosion. Their quarry was gone now, safely down to depth. He would not be surprised again. But, recalling *'Orrible*'s advice about depth-charging, Jay released his charges as near the datum as he could judge. The others, sharing his mood of frustration, did the same, until the sea boiled and spouted all around.

Afterwards, when the aircraft had reformed, Jay heard the observer's voice in his ear. 'Two of Andy's squadron, Boss. Andy himself and Jessop. Collided.' Andy must have made Jessop, as the weakest of his brethren, fly close to himself so that he could keep an eye on him.

They flew angrily up and down through the short night, flying search patterns from the Mull across to Ireland and back again. But there was no sign of their target, nor of the two Swordfish, not even a vestige of wreckage floating on the surface. The whole episode of the night before had vanished like a dream. The weather had cleared to the southward, and it was a day of almost maximum visibility. They could see beyond the Isle of Man and, to the west, well past the mountains of Mourne. Beyond them, clouds were massing, as though the fine weather was going to change. The convoy which had lost the straggler would be well out to Oversay by now, where the ocean escort would be joining. Jay and the others patrolled for hours, at fifty feet, looking for a periscope, or a trace of oil, or a piece of debris. But there was nothing. There was no sign of their friends, and their enemy was not going to give them another chance.

CHAPTER EIGHT

'You must look after your periscope. You must worship it. You must love it, above your mother, your wife, your girlfriend.'

Hansi presumed that Herr Onkel meant 'girlfriend', although he had actually used, purposely — to show what a hardened old seadog he thought he was — a much coarser, grosser word. Herr Onkel, as everybody called him, with his paunch, his little moustache, his puffy cheeks and his War Service Cross — commonly awarded for valuable service on the Home Front — was the chief lecturer on the U-boat captain's qualifying course, although Hansi sometimes found that fact hard to credit.

'Look after your periscope, I am saying,' Herr Onkel was saying, portentously. 'Your periscope will be your saviour in this world. Neglect it, and it will be your passport, for you and your crew, into the next. It is your totem pole, more potent than your penis...' Somewhere, maybe in the last war, Hansi thought, Herr Onkel had learned how to labour a point to death.

He shifted on his hard chair. The wind whipping off the Baltic pounded on the panes of the lecture-room windows. This must be the worst summer in living memory for much of the Baltic coast. It had arrived so late that one hardly noticed its coming. Now it seemed it might be about to leave early, before it had actually warmed anything. There was a spattering of rain against the glass, too. Hansi, sitting at his desk, was glad he was not at sea that day.

This building had once been a school, and everybody still called it the kindergarten. There were still echoes and remnants of its former existence, of rabbits and storks and all the impedimenta of childhood lessons, in the designs of elves dancing hand in hand around the lampshades, and in the little blackboard on the wall facing the course, which had a pink-painted wooden frame, with flowers picked out on it in blue and green. Beside it was a large line drawing of a Type VIIC, with all its compartments detailed and sectioned, and all its machinery labelled. Beside that were some old photographs of ancient warships, all dating from the Kaiser's war. Along the wall from that was another sheet, of British warship silhouettes. Somebody had crossed out the *Hood*. The *Hood*! They should be so lucky to get such a target to shoot at! Here, Herr Onkel, like everybody else, was obsessed by thoughts of submerged attacks against columns of dreadnoughts which advanced so slowly there was plenty of time to measure angles and distances and seconds. Nobody at this school seemed ever to have any conception of a surfaced attack, by night, or in bad visibility, which meant a hectic passage through ranks of ships, with only seconds to identify a target and lay off its bearing. *That* was now the normal way; the submerged ambush of a stately battleship belonged with Noah's Ark.

So far, Hansi had found the qualifying course, and Herr Onkel, equally tedious. But there was very little else to do except to concentrate upon one's work. Certainly, there was not much scope for entertainment in Neustadt, even if they had been allowed to go there. One could catch a train to Lübeck, of course, which was only about thirty kilometres away. Hansi had been there once, to walk about the wide market square and to see the spires and towers. There were tall red churches and short red men in Lübeck, as the saying went.

Lübeck, where the buildings and the citizens' heads were all made of brick, so they said. A surprising number of U-boat sailors came from Lübeck; they wanted to get away from the place, the Lordly Ones used to say. It was still a handsome town, with some of the atmosphere of the old sailors' city of the Hanseatic League. But everybody preferred Hamburg. A weekend in Hamburg might be the reward for passing this course.

Meanwhile, they had to make the best of the course, and of Herr Onkel. There were eight students, all roughly Hansi's age. One of them, Joldy Meyer, Hansi had known as a midshipman before the war and another, Karl-Friedrich, had served briefly in the same torpedo-boat flotilla before going to do the U-boat school a couple of training courses earlier than Hansi. Not surprisingly, Hansi was the only one with the Knight's Cross, indeed the only one with any decoration. He was very conscious that it marked him out, made him the target. The others watched and waited to see if he would make mistakes.

But the star of their course was undoubtedly Karl-Friedrich. He had the most amazingly accurate 'periscope eye'; he was able to judge a target's course, the angle off the bow, and the director angle, seemingly without having to think about it. It was a natural gift, like perfect pitch. But Hansi also noticed that whenever Karl-Friedrich made one of his very rare errors, or someone else made a mistake, he lost heart easily. He had no resilience, no optimism. Brilliant as Karl-Friedrich certainly was, Hansi privately decided he would never like to serve with him, and especially not have him as captain.

There might have been some excuse for Karl-Friedrich. Hansi had heard that he had recently had a very hard time. While attacking a convoy in the Atlantic two months before, their U-boat had come to the surface inadvertently in daylight, and almost under the nose of a destroyer. It was the engineer's fault, but they all had to pay the penalty. With such a heaven-sent datum starting point, the destroyer had wasted no time, or depth charges. The attack lasted six hours in all. Two more destroyers had come up and joined the attack. They dropped over two hundred charges. Hansi could hardly believe the figure. Surely three ships could not carry so many? It seemed they could, and that was another omen for the future.

But Karl-Friedrich's ordeal had not been over. A week later, they sank a ship off the coast of Ireland and surfaced after dark to make their best way home. But they had been stalked by unseen and undetected aircraft. If the aircraft had not mysteriously given themselves away by releasing an enormous explosive, with a huge fireball, immediately astern of the U-boat, they would certainly have sunk the boat. As it was, the aircraft must have had some unknown means of detecting a boat underwater, for they went on to drop their charges so close, and doing so much damage, Karl-Friedrich's boat struggled to reach St Nazaire.

That terrible experience, they discovered, had left Karl-Friedrich — understandably enough — inordinately sensitive to loud noises. A loud engine made him fidget. Any bang, or even the smallest and mildest pop, made him restless. He was not sleeping well. The training course slept two to a room in an old house by the harbour. It had been the customs officer's house and it still had an office on the ground floor, with a massive pair of weighing scales and an old Imperial Navy flag with the eagle, an eagle spread above the fireplace. Hansi shared a room with Karl-Friedrich, and every night heard him moaning before he went to sleep. One night he awoke to hear Karl-Friedrich screaming. He got up and went across to say something to him. He found him lying on his bunk, his body rigid as though in an epileptic trance, staring at the deckhead. He had gleaming sweat on his cheeks, and he looked like a man waiting for death, or already dead.

After some days of Herr Onkel's lectures, they went outside to a 'dummy' U-boat control room and tower. It had been fitted up to represent an actual U-boat, with range finder, attack tables, calculators, and an attack periscope which could be raised and lowered. In a loft above there were models of ships which were moved about by unseen hands. The whole building was an 'attack teacher', on which a class could 'get their eyes in' and make their mistakes without incurring any serious consequences.

When anybody made a mistake bad enough to have put the U-boat at risk, somebody up in the loft dropped bricks or some heavy object on the floor above. The noise was loud, but it was humiliating rather than dangerous. It was done to remind the erring student that, in real life, he would have endangered his boat and everybody in it. The banging was hardly ever through a fault of Karl-Friedrich's, but whoever's fault it was, the result had a punishing effect upon Karl-Friedrich. Every time the noise came, he crouched, and turned away his head, like a hound expecting to be beaten, while his face went dead white with fear and shock. Then he would gaze intently at the door of the attack-teacher, as though longing to escape into the open air.

After a time, Hansi and the others came to know of Karl-Friedrich's weakness, and made allowances for it. After his experiences, they did not blame him. But Hansi was astonished that neither Herr Onkel nor any of their instructors noticed anything. Karl-Friedrich had come with the highest recommendation from his former captain. On the course, he was clearly one of the most naturally gifted students they had ever had. But none of the instructors seemed able to see what Hansi and Joldy and the others could see: that Karl-Friedrich's tormented personality was cracking.

On the third weekend of their course, they moved to Danzig, along the coast, for operational sea training, using one of the old coastal submarines — the ancient Kanus, as they were called, from pre-war. On the Sunday afternoon, Hansi went ashore with Joldy to have a look round the city. He was curious to see it. Danzig was a prize of war. The Prussians had always resented having to make a present of it to Poland. Now Germany had taken it back. The 'Danzig corridor' had been a term on everybody's lips at the beginning of the war.

They went to see the church of St Mary, and were surprised to find it full of people, with music, and candles, and a service going on. There was an old priest standing by the door. He looked at their uniforms and at Hansi's cross, and silently held out an offertory bag. On an impulse, without thinking, Hansi put his hand in his pocket and gave the man all the money he had. He did not even look to see how much it was.

'Is that for forgiveness?' Joldy said.

Hansi shrugged and nodded at the sky. 'It does no harm to be on good terms with *the* Herr Kaleut, up there.'

The students had to get up very early, before dawn, and walk down to the harbour, where there was a motor boat to take them under the bridges and past the quays of old Danzig to the river mouth, where the Kanu was waiting for them. The course took it in turns to 'command' the boat — to give the helm and engine orders to take the boat to sea, to dive, order the amount of water in each tank, and bring the boat alongside again. One by one, they took the part of Herr Kaleut and carried out practice-dive attacks on an old tender which steamed up and down, at first steering straight and then, later, when they had

had more practice, zigzagging. After each attack, Herr Onkel and the Kanu's captain would discuss their performance, pointing out mistakes and suggesting improvements.

In general, they all did very well. In the quiet of a dived U-boat they all seemed to feel at home. There was only one incident, when Joldy failed to take the boat deep enough early enough after an attack. The Kanu's captain, looking through the other periscope, had to give the order to flood the emergency tank, or the tender-target would have run the boat down. It was a very serious error. In earlier days, when the U-Waffe was less hard-pressed for captains, Joldy would probably have been dismissed from the course.

As the days went by and Karl-Friedrich surpassed even himself, the others began to hope that his bad time was over, and he might be able to control himself. But one morning, when he was on the periscope and confidently rapping out a stream of bearings and ranges, a sailor passing through the control room happened to drop an empty bucket on the deck.

Although it made a hideous, sudden clanging, it was irritating rather than dangerous. Somebody even laughed, and the sailor looked a little sheepish. That would have been all, had it not been for Karl-Friedrich. For him, that was enough. It was the end. It was the final straw. The last threads of tattered nerves gave way. Karl-Friedrich began to tremble, to shudder, and then to howl out loud like a dog driven demented by a thunderstorm. He was shaking like a man in a fit, with no control over his muscles, and soon everybody in the control room knew by the sudden smell that one important muscle at least had betrayed him.

Hansi happened to be standing next to Karl-Friedrich, and as the wretched man swung round Hansi saw the terrified, hunted expression in his eyes. Karl-Friedrich leaped on to the ladder leading up to the upper hatch and began frenziedly trying to loosen the clips. Joldy went after him, grimacing at the smell, and hauled him down. But Karl-Friedrich tried again, with a frantic strength which took Joldy, still hanging from his shoulders, up the ladder with him. Again Karl-Friedrich was hauled down, but he fought and struggled, dipping and plunging like a maddened bull, and raved and cursed. Spittle spun from his lips and fell audibly on the deck.

At last, they managed to subdue Karl-Friedrich, while the rest of the control room looked on in horror. This was a brave man disgracing himself, through no fault of his own. He had been tried too far and for too long, until he broke. He was still shaking uncontrollably as Hansi and Joldy led him away to the petty officers' mess. He put up no struggle now, but just looked dazed and tired. They undressed him and cleaned him, sponging him as though he were a baby. Somebody produced some clean clothes for him. They threw his old trousers over the side on the way back to harbour.

It was a silent company who brought the U-boat alongside and secured it in Danzig that evening. They had, one and all, been given a terrible glimpse into a future which might be lying in wait for any one of them. All their own worst imaginings, their most private fears, too frightening to take even so much as the shape of a definite thought, had actually appeared before their eyes in the spectacle of that crazed and desperate man struggling to escape from a dived submarine. Poor Karl-Friedrich, it might have been better for him if he had died in that last depth-charge attack.

With Karl-Friedrich gone, Hansi was now unmistakeably the top man on the course. He always had, after Karl-Friedrich, by far the best periscope eye. He could make up his mind, even under pressure. Bangs and bricks on the deckhead above never ruffled him. Incidents invented and thrown in to distract him whilst he was carrying out an attack did not deflect him. He enjoyed it all, and enjoyed it more the longer it lasted.

All remaining seven passed, even Joldy. Hansi's name was at the top of the typed list pinned to the tiny blackboard. Herr Onkel asked them all what they would like to do, and gave Hansi, as the top man, first choice. 'You can either take over an operational *Frontboot*,' he said, 'or do a training job here in the Baltic somewhere, probably at Pillau or Gotenhaven. Or you can commission a brand-new boat.'

'Brand-new boat,' Hansi said.

'I thought you would say that. I have something special for you. Kiel for you. A Wonder Boat for Wonder Boy,' said Herr Onkel, enigmatically.

The night before their qualifying course dispersed, to go their various ways, they tried to hold a celebration party at a cafe in Danzig. But a curious incident happened at the entrance to the cafe, just as they were all arriving and trying to capture a mood that was jolly. A man in torn clothing leaped out of the shadows. He had a knife and slashed Joldy across the face, a grievous slashing cut on one cheek and over the bridge of his nose. The assailant vanished back to where he had come from, amongst the sounds of police whistles and voices calling. It was, as it occurred to Hansi at the time, just as though the police had been expecting the ambush but had arrived too late to prevent it.

Joldy was taken to hospital, and Hansi to the police station. Hansi could only tell the police what he knew: the attack had been so sudden and unexpected, a senseless act, the deed of a madman. The police asked what the man had been wearing, what he had said — if anything — what had he looked like; did he look like a Pole? They quizzed Hansi for a long time and finally, when Hansi was not sure whether they believed him or not, took him to another office, to another policeman in plain clothes. Hansi recognised him as a member of the Gestapo. This was even worse. The man seemed pleased to be given the chance to interrogate an officer of the U-Waffe. He looked at the Knight's Cross and smiled, in a manner which was only just short of contempt, as though such baubles meant very little inside here.

This interrogation had the same questions as before. Hansi was able to give no more satisfactory answers than he had before. Thus the questioning went on for most of the night. There was no question of going on with the party; in fact, Hansi was only just in time to get back to the customs house, collect his gear and catch his train.

It was only three hundred and thirty kilometres from Danzig to Kiel by sea, but by train the journey seemed everlasting. Hansi had to change trains at Stettin and again in Berlin, where he caught the train for Lübeck and Kiel. It was late in the afternoon before that train left, and it had hardly cleared the outskirts of the capital when there was an air raid and the train stopped. Obeying some common impulse, everybody got out.

The train had stopped, perhaps on purpose, in a deep cutting. Hansi climbed up the bank and lay back to look at the sky. He could smell cattle and flowers. As a city boy, Hansi could not identify the flowers, but he knew the authentic smell of summer. It had come at last. A long way away there was a faint thumping, as of bombs. Hansi could also feel the merest tingle of the earth beneath him. There was what sounded like a hooter or a siren. But it was all a very long, long way away. Hansi stared up at the blue summer sky, on this perfect evening. High overhead there were smoke trails, and smaller black puffs of smoke which appeared as if by magic. As Hansi watched, he caught sight of a tiny pinprick of light. It was an aircraft, miles over the earth, banking and catching the evening sunlight.

The guard came along the track, looking — as somebody remarked — more military than the military, with his medal ribbons in his lapel and his warlike peaked cap. The guard blew his whistle and waved his arms, and everybody climbed back in again. Hansi helped an old woman wearing a bonnet up from the track on to the carriage ledge.

It had been dark for some time when they reached Kiel. Hansi looked out of the window at the dark, silent buildings swinging by. They must enforce a blackout quite strictly here. There was not a light to be seen. The old woman sitting in the corner whom Hansi had helped off the track said, 'Three hours late. That is very good. Normally, much more.'

Hansi found that a small but disconcerting item of information. Trains in his previous experience always, or very nearly always, ran on time. It was part of normal life, an essential to an ordered existence. But now, it was a world in which Joldy could be attacked inexplicably on the street and where trains three hours late were considered good timing. Hansi for a moment had the unreal sensation that the very earth itself was trembling under his feet. He had a sudden glimpse of that terrible abyss into which Germany had plunged after the other war; his father had often spoken of that time, when nothing was stable, and neither money nor honour were worth anything. Surely, it was unthinkable that Germany should endure another such time as that.

Hansi was met at Kiel station by a tubby, grinning *Oberleutnant zur See* who introduced himself as Otto. He wore on his sleeve the winged staff of Hermes, the emblem of the supply branch. He shook Hansi's hand warmly, and seemed genuinely glad to see him. Otto led the way out to the open truck in the station courtyard. The driver, who was a soldier, not a sailor, swung Hansi's bags up on to the back of the truck. Otto and Hansi sat in front, side by side, next to the driver.

Otto made no apology for their transport. Instead, he said, 'You are comparatively punctual. Air raids are getting a little more common in Kiel these days.'

Hansi could see streets on either side cordoned off, and some building to the right showed a jagged roof against the lighter sky. There were figures of men in one street and somebody energetically bending and stooping to work a hand-powered water pump. The truck was stopped by somebody who held up a hand and then, seeing Hansi, waved them on.

'It's your decoration,' Otto shouted in Hansi's ear. 'To a Knight's Cross all things are possible.'

Hansi thought he detected a note of irony in Otto's voice, but he could not be sure. 'Are you connected with the U-boat arm?' he asked.

'Well ... I suppose I am. I do Herr Direktor's paperwork for him. I'm on the supply side, as you can see.' Otto held up his arm so that Hansi could see the insignia again. The truck stopped again, this time because a barrier was across the street and had to be removed. 'I haven't been to sea since I was a midshipman. No. I tell lies. I did go to sea once, for a few days, in the gallant old battlewagon *Schlesien*.' This time Hansi was sure of the derisive note in the voice. He knew, as Otto must also know, that *Schlesien* dated to the Kaiser's war, and had been a cadet training ship. 'We bombarded some wretchedly unfortunate people in the Norwegian affair. I don't think we ever hit anybody.' Hansi found himself involuntarily looking round for eavesdroppers.

They had come to another stop before a pair of very tall, dark gates. They opened when the driver sounded his horn. Otto produced some papers. The truck bumped over railway lines and the uneven surface of a dockyard road. Hansi could see high buildings on each side, and further roads opening to right and left. He thought he saw cranes at the end of some of them. He had been to Kiel before, many times, but in this dark, with not a light to be seen, it was totally unfamiliar.

They came to another, smaller gate, and then to a third, even smaller, where Otto produced more papers. It seemed that the smaller the gate the more papers Otto had to produce. The final gate was set in a high brick wall. Here the truck stopped and Otto got out. He led the way through a door, brushing aside a blackout curtain, along corridors which were themselves quite unlit, and finally turned into a large room so brightly lit it made Hansi blink.

It seemed to be half office, half laboratory, with glass-fronted bookshelves, dozens of glass utensils stacked in rows, a long bench with Bunsen burners and a desk, on which was a model of a submarine with an unusually streamlined, torpedo-like hull shape.

'Herr Prof, may I present to you *Kapitänleutnant* Hans-Dietrich Zschescher, our new recruit?'

While Hansi was still wondering about the informality of addressing the *Direktor* as 'Herr Prof', the man seated at the desk got up to shake hands. He was a large, burly man, with a walrus moustache, drooping, rather flabby cheeks which were nevertheless bright red, and very thick white hair. He was probably, Hansi guessed, about forty years of age.

'*Hansi!*' said Herr Prof. 'Welcome! May I address you as Hansi, if you address me as Herr Prof?'

'Of course,' Hansi muttered, still slightly taken aback by his reception.

'I am delighted our little project is to have the talent it deserves at last. I asked for one of the best, and here we are, with a holder of the Knight's Cross, and top of his class. Excellent! Couldn't be better. Let us drink to that, and to our new comrade. Would you have a glass of our schnapps, Hansi?'

'With pleasure, Herr Prof.' Hansi was surprised to see Herr Prof take up, not the usual bottle of spirits, but a glass decanter rather like a shaker with which to dispense medicines. Herr Prof poured a large measure into a tall glass.

'Cheers!' Hansi was about to put the glass to his lips when he saw the looks on the others' faces and paused. There must be some practical joke here, some trick played upon newcomers. He sniffed suspiciously at the liquid in his glass. It did not seem actually to smell of anything much, perhaps very faintly of sea water, like the lingering odour on rocks left behind by the receding tide. Hansi held up the glass to the light. It was clear, but perhaps with the merest greenish tinge and, now that he looked more closely, there was actually a bubble or two rising.

Herr Prof took the glass away. 'Look at this,' he said. He set a china dish on the bench and, from a cardboard box, took some wood shavings which he sprinkled on the plate. Then he poured the liquid he had given Hansi on the plate. At once, the wood shavings began to smoke vigorously, and then burst into flames.

Hansi was unable to control the instinctive movement of alarm which made him jump away from the bench. 'Good God! What's that? You gave me that to *drink*?'

Herr Prof bellowed with laughter like some demented buffalo. 'It's all right, I wouldn't have let you drink it. But *that* —' Herr Prof gestured at the smoking shavings — 'is the hope of Germany, Hansi. What you have just seen is the power fluid, the fuel of the future.'

The flames had gone out, and there was a not unpleasant smell from the ashes on the plate.

'That is the fuel for U-boats five, ten years ahead. It should be the fuel for U-boats *now,* if justice had been done. But that's a political matter. *That* —' Herr Prof, with pardonable theatrical emphasis, gestured again at the plate — 'may take rockets to the moon one day. It can already power an aircraft engine, more's the pity. The bloody Luftwaffe are after it all the time.'

'But what *is* it?'

'Perhydrol, Hansi. It is the stuff that silly blondes dye their hair with, but much, much more powerful. What is the chemical formula for water, Hansi? Ordinary tap water?'

Hansi frowned. It seemed such an unexpected, even frivolous question. 'Why, H two O. One molecule of oxygen to two of hydrogen.'

'*Exactly.* Now, supposing we somehow managed to add a second molecule of oxygen. H two O *two*. And that extra molecule of oxygen is man-made, Hansi, it's against nature. It will always be trying to get away again. So we help it get away. We decompose the stuff as rapidly as we can. You must look at this as a chemist looks at it, Hansi. When decomposed, two molecules of perhydrol produce two molecules of water, one molecule of oxygen, and some heat. A kilogram of perhydrol at eighty per cent strength, Hansi, produces as much oxygen as one point one five cubic metres of air. Think of that. From this fuel, decomposed, you get hot water, and steam, and *oxygen*. What does that suggest to you?'

Hansi shook his head.

'*Hansi* … Come, come, come. Put that steam through a turbine and then what? Why, you can drive something with that. We can go further. We can burn some extra fuel, some diesel fuel, in the oxygen and then put the whole lot, the steam and the carbon dioxide from the burning diesel *all* through a turbine. We shall have to cool it, of course. But that is all to the good. The cooling water will itself turn into steam and that, too, will go through the turbine. Do you understand now? That turbine could be put in a U-boat. A U-boat that will drive itself along underwater without needing to surface! Imagine what *that* could do!'

Hansi felt the force of the idea and its implications dawning upon him, as Herr Prof later said, radiantly, like the sun. It was simple. It was revolutionary. It was *brilliant*. The possibilities were boundless. With this magical fuel, a new world would open for U-boats. No need to surface to make progress or to charge the battery. No need to risk detection. No need to go near the surface at all. Just pump this perhydrol through the turbine. For the first time, in history, the true submarine!

Herr Prof had been watching the expressions, the realisation, on Hansi's face.

'I *do* see,' said Hansi. 'But why haven't we got this at sea?'

To Hansi's astonishment, both Herr Prof and Otto burst out laughing. 'Because of the office boys,' said Herr Prof. 'They keep on buggering us about. And the Luftwaffe keep on interfering. This is not a new idea. I myself have been working on it, on and off, for eight years, *long* before the war started. If they had listened to me you could have *started* the war with U-boats like that.'

'But where do I come in? I am not a chemist.'

'*Ah.* Indeed you are not. You are my seagoing expert. You are going to help me design a *fighting* U-boat to use this fuel. I know a lot about engineering and a lot of chemistry. But I know nothing of attacking ships at sea. You certainly know nothing of chemistry. But you *can* attack ships at sea. You have your certificate to prove that, hanging on a ribbon around your neck. My doctorate, my certificates, are on that bench, in those files. *Those* are our qualifications. Now let us have a proper drink. Perhydrol again...' Herr Prof laughed at Hansi's look of consternation. 'This time just a little, what our French neighbours would call a *soupçon,* no more than a teaspoonful, in spirits of wine. Leave it to stand for a couple of days, to get mature, and *voilà!*' Herr Prof uncorked a bottle and sniffed at the neck. 'This is last Thursday's vintage. This is the very best *T-Stoff Spezial,* Hansi, brewed in your honour! It will blow the top of your head off!'

Hansi tried it, and — when he had stopped coughing and his eyes had stopped streaming — he had to agree.

Later, when the *T-Stoff Spezial* had stopped scorching down his throat and he had become more or less inured to its fiery impact, Hansi followed Otto to his cabin high in the same building as Herr Prof's office and laboratory. It seemed that Herr Prof had his own self-contained quarters within the main research establishment. The window of the cabin was open. Hansi dared not put a light on, and undressed in the dark. A cool wind blew in from the sea. The night was very clear, with stars. Hansi could hear the lapping of water, but looking out he could see only searchlights. He went to sleep looking up at the glow of the searchlights, crossing and recrossing the deckhead of his cabin.

In the morning, Herr Prof showed Hansi around his 'parish', as he called it. It was a surprisingly handsome establishment, 'like a university' as Otto said, made mostly of new, red-brick buildings, with more being built all around. It was at the northern end of the naval yard, on the southern bank of the Kiel Canal, just below the point where the canal reached the bay. There were offices, and laboratories, and workshops, and a foundry, drawing offices and rooms full of filing cabinets, and even a long, luxurious-looking board room, with its own kitchens and servery. There were two concrete bunkers near the water, each holding ten great tanks made of aluminium, and each tank stored some twenty tons of perhydrol. The perhydrol itself was brought either by rail in specially fitted tanker trucks, or by sea in a converted oil tanker called the *Polyp*. There seemed to Hansi to be dozens of men around, all civilians, with hardly a uniform to be seen. They were working on a variety of projects, not just submarines, but torpedoes, engines of all kinds, guns and projectiles.

The all-pervading, guiding spirit of the works was clearly Herr Prof himself. All the ideas were his. The projects were all his. He signed every drawing, authorised every machine tool, and where a suitable tool did not exist, he designed it himself. He knew every man in his works, and what he should be doing, and how far he should have progressed. Herr Prof was designer, draughtsman, engineer, chemist, electrician — and, because so many of the buildings had to be made for their specific and unique purposes, also an architect.

But it was quite clear where Herr Prof's main enthusiasm lay. Hansi noticed the man's steps quicken as he led the way across *Polyp*'s deck and pointed down at the submarine which was secured on the seaward side.

'*There.*' Herr Prof's voice had a fatherly pride. 'My little experimental craft. My *Versuchsboot.*'

Hansi's first impulse was to laugh. There was the submarine of the desk-top model, but its splendid underwater lines were now hidden, and all Hansi could see was its stubby length, of some twenty metres, less than half the usual U-boat length, and its short, stubby tower, about one metre high at the most. It looked like a nursery toy, hardly worth the serious study of a war-waging navy. But, knowing that this craft was more precious to Herr Prof than any human child, Hansi controlled his feelings and congratulated Herr Prof on what he could see of the little *V-Boot.*

Beaming like any proud parent showing off a talented offspring's handiwork, Herr Prof led the way below. Hansi found himself once again amongst the familiar submarine tangle of piping, the same smell of oil and rubber, and the space even more cramped than usual. There was a crew of only five, but there was only just room for them. The turbine was at the after end, sealed off behind a bulkhead. Dived, it seemed that two men looked after the turbine, one man looked through the periscope, one man acted as helmsman and also kept depth, leaving one man — as Herr Prof said — 'for anything else'.

Hansi stood on the tiny bridge, looking about him. Before he realised it, somebody had let go the lines and the *V-Boot* was going astern, out into the stream. The only other person on the bridge was a man in a brown raincoat and a brown felt hat, who said nothing.

Hansi heard Herr Prof's voice shouting up the tower. 'Now for it!'

Hansi felt the submarine gathering speed with a noticeable physical sensation of acceleration. Soon the bow wave was climbing further and further aft along the casing. Astern, the following wave reared higher and higher, and above that, a plume of gas, or steam, or smoke, Hansi was not sure which.

'Twenty knots!' Herr Prof called.

The shore buildings of Kiel were swinging by, as though on a magic lantern screen. Hansi noticed a buoy, quite close, which passed at a tremendous speed. They really were travelling.

'Twenty-five knots!'

Hansi gripped the bridge rail in excitement. This was like being on one of those machines in a fairground. It was an unnatural, an *ungodly* speed for a submarine. Hansi was standing so close to the water he could hear it hissing and sighing and rustling as it went by. The bow wave had now climbed to the base of the tower and before it Hansi could see the submarine's bow, like a porpoise, forging steadily through the water.

Another buoy flashed by, and it suddenly struck Hansi that the man in the raincoat was taking no notice, was not taking any bearings, not keeping any look-out. Hansi himself did not know the harbour, nor even the general appearance of the Kieler Förde. He had no chart, had been given no course to steer, had no binoculars, was not in any recognised naval sense the officer of the watch, yet he was — to all intents and purposes — in command of a highly valuable research ship speeding at twenty-five knots along a restricted waterway.

Hansi looked down between his legs. There was not even a voice-pipe, so he had to call down the tower. 'There's two ships ahead!'

The *V-Boot* slowed, so suddenly, Hansi felt himself pressed by his own momentum against the front of the bridge. Clearly this little research boat was no joke; it had introduced new dimensions of speed and manoeuvrability into submarine warfare.

But Herr Prof had even more surprises. When the *V-Boot* had stopped, Hansi climbed down the ladder and stood at its foot, which was the only space left for him in the minute control room.

'Do we do a dived run now?' Hansi asked.

'No, no. We do those at night.'

'At *night*?'

'Yes. We have an escort of a *Schnellboot* on the surface to follow behind us. We mount a light on the tower and shine it upwards so that the *Schnellboot* can see it.'

Hansi looked carefully at Herr Prof. It was just possible this was another joke, like the *T-Stoff Spezial*. But when he saw Herr Prof was serious, Hansi began to laugh and shook his head. Truly, this was a realm of submarining quite beyond his previous experience!

But now Herr Prof's expression had changed from triumph to concern. He was looking at gauges on the bulkhead and comparing their readings with those on several large sheets of squared paper. Once, he leaned forward and looked through the glass porthole into the turbine compartment. It seemed that the turbine was held, like a wild and dangerous animal, in its own lair. Maybe, Hansi thought, that was not so far from the truth. Remembering the wood shavings and the *T-Stoff Spezial,* he wondered what might happen to a U-boat and its crew if such a beast ever got loose at sea.

Herr Prof and his chief mechanic, whose name was also Hugo, were muttering to each other. 'That's it for today,' Herr Prof said. 'Another blasted defect.'

Thus it was a chastened Herr Prof who climbed ashore after his *V-Boot* had plodded back, at a steady three knots, on auxiliary electric motors. 'It's one thing wrong after another,' he said to Hansi. 'I know it doesn't look good. But the boat is experimental. One cannot have an experiment without failures. Experiment means failures. That is the normal scientific progress. But times are not normal. I have too many critics. Too many interruptions and distractions.'

That, as Hansi discovered, was true enough. Herr Prof and his works had to suffer a stream of visitors. Many were scientists, engineers, and men from the various companies supplying the works with materials or services. But a disconcerting proportion were high-ranking Luftwaffe officers, with, very occasionally, naval officers from Berlin. The attitude of these visitors and the tone of their questioning made it clear that Herr Prof and his projects were still very much on probation and under constant review. Yet, while his visitors remained critical of Herr Prof's projects, especially the naval projects, they continued to bombard him with new ones. New specifications, experimental data, estimates of research costs, and new projections of likely performance would be demanded before Herr Prof had had a chance to provide earlier ones.

So far as Hansi was able to find out, there were — apart from the *V-Boot* and similar submarines — major research projects on a new and revolutionary engine for a high-performance fighter, a new and much faster long-range torpedo, and several engines for rocket propulsion. But requests for other weapons and engines arrived every month, many of them to be abandoned in their earliest stages.

'Look at this,' Herr Prof said to Hansi one morning, after a particularly heavy mailbag from Berlin. Herr Prof was standing at a workbench which had a board with dials and buttons on it, like the dashboard of a new and powerful motor car. Herr Prof played over the board, like a concert pianist at his keyboard, nodding at Hansi to keep quiet.

There was a grinding, clanking noise and from behind a metal screen emerged a contraption like a small tank. It was apparently radio-controlled, and Herr Prof was able expertly to make the thing advance, retreat, and turn from side to side. With its radio aerial exactly like an antenna, and its curious snuffling, grunting sound as it shuffled to and fro, it reminded Hansi of some grotesque, giant beetle.

'For the *Ostfront*,' Herr Prof said. 'It was to go and blow up Russian tanks. But it cannot catch a tank up!'

Herr Prof shrugged his shoulders expressively and skilfully manoeuvred the monster back behind its screen.

'They keep changing everything,' Herr Prof told Hansi one evening, when they sat in Herr Prof's office chatting after supper. It was something that Herr Prof seemed to find reassuring and enjoyable, as though he could unburden himself to Hansi as to nobody else. Hansi was distanced just the right amount — in age, and background and professional experience — to allow Herr Prof to unbend to him. It was a dirty evening again, with rain falling in sheets outside. The summer, such as it was, had long gone, and winter was coming on more quickly, it seemed, every evening. Herr Prof's spirits seemed to match the weather in gloom.

'The way we're going, Hansi, we're not going to have this new submarine in time. I know they keep on trumpeting about it, but I sometimes wonder if that is not to keep their own spirits up. I agree the Luftwaffe's claims are important. They must have a better fighter. They ought to have it *now*. They're still fighting the war with basically the same fighter they started with. Just as you're using basically the same U-boat. But the

Luftwaffe cannot *win* the war for Germany. The U-boat arm *can*. Or at least achieve a kind of peace with honour.'

Not for the first time with Herr Prof, Hansi looked cautiously at the door. Anybody could be listening.

'But by the order of the Führer, all technical projects which could not be completed in a year were cancelled.' Herr Prof laughed bitterly. 'It was going to be a short war. All over by Christmas, as they used to say. Just like *my* war, the time before. That was going to be all over by Christmas too. I'm not exaggerating, am I, Hansi? You do need new weapons at sea.'

'Of course.' It was odd that Herr Prof should so clearly be looking for reassurance. Hansi thought of all those black-framed photographs in Lorient. The last time he had seen them there had hardly been room for any more. But somehow they always managed to fit in another.

'Do they ever give you any briefing on what to do, what to say, if you were ever picked up?'

'Picked up?' Hansi still sometimes had difficulty following Herr Prof's shifts of thought.

'After your boat has been sunk. There *may* be survivors. You *might* be one of them, one day.'

It was a possibility Hansi hardly dared admit even to himself. 'It would be thought disloyal to the Reich even to think of such a thing. They never assume you might be captured. That would be almost treason.'

Herr Prof chuckled, as though Hansi had said exactly what he had expected him to say. 'Then the more fools they, if that is really what they think. You can bet your enemy has thought of it. It could happen to anybody at any time. They ought to give you a code to use in your letters home from the prison camps. All the U-boat captains should have one. You especially, you of all people. So you can write and tell us what went wrong. Save somebody else making the same mistake. I think I will make up a code. Something very simple, that the British censors would never suspect. Nothing written down. No complicated figures or formulae or transpositions. Just some key words, or a line or two of poetry. Yes, I think I'll do that.'

Knowing Herr Prof, Hansi had no doubt that he would indeed give it some thought, and in a few weeks or even a few days, he would produce something.

'It might even be worth losing a boat, a very old and obsolete one, say, just to get the word back on how it was done. That is taking the idea to extremes, of course, but that is the way we should be thinking. We should be more subtle, Hansi. Our enemy is. But I expect such a notion would be far too subtle for our lords and masters.'

Herr Prof used the same word for 'lords' as the U-boat sailors used for themselves, and the mere sound of it, coming so unexpectedly, gave Hansi a stab of nostalgia for all those long-suffering, hard-working, hard-swearing, oily, *smelly* human beings, who withstood such appalling living conditions, such stodgy, boring food, and such terrible weather. It would be wrong to say they never complained, indeed, they never stopped complaining. But, in a peculiar way, their complaints were not complaints at all, but willing and devoted acceptance.

Hansi considered Herr Prof's suggestion of a decoy boat. Like all Herr Prof's suggestions, it had a core of real possibility in it. It often happened that the more one thought of Herr Prof's ideas the more appealing and plausible they became. Indeed, why not find a U-boat, old but not too old, or the enemy would suspect, and man it with dead meat. Even put Karl-Friedrich in command … Hansi writhed with shame at his own callousness. That was a cruel, a despicable, a terrible thing, even to think.

Herr Prof liked to surprise Hansi, and now he had another one. 'Look at this.'

'But this is an English magazine!' It was of an expansive size, with large pages full of striking photographs, and all printed on good quality, pre-war, smooth paper. His father would have been interested to see it. Hansi had a sensation as though he were handling contraband. Surely it was not permitted to have such magazines in Germany.

'It's all right, it won't bite you. I get them through Sweden.' Maybe Herr Prof had special clearance to obtain them.

'Can you read English?'

'No, not a word.'

Herr Prof took the magazine, opened it to one page, and handed it back. 'There you are. Look at your enemy.'

It was a large photograph of three young pilots, all wearing flying overalls. They were smiling into the camera, wrinkling their eyes, as though looking into the sun. Behind them was an aeroplane which Hansi could at least recognise from the instructional silhouettes as a Swordfish, one of the obsolete-looking biplanes they still used.

'It says, "Three Fleet Air Arm pilots, at a northern airfield, pictured after a successful flight, when a U-boat was sunk off the coast of Ireland."'

'Is it true?'

Herr Prof shrugged. 'Possibly. *Probably*. I have no idea. But I want you to look at those faces. It pays to study your enemy. You've never seen an English naval officer?'

'Never.'

'Well, then. It also says the pilot in the centre of the three has a score to settle with the Germans. He has been a survivor himself this war, when his ship was sunk in northern waters.'

They looked so young and cheerful, grinning at him from the page. The one in the centre was a little taller, but no different from the others in his expression. Hansi looked long and hard at the faces. They did have a kind of coolness, almost arrogance, about them. They looked sure of themselves. In other circumstances, they could have been his friends.

Hansi suddenly felt an intense curiosity about these men. He wished he could meet them face to face. There was much he ought to know about them. He was conscious of his own ignorance. There were large areas of the war he knew nothing about, facts and thoughts and theories, all quite unknown to him. He *needed* that information.

'Where is this northern airfield?'

Herr Prof took the magazine back. 'Scotland, probably, looking at those hills.'

'Have you been to Scotland?' All at once, Hansi thought of Herr Kaleut, and his enthusiasm for travelling abroad. It was a memory more sharp and painful even than his yearning for the Lordly Ones.

'Several times,' Herr Prof said. 'It's beautiful, but cold and damp mostly. We're better off here in Kiel, Hansi, believe me, even in a winter like this. Now for our evening game.'

He took out his chess set and began to set out the pieces. He had been amazed and, it seemed, genuinely alarmed to discover that Hansi could not play chess, and had taken it upon himself to teach him. '*All* U-boat captains should play chess,' he said.

It was another severe winter and there was often ice in the river. One day, it seemed to stretch right across the Kieler Förde to Heikendorf on the other side. But the little sausage boat, as Hansi thought of it, was taken out most weeks for trials. It looked clumsy and awkward when it was alongside, but under way it moved readily under helm and hydroplanes. Herr Prof had fitted aircraft controls, with a joystick which he said had actually been taken from a Junkers bomber, and once in its own element, the little boat soared and dipped and turned as gracefully as a dolphin.

After a trial, Herr Prof and Hugo and the men in raincoats who never said much studied their readings and assessed their results. They always invited Hansi to join their discussions, asked his opinion, and deferred to his practical knowledge of U-boats. Hansi had always believed that scientists and researchers lived in a world of their own, far removed from the real world. So they did, to a certain extent. But here, neither Herr Prof nor any of his team ever seemed to lose sight of the fact that they were designing a weapon. All of them, even Otto, who went home to his little wife in Kiel every evening, treated Hansi with a curious deference, which was difficult to describe; it was as though they all realised they were not debating abstracts in some scientific forum, but building a seagoing U-boat in which one day men would be called upon to hazard their lives. As always, it was Herr Prof himself who made the point best.

'We always have to remember the story of David and the well at Bethlehem,' he said one evening. 'Do you know it?'

Once again, as over so many matters, Hansi had to shake his head.

Herr Prof sucked his teeth reproachfully. 'Such a pity. One can learn much about men and their motives from the Bible.' Herr Prof took down his leather-covered Bible. When Hansi saw what the book was, he felt again a shiver of guilt, as though he were now conniving at something which was against the law.

'It is in the second book of Samuel. Chapter twenty-three. Starting at verse fifteen. King David was in action against the Philistines and after a hard day in the field he found himself longing for a drink of water. And not just any water. It had to be from the well which was by the gate in Bethlehem. But at that time Bethlehem was in the hands of the Philistines. But when three of King David's strongest soldiers heard the King's desire, they fought their way through the hosts of the Philistines, drew water from that well, and fought their way back to the King and gave him the water. And do you know what he did then? No? Instead of drinking the water, he poured it on the ground, as a libation to the Lord of Hosts. And this is what he said.' Herr Prof took the marker out of the page. This was, as Hansi could see, a passage Herr Prof had often read and pondered. '"And he said, Be it far from me, O Lord, that I should do this: is not this the blood of the men that went in jeopardy of their lives? Therefore he would not drink it."'

Herr Prof put the Bible down on his desk and looked directly at Hansi. 'Now do you see? There is a lesson here for all of us who are on the outside of this war looking in. For all those who make the weapons without actually using them themselves. All those who write about it later, without ever having taken part themselves. Whatever praise or reward comes our way, whatever success we may have, we should never forget that our reward was only made possible by the blood of those who went in jeopardy of their lives. That should be enough to keep us humble.'

Hansi found himself greatly looking forward each day to his evening talks with Herr Prof. He had never enquired whether

Herr Prof was married. Certainly there was no evidence of a woman or a woman's presence. But he treated Hansi as a son.

'What are you going to do after the war, Hansi?'

'I shall be in the Navy, of course.'

'Of course. I was forgetting it is your career. You must survive the war, Hansi.'

'I very much hope to, and intend to. There are times, though, when I do feel that very few of us will survive. There's a bar in Lorient where we all used to go. And a wall. We called it the "Black Wall". It's covered with photographs. Absolutely covered. We must have lost *hundreds* of men in the U-boat arm.'

'Nevertheless, *you* must survive, Hansi. Germany will need young men like you.'

In the longer nights of deep winter, the bombing raids became more frequent. Life in Herr Prof's works was more and more interrupted. One night a bomb landed in the compound and shook the foundations of the perhydrol storage bunkers, causing a leak and a serious fire. Herr Prof said that if the storage bunker had not been kept scrupulously clean, there would have been an explosion. Nevertheless, in spite of the raids, activity seemed to redouble. Herr Prof was growing more and more preoccupied with another, larger *V-Boot*. There were plans to build in the spring, as soon as the ice and snow had melted, a new research outstation at Bosau on the Plöner See, a lake north and east of the city, between Kiel and Neustadt; there they would assemble and test new torpedoes and small submarines. Meanwhile, Herr Prof delegated more and more to Hansi, who had to travel around as Herr Prof's representative, not only to works and departments in Kiel, but as far afield as the factory at Springe, near Munich — an assembly of vast sheds filled with electric cables and glass tubing where the perhydrol was manufactured by electrolysis. There were plans, so Hansi had heard, to build a second and bigger factory somewhere in the Hartz mountains.

As the winter months passed and everybody looked forward to spring, Hansi began to have more and deeper misgivings about the final end and purpose of all Herr Prof's work. Hansi recognised, and freely conceded, that he was only a layman in these matters, but he could see no overall objective in the furious activity around him. Herr Prof was undoubtedly brilliant, and he was surrounded by other brilliant men, but their brilliance was not harnessed, as an electric current should be to light a bright lamp. Instead, it was dissipated through dozens of filigree wires, all elegantly wrought and turned, but all ultimately performing no useful function.

This basic uncertainty and lack of direction was shown most clearly one day, when it was announced that, because of the air raids, much of their equipment, stores and records were to be moved to Hela, along the Baltic coast. But nobody could decide which projects, apart from the *V-Boot*, were important enough to be moved to safety. In the meantime, fresh directives continued to arrive, fresh solutions demanded to new problems.

One morning, as he lay half awake and half asleep, Hansi had a vivid dream, which he was sure was inspired by Herr Prof's predicament. He dreamed of highly-bred horses being rigorously trained, one day for long distance races, the next for sprints, the third to draw ploughs, and then, most curiously of all, to haul a hearse.

Before any decision could be made about Hela, a party of dignitaries arrived from Berlin to inspect and evaluate the *V-Boot*. Everybody could see that Herr Prof was unusually nervous before the visit. 'These people can make or break us,' he told Hansi. 'Our little submarine is so advanced they can't come to terms with it. And of course the Luftwaffe have been gunning for it ever since we started.'

The visit was so important that the names of the visitors were kept secret, and nobody even knew how many were coming until they arrived in a fleet of cars amidst the utmost security. But Hansi, waiting on the freezing, windy jetty with the rest of the welcoming party, saw at once that BdU was there in person. He recognised Hansi and shook hands. 'I hope you will have a success story for us today,' he said.

The evaluation trials went very well. BdU, his chief staff officer, and the other visitors went, one by one, on board the *V-Boot* and were shown around. Then they all embarked in the *Schnellboot* to witness a dived run. The *V-Boot* dived, trailing a splash target specially devised by Herr Prof on the end of a wire, and worked up to full speed of some twenty-five knots, although the splash target was torn away at about twenty knots. But its departure far astern seemed to make the trial run even more impressive. Hansi could see by their faces that BdU and his staff were impressed.

Afterwards, they had intended to give BdU a meal. Otto had gone to some pains to prepare a banquet. But the chief staff officer, inevitably, was always looking at his wristwatch and trying to hurry events along. So, in the end, BdU only had a cup of coffee, standing in Herr Prof's office. Everything was still going well until BdU suddenly looked at Hansi.

'Well Hansi, as an operational U-Waffe officer, what do you think?'

Hansi intended to speak up enthusiastically and at once. But he had a sudden stabbing memory of his dream, which made him pause. He really only meant to collect his thoughts and make his response properly but, as he later came to realise, his seeming hesitation was fatal. It made him appear not as an enthusiast trying to find the right words, but as a doubter trying to let his superiors down as lightly as possible. That fatal pause destroyed the effect of anything Hansi said. The result was exactly the opposite of what Hansi had intended. Far from strengthening Herr Prof's position, he had seriously weakened it. Hansi saw the consternation on Herr Prof's face and knew that however hard he now tried, nothing would erase the image of his betrayal.

Herr Prof said nothing, then or ever, but Otto did.

'You're too honest for your own good,' he told Hansi. 'Or anybody else's.'

Six or seven weeks later, Herr Prof was called to the telephone in the outer workshop. He spoke for some time. Hansi watched him through the glass partition window with a sick feeling that he knew what was being said. He saw Herr Prof purse his lips and frown, but then he put down the telephone receiver and came back. He sat down again at his desk.

'Ah well,' he said, with a sharpness of timbre in his voice which gave it away for Hansi. 'It's all cancelled. The hull is going to be abandoned.'

'Does that mean the project is cancelled, the whole thing?'

'Oh, I doubt it. There will be other boats, I am sure. But this one is *kaput*.'

'Just like that?'

'Just like that.'

'Herr Prof, do you think I was responsible ... Do you think what I said ... had any...'

'No, no. Put your mind at rest. They were shooting for us all along. It's my fault if it's anybody's. I haven't handled the political side as well as I've handled the experimental side. I should have guarded my rear, to use a military term. But for you, it means you will go back to sea now. But I must warn you, and I look to you to spread this word as widely as you can. There are signs the Allies are getting to grips with the kind of *Frontboote* you have now. You are going to need something better very badly and very soon. I hope this is just a setback, not a final defeat. Because this is a very serious matter for the U-boat arm. There will be more delay now. That is inevitable. Production of the perhydrol will go more and more to the Luftwaffe, and the design of a U-boat for you will be put back and back.'

Hansi was still numbed by the suddenness of the blow. Herr Prof's calm manner made it worse. It would have helped if Herr Prof had cursed and sworn and jumped up and down, or got on the telephone to BdU or his staff, or somebody. As it was, Herr Prof was just lighting a cigarette and puffing at it.

'So that's that,' Hansi said.

'That is that.'

'After all that?'

'After all that,' said Herr Prof.

CHAPTER NINE

Boysie heard the Captain's characteristic footsteps as he stumped up on to the bridge.

'What's that ship, Mister?' The Captain's voice, as always, was pitched as though he were talking to a specially dumb dog. 'Didn't I tell you I want to know when any ship comes closer than one and a half miles?'

'Yes, sir.' Boysie knew it would do no good to remonstrate. But for the sake of correctness, and also on behalf of the radar operator, he said, 'Radar reported that contact, sir, and estimated it would pass three miles up our port side.'

The Captain did not answer. He was staring through his binoculars astern. 'Great *Goodman*!' he said. 'Did you ever see such a thing? All lit up like a Christmas tree. You'd never believe we were supposed to be at war.'

The destroyer USS *Edio Jones* was steering north at a brisk eleven knots, but the great liner from astern overhauled her and went ahead as though she were standing still. As the Captain said, the great ship was like a Christmas tree blazing lights. Beyond her, on the shore, there were many more lights, a long swathe of them, of red and blue and yellow and pink neon, as though every hotel and restaurant and bar in Florida was putting on a carnival firework display. On *Edio Jones*' port quarter, they could see a huge swatch of light, which was Miami, with a lighthouse flashing its steady sweeping beam.

When the liner came abreast, they could hear the sound of a piano. Dance music, at night, off the Florida coast, in wartime.

'Thelonius Monk,' somebody said.

The sailor on port lookout sniffed audibly. 'I can smell women, sir.'

'Keep your eyes on your sector.'

But Boysie knew exactly what the man meant. It was indeed a languorous wind, breathing contentment and ease off the land, bearing the perfume of spices and unguent oils.

'What's the time?'

'Half of two o'clock, sir.'

'Call me fifteen minutes before dawn. We go to General Quarters as usual.'

'Aye aye, Captain.'

'And don't shoot up the turtles!'

The Captain guffawed. Boysie made an answering sound, just loud enough to prove to the Captain that he had heard and was responding. But he was not amused. Any humour in the remark, and there never had been much, had long since been ground away by repetition. The day after Pearl Harbor, when *Edio Jones* had been on passage down to Bermuda, Boysie had sent the whole ship to battle stations for a ripple on the flat sea. He thought it was a periscope. Actually, it was a turtle, basking, or maybe on his way to a date on the beach. It had been a genuine mistake and surely, Boysie had asked himself at the time and often since, surely it was better to go to battle stations unnecessarily for a thousand turtles than to miss one submarine? But the incident had rankled with the Skipper and he never let go of it.

The Captain was a career officer, an Annapolis man like Boysie himself, but he was of another generation, and had a way of thinking which seemed as remote to Boysie as the Civil War. The Captain had served in the last war from 1917 to 1918. As a very young officer in a battleship, the Captain had seen — as he never tired of relating — lines of dreadnoughts at Scapa Flow. His officers now believed that their captain — this peppery little man, with his bald head fringed by a light skirt of mousy brown hair, like a tonsure — had left his professional heart back there in that misty northern fastness. Lines of great grey battleships, awesome and authoritative, their huge muzzles swinging round in search of a foe, menacing the far horizons with their thunderous discharge, *those* were what the Captain's heart truly yearned for. *Edio Jones*, at least, was in character. She certainly did date from the last war. But nobody relished this ceaseless patrolling of the east coast of the United States, searching for U-boats which never came their way, but simply went on sinking ships just over the horizon.

So far it had been another good year for the U-boats. Just how good, the American public had not been told. There were no convoys, and ships were free to go their own ways, radios squawking, lights flashing, music playing, doing everything but showing a sign saying 'Come and get me'. Then there was the 'bucket brigade', which was a sort of semi-convoy, where the ships were half escorted, half not. The main coastwise shipping routes ran a few miles offshore, and the ships liked to go from light to light, town to town, from St Augustine to Jacksonville, to Brunswick, to Savannah, Georgia, and on up to Charleston. Then it was from cape to cape, from Romain to Fear, to Lookout and then Cape Hatteras, where the famous geese come and go. 'Bucket brigade' ships steamed by day, laying up in protected harbours or behind net booms by night. It was not convoy, but it was better than nothing.

According to the Captain, and here his officers wholeheartedly agreed with him, convoy was in itself an admission of defeat, a defensive last resort, a duty for third-raters and deadbeats. Here, there was a certain irony, because the Captain had not thrived in his profession and was lucky to get any command, even *Edio Jones*.

Somewhere up the coast was the next destroyer, *Miray,* as old as *Edio Jones* and on the same patrol duty. *Miray*'s Captain had been in the same Annapolis Class as *Edio Jones*', and they had hated each other ever since. Unluckily, *Miray*'s captain was one name higher than *Edio Jones*' in the Navy List, and he always counted that as seniority. It was made quite clear to everybody in *Edio Jones* that their first enemy was not the Germans, or even the Japs, or even the US Army, but *Miray*.

The radar operator had been reporting a contact to seaward in a monotonously hypnotic voice. Boysie had acknowledged his reports as monosyllabically and automatically. Groucho, the operator was nicknamed, although he came from Tennessee, and had an accent as thick and heavy as molasses to match.

'Sir, this is radar, I have a fresh contact astern of that ship.'

Something in Groucho's voice made Boysie put down his binoculars and walk across the bridge, intending to duck under the blackout curtain shielding the radar shack door and have a look for himself. But before he could bend or make another movement of any kind, the sky to the east silently lit up, like a ghastly premature sunrise. By the time the noise of the detonation had arrived, there was a great corona of angry light on the horizon, with a curious purplish centre to it. It was followed by a green afterglow as the unnatural sun paled and went out.

'Holy Jesus...' Boysie pressed the button for the alarm rattlers and took a bearing of the explosion. 'Starboard thirty wheel...'

The Captain was behind him, and then beside him. 'Why haven't you ordered turns for flank speed, Mister...'

'Sir ... That'll be a U-boat for sure, sir. If we go any faster we won't hear him on sonar, sir. It's only five miles away, at the most...'

There was a second, smaller detonation, and a flash of flame which lit the base of what they could now see was a huge column of smoke, blacker than the night sky. Now they could actually hear it, a long, rumbling, groaning, as though that ship were protesting against her mortal wound. As it died away, it could have been seabirds calling, or it could have been a man in pain. Or men.

'Radar...'

'Contact faded, sir!'

'You *sure?*' The Captain ducked down into the radar shack and stared over Groucho's shoulder. Groucho braced himself for some form of reproof. He and all the younger sailors believed that the Captain did not trust what he so obviously considered such new-fangled gadgets and gizmos as radar. That was not, in fact, true, but the Captain's disbelieving manner and tone of voice made it seem so.

'It was there for just a couple of turns, sir, and now it's faded. Both echoes now faded, sir.'

'The ship has sunk, and the U-boat has dived,' the Captain said. Nobody could argue with that.

Boysie also braced himself as the Captain came back on to the bridge level. The Captain's temper was always held on a very short fuse, and Boysie guessed that he had only just restrained himself from chewing Groucho's head off. Boysie could even suggest the Captain's likely words: 'You and your newfangled kiddology. Great Goodman, sailor, when I need you you have nothing to tell me!'

Whatever the Captain might have said was averted by a report from the sonar watchkeeper. The bridge telephone rang and Boysie answered it. The ship had now gone to full battle stations and the sonar was manned by the sonar chief himself.

'Sonar contact, sir. Bearing zero eight five, range probably six thousand yards bearing moving left.'

Even in that moment of excitement, Boysie could still register his own sensation of wonder and disbelief: it was all happening, the reports were all coming in, just as they had exercised them so many times, only this time it was real.

The Captain gave a great whoop of triumph and anticipation. 'Steer zero eight five. Now we got it! Save your dollars, men, the South will rise again!'

Zero eight six. The bearing was now moving right. It had to be their U-boat, trying to evade them. As the sonar began to report regular and closer contacts, the target bearing steadied. The suspense and excitement on *Edio Jones'* bridge wound even tighter. Maybe their target really was unaware of them and was going to give them a free shot.

Boysie, as action officer of the watch, had the con at battle stations. For just a few seconds, he had the leisure to look around the bridge and check. The sonar was on its target and reporting steadily. The depth-charge crews were reported closed up aft and ready. The Captain was wearing his steel helmet, which Boysie had never seen him do before, even during a full battle exercise.

Boysie had taken his own cap off and was reaching for his own steel helmet on its hook under the bridge rail, when the target bearing altered rapidly left. Boysie was about to order a new course to port when a dark shape crossed from the port side, less than two hundred yards in front of *Edio Jones'* bows.

'All engines stop!' Boysie called out. 'All engines full back! Emergency revolutions. It's *Miray*, sir! She's cut across us!'

Boysie could hear the Captain gobbling with rage, and spluttering the words, 'Great Goodman!' Although he could not see the Captain's face in the dark, Boysie knew that it would be swelling and turning that terrible, ominous turkey-red colour it always did when he was enraged. With the tinkling of telegraph bells and the shuddering of the deck underfoot, as the ship's propellers began to turn astern and bite on the water, the shape of *Miray* drew slowly ahead. She had turned to port and was now steering a course roughly parallel to *Edio Jones*, after executing the rudest and potentially the most dangerous manoeuvre at sea Boysie had ever witnessed.

Boysie realised that he should have made their lookouts concentrate upon their sectors. They must all have been looking ahead, where they expected to see their target. He should have reminded them of their duty. As for himself, he had failed in his own duty; he might have checked that all was well inside the bridge and the ship, but he had neglected to keep a proper lookout. Neither he nor anybody else had noticed *Miray* closing on them, obviously intent upon the same target. There had so nearly been a collision. This had been *Edio Jones*' first real experience of war and they had nearly goofed it. That U-boat had nearly pulled off the coup of the eastern seaboard of the United States: one tanker sunk and two American destroyers in collision.

There was no longer any danger of colliding; indeed, *Miray* was rapidly pulling away and opening the range so quickly that Boysie reckoned she must have been doing all of twenty-five knots. There was no chance of her being able to hear or detect anything at that speed. But that evidently did not deter her captain from attacking. Soon there came the dull thump of depth charges. They burst midway between the two ships and *Edio Jones* actually had to steer through the curtains of descending spray which swept across her bridge like a brief monsoon. *Edio Jones*' bows dipped and rose as she went through the water turbulence caused by the charges. It was exactly like passing through a miniature storm.

The Captain was talking, or rather gabbling, to *Miray*'s captain on the TBS. 'Say. Nanson, old man ... what do you know?' But *Miray*'s captain was also talking back with just as much vehemence. For some time, both men yelled uncomprehendingly at each other.

'Piss off ... Let *me* speak, for Chrissakes. Great Goodman, boy, *will* you let me speak?'

'Joe, that you?' *Miray*'s captain's voice came through, as though from a long way away. 'You run out, Joe, and I'll charge him.'

'Charge him, cowboy!' The Captain whooped with glee. Listening to them both, Boysie was reminded of two boys on holiday, playing with a stray dog in the street. They were both cackling and hissing with laughter and excitement.

As though infected by their captains' mutual enthusiasm, both destroyers attacked in turn, jostling each other out of the way in their eagerness to run over their target, in a way which frequently jeopardised the safety of both ships and entirely ignored the rules of the road at sea. In a frenzy of depth-charging, each ship attacked and ran out and turned and attacked again. Hardly had the spray from one depth charge pattern subsided than another followed. Meanwhile, *Edio Jones*' sonar continued to report a stationary target, suggesting that the U-boat had been at least stunned into inaction.

Eventually, Boysie began to feel faintly suspicious of such a docile target. It seemed this U-boat was asking to be sunk. But the Captain had no such doubts. He continued to shout and bawl at *Miray* over the TBS and send *Edio Jones* wheeling and charging over the datum point, as though he were gripped by some mad blood-lust which made him long to smash and crush his enemy — or, at least, to smash and crush it before *Miray* did.

At last, the message came up from the fantail that they were out of depth charges. Almost at the same time, *Miray*'s captain reported that they were in the same state.

'Well,' said the Captain. 'How about that? I guess we got that sub good. Signal pad, signal pad. I'm gonna spread the word. Everybody's gonna know that *Edio Jones* has gone to war!'

But Boysie remarked that there was no answering elation from anybody on the bridge. They should all have been charged up by success. But it seemed that nobody wanted to cheer with the Captain.

At dawn they returned to the place of the attack. The sun rose over a dead, flat, eerily motionless sea, which glistened red in that early light as though some giant wound had been steadily bleeding into the water all night. *Edio Jones*' bows hardly cut a ripple in the unnaturally calm sea, weighted down by thousands of tons of oil spread upon its surface. There were acres of oily debris. It was amazing that one ship could contain so much. There were boards, and boxes, and spars seemingly stacked in rows, and what looked disturbingly like the heads of men, but were actually only casks. Everything was coated with gummy black oil. It was a dead sea, on which nothing moved, until the ship's side sent iridescent ripples, green and red and blue in the sunlight, spreading out for a short way until they subsided. The largest piece of debris looked like a float. *Edio*

Jones steamed alongside it. But it was empty, and hardly moved with the wash of the ship's passing.

'That's our U-boat,' the Captain said.

The others wanted desperately to believe him, but they all knew that this was not their U-boat. This could only be the grave of the tanker sunk the night before. She had clearly blown up and burned and disappeared with all hands. Now there was not even a corpse to mark the place of her passing. Normally, there should by now have been scavenging seabirds by the hundred overhead. There was not one. Even the birds knew enough to keep away.

A party of sailors had gathered on the upper deck amidships, ready to haul in survivors. But there were none. Eventually their conversation ceased, and a hush fell on them as it had over the whole ship. At last the general depression affected even the Captain, and all at once he seemed anxious to disclaim any responsibility for this desolation and eager to acknowledge that it was the tanker, sunk by the U-boat, and no handiwork of his which was causing this ghastly stain over the sea. It was still spreading. Maybe the wreck on the seabed would continue to seep its oil for weeks. But it was strange there were no bodies. The whole ship must have gone up like a gas oven when a match is put to it. Perhaps there had been high-octane fuel on board.

Finally, they did find a body, one corpse coated with oil, bedraggled like a wasp in a trap. It seemed he had no skin left, just bare, scorched flesh. *Edio Jones'* sailors could smell the gasoline on him. It was an eerily homely smell, one they all knew, like any filling station back home. The body was naked and there was nothing, nothing at all to identify it; no clothes, no dog-tags, not even a tattoo, because there was no skin.

The Exec came up to the bridge to report to the Captain. He was the ship's second in command and his battle station was in charge of the Combat Information Centre, three decks down below the bridge. If there had been anything untoward about their attack, the CIC should surely have known about it. Boysie tried to catch the Exec's eye, but he was more concerned with the disposal of the body.

'Nothing to do but wrap him up and bury him,' the Captain said.

'But not here, sir,' the Exec said. Everybody agreed. Everybody knew that would be wrong. It would have been an added obscenity to have dropped that man back into that foul, still, oily mass.

'Let's get out of this,' the Captain said. 'To some clean sea.'

Edio Jones steered east, away from the land, but the oil stain seemed to go on for miles. 'Goddammit and Great Goodman,' said the Captain. 'Are we never gonna get out of this?'

The Captain looked at Boysie in a way which Boysie knew well, as any man recognises the coming of a storm which he has experienced many times before. Just now, it was Boysie's fault. At times, everything was Boysie's fault: the torpedoing, the tanker, the weather, the war — it was all Boysie's fault. To a captain who came from Kansas City, it was all Boysie's fault if only because Boydell Merton III came from Boston and spoke what the Captain called 'that Ivy League lingo'.

Fortunately, Boysie was saved by a telephone call for the Captain. 'Ready for you aft now, sir, for the service.'

From the wing of the bridge, Boysie listened to the Captain reading the burial service. He read very well. The words floated up, disjointedly, to where Boysie was standing. *'The dead shall be raised ... The resurrection of the body...'* They had a semantic meaning, but no *real* meaning. What were they *talking* about down there?

There were proper waves out here, and Boysie could hear them lapping against the hull above the humming and crackling from the sonar broadcast, which had been left switched through to the bridge. All the time, like a great clock, the steady, searching, pinging noise sounded out, and fled away, unanswered by the sea.

But, as Boysie was idly listening, there came a reply from the sea, a firm, answering echo. *Ping?* went the question. *Doing!* came the reply. *Ping!* — 'the answer to every sonar man's fervent prayer.' *Doing!* — 'the perfect target acquisition.' *Ping!* — 'right on the money!' *Doing!* – 'you got it!' *Ping!* – 'one for the textbooks.' *Doing!* – 'straight out of Casco Bay!'

The sound was blurred momentarily, as though the searching beam were just shifting its grip and reassuring itself, and then it came again. *Ping!*, as clear as a bell.

The Captain came up the ladder two steps at a time and arrived on the bridge beaming. 'Here we go...'

Then he stopped, and everybody realised it at the same time as he did: neither *Edio Jones* nor *Miray* had any depth charges left.

Boysie had heard the Captain swear before, and expected now an extended virtuoso performance of deep intensity and sustained conviction. But the Captain merely bowed his head and bore his disappointment in silence.

'We'll send off an enemy contact report and ask for backup,' was all he said.

The reply from Key West was, 'Stay with it, Joe. Your picture is on the piano.'

The Captain bit his lip. 'What the hell does that mean? Sonar, keep reporting...'

'Course and speed steady. Course one-two zero, speed three knots, sir...'

The Captain shook his head again. 'Steady course and speed, it's *unbelievable*!' He went to listen for himself. When he came back on the bridge he said 'Great Goodman, Boysie, this is one for the book. Solid as the White House.'

It was indeed a remarkably steady, solid echo. The recorder tracing showed a perfect target track, keeping steady depth. It never varied, never altered course, never showed the least inclination to evade. After a time, Boysie began to wonder about the U-boat captain. He was acting like a novice. But the Germans did not send tyros all the way out here to the eastern seaboard. All the intelligence information was quite the opposite: they had sent their starting team, with the number one quarterback and half-back line. Boysie had heard that the U-boat crews could actually hear the sound of the sonar probe against their hull. They *must* be able to hear that steady pinging, so close. Why didn't that U-boat captain make a move? Why didn't he speed up, or change course, or go deeper? Why didn't he at least do *something?*

Meanwhile, *Miray* had joined and was keeping station on their starboard beam. She had no echo on her set at any time. Her captain could do nothing except make faces at *Edio Jones* until assistance arrived.

The first to arrive was a USAAF Catalina flying boat which flew very low overhead. They could see the pilot's face, see his lips moving, but for all the contact they made with him he might have been on another planet. He made no response to any of their signals or waves, and could be raised on no known radio frequency. Sitting in his cockpit as he thundered overhead, only a few feet away, he was still as remote as though he were on Mars.

Shortly after midday, and before any support had arrived, *Edio Jones'* echo disappeared. One moment they had it, the next it was gone, and gone for good, it seemed. The Captain browbeat the sonar chief and all his operators, swore at them, pleaded with them, threatened them. It was no good. Their lovely, clean, clear U-boat contact had gone, just as though it had never been. By the time the other destroyer came thrashing up from Key West, so that they could see her smoke miles away, the sea below was quite empty. *Miray* had never had a sonar contact at any time. The whole weight of responsibility therefore rested squarely upon *Edio Jones.*

Boysie could almost have found it in his heart to be sorry for the Captain as he stood in the centre of the bridge, head bowed again, the picture of disappointment. To have such a chance, not to have any depth charges, and then to lose it before anything could be done, that really was hard to bear. The Captain was a competitive man who hated to lose, and hated even more to appear less than one hundred per cent perfect at all times. It took him some time to accept that he had lost. He stayed at the sonar set, personally searching for their great big, fat, juicy target. But truly it had softly and silently vanished away. Boysie found himself pondering again on the nature of that U-boat captain. He had certainly fooled them all, just as Boysie had been writing him down as a novice.

When Boysie went down to the wardroom for a late lunch, the only other officer there was Dwight Brugher, the Sonar Officer himself, who was just finishing a cup of coffee. Now that Boysie thought of it, Dwight was more responsible for that forenoon's events than anybody.

'Well, what do you know?' Boysie said conversationally. 'The case of the vanishing U-boat. A case for Ellery Queen. Too bad.'

Dwight Brugher was at least two years junior to Boysie and, in Boysie's opinion, had it all still to do on board. He had only recently joined *Edio Jones*, and still did not know how to handle the Captain. That made him nervous, insecure, so that he jumped at the least rise of the Captain's tone of voice. Boysie regarded Dwight Brugher sardonically. He was going to have to learn a few facts of life, and fast, if he was going to survive in *Edio Jones*.

'What do you reckon, Dwight?'

'I'll tell you, Boysie.' Dwight looked cautiously around the wardroom. 'I don't think there ever was a sub there.'

Boysie paused, a fork full of coleslaw halfway to his mouth. 'You ... *What* did you say?'

'Never was a sub there.'

'You classified it. You identified it as a positive U-boat echo. You got Doppler effect. You almost told us his name and number...'

Dwight flushed. 'I know, I know. I know I did. But we all make mistakes. It wasn't long before I was convinced it was a will-o'-the-wisp. But I just daren't tell the Captain by then. Not after all that build-up. It was only a patch of cold water, moving along in a current, was all.'

'Would that give such a solid echo?'

'Well, you know yourself now it could.'

'Not until you told me, I didn't. *That* strong? I heard it myself. But *I'm* not the sonar officer.'

'You see, the sea ain't a homogeneous mass of water, all the same density and temperature...'

'I know that...'

'Yes, but it varies so much you wouldn't believe, especially off this coast. There's temperature gradients, and density changes so sudden it's like a solid cut through the water. It's like a whole new world down there. Sonar's not a precise science. You know they like to think it is. The Skipper thinks it is, I guess. An echo is an echo is an echo. But sometimes it ain't. It's like a whole series of shifting corridors, planes of silence, and corners of mystery...'

'Say, Dwight, that's almost poetic!'

'Well, it's true. I guessed the truth soon after we started to hunt it. I guess my chief did, too. The sea just warmed up with the sun. As the sun got hotter, the sea temperature just rose a little, just enough. Our little pocket of cold water just disappeared, like a drop of water on a hot sidewalk in the afternoon...'

'Say, that is poetry!'

It was indeed a vivid simile, and Boysie recognised its aptness and validity. He had learned something from this conversation. It definitely had seemed a firm enough contact, and nobody need feel ashamed at being deceived by it. It did seem now that they were mistaken. They could all learn from this.

'You'd better tell the Skipper. It's something we all ought to know.'

'I can't tell the Skipper. It's over now. We know what happened. We'll know next time...'

'But you must tell the Skipper, it's important...'

'Boysie, *don't* tell the Skipper.' Dwight was pleading now. 'We got it under control ... we can learn from it...'

'You're darned right we can learn from it! That's why we've got to tell the Skipper. It could be a matter of life and death to somebody, a natural phenomenon like this…'

'Natural phenomenon phooey. It's going to make the Skipper look a jerk. Please, Boysie? Boysie, *please*?'

For a moment Boysie thought he might yield to the pleading in Dwight's voice and eyes. The lesson had been learned and the man needed encouragement. He needed support, not criticism. But Boysie also recognised that this was vital operational knowledge. Lives might be involved. It might one day be a matter of life and death for somebody somewhere to have the information that under certain conditions on a certain day USS *Edio Jones* had tracked a non-sub contact for some hours. That was a great deal more important than Dwight's self-esteem. In any case, he had to grow up some time and stand up to the Captain. Better sooner than later.

The whole ship could hear the roar from the bridge. 'Great Goodman! Send me that no-good hog-washing sonar jockey! Where is he? I want him up here pronto! Send him to me.' The Captain had begun to hop up and down on one foot like an excited animal in a zoo, and when Dwight Brugher arrived the Captain just restrained himself from seizing him by the throat. 'You stand over there, Mister, where I can see you! What is this, Mister, what is this? You telling me you made a fool out of me and out of this whole damned ship? You made a fool out of *Miray* and her captain. Not that I give a goddamn about that. You made a fool out of Cinc East Atlantic. You made a fool out of the whole United States Navy. You telling me, you really telling me we followed a piece of cold water for four *hours*? *Jesus*!'

'No, sir.' Dwight directed a look of hatred and reproach at Boysie. 'We didn't make a fool out of nobody, sir. We honestly believed it was a sub contact…'

'You believed … And now you're telling me it was nothing but a…'

'It was classified as a sub contact, sir! It was … it was, it was … it was a matter of opinion.'

'Opinion!' The Captain spat the word out. It seemed he was, perversely, almost enjoying this scene. But, as so often with the Captain, he came perilously close to making himself look ridiculous. Chewing a man out was one thing. Making a Metropolitan Opera performance out of it was another.

'What rank are you, mister?' It was a ritual question, but still needed an answer.

'Lieutenant, sir.'

'Lieutenant *what*, mister?'

'Lieutenant jg, sir.'

'Jg. That's right. You're a lieutenant jg, and don't you ever let that out of your mind. You don't have opinions. *I* have opinions. *I'm* the only one around here who is entitled to have an opinion.' That was so patently absurd a statement that it defused the situation. From menace and likely tragedy, it degenerated close to farce. Too late, the Captain himself realised what he had done. 'OK, you can go.'

When Boysie got back to the wardroom again, he was left in no doubt about the hostile atmosphere.

'Here comes Judas Iscariot. Traitor jg.'

'Hey, that's not fair,' Boysie protested.

'How fair were *you*? Don't you ever think of your buddies? You sold Dwight here right down the Missouri River, on a fast-flowing tide.'

Boysie conceded that there was a loyalty to one's shipmates. But here there was a far greater loyalty. But looking around him, Boysie saw that he was alone. Even the Exec, a man he liked and admired and whom he had always counted as a friend and a supporter, was looking disapproving.

'But can't any of you see that there is a...'

'Save it, Boysie. Save it for your promotion board. They'll like it.'

Surprisingly, the Captain also liked it. The 'false echo' incident, as it came to be called, seemed to change his personal attitude towards Boysie completely and all at once from one of suspicion and wariness approaching hostility, to a cheery fellowship and a sense of fellow feeling. It was as though Boysie, to the Captain's amazed delight and relief, had suddenly shown himself to be on the Captain's side after all. For a day or so, Boysie could do no wrong in the Captain's eyes. Oddly, Boysie was disconcerted by this novel approach, which made him feel even more uneasy and even more of an outcast in the wardroom.

Happily, a signal arrived the next evening which changed the feeling on board completely. It was the Exec who appeared at the wardroom door, waving a signal. 'Back to Boston,' he said. 'Clean fire tubes. Fit new depth-charge gear and sonar. New radar. 'Bout time too, I'd say.'

Boston was their home port and a wave of joy swept through *Edio Jones* like a Pentecostal wind. Home to Boston, home of the bean and the cod, where the Cabots spoke only to Lodges, and the Lodges spoke only to God. Boston was Soldiers Field and Scollay Square, the Mystic River and Chelsea Bridge, the Cambridge Parkway and Harvard Stadium. Boston had Harvard, where Boysie's family still said he should have gone instead of breaking family tradition by joining the Navy and going to Annapolis. Boston had more Irish than anywhere in the world, and the best kosher butchers in the world, and the goldest dome of any town hall in the world, and the narrowest city streets in the US of A, and the worst and coldest cold-water tenements in the state of Massachusetts, so Boysie's father said — and he should know, because his firm acted for some of the city's biggest landlords.

There was that same agreeable buzz of excitement on board as they came up the Massachusetts coastline on a beautiful evening, with the sun setting dramatically on the hills behind the old town. Boysie knew the old familiar navigational and pilotage instructions by heart: when Fort Independence is abeam to port, port wheel, steer three zero zero, and so up the harbour. There was the airport to starboard, and its control tower giving a good leading mark ahead.

But it was not like peacetime homecomings. There was no crowd on the quayside, no wives, no girls, no families, just men waiting to take their lines. As somebody said, even Boston Navy Yard had heard about the war.

Boysie watched to see the shore telephone lines being brought on board and then slipped into the Captain's cabin, where the first line would be connected. It was perhaps the single, boldest act of all his two years in *Edio Jones*. He would be leaving the ship before she left Boston, and the Captain would be writing up his fitness report. If the Captain came in and caught him using his telephone, it would ruin two years' previous good service. But this call was very important.

'Hello, that you, Nancy?'

'Boysie, where are you speaking from?' Her voice had that same unmistakeable sharpness. Nancy, too, was a Bostonian born and bred.

'Navy Yard. Can't stop to say more now. Can you get a cab to the yard and pick me up? Have supper with me tonight? I got something to tell you.'

'What time? There's nothing wrong with you, or the ship is there? You haven't been *wounded,* Boysie...'

'No, no. Nothing. I just want to see you. OK? Make it about —' Boysie looked at his watch — 'about seven o'clock. Pier twenty-five.'

'I'll ask at the gate.'

'OK. Bye now.'

Boysie swiftly put the telephone back and stepped out of the cabin. He was just in time, by a whisker. The Captain was coming up the ladder from the upper deck, with several brass hats from the yard. Boysie turned silently, ran to the end of the passageway and down the ladder on the other side.

It was much later, when he had had to wait his turn for the wardroom telephone, that he telephoned his home.

'Henry.' His mother always insisted on using his second name, and her voice was anything but welcoming. 'Your father's in New York. He'll be back Friday. You coming home tonight? You should have told us.'

There was no explaining to his mother. 'I'll be back later tonight, Mom.' It was a pity his father was not there. But his mother would do. He wanted to make an entrance, with Nancy on his arm. He and Nancy had some talking and some planning to do, that is, if all went well.

Edio Jones' upper deck was full of activity already. Attitudes in the Navy had been transformed by the war. Even here, in Boston Navy Yard, there were changes. Six months ago, they would have needed six months' notice of *Edio Jones'* arrival. Now they just had a signal and went right at it.

The cab arrived alongside the gangway only a minute or so after seven o'clock. It was like Nancy to be punctual. Boysie went down to meet her. He was conscious of every eye in the ship upon them as he kissed her.

'Hey, not so fast,' he muttered.

'What do you mean, not so fast? Aren't you glad to see me? It's been over six months.'

'Yeah, it's been a long time.' For reassurance, Boysie felt the small leather pouch with the ring in it in his coat pocket.

'You're looking thinner. Much, much thinner. And somehow more determined-looking.'

'I am thinner. *And* more determined-looking. It's all those movies we've been seeing.'

Boysie gave the cab driver the name of an Italian restaurant on the fringes of downtown business Boston. The cab driver knew it. 'Best veal in the city,' he said.

They sat back, holding hands. 'This is like the old days,' Boysie said. They crossed the river and headed into the tightest, most crowded and narrowest of streets of Boston. One street led to the edge of Scollay Square. There were sailors on the sidewalks, and girls, in pairs, in parties, in packs almost. Boysie had always thought it strange the place had such a reputation, as 'the best run ashore east of Galveston, Texas'. It was not much of a square. Nothing architecturally, with just some cafes with floor shows, if you could call them that. Then a tavern, two movie houses, a sandwich bar, a liquor store with something wrong with its neon light so that it flickered on and off all the time, a penny arcade, a cafeteria, a drugstore, a handful more cafes. That was all. That was what made it great. But it was home, just like Beacon Hill, where his family had always lived.

The restaurant was on the first floor at the top of a wide, red-carpeted stairway. There were booths, and curtains on rails, and panelled walls, and red shades on the light bulbs. There was a smell of candle wax, and meat and spicy sauces. It was where Boysie's father, although he disliked Italians, sometimes took business clients. It was, Boysie knew, an odd place for him to take a girl. But it was the only place he knew that was formal enough for such an occasion.

It was also more intimate than Boysie remembered it. There were far fewer customers. The maître d' was a lot more welcoming and at the same time more defensive in his manners. It took Boysie a moment or two to understand why. Of course Italian Americans would be defensive. The Italians were the enemy now. It always used to be the Irish who were the fighters.

Boysie ordered a bottle of the house red wine and told them to bring it before they ordered.

'Just as impatient,' Nancy said.

'I feel impatient ... It's difficult to know how to tell you. But I feel I have to get on with my life. I just have the oddest feeling we don't have much time.'

'How long's the ship in for?'

'I don't mean that. I mean something more than that. I want to get certain things settled. Like us.'

'Like us. I'm *glad*.'

'I have something I want to ask you. But not just yet. Not yet. I want to try and wind down a bit from the trip.'

'Was it bad?' Nancy's voice showed her alarm. 'Was it dangerous?'

'No, not really. A ship was torpedoed near us.' Boysie had a sudden vision of that appalling sky, full of unnatural light, and that tower of smoke rising on the horizon. 'I think when I saw it go up, like a firework, something touched me then. Something touched my heart. It was like I could actually feel something physical against me. In secret, you know? I felt, for a moment, that could have been us.'

'I don't see why we've got to be involved in a war anyway.'

'Ah, now, Nancy, we have to. It's corny, I know. Over there in England they've been carrying it all by themselves. It's time we did something. Heaven knows, I don't have much time for Limeys. You show me a Boston Mick who does. I know it sounds corny. But it's true. It is a fight for democracy. It is. So don't laugh. It touches us too.'

'I'm not laughing. Have you ever seen a Limey?'

Boysie considered. 'No. Matter of fact, I never have. Never seen a German either, not a fighting one. I expect I shall one day. Sometimes I imagine what he'll look like. Blond, maybe. A big man. Giant. Aryan-race type. He might be just as frightened as me.'

'Are you frightened? I'd be *glad* if you were.'

'Well, as I was just saying, there are times when it makes you just a little bit thoughtful.'

'It must be a really funny feeling, fighting men you've never seen and don't know. Just a shape on the horizon…'

'Huh, it's worse than that, even. It's just a sound on a set. A sound in an earphone. It could be anything. Maybe just a fish. But the man says, that's a U-boat so you go to war on it, by golly.'

'You mean, it could be one of *our* submarines, with our boys in it?'

'No, no, that's not very likely. Much more likely to be a non-sub contact. Say, I don't know why I'm talking to you like this. I'm not even sure I *should* be talking to you like this.' On an impulse, Boysie got up and looked over the partition of their booth. The booths on either side were empty. In fact, the whole restaurant was nearly empty.

Briefly, but as though it were necessary for some measure of easing his conscience, he told her about the chase after the will-o'-the-wisp, the classification of the echo, the fruitless search, the vanishing contact, his own decision to tell the Captain, the reaction of the rest of the officers. But Nancy's response was quite unexpected.

'I agree with them,' she said. 'I can quite see how they all got mad with you.'

'But don't you see...'

'No, I don't see. I've said I don't see.'

'But it could be a matter of life and death.'

'It could be, but it wasn't, was it? So you just humiliated that poor guy and made him feel about two inches high...'

'But he's not important...'

'Not *important*?'

'Not *as* important. Not as important as the ship as a whole, and the way the war is going.' Boysie was dismayed by the turn the evening was taking. Nancy was often like this; she took up an opinion on an emotional basis and nothing then would shake her. They shouldn't be talking like this, precious near yelling at each other. 'I guess that guy was on the slide anyway.'

'Yes, and you gave him that final push over the edge.'

'*Nancy*. Well, maybe I did, at that. Don't you understand? A guy like that could get us all killed. We can't afford to be *polite*, Nancy. I'll tell you something, the enlisted men agree with me all the way down the line. Even the sonar crew themselves. They got no beef against it. They're realistic about it. They *approved* of what I did. One of them told me so. It was the sonar chief himself.'

'And that must have been good for your ego.'

'Nancy, *please*. I got something I want to ask you. Can't we talk about something else?'

'You started it. You're not like the rest of your family, are you?'

'You mean, why didn't I go to law school like a good little boy? Follow Pop into the family firm. And what a firm. The biggest in Boston, the biggest in New England, maybe the biggest outside New York. Well, maybe I'm not like the rest of them. Maybe I'm not civilised, if that's what you mean. But let me tell you this … we're going to need guys like me, uncivilised though we are. We've had all the *nice* guys. The nice guys stop when you declare war. It's the *nice* guys who got us into this…'

'My goodness, what a pompous, conceited, arrogant…'

'OK, I am. Whatever you say. But I know my job and all I am asking is the chance to get on and do it and not be messed about by people who're still thinking it's the good old piping days of peace.' Boysie himself was horrified by the arrogance of what he was saying. But the words just seemed to boil up and spill over of their own accord, driven out into the open by the sheer force of his convictions. And now that he had said them, he felt a curious sense of peace. It was a relief not to have to be polite about what he was doing. Now that Nancy had so inadvertently blundered into the subject, and he with her, it was best to be honest. Maybe Nancy was wiser than she knew herself.

'Well, don't let me stop you getting on with your appointed task,' Nancy was saying. 'I'm sorry to be taking up your valuable time like this. Surely you ought to be getting back to your ship, *sailor*…'

She had stood up. Clearly she was about to leave. The maître d' came cringing towards her, apparently under the impression that something in his restaurant was at fault.

'Bye bye, sailor. I'm going home now, and leave you to get on with your war…'

'Nancy, I was going to ask you to marry me…'

'*Were* you?'

'This could be my last chance to ask you. This is going to be a big year for me. The Skipper's sure to recommend me for command now. I got one more course to do in anti-submarine warfare at Casco Bay and that's it. The Navy's expanding so fast I could have my own ship by the end of this year. Think of that!'

'Great. That's *great*. Give me a call when you make Admiral. I'll be *out*!'

CHAPTER TEN

Times had changed at Lorient. There was no welcome on the jetty. There was not even a jetty, and no trees, no crowds, no brass bands and no girls. There was not even the open sky. They had shut out the sky with concrete and steel many metres thick. Looking from down river, there was a row of dark square entrances, each like the very portal of the underworld, set in a forbidding cliff of concrete. The whole vast structure looked as though it had been designed, exactly like a U-boat's hull, to withstand tremendous pressure, which of course it had.

As his boat glided inside, it took Hansi a few moments to adjust his eyes to the dimness. It was a huge underground chamber, lit only by daylight reflected from the entrances and by a row of subdued lighting on the wall close to starboard. To port was a larger Type IX boat with a badly damaged conning tower; something very drastic must have happened to that. On a bare concrete ledge stood the welcoming committee: five or six workmen in overalls, and one staff officer.

Somebody put out the gangway, but Hansi had climbed down from his bridge long before the staff officer had reached the casing. Obviously the staff in Lorient were in no hurry. Hansi saluted, and reported his U-boat alongside and correct after a patrol.

'Welcome.' Hansi remembered this staff officer from his previous stay in Lorient. He was not more than a couple of years older than Hansi and had risen in the U-boat arm by staying firmly on land. He had done a couple of patrols in the early days, what now seemed the easy days, and then made himself indispensable ashore.

'No girls,' Hansi said. It was a statement of fact, not a question. 'No band, no flowers. I know it's December...'

The other looked curiously at Hansi. 'You haven't been here for some time?'

Hansi shook his head. 'Months and months. *Years.*'

'That's obvious enough.' The other looked at Hansi's growth of beard, the red-rimmed eyes, the pallor of his cheeks. He sniffed at Hansi's U-boat leathers. 'Rough time?'

'Very.'

Rough time? That was a shockingly inappropriate, a brutally casual comment from the other. *Rough time.* Perhaps he was only trying to be considerate. But 'rough time' was just about the biggest understatement of the year, perhaps of any year, of the whole war. It had taken them seven weeks to get round the northern capes of Scotland and make the trip down to Lorient. The weather the whole time had been as bad as anything Hansi had ever experienced, as bad as in those terrible early days. At times, Hansi had felt that he had no other existence outside the sea. It had come in over the tower rail and flooded in and out as though it owned it. It had treated Hansi and his officers of the watch and his lookouts as primitive organisms which had crawled out of its element, and was now and for ever afterwards trying to reclaim its rightful property. For days on end Hansi had thought the sun would never be allowed to shine again, the sea never be smooth, his hands and body and clothes never be dry and clean and warm.

They had been pestered and harassed constantly by aircraft, sometimes at dawn, sometimes at dusk, and occasionally at midday. There was no pattern to the aircraft's appearances. They had been attacked twice. The bombs had dropped a long way off, considering how close the aircraft had been, but the explosions were bad for the crew. They hated them because they tended to come without warning. At least depth-charging meant that they must have made a preliminary approach to a convoy or a target. Everybody knew the risks. But aircraft appeared literally out of the blue.

Two days out there had been a report that the main engine lubricating oil was contaminated. Hansi had even suspected sabotage at Kiel. But it proved to be one of the youngest mechanician's mates. He was tampering with the samples. He would draw off a sample of oil to test it for salt water. Instead, he added salt water to it, and shook it to mix it up. He then showed it to the Engineer Officer, who had believed it the first time, but not the second.

It was obvious what the lad wanted, or rather, what he did not want. He did *not* want to go to war. He wanted to go back to the Baltic and stay there. He would now face a court martial in Lorient. The only reassuring aspect of the episode, for Hansi, was the reaction of the rest of the Lordly Ones. They had been genuinely horrified by their mate's treachery. Most of them looked as young as he was: they were in fact no more than nineteen or twenty, and looked only sixteen or seventeen. But they had all been genuinely angry at their shipmate's behaviour.

'The Flotilla Commander is waiting to see you in his quarters.'

That, too, was a change. In the old days, as Hansi was beginning to think of them, the Flotilla Commander would have been down here on the jetty to welcome every boat in person. But now that BdU had taken his headquarters away to Paris, Lorient had been downgraded, while its resident staff had upgraded themselves. When the cat was away the mice all thought the more of themselves. It was, Hansi supposed, just one more sign of the times. This was the fourth winter of the war and looked like being the worst, from every point of view. The *Ostfront* seemed bogged down on the Volga. They had never taken Moscow after all, after all that Wehrmacht boasting; they said they had got as far as a tram stop on the outskirts of the city. But they never got the tram. The Allies were ashore in north Africa. Rommel was a sick man, they said, and his *Afrika Korps* even sicker, they said.

Outside the U-boat pens — which had never been penetrated by bombs, they said — there were sounds of drilling, and shouts, and lorries' engines. There were men pouring cement and carrying bricks, and baulks of wood, and lengths of painted metal. It was like walking through one of the biggest building sites in the world, except that here and there were some twisted metal girders, and a car lying upon its side, burned out, and a great deal of smashed debris and powdered bricks, broken in pieces. Hansi had remembered Lorient as a pleasant little town. Now it was a fortress, and a fortress under constant siege, it seemed.

'They keep bombing us,' the other officer said. 'Almost every night. They never hit the bunkers. Or hardly ever. If they do, they do no damage. They never will, with the bombs they've got. But they kill a few more Frenchmen in the town each time.'

'But what about that Type Niner back there, with the conning tower? Something must have done that.'

'Ah, him. He was a little unlucky. They got him on the way in. They knew he was coming back.'

'*Knew?* How did they know?'

'Have you ever heard the Atlantiksender?'

Hansi had heard of it, even on the other side of Europe. It was a radio station which purported to broadcast from Germany, or at least from one of the occupied countries. It had the most astonishingly up-to-date information on U-boat movements, on U-boat personalities and equipment. It was so well-informed it was difficult to decide whether it was genuine or not. Hansi had been told that many U-boat sailors believed it really was broadcast from Germany.

'The French Resistance tell them a lot. They seem to know everything.'

The French Resistance. Hansi turned the phrase over in his mind. The French *Resistance*? The last time he was here that would have been a contradiction in terms. The French did not *resist*. The French came to an arrangement, accomplished an accommodation, arrived at an understanding. Not a *resistance*. The French always jeered at the Germans, saying that Germans only had two attitudes, either at your throat or at your feet. The Germans retaliated with another jeer: to retreat was to 'advance like Frenchmen', *ähnlich Franzosen vorstossen.* The French only had one attitude — pleading.

Outside, even just walking through the streets, Hansi sensed a new wariness. Maybe he caught it from his companion, but he did detect the slightest, faintest tingling of danger. But that was ridiculous. The French never threatened. They shrugged their shoulders. They came to terms. They were realists, the French. They took life as it really was.

'The police and the Gestapo have taken some of the locals in for questioning,' the other was saying. He did not use the usual word for 'taken' but another with more sinister connotations: *umfassen,* to embrace. The Gestapo had *embraced* some of the locals for questioning.

'We do have to be a little careful.' The other was still talking. 'Things have changed in the town since you were last here. Nothing much, but there are certain streets which are, well, not out of bounds exactly, not banned in any way. But let us just say they are better avoided, especially after dark. People get killed. Life in France is always full of *nuances*. It just means we have to be a little more aware of the *Lumpene Franzosen* and their little ways.'

Lumpene Franzosen. Once more, Hansi was struck by the phrase. The French rabble. What a very odd way to refer to the French. Truly things had changed.

'But surely we take hostages, for reprisals?'

'Oh, yes. We take lots of hostages. For reprisals. And we kill the hostages, too. But that wouldn't bring *you* back to life, would it, if it was in reprisal for you?'

There, Hansi thought, was the true staff solution. The man had calculated all the odds.

'I sometimes think...' the other was saying. 'No, that's not true. I *often* think, I *always* think, that the French are the most treacherous, self-seeking, selfish, calculating people in the world. They have done almost no fighting in this war, and they have lost almost every time they have fought. But I sometimes think they will come best out of this war. Better than us maybe. What sort of a trip did you have?'

'Rough. I've told you already. You've already asked me.'

'And we shall be asking you again, my friend.' The other gave Hansi a sharp look. 'We have to learn as much as we can from those who do come back. No, should I say, those who come back. We shall want to know everything that happened to you.'

That at least was an improvement, in Hansi's view. Two years ago they would never have bothered with such things. Maybe Herr Prof had had a word in high places.

The staff offices were no longer up in the main château but down in a connected series of shelters, like another set of bunkers, built in the grounds. The steps leading down smelled of damp, rather like the cellar under Hansi's home in Leipzig. Some of the notices on the walls were peeling off. The other had to explain to a sentry who Hansi was. They had to show identity cards, and submit to examination of the documents, and a slow silent scrutiny of their faces. It was all very different from what now seemed to have been the carefree days of 1940.

But Hansi was glad to see it. It gave him a great deal more confidence. Possibly they were now at last coming to grips with the nature of the war. Possibly war had finally leached out the weaker members and left only the stronger. The main staff office was much smaller than its predecessor — necessarily, since it had had to be dug out of the ground — and very much more crowded. There was the *Kapitän zur See*, the Flotilla Commander and two or three of his staff, and a cypher clerk wearing headphones. On one bulkhead facing the door was a large map of the Atlantic, covered with symbols and insignia. There were photographs and silhouettes of Allied aircraft. Through another door from an adjoining office, Hansi could hear high-speed Morse. Everything certainly had a new air of confidence about it.

Hansi's chief interrogator was a man he had never met before, called Krause. He was known as Kratzbürste Krause. Crosspatch Krause. He had an abrupt, suspicious manner, as though he never believed anything he was told. He took Hansi through the events of his patrol, day by day, watch by watch, hour by hour. Like a skilled prosecutor, he was quick to pick up a change of story, an amended detail, an omitted reference, an added embellishment.

The story that Kratzbürste extracted from Hansi was a grim one, by any standards. Even the most optimistic listener could not fail to be impressed by its implications — of an enemy who was growing ever stronger, more numerous, spreading his searches ever wider, and using more and better weapons. The U-Waffe was still achieving great successes, but the way was growing ever harder. Hansi did not spare his audience any details. He believed in realism. The more they knew the better. But he was surprised and not at all reassured by their air of optimism. Hansi knew that he had been fortunate to reach Lorient. They had struggled in, exhausted in mind and body, he and his crew. And they had found to welcome them, as their reward for their homecoming, the sight of those forbidding, defensive U-boat pens, the smashed tower of the U-boat alongside, the acres of rubble in the dockyard area and in the town, and above all the atmosphere of wary tension, as though the whole place and everybody in it was ready to take cover at a moment's notice. Yet, here was the flotilla captain, and his staff, all as happy as boys on holiday.

'We have more than two hundred *Frontboote* ready, and another one hundred and seventy boats in training and trials. We've *never* been stronger. Last month, November, we sank over a hundred ships. This month's figures are slightly lower, but still very good indeed. And we've only lost three boats so far, since the beginning of this month.'

'Oh?' Hansi looked up. 'Who were they?' It had made him shiver to hear Kratzbürste talking so confidently. Were none of these staff officers ever superstitious?

'Gilardone in U-254. Von Jakobs in U-611. And Bade in U-626.'

Hansi did not know any of the names. 'What were the causes, do we know?'

'Aircraft, most probably, in the Atlantic. Bade, we are not sure. It was off the American coast. None of them answered signals when they were due.'

'Did any of them have trouble with...' Hansi left his sentence unfinished, knowing his point would be taken.

'Not that we know. None of them took radio direction finding. We think the dangers of that are greatly exaggerated. We now have Metox to tell us. The first *Biskaykreuz* detected up to thirty kilometres. The Metox goes to a *hundred*!'

The Biscay Cross. What a contraption! Hansi had seen the aerials on earlier U-boats looking like flying bedsteads. It was fixed bodily to the conning tower and to train it on a bearing the whole boat had to alter course. It looked inefficient, even to a layman's eye. As somebody had said, almost *sotto voce,* any navy that depended on something like that did not *deserve* to win a war!

'So things are definitely improving in that respect,' Kratzbürste was saying. 'It seems we have been overestimating the enemy's capabilities with radio direction finding.'

'But boats are still being attacked without warning?' Hansi knew very well they were. He had been attacked himself, and his boat had Metox.

'Yes,' Kratzbürste continued, patiently, as though calming a fractious child, 'boats are still being attacked. But we have reports from the interrogation of a British airman. He says the Allies have got a device for locating the heat from diesel engine exhausts. Possibly an infra-red detector, or something like that. That could be the explanation. Personally, I think it is. Also, another British airman, shot down over Hamburg, let it slip that Metox transmitted radio waves which could be picked up. So we have to be careful, too.'

Hansi had a memory of something Herr Prof had once said. 'But let us suppose the Allies have developed a radio direction finder which can transmit at shorter frequencies than Metox can detect?'

Hansi was not sure of his technical grounds, and his hesitance when using such terms as 'shorter frequencies' was obvious. It gave Kratzbürste extra confidence. 'Oh, no no no *no*,' he said, and smiled indulgently, as though thankful to be on firm ground from where he could squash such ignorant speculation, and the other staff officers, including the flotilla captain, all nodded with him, to give him support from *their* positions of superior knowledge. 'No that is not possible. The scientists all say that shorter frequencies are not feasible. Not scientifically practicable. Not technically possible.' Kratzbürste flung his hand out so that the palm was flat, facing downwards, in a gesture of dismissal. 'No, Metox is the thing. Mind you, you still have to turn it by hand and it makes the very devil of a noise in your ears, but a good operator will tell you of anything within a hundred of kilometres. Plenty of time to dive out of danger.'

Hansi found himself resenting this lecture from this land-borne warrior. He had another memory of Herr Prof. 'But I hope we are still going on with research?'

They all looked reprovingly at him. 'That is not for you to worry about. *Kapitänleutnant*s are for going to sea. Not for research.'

Maybe, Hansi thought, *but even if that remark were true, it is* our *lives at risk.*

'Don't you worry. *Seekriegsleitung* are convinced we have the problem beaten.'

After that, there was no more to be said, on that or upon any other subject. The *Lordly Ones* in Berlin had pronounced.

Kratzbürste nodded at Hansi. 'Now, you can go back and sort yourself and your boat out.'

In the town, the Hotel Beau Séjour had been destroyed in a raid. So too had the old cafe with the cycling photographs. Hansi wondered what had happened to the old girl and her daughter in the Tyrolean dress. The whole building had been razed to the ground. Hansi passed the site. It was just a stretch of mud with not even a tin can on it. Everything had been scavenged from the place. There was a strip of wooden fencing. Most of that had been removed for firewood.

The U-boat officers were now quartered in a five-storey concrete building much nearer the U-boat pens, down towards the old quarter of the town and the fish market. The building, intended as the offices of the sardine-canning concern, had been under construction when the Germans arrived. It was still unfinished, but its lower floors were habitable. Somebody had left the window of the room Hansi was allocated open, and the rain was blowing in. The air was very damp and cold, as though that chilly Atlantic rain had been blowing in for months.

Junior U-boat officers now used another, much larger bar near the accommodation building. It had once been frequented by fishermen, but they, like the cyclists in the previous establishment, now kept clear. One thing was the same: the great wall running down the whole length of one side of the bar, covered with the photographs in their black frames and mounts. Once again, Hansi had that weird sensation that he knew them all: for one fleeting, terrifying moment they all looked like someone familiar. The caps were all at the same angle; the eyes under the rims, the lines of the faces — all had a family resemblance.

But when he looked around the room, Hansi could not recognise a single face. They all looked so young, they made Hansi feel positively middle-aged, as though he were himself a survivor from another age. Herr Kaleut used to tell the tale of a Breton sailor who came back to his home town and found that he did not know anybody, although they all seemed to know him.

'What will you have, Hansi?'

Hansi frowned at the familiarity of that name, which the other had used several times, just as he kept on using the personal pronoun *du*. It was a small thing, but Hansi resented it. He did not respect this man. He hardly knew him. Yet the other was behaving like a bosom companion who had shared a dozen war patrols. Nobody had done that. In fact, now that Hansi came to it, nobody had survived a dozen war patrols.

'Champagne, of course.'

Champagne, as Herr Kaleut used to say, *is a great healer.* Herr Kaleut: that was the second memory of him Hansi had had that evening. Hansi had not thought of him for months. But Lorient brought him back — his voice, his wry humour, his fatalism. Fatalism had caught up with him.

'Cheers, Hansi.'

'Cheers, indeed.'

'Did you know we're planning a new exercise for the New Year? It's going to be a great *Razzia* on the convoys.'

Razzia. Once again, Hansi pondered upon the use of that word. *Razzia*. There seemed to be a second language in this place, used by the staff. *Razzia* meant a police swoop, a mass rounding-up of criminals — or, Hansi had heard, other undesirables in the Reich, and in the occupied countries. *Razzia* implied a helpless or at least a guilty prey, malefactors too frightened or too taken aback to resist or evade. That was certainly not true of the air and surface convoy escorts. They were only too ready to resist.

Hansi looked cautiously around the room.

'Pah,' the other said. 'Careless talk, you mean? We're quite safe here. No. We're planning something good, something big, for the New Year. Codenamed *Niederschlagen*!'

Hansi could not stop himself this time expelling his breath in one short, sharp burst of mirth, which sent stinging champagne up his nostrils so that he had to sneeze and cough, which, luckily, helped to hide his laughter. *Niederschlagen*. 'The Knockout Blow'. Oh, would it were so simple! A knockout blow implied that the opponent had a chin, a vulnerable part. This enemy had no chin, or rather he had a thousand, a *million* chins. Punch one and he grew a hundred more. That was not to say all was hopeless. Hansi quickly corrected himself. That was a dangerous line of reasoning.

'I wish it were so simple.'

'What do you mean?' The other was looking suspiciously at him.

'That very word suggests all we have to do is to have one more strike. One more heave, as the coalman said, and we'll win.'

'Well?'

'I wish it were like that, truly.' The expression was hardening on the other's face, and Hansi hurried to repair the impression he saw he had made. 'I'm not saying that all is lost.' Of course he was not; but even to say that was worse still. Hansi plunged on. 'Far from it. Of course I'm not saying that. The U-boat arm will do much more to win the war than all that pissing about in the Russian snow. All that will achieve is frostbite.'

The other laughed, and Hansi hoped he had repaired the situation. He could feel the champagne beginning to affect his head. Normally, Hansi had a hard head for liquor, but it was some time now since he had had any and, after the strains and anxieties of the last patrol, perhaps he was more susceptible.

There was the sound of table legs sliding across the floor and the crash of breaking glass. Somebody went sprawling heavily nearby. Somebody else standing next to Hansi said: 'He's working it off. He was in that Type Niner when she was hit. Lucky not to have his head blown off.'

Hansi swung round. All his natural caution had been dissolved by the alcohol. He did not care who was listening. 'But didn't his Metox tell him...' Hansi did not complete his question. He could tell how silly the words sounded even as he was saying them.

The big man next to him formed the word 'Metox' silently upon his lips, miming his contempt. *Metox Scheisse*, he was clearly saying.

The man from the Type Niner had got to his feet again. He was swaying. He opened his mouth, and he was sick, profusely and comprehensively, all over the table. The sound of the vomit falling was like waves splashing upon the table's surface. There was a tremendous cheer from everybody. The sick man blinked, and grinned, and waved his arms as though conducting an orchestra.

Hansi felt himself being caught up and carried along by the atmosphere of feverish excitement in the room. This was a cynical seizure of the passing moment. It was good to see them enjoying themselves.

Hansi looked again at the big man standing next to him. He had already remarked that the faces on that wall looked familiar. Maybe it was just the champagne, but this man really did look familiar.

'Don't I know you at all? I just get the impression that...'

'You knew my brother. I am Reinhardt. You knew my elder brother, Karl-Friedrich. I am his little brother.' Reinhardt grinned briefly. He was well over six feet tall, and burly to match his height.

'*That's* it!' Hansi could see the family resemblance clearly now. But this man was much more cheerful, a brighter version of his brother. Karl-Friedrich was the dark side, this was the light. It was a pleasure to meet him.

'How is Karl-Friedrich?'

The bright face clouded over. 'I am sorry to say that my brother shot himself. He could not go on.'

'But why didn't I hear? How was it I did not know?'

'It only happened a week ago. In the sanitorium where they sent him. You were at sea.'

'I am so sorry. But how did they let him have a gun?'

'*That* is being investigated.'

'I always felt we should have done more for Karl-Friedrich. He was a very able U-boat officer. He had a good eye, you know. Brilliant, in fact. Basically.'

'Basically, I know. He was good. But you needn't be sorry about it. Don't feel at all responsible. You could have done nothing for my brother. He was already dead, in everything but name.'

'It is still a great pity.' Hansi felt himself relaxing at last. It was not just the champagne. It was Reinhardt's company. It was an immense relief to meet a man he could befriend. It was like shedding a huge and anxious load which had been troubling him for months, perhaps years.

They were standing on a raised dais in one corner of the room, and Hansi noticed that, by some unseen act of protocol, all the officers drinking at this level were U-boat captains. The others drank at the lower level, at the long bar which curved round and extended down the facing wall. Amongst the crowd, Hansi saw his own first and second watchkeepers, and his Engineer Officer, and he wondered: who, then, was in charge of the boat? He ought to have checked that there was a shipkeeper, just as he ought to be thinking of paperwork, repairs, defects, all the myriad problems of running a boat. He ought to be down there, seeing that everything was being done properly.

'I should let all that go for tonight,' Reinhardt was saying. 'You've had a very hard time. I can see that in your face. You have the same look as Karl-Friedrich had sometimes. Why not enjoy yourself tonight, your first night?'

'Of course. I sometimes think I have lost the knack of enjoying myself. Just lost the way of it.'

Reinhardt nodded. 'I know the feeling exactly. Let's go to the Snake Pit.'

Outside, it was raining, very cold, and windy. Hansi turned the collar of his jacket up and dug his two hands down hard into his pockets. He began to jog lightly down the street, jerking his head from side to side, to clear the alcohol fumes, while his Knight's Cross bounced on its ribbon around his neck.

'You are fit enough,' Reinhardt said.

The Snake Pit was just the same, not bombed, and not redecorated either. Even the women were the same. They certainly looked the same, though a little older. *Like all of us,* Hansi thought. They all looked as though they had undergone a number of war patrols, too.

'These are not whores,' he said to Reinhardt. 'They're secret weapons.'

The place had the smell of a bordello, but an atmosphere curiously like a clinic. Clinical was the word for it. These women were not courtesans. They provided no entertainment, just a service, quick and moderately efficient. Cheap but not cheerful. Hansi saw some faces from the flotilla and the staff, and one high-ranking jacket hanging upon a peg. It was all chillingly brief and impersonal. A most intimate and tender act was reduced to a financial transaction. Hansi felt, in some odd way, cheated. Perhaps eventually there would be time, not for Hedwig or any of the women at home, and certainly not for women such as these, but for someone.

'Don't worry.' Reinhardt had seen the hesitation on Hansi's face. 'Think of it as cough mixture. I am still laughing at your remark about secret weapons. Very true! That was a typically French remark, did you know?'

Perhaps, Hansi thought, as he let his weight down upon the woman, *this is like France. Yielding for commercial benefit. Violation for profit. Fruitful, in the end.* That was very French.

The woman had already covered herself up again. Hansi could not be sure, but she seemed never to have looked him directly in the eye at any time. Did they never say anything? The thought crossed Hansi's mind that if these women engaged their clients in conversation they could be valuable to the Resistance. He stood at the end of the bed and waited, until the woman was forced to look at him, very briefly. There was not even the faintest flicker of interest. In a way, it was worse than active contempt.

When Hansi got back to his room he stretched out on the bunk and had time to become aware that it was damp before he fell asleep and slept like a solid log. The rain was still blowing through the open window when he awoke. There was a pool of water on the floor beside the window. Hansi felt sore and bruised all over, as though he had been beaten. He would have liked to have stayed in bed, but it was time to go down to the boat.

The Lordly Ones had heard a rumour that the boat was to sail just before Christmas. Naturally, they looked to Hansi, their Herr Kaleut, for confirmation or denial. Hansi had still not grown accustomed to the feeling of being himself 'Herr Kaleut' for a crew of young shavers still wet behind the ears. There was, as his own Herr Kaleut used to say, a part to be played in being a U-boat captain. One was expected to react in certain ways, respond in other ways, behave as though upon a peculiar kind of professional stage.

'Is it true, Herr Kaleut? Do we sail before Christmas?' The questioner was the radio operator, the *Funkmeister*. He was a tall, gangling youth from Saxony, with a shock of flaxen-coloured hair. He seemed to have little coordination over his arms and legs, but he had proved to be an astonishingly successful centre forward for the football team. From out of that flailing storm of seemingly unrelated limbs the ball would suddenly emerge, propelled towards goal with astounding velocity and accuracy. He was a good sailor, a good hand, and a good radio operator. He was very popular with the rest of the crew, who affectionately called him Kuddeldaddeldu. Kuddeldaddeldu also operated the Metox. He had done a special course on it. He said it was a remarkable instrument, and he had faith in it. That remark alone encouraged the Lordly Ones more than any reassuring pronouncements from the staff, and Hansi was grateful to Kuddeldaddeldu for it.

'I don't know,' Hansi said. It was annoying to have to admit one's own ignorance. 'I shall ask the flotilla staff again.'

But the staff continued to say they did not know, until one morning, when the whole town seemed to wake up knowing the news. They were to sail on the shortest day of the year. That, too, was a reminder of Herr Kaleut for Hansi, and he felt a shiver of premonition. St Lucy's Day again, and because of the tide, they would sail again at midnight.

The news was confirmed on the next broadcast of the Atlantiksender. Hansi was always surprised to note how openly the Lorient staff listened to it, when an ordinary U-boat sailor was forbidden under pain of the severest penalties. For the French, to be caught listening to the Atlantiksender meant deportation to the labour camps, or worse.

Hansi himself listened with the same feelings of guilt, as though he were taking part in some clandestine ritual, as he had felt when he looked at the pictures in Herr Prof's illustrated papers from England. It began, as always, with its signature tune, a very popular German music hall song called *'Es war in Schöneberg im Monat Mai'*, to which the sailors had put their own words: *'Ich war in Lorient in einem Puff...'*: 'I was once in a brothel in Lorient...' The Sender knew of that version; one of their regular and most well-liked broadcasters — a woman named Vicky who called herself 'the sailors' sweetheart', dedicating every programme to 'her dear boys in blue' — had more than once let slip that she knew of the sailors' version.

The Sender was always easy listening. German radio broadcasts were always very formal and correct, always using the correct grammar. The Sender was the usual *Deutschhochspiel*, with no regional accent or inflexions, but it caught the ear; it was slightly confidential, almost cosy, somehow disarmingly friendly and knowledgeable. This, the listener felt, was someone who knew how things were, who knew the score. He was speaking apparently from somewhere not too far away, maybe one of the ports on the northern French coast, or possibly from Paris. He sounded like a neighbour, and a very well-informed neighbour at that.

'...And all you little kippers at Lorient, you must be kicking yourselves over that Type Niner which was hit the other day. You were lucky, Wilhelm Steiner and all your crew. You only have a headache. Next time it could be your head. It really is your own fault. You would think the flotilla staff, old Kratzbürste and the rest of them, down there in their little rabbit hutch at Kerneval, you would think they would learn from experience. They always let you approach the harbour along the same bearing. You're not buses, you're trams! A blind man could find you by tapping along the kerb...'

Then the Sender said something which made every hair on the back of Hansi's neck literally stand out in bristles. 'Hello, Hansi ... Hansi-Dietrich Zschescher ... You had a good round trip, with just one or two misadventures. It's that Metox. It'll get you in the end. I shouldn't put too much faith in it. But you will be very welcome at Lorient, Hansi. The flotilla needs a good centre-forward, and you have brought them Kuddeldaddeldu. Now, that reminds me, for all you listening at sea: the football scores...'

In his surprise and alarm, Hansi had opened his mouth to speak, but the others had waved him to silence. One of the staff had a tape recorder, and there was also a shorthand writer, to take the full Sender's text down, just as it was said.

'I hear you're sailing on the shortest day, Hansi. It may be your shortest trip, too. Now —' there was a slight pause as though the Sender were shuffling papers — 'the bomb damage over the last weekend. In Lorient, in the Place George Clemençeau, where the Rue Victor Masse ends, and in the Place Alsace Lorraine, near the site where the old Hotel Beau Séjour used to be, before *that* was bombed...'

The Sender was talking about a raid which had happened just before Hansi had arrived. He could see from the looks on the faces of Kratzbürste and the other staff that the information was accurate. How the devil could the Sender know so much? While Hansi was still asking himself that question, the Sender went on to remind sailors at sea that high officials in the National Socialist Party were exempt from front-line service, by special decree of Goebbels' propaganda ministry, and gave the number and date of the decree. Instead, Party officials could join the forces for a short token period and then return to their work on the Home Front. The Sender had a list of officials who had recently returned to the Home Front.

Next was an item about a typhoid outbreak in the *Kinderlandverschickungslager,* the special camps for evacuated children located in the Eder district near Kassel, chosen to be far from the bombing. The Sender spoke as though his listeners already knew of the outbreaks; he was now congratulating the camp doctors on their selfless and almost hopeless task.

The Sender reminded his listeners that if their homes were bombed they were entitled to apply for compassionate leave under OKW order number 967/42g dated 28 August 1942. He advised them to apply for leave at once and to insist upon their entitlement. Lastly, the Sender urged his Service listeners to desert. The authorities would threaten reprisals against your families, he said. That was not possible, he said, because 'they do not know who is missing because he has been killed, and who is missing because he has deserted.'

Hansi did not know whether or not that was true, but he could see from the faces all around him that it might as well be true.

The programme turned to dance music, and somebody turned the set volume down.

'It's propaganda,' Hansi said, although he knew it was not. Most of these news items had the uncomfortable hard ring of truth.

Kratzbürste shook his head. He was looking unusually thoughtful. 'It *is* propaganda,' he said. 'But of a very special kind. It is difficult to know what to do about it. One example: he talks freely about Metox. How can we tell the sailors not to talk about Metox when he broadcasts it far and wide as though everybody in the world knows about it. Sometimes they put the Führer himself on, and it is a recording of a true broadcast by the Führer. But, whether by accident or not, they put it just after a news item about the scarcity of contraceptives in somewhere like Neustadt or Lübeck. What effect do you think that has on sailors listening?'

Nobody had dared to laugh. Kratzbürste's voice showed how worried he was. For the first time since he had met Kratzbürste, Hansi had the impression that the man felt that he was being *intellectually* bested, and that hurt more than anything else.

Hansi had expected that after the Sender's revelation of their sailing date, the patrol orders would be changed. But to his amazement plans went ahead. It was as though the Lorient staff lived in a hermetically sealed world of their own; they listened to what the Sender said, were concerned about its possible effects, but did not allow it to affect their own plans in real life. Hansi protested against their sailing date as strongly as he dared, but he was overruled. Furthermore, there was to be no chance of a shake-down cruise. They would go straight on patrol, and with a crew who were mostly raw. Several of the 'experienced' men had been replaced by new recruits from the pool in Lorient. Despite his anger and consternation, Hansi had to smile at the staff use of the word 'experienced'; anybody who had been on one patrol was now 'experienced', and Hansi himself was as 'experienced' as Methuselah.

Hansi had a formal staff briefing on the eve of sailing. This, too, was an innovation which showed a more professional outlook compared with Lorient in the old days.

'We've had instances of boats returning prematurely,' Kratzbürste said. 'They were surprised and attacked from the air. We suspect they had turned their Metox off because they did not like the noise it made.' He looked at Hansi. 'I hope that will not happen to you. We will check the weather forecast with the Luftwaffe.'

Hansi only just suppressed his giggle. Check the weather with the *Luftwaffe*? The Luftwaffe would not know whether it was Wednesday or Christmas, let alone whether it was going to rain or not.

In the event, the Luftwaffe forecast was for a cloudy start, clearing from the west to give a fine bright night. The sailors brought on board a Christmas tree and green branches before they sailed at midnight — in a snowstorm, the first of that winter in northern France. Going down harbour, the snow whirled ever thicker around the U-boat, so that Hansi could hardly pick out the dim stern light of the minesweeper they were following. As the estuary began to broaden, the visibility dropped almost to nothing, so that Hansi had to creep cautiously out, steering by magnetic compass. He did not see the minesweeper again, and missed its farewell signal, if it had ever made one. But he could tell by the lifting of the U-boat's bows, steadily rising and falling, that they were reaching the open sea. One larger wave slapped heavily, like an omen, upon the forward casing, and its ice-cold spray flew over the bridge and stung Hansi's cheeks and mouth.

Further out, where the depth of water below the keel increased, Hansi took the U-boat down for a test dive, to catch a trim. Considering the inexperience of his Engineer Officer, and of everybody else, it was not at all bad. They surfaced and got on both diesels, steering out into the Bay of Biscay on Christmas Day. Half an hour before dawn, as Hansi was preparing to dive, the aircraft appeared overhead.

There was no warning from the Metox, which was switched on at the time, not a squawk of alarm from anywhere, no sighting by any lookout, no sign or sound of any kind. One moment the U-boat was alone and unmolested, and the next the attacker was actually right over their heads.

Luckily, the bombs were poorly aimed, and dropped a hundred metres or more on the starboard quarter. The Tommy airman, as usual, had been much too eager. He was out for line, because he had not waited to get on the proper course, and he was out for range, because he had been in too much of a hurry, too anxious to get overhead before the U-boat went down.

Hansi decided to stay dived until it was dark again, which was not long at that time of year. Every hour he brought the boat to periscope depth, but all he ever saw was the dreary wash of grey sea and grey sky. The tide changed, and Hansi reckoned that for much of the day they were only just stemming the tide at their dived speed. It was a cheerless and dispiriting start to the patrol.

Dusk came early, and they were able to surface soon after four o'clock. They started both main engines, blew round the main ballast tanks, and began to plunge westwards and northwards again into the open Atlantic.

Kuddeldaddeldu had been puzzled by the failure of his Metox, and unable to explain it. He brought the Metox up to the bridge himself. It was the very latest type of *Biskaykreuz*, and Kuddeldaddeldu rigged it himself, carefully tested the circuits, checked that voltmeter and ammeter were reading correctly, and that there was no signal except the regular tuning signal. When he was satisfied, he held up his thumb.

'Make sure you get it this time!' Hansi shouted to him, over the steady drumming of the engines. Kuddeldaddeldu nodded and held up his thumb again, and went below to keep watch.

It was the blackest of all nights, and perfect for U-boat warfare. *The year's midnight indeed,* Hansi thought. There was not the slightest lifting of the darkness, not even a glimmer of the wake astern. It was so dark Hansi could only sense, not see, his own hand in front of his face.

But once again, after they had been on the surface barely half an hour, they were caught. This time the attacking pilot seemed to have profited from the other's experience, and his bombs very nearly obtained a direct hit. The U-boat seemed to stop in its headlong progress, and rear up, and plunge down again, like a horse with an axe laid to its neck. Hansi pressed the diving hooter and fell down the ladder after the lookouts, while the roar of escaping air and the reverberations of the explosions all mingled together in one long dreadful booming shudder of sound.

For a long time, Hansi did not know whether his boat was diving or sinking. They were still over the continental shelf, so at least they did not have to reckon with the awesome abysses of the far Atlantic. The U-boat hit the bottom of the sea with a shattering impact that shook every tooth in Hansi's mouth. While he bit his tongue on the shooting, agonising pain, voices all around him cried out in terror. The hull groaned and shrieked as it wormed and wriggled, like some great wounded lizard, across the rocks and shingle of the sea bed. It made a noise as though the sea itself were protesting against the intrusion of this monstrous foreign object, as though even the sea was rejecting them.

Reports of flooding were coming in from every compartment, but the worst seemed to be aft. Hansi went to look for himself, and he could hear the noise of the water rushing in as soon as he left the control room and began to walk aft. The Engineer Officer was crouching in the aftermost, narrowest part of the hull, just above the propellor shaft glands and the rods and cylinders of the after hydroplanes operating gear.

'A seam has split,' the Engineer Officer said. 'Wrenched apart, Herr Kaleut. We have the pump going and we should be able to control it. But I doubt if we could dive to full depth. I think we should go back.'

'Never. What else?'

'Rudder's jammed amidships, Herr Kaleut. We hope we can move it by hand. Emergency hand steering may be usable.'

'What else?'

'Salt water in the main diesel lubricating oil. I have not seen it for myself, but I am told it is the real thing this time.' He exchanged glances with Hansi and shrugged his shoulders.

'Can you run the engines?'

'We hope so, Herr Kaleut. They may get us back. But no more.'

Hansi had instinctively dismissed the suggestion of returning from patrol early. But it now seemed there could be no question of continuing, indeed they might be lucky even to get back to Lorient. That was now the very most they could hope for. The first problem was to regain the surface. The second would then be to propel themselves back to harbour.

In fact, the boat came to the surface without any great trouble. Hansi ordered all main ballast tanks blown with high-pressure air. There was a heart-stopping moment or two when the boat would not move off the bottom, as though it were actually reluctant to go up and meet further punishment. But then the deck shifted, and tilted, came alive and moved, and they began to rise. Once the boat was going up it was impossible to stop. Hansi had intended to try and catch a trim at periscope depth and wait and see if there was anything up there. But nothing would prevent the boat soaring on and upwards until it lay, wallowing and swinging from side to side, in the surface swell.

The night was still as black as ever, but the wind was getting up and the sea with it. Hansi was relieved to hear both diesels starting and to feel the joyful shuddering underfoot as the boat surged forward under power although, as the engineer said, it was a matter of hope and conjecture how long the main bearings would last with such poor lubricant. Hansi ordered full ahead. They blew round the main ballast tanks again to give the maximum buoyancy. It was going to be a dash for safety. Having spent the day before submerged, they only had about thirty miles, or perhaps two hours, to endure.

But within seven or eight minutes of surfacing, just long enough, Hansi calculated, for the waiting aircraft to pick up the echo on its screen and close the distance, they were attacked again. This time there were no explosions at first, but a blinding light approaching from astern. The millions of candle power seemed to stun the senses, to deprive Hansi of all his reasoning powers. He could think of nothing to do, make no decisions. His whole being seemed battered down into cowed submission by the almost physical power of the great light. Then came the explosions, near, but not so near as the ones before. The attack had been bungled. They had been too eager again. Nevertheless, Hansi knew that for the first time in the war his enemy had had him at his mercy. For a few seconds, Hansi had been helpless, and as near death as he had ever been.

They could not dive. With that leak they would never surface again. Hansi roared down the tower for the 20-millimetre guns' crew. They came floundering up, after what seemed an age. Hansi could not see them, but he knew by their actions, by the movements of their bodies, that they were all terrified. He felt for the gunlayer's body and clapped him on the shoulder.

'Fire at the light!' Hansi bawled at the man. 'Do you hear me? When he comes back fire at the light and keep on firing! Don't wait for another word. *Fire!*' He pounded the man on the back until he felt him nodding that he understood.

The light returned and this time they were able to meet it with a stream of tracer. There were more explosions. Hansi knew that anything close now would finish them. But the gunfire did make the light more cautious. The bombs dropped even further off. Hansi ordered the wheel hard-a-port and then hard to starboard. He could see the flashes from the gun's barrel although curiously he could not hear a sound. Shaken as he was, Hansi realised why they were still alive. The bombs had been too far away and had exploded too deep. The damage was bad, but not lethal. Hansi forced himself to grin. His enemy had just had a chance to kill him and had missed it. Hansi knew now they would reach Lorient. They were going to survive. *Christmas in Lorient after all,* he thought.

But for the moment Lorient was closed to them, and hostile. The harbour would only be cleared and opened for them when a U-boat or any other vessel was expected, when signals had been sent, emergency recognition procedures carried out, when reassurances had been given that the vessel approaching from the sea was not an enemy but one of their own side, and badly needing help.

Hansi had just ordered the sequence of emergency recognition signals to be sent when the port main diesel stopped. Hansi had just become aware of it when the starboard engine also stopped.

'It's the oil, Herr Kaleut,' the engineer was shouting up the voice-pipe. 'It's like gum. The pumps won't pump it any more.'

'Can't you get the engines started?'

'No chance of that. They are seized solid. It is a miracle they have lasted as long. You can stand a spoon up in the oil.'

'We can make it on electric motors.'

'The starboard one is defective. There are flashes and short circuits every time we make the breakers, Herr Kaleut. It's no good.'

So it was on one electric motor, with a battery almost flat, hand steering, a wrecked stern, and pumps working at full speed to keep the water level down, that Hansi's boat came alongside again in Lorient, less than thirty-six hours after it had left. There were some long faces amongst the reception committee waiting in the U-boat pen, and some even longer ones in the staff bunker when they heard Hansi's account of what had happened.

But the Lordly Ones did not bother to conceal their delight at their return. They did not seem in the least concerned by the dangers they had survived. Christmas ashore was well worth a spot of bombing from the air.

The jubilation of Hansi's sailors aroused the suspicions of the staff. Hansi was at first amused, and then alarmed, by whispers that his damage had been all too convenient. To Hansi it was a fantastic suggestion. Nobody could *arrange* to be attacked. Nobody could calculate the odds so precisely as to be damaged just badly enough to have to return, but not so badly as to be sunk. The idea was preposterous. Surely, even a staff officer could understand that?

But it seemed not. *Leitung* meant 'staff'. But there was an old saying, *Eine lange Leitung haben*, which meant 'to be slow on the uptake'. It was not much of a joke, and it could be dangerous to make it. But Hansi found himself thinking of it more than once during his first interview — which was more like an interrogation — with the flotilla captain and his staff. At first, Hansi put their attitude down to the natural obtuseness of staff officers. He had expected sympathy, or perhaps even praise for having rescued his boat from a difficult set of circumstances. But he found that the atmosphere was not sympathetic, nor even neutral, but actually hostile.

'The Führer is not keen on the Navy,' the flotilla captain was saying. Those words alone were enough to strike a warning bell. Matters must be serious for the flotilla captain even to think such a thing, let alone say it out aloud. 'There must not be the faintest suspicion anywhere that the Navy is not trying hard enough. Admiral Dönitz himself is concerned that some U-boats may be giving up too easily...'

'Giving up too *easily*?' Hansi's incredulous voice made them all look up sharply. 'Sir, I have just brought my boat back, after great dangers to our lives. The stern of the boat was flooded because the hull was breached by bombs. The steering was jammed. We had no main diesels and only one main electric motor. We were bombed three times, out of the blackness, with no warning. Not *trying* too hard? If that refers to us that is an accusation against our honour...'

'Not unless you understand it to mean that,' Kratzbürste said. 'If the cap fits, you must wear it.'

'But that is an insult!'

'There is the strong suggestion, suspicion even, that you had your Metox switched off because of the noise it made...'

'Switched off ... Metox ... Because of the *noise?*' Hansi found himself gasping for breath, for words, for himself to be believed, for this nonsense to be refuted once and for all. 'No matter how awful the noise is...'

'So you do admit it is bad?'

'Of course it's bad. Everybody knows that. But no matter how bad it was, it is not as bad as the sound of bombs exploding beside you. Nobody but a lunatic would switch Metox off. Nobody would deprive themselves of any means, any means at all, of knowing when an aircraft is coming at you. Nobody would be so foolish...'

'Oh, yes, they would,' Kratzbürste interrupted.

'Who? Tell me, somebody!'

'A survivor from U-457. A fishing vessel in the Bay picked him up. He was the only one. He was almost dead. But he was alive long enough for them to ask him when they got him back. He wouldn't say anything, but they played the sound of the Metox in his ear...'

'But that's torture!'

'So *you* say. It did it. He howled and cried and screamed. It reminded him, you see.'

'But that doesn't prove anything! Who was he, this survivor?'

'He was the chief boatswain's mate.'

'But he wouldn't hear the Metox! Only the operator would hear it, in his earphones! This survivor wouldn't even know what to listen for. It's a skilled business. Maybe he associated that sound with the last moments of his boat and his shipmates. But what that man said is no proof of what happened in that U-boat with the Metox!'

Hansi saw that he had scored a major hit. There was definite doubt on those faces which had been accusing him. But Kratzbürste seemed immoveable and implacable.

'Your Metox operator, is he reliable?'

'Of course he is...'

To Hansi's dismay, the interrogation was now proceeding as though he had said nothing in his defence. The others took their cues from Kratzbürste's certainty. Eventually, Hansi went back to his boat, furious at his treatment. He sent for Kuddeldaddeldu.

'Did you at any time switch off the Metox, because of the noise, or for any other reason?'

'No, Herr Kaleut.' Kuddeldaddeldu looked genuinely puzzled. 'Why should I do that? The Metox didn't make any noise, not at any time. I had no signal at all for any of those attacks. That is what puzzles me. There was nothing wrong with the apparatus.'

'That is what I thought, I wanted to make sure. Thank you. You can go back to your carol practice now.'

It was the most miserable Christmas Hansi had ever spent. For no reason given, none of his officers or crew were allowed leave. There was mail on Christmas Eve, with letters from home and some presents. Hansi had a box of cigars from Hedwig and some homemade marshmallows from his mother. In his letter, his father seemed depressed; he had failed to get promotion to Senior *Blockführer*, and the news from the east refused to get better.

The Lordly Ones had a carol service, for which they had practised hard, in the control room. Inevitably, it aroused memories in Hansi of that other carol service what seemed like a century ago. As he heard, and sang again, *Stille Nacht,* he could see Herr Kaleut's pensive face on the other side of the periscope standards, looking at him and smiling. Hansi found his eyes streaming with tears again. That was the most frightening aspect of the war. Tears came more easily all the time. The war should be hardening them. Instead, it was making everybody more vulnerable.

It was raining when Hansi walked up from the boat to the hotel. It stopped raining and began to snow. The wind blew from the north in tremendous gusts, which swept the smoke from the chimneys down to street level. There were several air raids a week now, sometimes one or two a day. There was even an alert on Christmas Day. So much for the old stories of a Christmas truce in the Kaiser's war. No truce here, from the enemy or the weather. Hansi saw in the staff offices signals from U-boats at sea reporting the most appalling weather of the war, of constant storms surpassing in duration and ferocity even those of two years before.

Kratzbürste was unimpressed by the signals. With the inimitable staff officer's philosophy, he remarked that he did not believe the Atlantic weather was any worse in recent years. It was just that there were more ships and men out there to experience it and to complain about it. That, Hansi thought, was the typical staff officer's solution, and what made it even more annoying was that it was very probably true.

New Year's Eve should have been merrier. Hansi spent almost all of it in the cafe with Reinhardt. They drank champagne at first, and then, when it made them thirsty, they went on to brandy and water. But as the day drew on and night fell, the alcohol seemed to depress them. They sat at a table by the window, toasting the new year of 1943. It seemed that both the blackout and curfew had been relaxed for that night. There were Frenchmen passing by in the street and looking in through the window. They were not envious. They showed no emotion at all. As a nation, the French were still *collaborateurs*, to use their own word.

Two days later, there came news of a disaster for the Kriegsmarine, somewhere up in northern waters. The Führer was an Army man, everybody knew that, and always suspicious of the Navy. Before the war, and throughout German history, even before Bismarck had pulled all the sovereign states into one Reich, the Army has been everybody's favourite, and the Senior Service. That being so, it was all the more necessary for its very survival that the Navy should appear to be successful.

The story first emerged as rumours in the staff office. It took some time for a version of the facts to appear. The Atlantiksender, inevitably, had a full account. Hansi listened bitterly to that cheery, gossiping voice. It would have been better had the Sender betrayed any jubilation. Instead, he related it as though it were the most natural series of events in the world, no more than any reasonable man would ever have expected.

The more one heard, the worse it seemed. A strong task force — of a battleship and a heavy cruiser — had actually come across an English convoy somewhere to the north of Norway in the Barendts Sea, on its way to reinforce the Russian front. It should have been a massacre. They should have fallen upon those fat morsels like wolves upon the fold. Unfortunately, the sheep had fought back with surprising skill and bravery. The German ships had been fended off, diverted, fooled, bluffed, made absolute idiots of, by a small force of English destroyers. The commander of the German force had hesitated, lost his chance, and the greatest day of his career had passed him by. It was bad for him, and even worse for the Navy. Raeder had promised the Führer a great victory. The Führer had for once believed him. Instead, the Führer had been given a fiasco and, to rub salt into it, he had heard it first from the British radio broadcasts.

Shock waves from the force of the Führer's rage stretched out to the furthest limits of the Kriegsmarine. The surface ship navy had been to blame, but it seemed the whole Navy had to bear the Führer's sarcastic fury. Even the U-boat arm was somehow implicated, and stained with the disgrace.

The defeat in the north had immediate personal repercussions for Hansi. More interrogators arrived, from Paris and then from Berlin, to question him about the circumstances of his premature return, 'premature' in their opinion, at least. Clearly they were seeking a scapegoat, and having for some reason decided to step around Hansi himself, they seized upon Kuddeldaddeldu.

They were convinced, they said, that Kuddeldaddeldu had sabotaged his own equipment. If he had not sabotaged it, then he had failed to keep it in proper repair. If it was not that, then he had failed to report the signals when he should have done. If not that, then he had misunderstood, through incompetence, those signals. If he had not ignored them, then why had he not reported them? If there were no signals, as he still insisted, then the equipment must have been badly maintained. Or, if not badly maintained, then it must have been sabotaged. The questioning went on and on, returning in a circle in this manner.

Kuddeldaddeldu, who had been confident of his own competence and had treated his inquisitors at first with good-humoured tolerance, eventually took fright. He appealed to Hansi to support him. Hansi tried, but had no more success with the staff on his crewman's account than he had on his own. Besides, the constant, grinding suspicion had aroused misgivings in Hansi himself about the efficiency of the Metox.

This had a further and disastrous effect; he was only unsure about the equipment, but the interrogators assumed he was unsure of Kuddeldaddeldu.

It was as though Hansi and his whole boat had been marked out as scapegoats. Everybody knew that other U-boats had been attacked, many times, from the air. Other U-boats, too, had had no prior warning from the *Biskaykreuz*. It seemed that somebody's reputation was at stake, and that reputation demanded it be proved that Hansi's Metox operator was at fault.

They came for Kuddeldaddeldu — or 'embraced' him, as they called it — in the early hours of the morning one day in January. Hansi knew nothing of it until he went down to the boat later that forenoon. The U-boat, as usual in dockyard hands, was a depressing and an infuriating sight, and by the look of things, likely to be so for weeks to come. Most of the casing aft had been removed and there was staging around the stern and the propellors. Everywhere Hansi looked there were cables, pipes, and trunkings, and the sheer filth of a dockyard. Shore workmen were always filthy. These were filthier than most, and getting filthier as the war went on. Just to look at the mess they made made Hansi indignant. They made a pigsty wherever they went and whatever they did. Were their own homes like this? Did they make this disgraceful squalor beside their own firesides, for their own wives and children to live in? Or was it just sailors' living conditions they treated in this way?

A group of his ship's company were standing on the fore casing, and the Engineer Officer, seeing Hansi on the concrete jetty side, came across the gangway to speak to him.

'They came at four o'clock this morning, Herr Kaleut.'

'Who did?' No normal naval business was conducted at four o'clock in the morning.

'Special naval representatives, they called themselves. They had authority from Berlin.'

'Why wasn't I informed? Who gave authority for this?'

The Engineer Officer did not reply, but his shrug of the shoulders and his expression told Hansi why he had not been informed. But it was preposterous that a sailor in the Kriegsmarine, who had been neither charged nor convicted of any offence, who had done nothing more than his duty, should be taken away in this manner.

But on the way up to the staff offices, Hansi's anger cooled. He knew that it was no good to protest. It would achieve nothing. It might even have consequences for himself and the rest of his ship's company. It would do no good.

Nor did it. There was no information at the staff bunker. *Alle ist Nebel.* 'All is fog.' Those aircraft had come out of the darkness, and the same darkness had swallowed up poor Kuddeldaddeldu. The demeanour of Kratzbürste and the rest of the staff made it clear that, for his own good and for the good of his boat, he should enquire no further.

It was, as Hansi confided to Reinhardt that evening, his biggest betrayal. It was by far his most serious lapse in loyalty. As the war went on, the betrayals became more grave and more damaging, when one would have expected one's sense of purpose to grow clearer. There was now the real fear that the blackness which had taken poor Kuddeldaddeldu might take Hansi, too. But Reinhardt, like the Engineer Officer, could give no information. He did not know, either.

But then, one blustery day in February when a west wind was blowing off the sea and shaking all the chimney pots, a signal arrived which changed all attitudes at once. Kratzbürste seemed almost reluctant to tell Hansi what it said.

'They have found a bomber, crashed in Holland. It had some equipment fitted. A shorter-wave radio direction finding set.'

It took Hansi some moments to appreciate the implications of that. 'So, it *is* possible to have a shorter wavelength set. So short that the Metox could not pick it up?'

'Yes.'

'You say yes. Are you not going to say any more? We were told on the very highest authority that shorter wavelength sets were not technically feasible. We were questioned for hours. We were accused of sabotage, of cowardice. If the cap *fits,* you told me. Now you tell me they *do* have a set with a shorter wavelength!'

Kratzbürste shrugged. 'We must review the situation in the light of the latest information. That was what we believed then. Now we know better.'

'But what about my Metox operator, who was right after all?'

Kratzbürste shook his head and shrugged. For once, it seemed there was no staff solution.

That night Hansi touched glasses with Reinhardt. 'To absent friends,' he said.

'To absent friends. Talking of that, the Atlantiksender mentioned you again this evening.'

'Oh?' That normally boded no good at all. Hansi now purposely avoided listening to that voice, which he had grown to hate.

'He says you're going to sea at the weekend. To replace Siegfried Flister, who is ill. They need an experienced captain to take his place.'

'Is that right?'

'Siegfried is certainly ill…'

'So it's right.'

'You know the Atlantiksender, Hansi. He is always right.'

CHAPTER ELEVEN

The Captain had a very long nose, and a very supercilious manner to match it. He treated Jay and the rest of his officers with a lofty disdain, rather as a landlord might regard his somewhat scruffy tenants. Jay had been delighted to overhear one of the RN liaison officers in New York, on their first evening in the main downstairs bar of the Barbizon-Plaza Hotel, come up and greet the Captain. It seemed he had been in the Captain's term at Dartmouth, years before, and he called the Captain 'Sniffer'. *Sniffer.* It was the perfect name, and Sniffer the Captain henceforth became.

Sniffer was an odd choice, it seemed to Jay, for this ship. He was a gunnery officer who had been promoted Captain just before the war and had spent some years in the Admiralty. Sniffer made no secret of his ignorance of flying and fliers, indeed he almost seemed proud of it, as the old type of aristocrat might have disdained any knowledge of machinery. Sometimes, when Jay was trying to explain some basic aspect of carrier life to an obviously disbelieving Sniffer, Jay wondered at the Admiralty's policy of choosing such men to command such ships; surely there must, by this stage in the war, be enough aircrew officers of Commander's and even Captain's rank who at least knew which end of an escort carrier was which?

The ship herself was an oddity, a thing of squares and boxes and rugged frames. Functional was the very word for her, cheap and cheerful, a 'Woolworth carrier', as somebody once said. But there was nothing cheap or makeshift about her equipment. Jay and the others had long since ceased to exclaim at her size and fittings. She was nearly five hundred feet long, with a flight deck nearly four hundred and fifty feet long, and at full complement she would carry eighteen aircraft in a closed hangar. Then she had nine arrestor wires, and three crash barriers, and two aircraft lifts, and even a single United States Navy H II catapult. Her gangways were narrower than in a British ship, and her compartments more tightly organised. Her cabins were bigger, her wardroom smaller, and there was no wardroom anteroom. Evidently, despite being a gregarious race, Americans did not look for communal living at sea, preferring to stay in their cabins, or staterooms as they called them. But the sailors' mess decks were larger and had bunks. There was a laundry and a cafeteria for self-service meals, both of which had been retained in the face of reactionary pressure from the Admiralty in London to remove them, on the grounds that they took up valuable space and 'made the sailors soft'.

Jay was one of the advance party of officers and men who had made the week-long train journey westwards across the United States to Portland, Oregon, to take the ship over from her builders and to commission her under the White Ensign. In their brand new ship, and still feeling their way around in her, they had made the voyage of so many of their predecessors: down the west coast through the freezing fogs off Seattle, to San Francisco, down and through the Panama Canal, up to Norfolk, Virginia, the 'Pompey' of the United States Navy, and so to New York. Shortly, they would sail eastwards with their first homebound convoy.

There were six Swordfish on board. The ship would embark more, up to squadron strength, in the United Kingdom. Meanwhile, no space was wasted in any ship going across the

Atlantic. The hangar was filled with stacked fuselages and dismembered wings of more aircraft, to be reassembled and flown on the other side. Jay had had no chance to work up his aircrews, or even to practise basic tactics. He recognised amongst them many of his former pupils, and he thus had to rely upon his own training, and hope they remembered what he had taught them. He had watched them do some deck landings on an American escort carrier out in Long Island Sound. They seemed safe enough, at least, and he would have to take their antisubmarine expertise very largely on trust. Jay's main preoccupation now was to learn their names and something about them.

Jay had been surprised, and at first somewhat disconcerted, to find himself not just the only straight-stripe RN officer in his squadron, but one of the very few on board. The only others were the Chief, a Lieutenant Commander (E) RN, and Sniffer himself. Even the First Lieutenant was RNVR. He had a very red face, a stocky body, with a loud voice and a blustering, somewhat domineering manner. Jay suspected that these last were to compensate for a certain lack of experience, and a certain awe of Sniffer. He had the nickname Biffer. Biffer and Sniffer. It sounded like a music-hall comedy act. They were a curiously ill-assorted pair, and it remained to be seen how they would react to each other when they were properly in commission. Jay was not the only member of the wardroom to forecast squally times ahead.

The rest of the wardroom were a mixed bunch of RNVRs and RNRs, with some of the engineer officers being hardly officers at all; at least, they themselves appeared not to want to be treated as officers. They began by coming into the wardroom in their steaming boots and oily overalls, until Biffer spoke sharply to them, whereupon they challenged him to clarify their status. 'We are engine-room artificers,' they said. 'Why don't you treat us as engine-room artificers?' It seemed they had signed for service, under some form or other, a T124X. Jay hardly knew what that meant, but apparently it brought Merchant Navy personnel under the Naval Discipline Act; thus these men were in the Royal Navy, but not of it. Jay and the rest of the officers in the wardroom found the T124X attitude hard to understand. It was a very human trait, recorded as far back as New Testament times, to want somebody to say, 'Friend, go up higher'. Warrant officers in the Royal Navy could scarcely wait to ship a thicker gold stripe on their sleeves on promotion to senior rank. But such aspirations did not apparently appeal to these surly, bad-mannered men, with accents from the north-east of England and the south-west of Scotland, and one — the dirtiest, surliest, foulest-mouthed of them all — from Cardiff.

When Jay first saw the T124X men, and marked their table manners, he was curious to see how Sniffer would react to them. He ignored them. He had never been known to address so much as a single word to any of them, not even to ask their names. They, for their part, treated him with a kind of distant reluctant respect which shaded out of contempt.

Biffer treated the T124Xs with a wary reserve, which was most unusual for him. Biffer always met people head on, as though bent upon collision. He had been a salesman before the war, he told Jay, although Jay could not imagine him ever being a successful one. He had joined the RNVR as an ordinary seaman in 1939. He was commissioned and came near the top of his course at *King Alfred*. He had served at sea almost constantly ever since. Thus, his manner seemed to suggest, his appointment as First Lieutenant was only his just due for services rendered. Of the oddness of their new ship, and the exotic natures of some of their new messmates, Biffer said to Jay, more than once, 'Well, it's a new war now, isn't it?'

It certainly was, as the convoy conference — the first Jay had attended for more than two years — demonstrated. It was held in a large warehouse on one of the wharves. It was a large building, but only just large enough. There were, Jay estimated, nearly four hundred people present. Jay wondered at the lack of security. The two US Navy bluejacket sentries on the door, with their white caps, white belts and truncheons, had nodded at Jay's uniform, but did not try to check the credentials of the merchant ship masters in their best 'Sunday go to meeting' suits. Theoretically, anybody in a grey serge suit could have walked in and obtained the most intimate details of a large convoy.

It certainly was a large convoy, a *very* large convoy, of nearly ninety ships, of twelve nationalities. There was a Convoy Commodore and two Rear Commodores. There was a close escort group, of destroyers and corvettes, with an American escort group to take them from New York to the latitude of Newfoundland, where a Canadian group from St Johns would relieve, and take them as far as a mid-ocean meeting point, where they would be reinforced by a group from Iceland. Nearer journey's end, a group would come out from Londonderry to meet them. Also, in the deep field, were two support groups, each with not less than six ships, ready to join the convoy escort at any time and strengthen its defences. They would be available to stay with a U-boat contact and hunt it to destruction; not like the old days, when the escorts often had to abandon a promising attack so as to rejoin their convoy. There were two rescue ships fitted out for picking up survivors, and three oilers, fitted for refuelling escorts at sea. There would be long-range air cover from Newfoundland, from Iceland and from Coastal Command at Ballykelly, with no less than five air squadrons — USAAF, RCAF or RAF — flying everything from Catalinas to very long-range Liberators, from Hudsons to Sunderlands, tasked to support the convoy. Jay's Swordfish would provide close air cover around the convoy and a quick reaction anti-submarine striking force to back up the surface escort.

Jay sat in one of the back rows of the conference, listening to all the plans and preparations for this colossal convoy as they were expounded. The passage of this convoy was a major naval occasion, equivalent to a fleet action. This was no longer a huddle of unwary merchantmen with a scratch escort. This was a huge military operation. Jay felt suddenly humble, like a common foot-soldier who had just emerged from his private and messy hand-to-hand skirmish and come out on to the broad, clear plain of a major battlefield, where vast formations were taking up their positions.

The Senior Officer of the close escort was Gussie. His hair was a little greyer, and his face a little more lined, but he now commanded a frigate, and he was plumper and looked generally more successful and more cheerful. He also wore the ribbons of the DSO and the DSC.

'You must have wondered why I didn't write to you about your gongs, sir. I'm afraid I must have missed them. I don't know why.'

'Never mind, Jay. All you flyboys always got your heads in the air. You never notice what happens to us fish-heads down below. Tell me, is Sniffer *your* captain?'

'Yes, he is, sir. Do you know him?'

'Believe it or not, he was actually in my term at Dartmouth. He prospered in the pre-war Navy. I didn't. I never liked him much. In fact, I always thought he was a pompous little prig, between you and me. I married his girlfriend, too.'

That postscript, so absolutely typical of Gussie, brought back happy memories for Jay and made him laugh until his ribs ached.

Whatever their relationship had been in years past, the present meeting between Sniffer and Gussie did not go well. Jay decided afterwards that it was probably Gussie's medal ribbons which caused the trouble. Sniffer could hardly take his eyes off them. It must have been galling for Sniffer to see somebody whom he had thought he had outstripped in the professional race now so visibly overtaking him in what everybody knew was the real business of their profession.

'You didn't miss any of your golden moments, Gussie.'

'I don't know about that. I've missed a few, I feel.'

Jay remarked on the absence, almost studied, of the word 'sir'. In any case it was absurd to expect term-mates to call each other 'sir'. But Jay sensed that Sniffer, nevertheless, had expected it.

Gussie did show a reluctant deference to Sniffer's rank, as the two of them exchanged cautious conversation. It had clearly been some time since they last met, and they had moved in different worlds. As they swopped gossip, each inquiring after absent friends and term-mates, Jay eventually came to realise that Gussie was waiting for something. His conversation was perfunctory, as though it were only sparring before the real business. After a time, Jay guessed what it was: Gussie was waiting for an invitation. He and Sniffer were to be colleagues for this convoy. Their mutual understanding was going to be vital for the convoy's safe passage. It would be a serious matter, and have a noticeable effect upon the war effort, if anything went awry with a convoy of this size. It would be essential for Gussie and Sniffer to have a common understanding, to avoid unnecessary and irritating signalling. More could be said in ten minutes' conversation than in a thousand signals. What Sniffer, as the senior Active List RN officer present, should now do was to invite Gussie and his fellow escort captains, Jay and the Air Direction Officer, the Commodore and his Rear Commodores, to a council of war, followed by lunch in his cuddy. There, they would all be able to put a face to every name and weigh each other up. That might be worth many lives in battle.

At last, in a decision which was actually visible to Jay, Gussie broke with convention. 'I'm just going back to my ship,' he said to Sniffer. 'I know we're both very busy today. But I wonder if you would like to have lunch with me? I could invite some of the captains from my group, and we could have a talk about affairs generally?'

Sniffer looked ostentatiously at his wristwatch. 'No, no,' he said, briskly. 'No, no. Sailing tonight. Got to get back. Lots of things to do. Kind of you.'

Jay was about to accept the invitation, for himself at least, but a look from Sniffer warned him.

Gussie was clearly just about to say something else when Sniffer abruptly turned on his heel and left them. They watched him go up and engage the Convoy Commodore in conversation. But Sniffer was obviously not conscious that he had been rude. He simply had never bothered to consider the effect of any of his actions upon anybody else. He had finished what he had to say to Gussie. He had something to say to the Commodore, so he left one and went to the other.

Jay had noticed a young US Navy officer, who had been waiting his chance to join them. As Sniffer left, he came forward, with his hand outstretched.

'May I? My name is Boydell H Merton. I'm from Boston.'

Jay and Gussie concealed their surprise and shook hands. 'How do you do?' they both said.

'Everybody calls me Boysie. I'm the Skipper of *Muskogee*. It's a very old destroyer, one of the oldest in the Navy.' The young man's face was apologetic, but still proud. 'I shall be part of the escort group when you sail. It'll be my first.'

'Your first convoy?' Gussie asked sharply.

'Ah, no. Not my first convoy. My first in *command*. I'm just out of the egg, command-wise.'

Gussie laughed out loud. 'Just out of the egg, command-wise. I must remember that one.'

They were both conscious they were being sized up. The young man's thoughts were almost visible: *Are these Limeys any good?*

'I saw your wings. I guess you must be the high-priced aviator on that flat-top?'

'That's me exactly,' said Jay, grinning. 'High-priced aviator. Yep, I'm the squadron CO.'

'Pleased to meet you. We've never operated with a flat-top before. We've often felt we needed one, real bad.'

Suddenly, Gussie and Jay both began to pay extra attention. This was exactly the sort of discussion they might have had with Sniffer. It seemed strange that they should now be getting down to it, standing outside a warehouse with a young stranger who had been eavesdropping on their conversation.

'How would *you* say aircraft could be best used, Boysie?' Gussie asked. 'What are you looking for us to do?'

'Well, you'll keep the U-boats heads down, for a start, while we all get past. But you know all about that. But if a sub comes too close, why, I guess it'll be the old one-two, *one-two!*' Boysie punched the air, with both fists, right and left, left and right.

'Surface escort and air escort working together. Whoever detects the sub first, directs the other on. If we get a radar contact or a huff-duff, we give the aircraft the range and bearing, so he can get over it fast. If the aircraft gets a radar or a visual, he gives the tin-can the word. Whoever gets there first attacks first, and if he misses or just pricks him, why, then the other has a go. Air and surface, surface and air. One-two, *one-two*!'

Gussie nodded. 'Actually, we've been trying out some ideas like that for some time. Trouble is we've never had long enough exercising with the aircraft and the escorts together. It needs some understanding and co-operation between the two.'

'Well, maybe we can try some things out this trip. But I'm only the junior dogface. Say, would you like to meet our group leader? He's the Senior Captain. Come over and meet them all?'

It was a splendid and valuable suggestion. They should have acted upon it days ago. But the American destroyers were over in another part of the harbour. 'I'm sorry,' Gussie said. 'I'd love to. But there's no time today.'

'Well, it was still nice to have met you. We'll look out for you. Have a safe trip.'

'There's a really keen spirit,' Gussie said. 'I like the look of him. That's a good officer there. He's got what they call the "can do" attitude. All the right ideas.'

Sniffer came back and nodded to Jay. 'Come on,' he said, and led the way, without another word to Gussie.

The first ships of their convoy began to sail a few minutes after midnight. The departure of the whole convoy would take some time, with ships moving out into the Hudson and the East River from more than a dozen berths and wharves, and some ships joining from the Hoboken and Jersey side. The convoy would not begin to take its final shape until all the ships had passed through the Narrows.

Jay stood on the flight deck, watching the departure take place against the spectacular background of New York. It really was one of the wonders of nature, or rather one of the wonders of man which lived up to its description. In fact, one could say, like the Queen of Sheba, *Behold the half was not told me.* Those great buildings by night made canyons and slabs and fields and planes of lights, in bars and dots and strings and swathes. It had been created haphazardly, to no previous plan, but it presented a collective aspect of harmony, very pleasing and reassuring to the eye. The moon was just rising, a full moon, a hunter's moon. *Moonlight over Manhattan,* Jay thought: it could have been one of their own song titles.

Leave had closed on board at four o'clock that afternoon. Jay was surprised by the small number of men adrift. None at all from the air department That was the gift of the ladies of New York to the war effort. There were hardly ever any leave-breakers when a ship sailed. New York was now the finest run ashore in the world for sailors, and New York women had exerted themselves to be hospitable. But New York was also the biggest staging post for shipping in the world, with convoys leaving and approaching from the south, the north, and the east. Nobody had ever given the ladies of New York credit for getting the men in those ships back on board in time. They should all get a medal.

It was bitterly cold on deck. Frost particles were already shining on the great expanse of the flight deck. The moon was reflected on it, as a huge silver pool on its surface. Men walked across it, in silhouette, their breaths smoking in the dry, cold March night air.

The great convoy, assembling in the moonlight, made a sight more thrilling than any photograph or painting. This was indeed a naval occasion. There ahead was a long tanker, turning itself laboriously in the stream to face the sea. Beyond it were more ships, their wakes clearly visible in the light of the moon. Lights flashed on shore, and there were hooters all around. As the shore fell away to either side, so the convoy seemed to expand to fill the space. Jay thought of the convoys early in the war, a gaggle of undisciplined and resentful merchantmen. They hated being in convoy, but were too afraid to go alone. But these ships were moving and handling themselves almost like a fleet which had exercised for months. Actually, many of these merchant ships must already have sailed in several convoys. Many of these masters and officers probably had much more experience of handling ships in close company with others for long periods than most professional naval officers. Now, they were streaming out to take up station in their appointed columns as confidently as any pre-war destroyer flotilla.

Jay went up to the bridge to stand, noticed but, he hoped, unspoken to, behind the Captain. The bridge was tiny and seemed to be fitted together out of parts, like something from a schoolboy's kit. There was nothing ornamental: room for everything, just enough and no more. The whole ship had been designed and built for a specific purpose, and there was nothing over for frills or favours. The piping and machinery layout below was utilitarian. The decks were covered in a plain but hard-wearing material. The only polished surfaces in the whole ship were probably the nameboards, placed beside the gangways when the ship was alongside; the builders had made and presented them, together with a silver model of the ship's crest.

Jay left a message in the ready room for a shake early in the morning, and went down to his cabin. That too was functional, like everything else. There was a single bunk, and a wash-basin, a chest of drawers, and a wardrobe. But it was large enough and just what was wanted. Jay had had to fight a battle with Biffer over proper cabins for his pilots and observers. All of them, except Johnnie Johnson the senior pilot, were Sub-Lieutenants, and Biffer, drawing upon some vestigial memory of his own days as an RNVR Midshipman in a battleship, had insisted that they form a gunroom. He took some convincing that Jay's aircrew were not officers under training, like gunroom officers pre-war, but fully trained ship's officers with full responsibilities, and were entitled to cabins.

That battle had been won, but Jay was still fighting another over a suitable mess deck for his aircrew ratings. The Telegraphist Air Gunners — the TAGs, as they called themselves — considered themselves the elite of the lower deck and entitled to a mess deck of their own. The rest of the lower deck looked upon them, flying and mixing with officers as they did, as 'neither fish nor fowl nor good red herring'; they were in a similarly invidious position as the rating pilots had been at the outset of the war. Jay had a sudden memory of Bracewell, and wondered what he was doing. The last Jay had heard, Bracewell had had to lose some toes, and could not go to sea.

The mail had arrived on board just before sailing. That was another of New York's efficiencies. There were three letters from Sarah, the latest only three weeks old. Just to see her handwriting again at once summoned those memories of his eighteen months in Scotland. It had seemed at the time a deliciously long period, stretching out into infinity. Looking back on it now, it seemed to have passed in a flash. They had seen the seasons change there. He had sat out on the same hillside, in summer, and in a biting east wind, to watch the Swordfish on the range dive, and bomb, and climb away again. They had walked together on that same stretch of beach, barefoot in summer, wrapped up in winter when the waves thundered on the sand and piled up great tangles of driftwood overnight. It was typical of Sarah that she always examined the debris closely for ships' names or any other information. 'There might be wives and girlfriends,' she had said, 'who want to know what happened to a ship. *I* would want to know, if you were in a ship.'

They had both been reluctant to admit they were in love. Like anybody who had once been burned, Sarah was afraid to risk any further hurt. Jay too had been afraid of allowing any part of himself to be made hostage. The constant stream of faces passing through on courses, so many of them that in the end he gave up trying to put names to any of them, had induced a feeling of fatalism in him. Sometimes he was afraid he would not survive the war, and he was even more afraid that in the event he would not care. *I'm the oldest inhabitant here,* she wrote. *We've got a new captain, and new people all around. More and more training classes, with younger and younger pilots! Better looking, too!* Jay read through her letters and, as he went to sleep, made up his mind that he would certainly ask Sarah to marry him as soon as he got back home. He should have asked her a long time ago.

Jay woke to the tap on his cabin door and to the sound, from far away, of the ship's siren. When he went out on the small walkway under the flight deck edge, the fog was so thick he could not see the stern of the ship. But he could tell by the vibration that the ship had not slowed down. There was no ship in sight, but Jay fancied he could actually hear the rustling of another ship's wake only a short distance away.

The fog had not dispersed when the sun came up, and there was still no sign of any other ship. But the convoy was still standing on, relying on radar to keep them together. They had all learned that the best way in fog was simply to press on, and it was remarkable to see, when the fog eventually lifted, the convoy still in its proper ranks and columns, ploughing steadily onwards. The one thing not to do was to deviate from the convoy course and speed. It required an act of faith from every ship's captain, but it was the only way.

After breakfast, when flying should have begun, the fog was still closed tightly around the ship. Jay took the chance to brief his squadron. They all gathered in the ready room — the pilots, the observers, the TAGs, and Jay had also asked the senior airframe and engine fitters. The ready room was almost luxurious, by the standards of the ship, with comfortable armchairs, strip lighting over the blackboard, main room lighting which could be adjusted for brightness. There was also an annexe, with bunks where crews at readiness could rest and keep their eyes adjusted for the dark. The compartment was stuffy with cigarette smoke. Jay, a non-smoker himself, had been surprised to find that everybody else in the squadron smoked heavily. That was the United States for you, as somebody said.

'Our squadron,' Jay said, 'will be watch on, stop on, for the whole of this trip. We shall have at least one, probably two crews in the air at all times, with another stand-by. I'll make out a sort of flying programme for every day, putting in everything I know about the situation. But I shouldn't put too much faith in the flying programme. Something might happen at any time. Our job, as you know, is to look after the convoy.

We shall fly anti-submarine patrols regularly, out ahead, and to either side and we shall respond to any detections anybody gets.' Jay looked along the rows of young faces. A stranger might think them all too young. But this was a young man's job. It needed young eyes, young limbs, the flexibility of youth, the quick recovery of youth from fatigue and strain. Jay had to admit to himself that he found it difficult to know all his aircrew's names. They all seemed to have the same young faces, with blue eyes and brown hair on top. But the names were beginning to come to him now.

'You can see from the vis this morning that the weather is going to be one of our main bugbears. We should be flying now but it's too clagged in. Met says it's going to clear about midday.' Jay shrugged and drew the sides of his mouth down in a grimace, and he was rewarded by laughter.

The Met Officer was an Instructor Lieutenant, a classical scholar from Cambridge, a sensitive youth with two brand new RNVR stripes and a tendency to give a great uncontrollable start whenever Sniffer spoke to him. Jay was awaiting the day when the forecast was demonstrably wrong, or, more likely, Sniffer simply disagreed with it. Meanwhile, the forecasts had had an element of inspiration about them. Clearly one needed a touch of the fey for weather forecasting, a brush of that same talent possessed by readers of bones and markers of bird flights of the ancient world. The Met Officer himself said it was a branch of haruspicy. 'I'm a haruspex,' he said. 'An inspector of entrails.' Thus everybody on board henceforth called him Harry Specks.

That morning, Harry Specks said, the fog was only a shallow bank. Once above it, there would be clear sky and maybe even some sunshine. It was he explained, a matter of the effect of cold arctic water meeting the warm Gulf Stream. The problem was to persuade Sniffer to turn back into the wind merely on the strength of Harry Specks' opinion.

It was already clear that the weather was not the only obstacle to flying. Sniffer was another. He had an almost obsessive sense of order. He hated any break in ship's routine — unusual courses, unexpected events. A ship out of station was an offence to him. Any unscheduled happening was an irritation. He liked to steam along at the course and speed of the convoy, or rather, what he imagined them to be. He took station on the convoy's starboard beam, some twenty miles away, and kept radio silence. Gussie's TBS appeals for information on the carrier's course, speed and position were ignored.

The major cause of disruption in Sniffer's life, and thus his greatest source of anxiety, was flying. To fly off aircraft meant steaming into the wind. This convoy was steering north-east. The prevailing winds were westerly or north-westerly. To fly off, Sniffer would have to turn in and steer towards the convoy's starboard flank or down towards the convoy's rear. He hated to do either and, as the forenoon wore on and the weather, as Harry Specks had said, showed signs of clearing, so Sniffer's distress increased. Jay could see him growing more and more uneasy, screwing up his face in his anxiety and chewing his lip furiously.

Sniffer's anxiety showed most clearly in his ship-handling. He had a habit of turning up into wind only at the last possible moment before flying-off was due, and similarly turning away out of the wind when the last aircraft was barely airborne from the deck. When landing on, Sniffer would have the ship into wind the shortest possible time before the aircraft landed on, and would begin turning out of wind as the last aircraft was crossing the round-down.

Towards noon, the fog did begin to disperse, just as Harry Specks had predicted. Jay and Johnnie Johnson took off, the first aircraft of that convoy. The air was clear above the convoy, but the fog still lay in stretches, with the tips of ships' masts sticking up through it. Jay checked the ranks of the convoy. Everybody was in place, present and correct. There was something enormously reassuring about that great concourse of ships, moving steadily onwards. Whatever happened, the convoy would go on. U-boats might attack, ships might be sunk, but at the end of the hour the convoy would still have advanced its sixty-minute run. It was the sheer statistical certainty of that which would in the end defeat the U-boats and win the war; it was as though the Allies had the assistance, not just of armaments, but of mathematics.

Jay landed on after Johnnie Johnson and, as he had anticipated, he found the flight deck slipping sideways from underneath him as he came on. Sniffer was up to his old trick again. Jay had hesitated to broach this subject, but now he felt it was time, before somebody went over the side unnecessarily.

On the bridge, Sniffer was sipping a mug of cocoa. 'See anything?'

'No, sir.'

'Thought you wouldn't.'

'Well, sir, it's still early days. The visibility is none too good, even if it has cleared up a bit. We didn't get any indications from the surface escorts.'

'Nor will you.' Sniffer seemed almost pleased to be able to express such an opinion.

'I don't know, sir, give them a chance...'

'I *do* know. A bunch of incompetents. They wouldn't know a U-boat if it got up and bit them on the arse.'

Somehow, the contempt, and the tone of voice and the words in which it was expressed, seemed to Jay so much more shocking from Sniffer's lips. He had not realised that Sniffer hated and envied Gussie so much. Jay decided not to mention Sniffer's ship-handling. This was not an opportune moment.

Two hours later, there was a U-boat report. It had been heard transmitting from a bearing directly astern of the convoy. Either it was shadowing, or just possibly the convoy had actually run over it without detecting it or being detected. But now the Long Stop was awake, and on the surface, and transmitting to the rest of its group.

Jay took off, this time with his second aircraft flown by a lad who was always known as 'Crasher', although he seemed steady enough and competent. Maybe it referred to some incident in his early training. Jay had always meant to ask him, but kept on forgetting.

The wind was still just north of west and with the convoy still heading north of east, Sniffer had to steer in towards the convoy again. Looking back, Jay saw the bows begin to swing away as Crasher's Swordfish barely cleared them. That was a very close thing indeed.

The visibility improved astern of the convoy, as though better weather were being blown towards them. There was even the hint of the palest, most fleeting ray of sunshine, enough to brighten the wave-tops and raise the light level several times over. It should make a U-boat easier to find.

The huff-duff signal strength and direction had estimated the U-boat's position at fifteen miles range, astern of the convoy, and apparently steering a parallel course. Jay worked out his approach so as to fly out to one side and then turn in and fly at right angles to the convoy's wake, hoping to surprise the U-boat on its port beam.

But there was nothing there. Jay flew over the datum position, but could see no sign of a U-boat, no periscope feather, no trace of a wake. He flew out, turned, and flew back. Jay was sure the U-boat was there, but obviously he was no beginner. Jay turned parallel with the convoy's track and flew on an opposite course. Just possibly the U-boat had slowed down after transmitting, having decided it could no longer make an attack and had fulfilled its part by transmitting a report to its fellows up ahead. But again, there was nothing.

When Jay turned for home, he was some fifty miles astern of the convoy and he noticed, as he set course to rejoin, that the wind had strengthened and gone round towards the north. That was why the weather had cleared. The wind was now blowing from almost directly ahead of the Swordfish. It would make it a long flight back. Looking at his fuel gauges he saw, with a stab of concern, that he had only just enough. There would be no scope for any of Sniffer's antics. As a precaution, Jay jettisoned his depth charges. They detonated some way astern with satisfactory water spouts. Maybe that would frighten the U-boat, if nothing else did.

Jay approached the rear ships in the convoy with care. Nobody was any the less quick on the trigger now than they had been in the early days. They still fired at an aircraft first and identified it later. As he crossed the rear ships, Jay saw another Swordfish fly past him. It waggled its wings and Jay saw the fuselage code, 5F: that was Johnnie Johnson, going to take up the search. Evidently it was not worth sending a second Swordfish. There was not much chance of a sighting now; but while there still was a chance, they had to go on trying. Meanwhile, Jay's own preoccupations were with getting back safely on board. He could see below that the waves were still increasing in height and length. For a fleeting moment, Jay wondered whether it was wise to despatch Johnnie Johnson so far astern of the convoy, with the wind direction where it was, and still strengthening.

At last, the carrier deck was in sight ahead. Once again, Sniffer was only just into the wind by the time Crasher crossed the round-down and, once again, Jay saw the flight deck tilting and swinging as he himself touched down. That one had been even closer. This time, Jay made up his mind he must protest. But again, he found Sniffer fuming about something or other. This all had echoes of that other captain, off Norway so long ago.

In the wardroom, the Welsh T124X engineer was having a cup of tea and some toast. He had, as a concession to Biffer, put on a collar and tie. But there was a dark thumb print on the collar. The man's fingernails had broad black rims of oil, and one nail was broken. The fingers were inlaid with grime.

The man's conversation was as disagreeable as his toilet. He was talking to another of the T124Xs, loudly enough for Jay to overhear. It was the usual ignorant tirade against aircrew 'flyboys': how they were 'Brylcreem boys' who did none of the hard work and got all the credit; how their wings on their sleeves were 'golden leg-spreaders' for all the girls; how they were overpaid and underworked. Every aircrew had experienced this sort of abuse, normally in pubs near closing time, from drunken sailors. But this man's voice was so jarring and his language so abusive that Jay was about to rise to the fray when there was the crash outside of a larger wave, and the deck sloped suddenly. The sea was still getting up and, by the sound of it, so was the wind. Jay thought of Johnnie, miles astern, looking for that U-boat. It was high time to recall him, if he was not already on his way.

But there was no sense of urgency about Johnnie and his recall anywhere in the island. Even in the radar office, they were sitting calmly looking at his echo on the screen. The radar office was as functional as everywhere else, just big enough for the radar sets and the men who watched over them. There was a thick hot fug in there. The radar watchkeepers were chain smokers and they kept the radiators full on twenty-four hours a day.

Jay stood for a while, watching the band of light sweeping round and round the orange screen, lighting up the small blip astern of all the other echoes every time it passed.

'How far is that?'

'About sixty-five miles, sir.'

'Sixty-five ... you *sure*?'

'Yes, sir. We're keeping a log of him. The datum for that U-boat is dropping astern all the time, and so in the centre of his search pattern, sir.' The watchkeeper's voice was scornfully patronising, as though an officer and a squadron GO ought to have such elementary facts at his fingertips.

This time Jay did not hesitate. 'I think that Swordfish should be recalled *now*, sir.'

'Whatever for?' Sniffer clearly thought the suggestion preposterous.

'I think it quite possible he might have difficulty in getting back to the ship, sir.'

'Why on earth should he have any difficulty?'

Jay looked at the anemometer dial on the bulkhead. Its needle was swinging rapidly, from thirty knots up in gusts to thirty-five and even forty knots. This was going to be a full gale; indeed, it was not far off that now.

'Well, sir, a Swordfish does about eighty knots. He's sixty-five miles astern now and he's got a headwind of about thirty-five knots and still increasing, sir. It'll take him two hours to get back at that rate. He's only going to do thirty or forty knots over the ground. There's the question of fuel, sir.'

'No doubt your senior pilot knows his own position better than anybody else. He should be on his way back now. There's no question of recalling him. We are keeping radio silence.'

'Could we tell him to ditch his depth charges, sir?'

'Certainly not.'

Jay had known the request would be refused as soon as he had made it. He was sorry he had mentioned it. He should have quietly briefed Johnnie beforehand to do it if he were in any doubt. Jay saw Sniffer frown, as the implications of the request sank in. To Sniffer's sense of correctness, the notion of ditching perfectly serviceable depth charges would be anathema. Depth charges were naval stores. People had to account for them, muster them, record their numbers and their service histories on special forms. They would be on somebody's charge, perhaps even Sniffer's own.

'Certainly *not*,' said Sniffer again.

For Jay, the time for observing correct procedures in addressing the Captain was now past. 'Could we slow down a bit, sir, please?'

'Certainly not. There might be more U-boat transmission up ahead. We must keep up with the convoy.'

'Sir, I must tell you that there is a real chance that Swordfish might be lost. Could we signal the stern escort to stand by in case she is needed?'

'Certainly not, and I am beginning to find your constant suggestions extremely tiresome. We are keeping radio silence. I'm not going to jeopardise my whole ship for one man.'

'One crew, sir.'

Sniffer gave Jay a sharp look, suspicious of insolence. 'One *crew*, then.'

'But sir, I must insist ... the U-boat transmission, sir. We have been sighted. We would be giving nothing away...'

'*No.*'

At that, Jay knew what the outcome would be. He saluted, left the bridge and went down to the radar office to watch the screen. For a time, it did seem that Johnnie was closing the ship. Maybe he had ditched his depth charges. But Johnnie was a very conscientious man and would probably jib at that. Jay watched Johnnie's blip, almost stationary relative to the ship. It was about twenty miles away. And then, on one sweep, the blip was gone. On the next, it had returned, but much, much smaller and less clearly defined. Jay continued to stare at the screen, hoping this was a temporary aberration, that Johnnie's echo would be regained.

The watchkeeper looked up at Jay. 'The range of that small echo is opening now, sir. It's the wreckage of the Swordfish, sir, for sure.' The man's voice was apologetic, ashamed. He knew now, too late, why Jay had been so concerned.

Even the small blurred echo had now disappeared. Johnnie and his crew were gone. Jay knew that the fault was his. This was a new ship. This was their first convoy. This was their first day of air patrols. They were all as green as grass. Just out of the egg, as that Yank had said. It had been *Jay's* business to make sure that nothing like this could ever happen.

In the ready room, everybody was still watching the sweep-hand of the clock move round. It was not impossible, not *quite* impossible, that there had been some inexplicable atmospheric freak, some defect in the radar set itself, which might have caused Johnnie's echo to fade. He might, *just,* still appear astern of the ship and bring his Swordfish on to the deck, as large as life and twice as natural. But when the minutes passed the uttermost limits of his fuel consumption — beyond even the most optimistic estimate, even if his tanks had been overfilled, even if they were idiosyncratically, abnormally capacious — there was no longer any doubt that Johnnie was gone.

Somebody was at the ready room door. 'Captain would like to see you on the bridge, sir.'

Sniffer was leaning against the forward rail of the bridge, staring through his-binoculars at something ahead. He seemed to sense Jay's approach and turned round.

'I owe you an apology. I could have done more for that crew. I am very sorry indeed. You must put it down to my ignorance, which was inexcusable.'

'Thank you, sir.' There was no more to be said after that.

Johnnie had never said a word. He knew the ship was keeping radio silence and he had not broken it, even to ask for a short transmission for direction finding. He had not even said goodbye, when it no longer mattered. It was the most terrible of deaths, which left nothing for anybody to remember: no violent crash on deck, no injuries, nothing to see except a blob of light which died out.

Yet Jay found that he felt no grief for Johnnie. He literally felt nothing at all. He had hardly known him, above a purely squadron acquaintance. He could not even remember, for the moment, the name of Johnnie's observer. It was a lad called MacPherson, or MacSomething.

'What was that observer's name, somebody? Johnnie's observer?'

'Ferguson, boss. Ferdie Ferguson.'

'Thanks.'

Jay would have to look up the names of their next of kin and write to them, although what he could possibly say to them, for the moment he had no idea.

The wind increased as the day went on to a full gale and more than a gale, blowing from the north-west on the convoy's port beam. Enemy activity, brief though it had been, died away completely. Evidently Long Stop's transmissions had not been received by other U-boats, or if they had, they were not acted upon. There was one brief cheep of a transmission after dark. The forward escort on the portside ran the bearing down, but found nothing. Gussie had most of his escorts on the windward portside, remembering from the old days how U-boats liked to attack downwind. But the night passed, and the next day, as the convoy clawed its course north and east towards Greenland, past the latitude of Sable Island, graveyard of so many ships in the days of sail and not a few in steam. The gale blew unceasingly from the north-west, and the little carrier rolled twenty degrees either way. There were constant showers of heavy, blinding snow, so there was no flying.

It seemed a very orderly, good-humoured convoy. There was very little signalling, both Gussie and the Commodore holding their peace as long as possible. The ships made almost no smoke, and kept very good station in the prevailing conditions. It was as though everybody, convoyers and convoyed, had become professionals.

Despite the weather, one U-boat at least had held on. On the third night there was a very lengthy transmission from right astern. The huff-duff operators could distinguish between individual U-boats by their operators' touch on the Morse code key, and they confirmed that this was the U-boat which had reported earlier. Long Stop, it seemed, was a very persistent tracker.

During that night, the wind moderated and veered to the north, and with the sun — like a dawn chorus — the U-boats piped up. Long Stop was still astern, and there were more transmissions from ahead and on the starboard bow. By the end of the day, the convoy would be within range of Liberators flying from Iceland. But meanwhile, the surface close escort and Jay's Swordfish would have the day to themselves.

Jay slept in the bunk space next to the ready room. He was up and shaved well before dawn, and had a breakfast of bacon and eggs and fresh white rolls in the ready room. The ship had ample refrigeration space and they were still on the splendid American food. The ship's cooks were also T124X men, but they seemed to take a different attitude to the engineers, being pleased and proud of their work. The food on board was better than that on any warship Jay had ever served in.

With the expected pipe 'Range two Swordfish', the tempo of events began to accelerate. The ready room filled up with figures in flying suits. Numbers and letters were rapidly scribbled on the blackboard, there was a babble of voices, cups of hot coffee on the ledges, and everybody puffing away at cigarettes. Jay went up to see Sniffer, and found him poring over a signal log. There were certain incoming signals which nobody but Sniffer was permitted to read.

'Here we are, Jay,' he said. 'Today's the day, it looks like. Transmissions all round the clock. The U-boats are going to make their bid today.'

As Sniffer was speaking, Jay felt the detonation through the soles of his feet. Sniffer put up his binoculars, but they were too far from the convoy. The TBS speaker on the bulkhead crackled. It was Gussie, asking for Sniffer's position course and speed, and giving some news.

'It was the end ship in the starboard side wing column...'

That meant, almost certainly, that Long Stop had caught up during the night and had overhauled the tail-end Charlies in the convoy. He had already picked off the starboard wing man. He might even now be on the surface, trying to work his way around and get ahead of the convoy.

With a thumping heart and a dry mouth, Jay recognised the same excitement of two years before: the messages, the contacts, the explosions — there was an almost audible humming in the air of activity and threat.

Jay was airborne just before dawn. He noted ruefully the flight deck sliding away as he left. Sniffer's remorse was not all that deep, or long-lasting. Jay flew first close to the convoy, to check that Long Stop was not still on the surface, trying to get ahead. But there was nothing there, so he flew up the convoy's starboard side and ahead, where the U-boat transmissions had clustered thickest. Below he saw a US destroyer plunging and dipping, and steering in the same direction. According to the screening diagram that was *Muskogee,* their keen young friend from New York, Boysie H. Whatever his name was. Jay thought of waving at the figures on its bridge, but he had his hands full to keep the heavily laden Swordfish in the air. The depth charges felt like millstones. The Swordfish had almost got to the end of its considerable capacity. The latest Stringbags, with a crew of two, a radar set, and depth charges or rockets, now needed rockets themselves to help them off the flight deck.

Jay heard the voice of Sonny, his observer, speaking in the tube. He had a radar contact. It was a bold and bright one, apparently, a grade-A target. The visibility was poor. Without radar they would have been almost blind. But now it was the U-boats who were blind.

It was Sonny's voice again. The target was still standing on, still closing. Whoever he was, he was a confident customer. He seemed to know exactly where the convoy was, and was boring in on it as though he were quite sure of success.

It was vital to get over the target fast. This man would give them no second chance. Jay discarded any plans to swing round and approach from astern or from the beam. He would have to take the target head on, like a charging bull.

The range was coming down rapidly. Sonny was reeling off the figures. The visibility was still less than a mile. Jay knew he would have only a few seconds to pick up his target, make the last adjustments to his course, and attack.

And there it was, the first U-boat he had ever seen. It was dark grey, but somehow lighter in colour than he had expected. Spray was breaking over its tower, and as he watched he saw the long lean forward bow rising out of a wave, cutting through the water like a great black knife or a shark's fin. It really did look exactly like all those clichéd shots from the pictures. The sight of it, the colour, the texture, the ratio of length to width, the wisp of faint wake, would have told even the most ignorant what it was.

The U-boat had seen them. The shape was already diminishing. The man was diving. But with luck he was going to be a second or two too late. Jay flew overhead and the charges dropped away. He heard and felt them detonate, turned hard to starboard and flew back over the spot. He could not have missed. It had been the most splendid target, one straight out of the training manuals. He could not possibly have missed, given such an aiming point. He could guarantee to drop a depth charge on a clothes peg and drive it into the ground more often than he missed. But there was no sign of a hit. Nothing surfaced, and there was no trace of oil or debris.

Sonny had dropped a smoke flare. It ignited properly and its white trail drifted down wind. There was Boysie Whatnot's destroyer coming up at full speed. Jay circled overhead to mark the spot, but *Muskogee* had already slowed down, like a hunting dog suddenly getting a whiff of its game, with a head-high scent. *Muskogee* had the attack flags flying, and clearly had a sonar contact.

As Jay watched from above, the destroyer ran over the smoke flare. Four charges flew in the air, looking like wood chips flying from under a chopping axe. In a short time, there were great gouts of water from astern.

Muskogee altered course, ran out, turned and steamed back. Again the charges flew, the sea spouted, and subsided again. *Muskogee* rolled in a tighter turn. Her flags were still flying, and she came back eagerly, as though excited by blood. For a brief moment the ship seemed to hesitate, like a man poising himself before making quite sure his rolled newspaper smashed an already injured fly to the window pane.

This time, there was no possible doubt about the hit. Jay saw the oil rush to the surface and spread out, with dots like particles of flesh mixed into it. It looked like some great pustule bursting under the surface and belching out blood and pus and tissue. There were huge bubbles, and a brown stain, and pieces of wood or debris of some kind. That last pattern of charges must have exploded right alongside, above and below the U-boat, and simply broken it into fragments.

Jay flew round and round, awed and almost afraid of what he could see. The stain seemed to be still widening. Debris was still coming to the surface in the middle of a great mess of oil and crushed and smashed bits and pieces. *Muskogee* had slowed down and Jay could see some sailors in her waist, lowering buckets on lines. Souvenirs. The Yanks loved souvenirs. But they would need that evidence.

'Sonny, get out your lamp and make to that destroyer, "Congratulations, is that your first today?"'

It took some time to pass the message. But eventually a surprisingly large and very bright signalling lamp began to flash an acknowledgement. The Americans evidently designed everything on a large scale.

"Thanks," the lamp said. "That was the old one-two."

CHAPTER TWELVE

Through the attack periscope, Hansi watched the biplane fly across their track and out to the port side. Just as he was hoping it would carry on, it turned, and flew back. Clearly it was searching. What was more, it knew where to search.

That aircraft must have come as a result of his attack. It had, Hansi congratulated himself, been one of his better attacks, perhaps even his best. It was getting harder and harder, these days, even to approach a convoy at all. But he had followed this one in weather which would have deterred all but the most determined U-boat captain. He had closed the rearmost ship, coming down upon it in a sudden dart, and sunk it before anybody knew he was there. Then he had slipped astern, well out of sight, and dived. In the old days, he might have stayed on the surface, and hauled around and tried to attack again later in the day. But there was a line between duty and foolhardiness which Hansi had no intention of crossing. Even now, that aircraft knew the boat was there somewhere and things could still go wrong. Indeed, perhaps he should not stay up looking at it. Hunters always said you should never stare too long at your prey; it would eventually become aware of you.

The periscope slid downwards. Hansi stood back and folded his arms over his chest. That was a very antiquated-looking biplane. Like something out of the Kaiser's war. A single-engined biplane like that, hundreds of miles from land: that must mean an aircraft carrier somewhere. Everybody knew the aircraft carriers were beginning to sail with the convoys.

Confirmation of that would be worth reporting at the next routine message to BdU.

'Up periscope!'

The aircraft was still there, crossing and recrossing. Hansi was able to pick up its flight at once. By an odd trick of his hearing, he fancied he could even hear the steady drone of its engine.

'Down.'

Once again, Hansi considered the biplane. Now why should an aircraft arrive at the one point in the middle of the wide ocean where there was a U-boat, and begin its search there? It was true it had not seen their periscope, and in that weather it almost certainly never would. But that pilot was behaving as though he had been briefed to look here. Hansi wondered, not for the first time, *Does the enemy know something we do not?*

Hansi looked at the control-room clock. It would soon be time for the next broadcast to BdU. Every boat had to signal at certain set times. They were allowed some latitude. But if a boat missed a couple of allotted times, BdU started to get restive. Hansi would soon have to signal his routine information about fuel remaining, torpedoes remaining, and the weather. That convoy up ahead was a very big one, and the others in the search 'stripe' ought to know of it.

Nevertheless, as the signalling time came nearer, Hansi was reluctant to come to shallow depth and begin transmitting, almost as though it were an extra risk he preferred not to have to take. He would not have been able to express his misgivings in so many words, but he had noticed from his own experience, and it had been confirmed by hints in conversations with other captains at Lorient, that a radio transmission was mysteriously often followed by an attack. It had happened too often to be put down to coincidence. It seemed unbelievable, but it seemed that the radio transmission itself was the trigger which set off an attack. It was as though the enemy actually had some means of detecting the transmission and using it as a guide. Somebody — it had been Reinhardt, Hansi recalled — had tentatively mentioned this possibility at a staff briefing. But the staff had mocked at such a suggestion, as though it were just a madman's ravings. When Reinhardt had, rather diffidently, tried to press the point, quoting from his own experience, the staff as one man had jeered at him and called him a crank.

Hansi heard two detonations up ahead, but a long way away. It could mean something, it could be nothing, but Hansi saw the winces on the young faces around him. None of them had experienced depth-charging, but they had heard about it. They were getting ready for the agony before they had even come near to it.

Just before dark, Hansi had the periscope raised again. He looked very carefully and cautiously all round, through three hundred and sixty degrees of the horizon and overhead to the limit of his vision. He looked three times, each time more slowly and painstakingly. There was nothing. Then, slowly and carefully, as though the boat were already suffering from some painful wound, they surfaced.

The main diesels were coughing and roaring, and sending out their streams of smoke and froth, when Hansi first became aware of the discoloured water just ahead.

'Stop together!' Survival nowadays meant being able to dive at once.

Hansi looked through his binoculars. The sea just ahead was definitely a different colour, even in the fading light. The wave shapes were damped, as though oil had been released. The water surface was speckled and mottled, as though sprinkled with sawdust. There was even the suspicion of a smell, like *cooking,* on the wind. The boat's bows were cutting into what resembled the waters of a river estuary, with floating sponges, and small sticks of wood; the very texture of the water surface was studded with the shapes of debris, hidden under the oil, and by God, with a sudden shiver of premonition, Hansi recognised a whole sausage, a large *Wurst,* exactly like those which swung in bunches down below in his own U-boat.

The boat had stopped now, and was drifting alongside a great tangled mat of debris, so thick and congested it looked like flotsam gathered at the brink of a river weir. Hansi bellowed down the voice-pipe for two hands on deck, with buckets and lines.

'Trawl, *trawl!*' he shouted at the puzzled sailors when they arrived. 'Get what you can.'

They did not get much. But it was enough. The main item was a ragged scrap, several centimetres square, of a leather watchcoat, of a very familiar colour, material and thickness. Hansi turned it over. He held it close to his eyes. The sun was down but he could read the letters stencilled on the lining: - TTO TOPF--.

Hansi had to swallow hard to keep down the saliva flooding into his mouth. This watchcoat had belonged to Otto Topfer. He was, or rather, he had been, Reinhardt's second watchkeeping officer. This lifeless piece of material spoke to Hansi from the grave. It was irrefutable evidence. This appalling soup, this mess, through which his boat had steered, was all that remained of Reinhardt and his crew. There could be no doubt. Reinhardt and his crew were gone. Those distant rumblings Hansi had heard might even have been Reinhardt's last battle. These scraps, these shreds, these sweepings from an abattoir, were all that was left of the bodies of his friend and those who had gone to sea with him. He had actually been looking at the shattered corpses of his fellow countrymen. Hansi remembered Herr Kaleut once talking of a Greek sea battle long ago when they had trawled in the bodies afterwards like tunny fish. But at least those bodies were whole. When the last day of judgment came and the sea gave up its dead, what would the sea give up from this spot?

A voice calling up from below reported that the signal to BdU had been passed and acknowledged. They could head for the convoy again. Hansi gave the orders for course and speed. For the first time ever, he felt that his resolve for battle had been badly shaken. The sight and what he now realised must actually have been the *smell* of Reinhardt's fate shocked him more than anything else in the war. It showed, if any more proof were needed, how very difficult a convoy attack now was. In what Hansi had come to think of as the old days, Herr Kaleut had descended upon a convoy almost light-heartedly. It had been a dangerous business, a very dangerous business indeed, but it had never had the constant many-layered menace of today. Every convoy now had aircraft, which came overhead as though they knew just where to look, and destroyers appeared out of the smother, as though they knew just where to steer. Meanwhile Hansi, and Reinhardt, and everybody, were still going to sea in basically the same U-boats, with some minor additions, as they had at the outset of the war. Whether Herr Prof's marvellous new designs had ever been built or not, they had certainly not appeared in operational service.

For half an hour, Hansi steered at full speed at right angles to their original course just in case a destroyer came down the wake of the convoy. This might lose them some ground on the convoy, which was already some thirty or more miles ahead, but it might also mean survival for another day. The Lorient staff might scoff at the notion that the enemy could have some means of locating signals. But the Lorient staff did not have to go to sea and put their notion to the test. Reinhardt must have been approaching the convoy for an attack from ahead and on its starboard bow when he was sunk. Hansi wished he had more information on where Reinhardt had been and what had happened to him. In the old days, one could learn a lot by listening in the bar at Lorient. With fewer and fewer boats returning from sea these days, there was less and less reliable first-hand information.

From his chart, Hansi estimated that they had been about thirty miles behind the convoy which, in that half an hour, would have moved on about four miles, possibly less. In the same time, the boat had made about seven miles at ninety degrees. Had they steered on after the convoy, they would have caught up some three miles, leaving the convoy still some twenty-seven miles ahead. Now, the boat was at least thirty-five miles from the convoy and down upon its starboard and leeward quarter. When they turned to port to close the convoy, they would have the wind abeam and should be able to catch the convoy up at a relative closing speed of about ten knots. That would mean a three-and-a-half-hour pursuit, on the surface, a most dangerous undertaking. But with luck they should be in amongst the rear ships of the convoy well before midnight. There would then still be hours of darkness left to make the attack and the escape.

There was only one major disadvantage — the moon, which was at its full the day after tomorrow. The previous night it had been brilliant when it emerged from cloud and had lit up the sea like a stage. In the old days the *Propagandakompanie* would have called it a hunter's moon. But not now. Moonrise was at nine o'clock and already there was a lightening of the horizon down to the southwest. It was going to be a white night, and Hansi considered whether it was wise to press on. This was a most unusual caution for him but tonight, after seeing what had happened to Reinhardt, Hansi had the most unusual sense of foreboding.

Already, there was a mysterious glow on the rim of the conning tower and the sides of the periscope standards. As Hansi watched, it brightened into a ghostly glare. It was St Elmo's fire, which superstitious sailors always said presaged a death on board. But Hansi also remembered talking to a U-boat captain at Lorient long ago who said he had seen this same fire all over his boat when he was attacking an aircraft carrier on a Gibraltar convoy. He said the carrier had seen him, and so had the escorts. But he had gone on, he said, and he had sunk the carrier, and he had got away again. Surely that was a much better omen.

But his lookouts were outlined in the same fire, too, and Hansi could see it was frightening them. It had no substance, like a firefly or the chemical glow of rotting wood. Hold one's hand to it and there was no reflected glow. But it must make the boat more visible. Hansi dived to wash it off, but every time he dived he knew that it was reducing his own power to influence events.

While dived they had a hydrophone bearing. The bearing of the convoy screws was drawing right, and growing ever fainter. They were dropping behind. They had to steer always and ever more to starboard to try and head the convoy off. Every hour they dived to check the hydrophone bearing. On the third dive, when Hansi estimated they were about ten miles astern of the convoy, there was a new noise. A destroyer had left the screen and was coming back to look in the convoy's wake. They heard it go down their port side, further and further, until it was on the boat's port quarter.

Looking at his chart and plotting the destroyer's approximate course, Hansi saw that it was steering directly down had been the boat's bearing from the convoy when they had transmitted to BdU. That was another ruse: to wait before going towards the transmitting U-boat, hoping to have lulled its captain into a state of false security. It might have worked, had Hansi not remembered Reinhardt's remarks to the staff at Lorient. Hansi had no doubts now that the enemy did have some means of locating radio signals. It was not so outlandish, after all; the Luftwaffe had a system for directing bombing raids and even, so Hansi had heard, for directing night fighters. Hansi made up his mind that this time he would argue the point hard to the staff at Lorient. It was idle to deride the idea as impossible; the facts showed that it was possible, and that the enemy was making use of it.

On the next dive, the destroyer's propellor noises were coming up the boat's port side again, obviously to rejoin the convoy. They heard it pass, overtaking them. It occurred to Hansi that the destroyer, having run down that bearing and, so to speak, cleared it, would not now expect a U-boat to approach along it. That destroyer must have carried out a search, listening and looking, with Asdic and whatever radio location apparatus it must have. It would have seen nothing, heard nothing, detected nothing. That band of approach would now be deemed clear, at least until morning. So if Hansi moved over into it and resumed his original course, he could attack the convoy from dead astern, a direction which the escort would not expect. They would lose a little distance again, moving over, but it would be worth it.

The next dive — and the last, Hansi calculated, before their attack — showed the convoy's bearing moving rapidly right. It had zigzagged to starboard and thus cut down the distance the U-boat had to travel. Hansi was able to turn on to the convoy's course a full fifteen minutes earlier than planned. That was an unexpected gift from the Gods. On such small hinges did battles turn.

Hansi hoped to approach within some three miles of his target before diving. He rang down full ahead and told the engineer down the voice-pipe that 'full' meant 'full and a half' — he must give it everything. The sea boiled and foamed over the casing, and the exhausts drummed out astern. The moon herself had appeared first as a great red glowing blur on the horizon, like a ship on fire, and in fact the port after lookout on that sector had reported it as such. It rose steadily above a hard, straight horizon line, which probably meant stronger winds to come with the daylight.

The moon was so bright it gave an optical illusion of being a huge silver orb only a few metres away from the U-boat. Hansi had to prevent himself staring at it for too long, and he looked closely at the lookouts on that side, lest they too were being tempted by the goddess. There was the flick of a speck across that great shining face, and Hansi involuntarily ducked and tensed. But it must only have been a seabird.

The moon had driven away St Elmo's fire, or maybe it had drowned it in her own radiance. It was the most splendid moon Hansi had ever seen in his life. It was like a great soothing light, sent from the heavens, which calmed even the waves and reduced the wind to a breeze which breathed of success. The U-boat rose and plunged, and each plunge threw up showers of spray which gleamed like pearls. Hansi stood at the front of his bridge, feeling the wind across his face and drawing in deep breaths of sheer delight.

There was another blemish on the moon's perfect surface, a larger one, and slower. Maybe another bird, but Hansi could not afford any chances. It was just as well. He heard the engine roar overhead, and he crouched for the most fleeting fraction of a second in the tower hatchway, looking up. He could see the moonshine on the fuselage. It was another of those biplanes.

As they went down, Hansi braced himself for the inevitable explosions. That pilot *must* have seen them. It was as bright as day up there. From that low height, the U-boat must have stood out like a black wart on the silver sea.

But as the silence lengthened, and the faces all around him began to lose their expressions of terrified waiting, Hansi realised that the aircraft must have missed them after all. It all went to prove one of Herr Kaleut's sayings: never assume that the enemy would do as you expected, or see what you expected.

Hansi was irritated by the expressions on his crew's faces. They had no right to expect the worst automatically. Good God, the battle had not even *started* yet. They had been so easily cast down. Now, a moment's respite buoyed them up again. They were like children. Hansi had to think hard before he could put a single name to any of their faces. He simply could not remember their names. For a U-boat captain, that was a very bad sign, like a workman not even recognising his everyday tools.

Hansi looked again at the clock. They could not afford to stay down too long if they were to have any chance of overhauling the convoy. It was tempting to stay here. They had carried out one successful attack, more than most U-boats could boast these days. They had reported the convoy's position, course and speed, and likely numbers, for those U-boats ahead. They had done enough, and many would say more than enough. Hansi had heard whispers of U-boat captains who had been tempted and yielded. Hansi recognised the temptation, but put it from him. He now had the memory of those pitiful shreds of flesh on the surface of the sea. This convoy's escorts had done that to his friend.

At periscope depth again, Hansi had yet another cautious look round the horizon. The moon was now like a spotlight glare on the sea, making it impossible to know whether there was anything over there in its path. Meanwhile, that convoy was still marching away. Every minute Hansi deliberated, every minute the boat stayed submerged, meant that much more distance to catch up. Not for the first time, Hansi felt that it was not fair to put one U-boat against such a convoy, which seemed even to have the laws of physics on its side.

Hansi swung the periscope round as slowly as he dared. He had to cover the whole horizon as quickly as he could, but he had also to risk the quick flash of moonlight on the top periscope glass. It would be comparatively faint in the moon, but it would be enough. There was always somebody there to see it. That was another of Herr Kaleut's old sayings: if there was any way things could go wrong, they would.

Hansi's decision to surface was finally hastened by the incompetence of his engineer, another very young man on his first war patrol who seemed not to have the faintest idea of the principles of trimming the boat. Long gone was Hugo, who could balance a boat on a wet handkerchief for hours on end. This man pumped and flooded, flooded and pumped, sloshing water around like a milkmaid pouring milk from pail to pail. As the boat steadily lost depth, Hansi had to crouch lower and lower to keep the periscope from sticking up too far above the surface.

'Keep me down, you clumsy dolt!' Hansi shouted. 'Keep me down ... *down!* Do you want to surface in front of a destroyer?'

Hansi heard the sharp intakes of breath all around the control room. He must not threaten them like that. These were not the crews of yesterday. Their morale was still excellent, for all the enemy's taunts and jibes. Every day the Allies claimed that the U-boat crew's mettle was cracking. It was not true. All the same, he could not take liberties with it.

The boat surfaced with the tower only, leaving the casing awash. It was a tricky piece of trimming. The boat was almost unstable at that low state of buoyancy, and might well slide back under again, leaving Hansi on the surface. He shut the upper hatch and stood on it in case that happened. That also prevented the lookouts coming up with him.

Once again, for the thousand thousandth time, Hansi made one rapid sweep around the horizon, in case he had made a terrible error and surfaced in front of a stopped destroyer. Then he scanned sea and sky carefully and slowly, in sectors. There was nothing except the moon, larger, brighter and closer than ever. It seemed to have gained enormously in brilliance and intensity whilst they had been down. That was the direction of danger. An aircraft could easily come gliding in unseen along that brilliant carpet of light which led straight to the U-boat.

This time, there was no warning at all. Hansi did not even hear the engine sound overhead, had no inkling of danger, no pricking of the thumbs. Hansi could not guess from which direction the aircraft had attacked, but he knew it must have been stalking the boat. In that split second when he saw the black shapes of the charges pitching into the sea close at hand,

Hansi knew that there could be no doubt whatever that enemy aircraft had some means of locating a boat in the dark. In the dark, in mist, fog, cloud, in rain or shine, sunshine or moonshine, night or day, the enemy could find them.

The two explosions, one on either side, straddled the boat so close the water fell in torrents on Hansi's head as he bent down to open the hatch. Somebody, he could hear by the escaping air, had already given the order to dive, and he did not have much time. The whole U-boat hull rocked and shivered, with that awful bodily trembling which Hansi had experienced in that other U-boat and had forgotten. Now that memory came back. This was a mortal blow. This might be their last dive.

Below, as the deck angle steepened sharply, Hansi had to shout to make himself heard over the yelling and yammering voices. One man was lying, apparently rigid with terror, on the control room deck. Summoning all his own strength of mind and purpose, Hansi gave his orders in a louder voice than usual, and stood as still and calm as he could in the centre of the control room, trying to act as a focus for order and discipline. His ship's company, he could tell by the feel of the boat, was near to panic.

Matters were already almost beyond control. From the deck angle, the boat seemed to be sliding down an ever increasing slope, accelerating towards the bottom of the sea. Hansi ordered full astern, and both hydroplanes to hard to rise.

'Port shaft jammed, Herr Kaleut!'

'Full astern, I tell you!'

'Main motor fuses have blown, Herr Kaleut!'

That was quite possible. A jammed shaft would need an inordinate amount of electric current to turn it, enough, possibly, to blow the main motor armature fuses.

The depth gauges were still madly unreeling, to greater readings than the boat had ever reached before. They were still going down.

'Blow all main ballast tanks!'

The air bottle group pressure gauges flickered wildly to and fro.

'Use it all!' The pressures were going down as the air was released from the bottles.

'*Starboard* shaft jammed, Herr Kaleut!' The voice from aft — Hansi could not put a name to it — seemed calm enough.

'Can you do nothing?'

'We'll try, Herr Kaleut. Both shafts were distorted in that attack, and now the hull gland packing is damaged. The water is coming in extremely fast.' The voice had bad news, but was nevertheless reassuring. Hansi was grateful to its owner.

'Who is that speaking?'

'Johann Achilles, Herr Kaleut. *Maschinenobergefreiter.*'

'Well done, Achilles.' Hansi had no recollection of the stoker's face, or anything about him.

Hansi could not be sure, but he fancied that the frenzied swinging of the depth gauges' needles was slowing down. In a moment, he saw they had stopped. The U-boat had paused in its downward plunge, at about one hundred and fifty metres, a colossal depth.

'Stop blowing.' Hansi did not want to use any more air than he had to. Once the boat started to rise, if it started to rise, decreasing sea pressure would allow the air in the ballast tanks to expand. That would be the same as using more air. 'Pump from all trimming tanks as fast as you can.'

'The pumps won't discharge to sea at this depth, Herr Kaleut.'

That, too, was true enough. The boat was well below its designed diving depth. And it had definitely caught a kind of trim at this enormous depth. Hansi motioned to three men at the back of the control room.

'Walk forward.'

The deck tilted slightly as they did so. So, at least something about the boat was still responding. But as Hansi waited, the deck began very slowly to tilt aft again. It must be that water flooding in through the stern glands. Hansi walked to the after control room door to listen. He could hear it, a steady, terrible thundering of water. There must be tons of it back there by now, at this depth. They must reach the surface and pump out, or those waters would flood the main motors and that would be that.

But the depth gauges were certainly unreeling, very slowly at first, but then more confidently, as though the boat itself was gaining confidence. Hansi felt all their spirits rising with the gauges, although nobody knew what would happen when they surfaced. Unless that pilot was an idiot, he would still be there, flying around and waiting for results.

There was a furious knocking from aft. Hansi did not reprove them. Normally he would have silenced instantly any noise, but repairs now were their only hope. Noise no longer mattered; in fact, noise was a sign of life. As long as they could still make a noise, they still had a chance.

The depth gauges had steadied at about eleven metres. That was better, but not good enough. As the boat came shallower, the pumps could start pumping out water, while the expanding air in the ballast tanks had driven out the last of the water from them. But water was still flooding in aft, making the boat heavier. A state of equilibrium had been reached, but soon the boat would start to go down again. Something desperate and immediate was needed, or they might never reach the surface. The boat must be *driven* upwards.

'*Stand by main engines!*' Hansi felt the shock waves of the order travel through the boat. It was an unheard-of command. The engines could be started underwater, but they would draw their air from inside the boat and very soon cause a vacuum. It was a last, desperate measure. But it might just work.

'Stand by surface induction valve. Open it as soon as I give the order!'

The vacuum drawn in the boat would make it very difficult, if not impossible, to open the upper hatch against atmospheric pressure. That induction would have to be opened quickly, underwater if need be.

'Start main engines. Full ahead together!'

'Not ready yet, Herr Kaleut!'

It was several minutes before they were ready. Hansi watched the depth gauges begin to sink again, like the boat.

'Main engines ready!'

'*Start main engines! Full ahead together!*' Giving the orders, Hansi had no idea whether they were capable of fulfilment, but he just had to hope so.

There was a delicious rumbling from aft. Hansi felt his eardrums popping and clicking as the air was dragged out of the boat. The deck angle steepened upwards. The depth gauges were moving. Hansi watched until he judged the tower was almost on the surface.

'Open surface induction valve!'

For some long moments there was a steady drumming noise of water. Hansi thought they were lost, after all. But then the air pressure increased, he was through the lower hatch, up to the upper hatch, and had it open. The U-boat lay on the surface, wallowing, as though exhausted by its efforts. But once the boat was on the surface, Hansi knew by the feel of the deck as it rolled and heeled under his feet that the boat was stable for the time being. It was not going to slide back under, not yet.

The lookouts and the guns' crews had followed Hansi up. The boat would probably not be able to dive again for some time, if ever. Anything more that had to be done, would have to be done on the surface. They could at least pump water out, and very probably match the incoming water. They might be able to make some repairs to the stern glands. But not with the shafts still turning.

'Stop both!'

The moon was now much higher and smaller and, as Hansi looked, it went behind some strands of cirrus cloud. That probably meant the wind was coming. It was still a most beautiful night, with stars shining, but the air temperature had dropped. Maybe there would be more snow during the day.

The guns' crews were in position, and in the moonlight Hansi could see them moving, training their barrels to and fro and up and down. The boat had one 3.7-centimetre FlaK cannon on a mounting aft, behind the tower superstructure, and two twin-barrelled 2-centimetre FlaK cannons mounted, port and starboard, either side of the tower. This layout meant that the boat had maximum fire-power astern, a certain amount to either side, and virtually nothing at all ahead.

'Herr Kaleut, we can go ahead now, on the starboard shaft. On main diesel.'

'Very good. Well done, Ing. Very, very well done.' It was indeed the best news of the day. They had one shaft, and the rudder was still working, and the boat was still afloat. As Herr Kaleut would have said, it could be worse.

Hansi set a course to steer south-west. That was away from the convoy, and an admission of defeat. He should be following the convoy. But that would be to sacrifice his boat and crew unnecessarily. If they could remove themselves from the battlefield, they could perhaps lick their wounds, patch themselves up, and fight another day. There were always more convoys on the way, just as there were always more fish in the sea.

Hansi sighted the first aircraft just before dawn. It was shadowing the boat. He followed it in his binoculars as it flew round; once, the dying moonlight actually gleamed on its wings as it banked. The guns' crews followed it with their barrels, training round to the limits of their sectors, and quickly training back to pick it up again as it came around. It was well out of range. Hansi was tempted to fire. But that would only confirm their position, and they might need every round of ammunition before the day was out.

'Can we go any faster?' Hansi bellowed down the voice-pipe.

'Not yet, Herr Kaleut. Maybe in half an hour.'

That might be too late, Hansi reflected. Their attacker had already made one big mistake in holding off. They must know the boat was damaged and probably could not dive. If Hansi had been in that aircraft, he knew he would have already made one or two passes over the target, or near it, if only in feint. It would have tested the U-boat's temper. It might have fired back and jammed its guns. At least it would have expended ammunition fruitlessly. Hansi knew, even if the aircraft's pilot did not, that the U-boat only had a certain amount of ammunition in ready-use lockers, waterproof and pressure-tight, beside the gun position. Anything more would have to be passed up the tower by hand. As it was, because this aircraft had left them alone, Hansi's gunners had a priceless half an hour or more to clean their guns of verdigris and salt-water grease, to work their breeches to and fro, train and elevate the guns to their fullest extents, ease springs, check sears, and free cut-outs, and clean the ready-use ammunition. They were as ready now as any U-boat gunners had ever been.

Hansi caught the eye of the gunner on the starboard side 2-centimetre. The lad grinned. His name was Alexander; that was one name Hansi *did* know. He was very young, quite beardless, not even the slightest sign of stubble on his smooth chin. But he was a deadly gunner. He had shot very well at the target drogues in France. But that was in broad daylight, with a firm footing beneath him. It remained to be seen how he would do now.

The first attack came just as the sun appeared over the horizon. The beautiful night was clearly turning into a beautiful day — of sunshine, with high clouds, a brisk wind chipping spray off the wave crests and creating white horses. This was U-boat weather, when it was difficult to spot the feather of a periscope. Ironically, it was the one day they could not dive.

The aircraft attacked with the sun behind it, obviously hoping to confuse the gunners. But in fact that was another mistake. It brought the aircraft in on a bearing almost astern, where the boat's fire-power was greatest. The gunners could see the aircraft, silhouetted against the light, perfectly.

'Fire when ready!'

Hansi had no time to check whether they had heard the order. They must have done, because all three gunners took the aircraft under fire — the 3.7-centimetre first and the 2-centimetre guns a second or two later — when their target was just over a thousand metres out.

The shooting was excellent. The tracer soared up seemingly through the biplane's wing struts. The aircraft lifted suddenly, and banked, and flew out to one side. It was a hit, undoubtedly it was a hit! There was a puff of smoke from the engine.

The biplane was struggling for height. It had turned back towards the convoy and its carrier. Then, calmly, with no splash, or fuss, or any sound, it disappeared into the sea. Hansi found himself cheering and slapping Alexander on the back. He, and the port-side 2-centimetre gunner, and the layer and trainer of the 3.7-centimetre, all cheered and shouted at the tops of their voices. In the midst of their cheering, there was a tremendous detonation, followed at once by another.

The men on the bridge stopped cheering and looked at each other. There was nothing out there except the crashed aircraft. What could have caused that explosion? Who could have dropped depth charges?

Oddly, it was Alexander who suggested the truth. 'It could be the aircraft's own depth charges, Herr Kaleut.'

Hansi recognised the true solution. As the fuselage was sinking, it had reached the depth at which the hydrostatic fuses were set to detonate. The charges should have had safety devices. Maybe they did, and maybe the gunfire had damaged the mechanisms.

'One to paint on the tower!' Hansi called out. In the hubbub of exhilaration, Hansi barely heard the port after lookout's report.

There was a second aircraft approaching from the port quarter.

Hansi turned the boat stern on to the attacker. This time, he would wait, and then jink from side to side as the charges were dropped. They had caught him napping in the dark. He would not be caught so easily again.

But once again, the guns were in action and took the aircraft under fire some distance away. Alexander was shooting like a man inspired. The aircraft appeared to cross the U-boat's stern from port to starboard. Alexander's tracer met it. After a very short burst of fire, the aircraft seemed to stop dead in the air for an instant. Looking through his binoculars, Hansi saw the propellor actually stop revolving, and then begin wind-milling as the aircraft pitched forward. Hansi looked directly into the pilot's eyes, clearly visible in the magnification of the binoculars.

The aircraft carried on gliding towards the U-boat, and for a moment Hansi thought it was going to crash upon the after casing. But it settled in the water, only about two hundred metres in their wake. It was the nearest they had ever been to an enemy.

Hansi watched two figures climbing out of their cockpits and on to a wing. They had some sort of dinghy or rubber boat. It was bright yellow, and for a few seconds it thrashed about, in a grotesque way, as though it had a life of its own. By the time Hansi could see the two heads in the dinghy, the aircraft had sunk.

Nobody cheered for this aircraft. The same lookout, who was sticking to his sector and his duty admirably, had made another report. There was a destroyer on the horizon dead astern. Hansi saw that she was at full speed, with a white bone in her teeth, smoke swirling from her funnels, and her stern set hard down. She was closing rapidly and, with the U-boat's own limited speed, she would catch it up within a few minutes. To Hansi, now that he saw the destroyer approaching, the wonder was not that she was there, but that she had taken so long to appear.

Everybody on *Muskogee*'s bridge now had the target. They had had it on radar since leaving the convoy screen. Boysie had picked it up through binoculars and now he had it plain. That speck was a U-boat, surely: the first Boysie had ever seen outside of newsreels and photographs.

This one must be Long Stop, whose signals had betrayed the convoy to the group of U-boats up ahead — who were even now gathering for the attack. The first contacts with them had been made during the night, and the Escort Commander had been very reluctant to let Boysie go. Like all Limeys, he was a cautious S.O.B. He liked, as he said, to keep his troops together. He did not want them 'to go swanning off on their own', as he told Boysie on the TBS. In the Escort Commander's opinion, Long Stop was finished as a fighting force and no danger to the convoy; he would rather keep his escorts together for the attacks to come.

That had not been enough for Boysie. He had pressed the point. He had, after all, tasted real blood the night before. That was the real McCoy. *Muskogee*'s medics said the debris they had picked up was the real thing: human flesh and viscera. They had all been delighted. That was what they had trained for. They might be the oldest destroyer in the escort but they had just come swanning up and nailed the U-boat right where it lived. Boysie could still feel that warm glow from the signal of commendation, and he could hear still the hooting of the sirens as *Muskogee* passed through the convoy. He longed to hear that again. Maybe it was that success which had influenced the Escort Commander. More probably, he resented the way Long Stop had closed his convoy and sunk one of his ships. Anyway, apparently against his better judgment, he had released *Muskogee* to find and finish Long Stop, with support from the carrier's aircraft.

It was now a question of how long that U-boat would stay on the surface, and would that be long enough? *Muskogee*'s sonar was useless at this speed, but the radar contact was solid. Boysie had called down several times for more speed. The black gang were certainly doing their best. *Muskogee* was clocking thirty-two knots, more than she had done, Boysie suspected, since her trials in 1919. She was reliving the days of her youth. There was black smoke pouring from all four of her funnels, but that did not matter. Speed was of the essence now.

The moment that U-boat saw them, which would be any time now, it would dive, and then it would be another ball game. Boysie had already passed the word to the forward 4-inch to fire when in range. The chances of a hit were remote, but it might make the U-boat dive prematurely. Boysie pondered the question: what *would* Long Stop do? It was a nice choice for him. Did he dive or stay? He was vulnerable either way.

Boysie had seen the aircraft overtake him and fly on ahead, but he had seen no sign of them since. The port bridge lookout shouted. Boysie trained his binoculars on the bearing he had reported. It was a yellow speck, like a dinghy — a small boat of some kind. Boysie could not stop now, not with the enemy in sight. But he could signal the rescue ship, which was astern somewhere; that was its job, to hang around behind the convoy and pick up the remains.

The forward guns barked, so suddenly and unexpectedly they made Boysie jump in spite of himself. There was no sign of a splash. It must be very short, or way over. That black speck was much bigger now. It was throwing up spray and a suspicion of brown hazy smoke in its wake. He must be flogging his engines hard. But it was odd he was only making ten knots. They were coming up on him very fast. Why don't he go faster, or dive? The plot reported a closing speed of more than twenty knots. It was only a matter of minutes now. Boysie could even see heads on that conning tower, just tiny black dots — excrescences, no more.

The guns fired, again, and again. There were splashes now, to port and over. From below on the gun deck, the guns' crew's shouts came up on the fierce wind. That U-boat was either wounded or loco. He was zigzagging, but still only at half speed. He didn't dive, and he didn't go any faster. *Maybe,* Boysie thought, *he knows something we don't know.*

It seemed he did. There was a shout from the starboard bridge lookout, who pointed down at the water. Boysie raced to the rail in time to see the faint disturbance of a wake passing very close down the starboard side. It had missed by no more than a whisker. Some quirk of wave or wind had diverted the torpedo just that critical amount, or Boysie and those of his crew who survived would have been waiting and hoping for the rescue ship.

That was a brilliant attack. A torpedo aimed 'down the throat' like that, on an attacking destroyer close to. Long Stop must be a poker player, and he deserved better. There was a gunslinger who was not afraid to draw on the Sheriff.

The forward guns were silent now. They were reported jammed. The Bofors on each wing of the bridge were also manned. They would be in range any moment now.

The target had altered to starboard. Boysie followed. He had not decided upon any specific attack yet. This U-boat was going against all the rules. It was not trying to escape on the surface, and it had not dived, as it should have done way back. This one was not in the training manual. Looking through his binoculars, Boysie saw the array of guns on the U-boat's conning tower and on the superstructure aft of it. There seemed to be dozens of them, and Boysie seemed to be looking right down their barrels.

Both wing Bofors were firing now, and Boysie could not hear himself speak. He could see foaming splashes all around the after end of the U-boat, but not on it. Their shooting was terrible, not in the same league as their sonar and depth-charge work. Boysie made up his mind he would do something about that.

The U-boat turned hard-a-port and Boysie followed, but the U-boat had a much smaller turning circle. *Muskogee* and all her sisters took more room to turn than a battle-cruiser, and Boysie was forced to cast out far to starboard of the U-boat's wake. It seemed that the U-boat had noticed that, because no sooner had Boysie got on his tail again than he turned again, and again *Muskogee* plunged away, opening the range. Boysie had to slow down. This was like trying to corner an agile young steer on a horse that could not be turned or stopped.

Boysie noticed that the U-boat kept turning to port, never to starboard. That could mean he had only one shaft, the starboard one. That could also account for his lack of speed. Boysie was just making up his mind that next time he would jump to port first, when there was a grinding, smashing noise all along the bridge rail.

The starboard lookout was lying on the deck. The sonar talker, with his earphones still slung round his neck, lay on top of him. The double barrels of the starboard wing Bofors were pointing to the sky, one of them twisted into a noticeable bend. One of its crew was still alive and struggling with the training handle, his face gritted with the effort. The U-boat's gunners had won the first encounter, spraying the whole starboard side of *Muskogee*'s bridge.

The U-boat was heading back towards the convoy again, but still turning to port. Boysie once again ordered full port wheel and, as *Muskogee* heeled well over to starboard, Boysie heard the port side after Bofors firing, at last, across the broad creamy crescent of wake left by their turn. But the port side guns were no better than the starboard. Those heads on that U-boat's tower seemed unmoved. Those barrels trained round again and Boysie felt himself looking down them once more. This was *ridiculous*. They should have put paid to this customer by now, dangerous though he was. Everything was in the destroyer's favour, but here they were, still waltzing round this U-boat unable to get to grips and finish him.

Boysie felt a sharp pain in his right shoulder. He must have taken a fragment of shrapnel without noticing it. But now that he had, it was very painful indeed. His bridge was hardly recognisable now that he looked more closely at it. Most of the starboard side bridge bulkhead had been smashed flat, with all the equipment and fittings on it. There seemed to be nobody left alive but Boysie. The ship's head was falling off to starboard, and nobody was doing anything about it. The ship's broadcast, when Boysie tried the key, was dead. The voice-pipe to the wheelhouse had been snapped off near the deck. Boysie had to get down on his hands and knees and bellow at the stump.

'Wheelhouse?'

'Hanker's dead, sir. That last burst got him.' The answering voice was totally unknown to Boysie. 'We're putting steering in emergency now, sir!'

The U-boat's fire, for its weight of shell, had been devilishly well directed. It had inflicted a stunning blow. They must have aimed specially at the bridge.

Looking aft and down at the upper deck, Boysie saw two sailors, both carrying machine guns. He had given no orders to break out small arms. But the word had evidently got around.

Muskogee was now lying broadside on to the U-boat. Arcs of fire from forward and after 4-inch guns were both now open, and to Boysie's relief both turrets opened fire. This time, they got a hit: a brief flare of flame and some smoke from the U-boat's tower. Its bow rose up and then sank again, and stayed level. It seemed to stop for a moment. Boysie could see none of those heads.

Boysie could hear a voice from somewhere asking a question. It was the wheelhouse, reporting steering back, and asking for a course to steer.

'You see that U-boat? Steer for that. Pass the pipe, stand by to ram...'

Boysie did not really believe he would ever succeed in ramming. The U-boat would surely never stay still long enough. But it did. The impact was surprisingly slight. He had imagined a great rending, tearing noise, but there was nothing like that. *Muskogee*'s bows rose for some way, and then seemed to stick at that angle. Boysie could actually see parts of the U-boat, dark grey and sea-stained, and dripping wet, on either side of the bows. It was exactly like spearing some giant metal fish.

'All engines full back, all engines full back...' Boysie fell to his knees again, looking for the voice-pipe stump. The order was acknowledged, but the ship did not obey. There was no movement. *Muskogee* seemed to have stuck upon her prey. But now, as Boysie watched in perplexity, the U-boat swung from under *Muskogee*'s bows and lay alongside, with its bows pointing towards *Muskogee*'s stern.

The heads had come back on to the U-boat's tower and, as Boysie watched, a sailor manned the double-barrelled gun on the starboard side. The gunner fitted his shoulder carefully into the padded rest and began to train his gun from side to side, pumping shells into *Muskogee* at point-blank range. Boysie could feel them hitting. There was another, taller man standing beside him, wearing a uniform cap with a white cover. He was bending down and speaking into a voice-pipe. The man in the cap straightened and looked up at *Muskogee*'s bridge. Boysie guessed that he was probably looking at Long Stop himself.

The U-boat was sliding slowly astern, its hull grinding against *Muskogee*'s as it went. A larger wave lifted it and flung it against *Muskogee*'s side with an impact which Boysie could feel above the noise of that gunner. A few of those would hole the destroyer's hull.

Boysie lay flat on the deck of the bridge and crawled forward until he could look out over the starboard side. That U-boat gunner and the man in the white cap were dominating this battle. They were too close for the destroyer's 4-inch to depress far enough to hit them, and they had wiped out all the Bofors gun crews on that side. That gunner was as quick as a cat. He swung his gun to and fro whenever he saw or heard anything, and blasted it.

Boysie crawled back from the edge, and as he passed the voice-pipe stump he heard a babble of voices from it. The ship was making water fast up forward, as a result of damage caused by the ramming. There was more flooding amidships, where some part of the U-boat, probably its hydroplanes, had punched a hole in the hull beneath the water-line. The U-boat was still working its way aft, and would very likely cause more damage as it went. Already, *Muskogee* had a noticeable list to starboard. Boysie was having to crawl backwards uphill. He kept on crawling until he felt his toe touch the top ladder coaming on the port, disengaged side. Carefully he lowered himself down the ladder. Looking through the rungs of the ladder, Boysie saw two of his crew, wearing steel helmets, setting up a machine gun in the cross passageway just forward of the funnels.

Boysie stared at them. This was fantastic. This was like street fighting, at sea, in his own ship.

He climbed down the ladder and slipped into a compartment on the upper deck. It was a bosun's store, containing ropes and stages and paint pots, odds and ends — a sort of glory hole, impossible to clean up for inspections, which had been the refuge and the despair of two generations of sailors. But it did have a porthole looking out on to the starboard side.

For a moment, Boysie thought the gunner was looking right at him. His line of sight was directly opposite the U-boat and at the gunner's eye level. *Muskogee* had settled in the water that far already. The gunner was not firing, but he was ready. His whole body showed that he was ready for the least sound, the slightest movement. He had cleared the upper deck. Squinting downwards, Boysie could see two bodies lying by the guard rail. This gunner had made a butcher's shop of Boysie's ship. He was going to go on until he had killed them all. Even now, he had heard something and, with one swift, fast-footed movement, he had trained his gun aft and sent more shells belting into the ship's hull. He had the reflexes and instincts of a natural hunter. He was probably enjoying himself. Every now and again, Long Stop in the white cap tapped his gunner on the shoulder and pointed something out to him, and the man would dip his body or flex his shoulders, round would come the gun, and more rounds crashed into the superstructure somewhere over Boysie's head.

Boysie could feel his ship rolling sluggishly. It was not moving naturally to the send of the sea. It felt waterlogged. Boysie could not remember now what his last order had been. Did he stop the engines? Were they supposed still to be going astern? Certainly, by the look of it, the ship was now stopped, locked together with the U-boat. The surface of the sea was much closer to the upper deck. The water must have come in, hundreds of tons of it, at a phenomenal rate — far faster than their hull pumps could handle it.

There was a sailor crouching beside the compartment door. Boysie did not know whether he was frightened, or wounded, or just resting.

'Pass the word, sailor. All hands on deck, port side.'

The sailor said nothing, but just nodded at the hatch from the forward fire room. Men were coming up through it as though the devil was after them. 'The water's almost up the ladder, sir. She's a goner, sir.'

'I don't believe it!'

The man shrugged, as though to say, *Believe what you like*, and Boysie remembered that he had just himself ordered all hands on deck. The man must think him mad.

The firing from the other side had stopped and a voice called out: 'He's out of shells! Come on, we'll get him now! Come on!'

With a weird sensation that this was not actually happening to him, that this was all a feverish dream, Boysie ran through the cross-passage with the rest. On the starboard side, he stopped, before a most amazing sight.

The crew of the U-boat were abandoning ship. Men were streaming up through the tower, all wearing some kind of rubber apparatus, like a bellows with tubes, on their chests. They climbed over the bridge rail and spaced themselves out along the fore casing. The U-boat had sunk so much that the sea was lapping at their shins as they stood. Nevertheless, two or three of the men were feeling about under water. At last, they obviously released some catch, and pulled up four lids. They took out bright yellow bags. More apparatus. Probably dinghies.

The gunner had left his post, but Long Stop in the white cap was still there, shouting instructions in German to the others. He seemed suddenly to notice Boysie and *Muskogee*'s sailors staring at him. He lifted a revolver, pointed it at Boysie and fired.

Boysie had no idea where the bullet went, but *Muskogee*'s sailors gave a great collective roar of rage and stormed towards the U-boat. They were too late. As they moved, the sea flooded in over the upper deck coaming. It was just like a child's toy being swamped in the bath. Boysie had had some vague memory that the captain should be the last to leave his ship, but he was given no choice. A wave some two or three feet high flowed along the upper deck from aft and carried him off with it. One moment Boysie had been standing on deck, the next he was underwater and swimming for his life. When he came to the surface, the ship was gone. *Muskogee* had behaved like the perfect lady. There had been no histrionics, no shrieking of escaping steam or suction dragging her people down with her. She had simply sunk, and left them all behind, sorry for having so embarrassed them.

The sea was very cold, and very much rougher than it had appeared from *Muskogee*'s deck. Just in front of his eyes and not very far away, Boysie saw what looked like one of *Muskogee*'s floats. He struck out confidently towards it, but it skimmed away from him as he advanced. He swam as hard as he could, but could get no nearer. He could see the faces of some of his own sailors sitting in the float and waving to him. But they might just as well have been waving from the moon.

Boysie stopped swimming and began to tread water. He felt something nudge his shoulder. Close to his face, so close that its appearance gave him a shock, was a shining yellow surface. Above it, was the face of Long Stop, looking down at him. Close to, the man had dark stubble on his chin and dark shadows under his eyes. Goddammit, he was *still* wearing that white peaked cap with the eagle emblem. He put out a hand and Boysie seized it.

Boysie was astonished by the man's strength. Boysie seemed to hurtle up out of the water and crash face down on the dinghy's bottom, gasping and fighting for breath. When Boysie had wriggled round to lie on his back, he saw two other men in the dinghy. They were all wearing that rubber apparatus with the bellows and the hoses. Long Stop said something to them which Boysie did not understand, and then he looked at Boysie. His expression was unmistakeable. *What else could I do?* he was saying. *What else did you* expect *me to do?*

Boysie felt that some response was now required of him. 'Thank you,' he said. 'Appreciate it.' Long Stop and the other two all grinned briefly.

The sea was now very much rougher than it had been. It kept slopping in over the sides of the dinghy. Irritably, Boysie flicked it away with his hand. It had no business to come in here. This thing was supposed to save their lives. But the movement wakened the wound in his shoulder. It felt red hot, as though plunged into a molten poultice. But as he clenched his teeth against the agony, Boysie also became aware of the smell of oil from the man next to him. There was a whiff of something else, perhaps *eau de cologne*. It was a curious mixture, of machinery and effeminacy.

Long Stop and the other two had begun to sing. It was not a strident, threatening Nazi marching song, the kind Germans were always singing on the newsreels, but a jaunty optimistic, little tune, which seemed to suit the hazards and uncertainties of a sailor's life. Boysie could not understand the words, but it seemed to him that he understood its sentiments. *'And it did get worse, the very next day…'* they seemed to be singing, and Boysie agreed wholeheartedly with that. So the rescue ship found them, less than an hour later.

In the event, Boysie's shoulder wound was too much for him. He found that he could not, by himself, put the bowline strap under his arms. It was Long Stop and one of the others who did that for him, and gestured to the deck above to hoist. As Boysie dangled in mid-air, his shoulder crashed against the ship's side, causing so much pain he could not stop himself screaming out loud. But when he reached the rescue ship's upper deck, he waved away the stretcher indignantly. His arm might be hanging numb and useless, but at least he could still walk. So they led him forward to a large, brightly lit compartment.

There was more than a score of men in there, some in uniform, some in overalls, some in vests and underpants. Some had oil streaks or blood on their faces. Boysie could recognise nobody from *Muskogee*. He felt he ought to assert himself, assert his authority. He was the captain of a United States ship. Old maybe, but still a warship. But he had ceased being a captain from the moment he was washed off the upper deck. Since then, he had been picked up, and hauled out, and tossed around, and dangled like a sack of beans.

Boysie walked meekly across the compartment. He had sat down on the deck, with his back to the bulkhead, before he recognised the man sitting next to him.

'Say, you're the Limey pilot I met in New York City! Remember me, at the convoy conference?' The man did not answer. 'Ain't you the high-priced help from that flat-top? You must have been in that aircraft.'

The man's face was white with shock. He pointed, with the crook of one finger, at his jaw.

'Your jaw's broke, is it? Well it's good to see you again. It could have been better. On the other hand, it could have been a hell of a sight worse.'

This time the man did nod, and immediately winced with the pain.

Next were Long Stop and the other two. Long Stop saw Boysie sitting against the bulkhead and at once walked across and sat next to him, in a clear gesture of friendship.

One of the rescue ship's officers, a bright young man with a clipboard and a brisk manner, came in and stood in the centre of the compartment.

'*Right,*' he said. 'Let's have some names, as the copper said to the whore.' He saw Boysie, with Long Stop on one side of him and the Limey aviator on the other. 'OK,' he said to Boysie. 'Let's get some details down. Which of you is which?'

A NOTE TO THE READER

If you have enjoyed this novel enough to leave a review on **Amazon** and **Goodreads**, then we would be truly grateful.

Sapere Books

Sapere Books is an exciting new publisher of brilliant fiction and popular history.

To find out more about our latest releases and our monthly bargain books visit our website:
saperebooks.com

Made in the USA
Coppell, TX
12 September 2023